The Good Men

RIVERHEAD BOOKS

a member of

PENGUIN PUTNAM INC.

New York

2002

Charmaine Craig

The Good Men

A Novel of Heresy

Riverhead Books
a member of
Penguin Putnam Inc.
375 Hudson Street
New York, NY 10014

A list of permissions can be found on page 401.

Library of Congress Cataloging-in-Publication Data

Craig, Charmaine.
The good men : a novel of heresy / Charmaine Craig.
    p.   cm.
ISBN 1-57322-197-X
1. France—History—14th century—Fiction.   2. Pamiers (France:
Arrondissement)—Fiction.   3. Montaillou (France)—Fiction.
4. Heretics, Christian—Fiction.   5. Trials (Heresy)—Fiction.
6. Inquisition—Fiction.   I. Title.
PS3603.R35 E29   2002   2001019519
        813'.6—dc21

Printed in the United States of America
1   3   5   7   9   10   8   6   4   2

This book is printed on acid-free paper. ∞

Book design by Judith Stagnitto Abbate
Maps © 2002 by Rodica Prato

MONTAILLOU AND ENVIRONS IN THE SOUTH OF FRANCE

↑ To Limoges

To Bordeaux

Figeac

Cahors

Garonne River

N

F R A N C E

Albi

Garonne River

Toulouse

Hers River

Saverdun

Belpech

Carcassonne

Béziers

Aude River

Pamiers

Ariège River

Limoux

Varilhes

Foix

Tarascon

Junac

MONTAILLOU

Quéribus

Sabarthès

Prades d'Aillon

Perpignan

Ax-les-Thermes

A N D O R R A

P Y R E N E E S

Baga

Sègre River

S P A I N

MEDITERRANEAN SEA

Barcelona

Kingdom
of
SCOTLAND

Kingdom
of
IRELAND

WALES

Kingdom
of
ENGLAND

ATLANTIC

OCEAN

Paris

Kingdom
of
FRANCE

HOLY

ROMAN

EMPIRE

Kingdom of
NAVARRE

Montaillou

Provence

Kingdom
of
CASTILE

Kingdom of
PORTUGAL

Kingdom of
ARAGON

Papal

States

Kingdo

of

Kingdom of
GRANADA

NAPLE

EUROPE
circa 1318-1325

SEVEN YEARS ago or thereabouts, in summer, the rector Pierre Clergue came to the house of my mother while she was out reaping. He incited me to let him make love with me. I consented. I was a virgin still, fourteen years old, I think, or perhaps fifteen. He took me in the barn where the straw is kept, but not at all violently. Afterward he made love with me often, until the following January, and always in the house of my mother. She knew and was consenting. It happened mostly during the day.

In January, he gave me in marriage to my late husband. . . . After that, he still lay with me often. . . . My husband knew about our lovemaking, and did not put up resistance. When he asked me if the priest had lain with me, I said yes, and he told me to take care it should be with no other man. But the rector did not make love with me when my husband was home, only when he was out.

I did not know Pierre Clergue was, or was said to be, a relative of my mother, Fabrisse. I had never heard anyone say so. I did not know she was related to him by blood in any way. Had I known she was a relative of his—although an illegitimate one—I would not have let him near me. Because it gave me joy and him also when we made love, I did not think that with him I was sinning.

FROM THE DEPOSITION OF
Grazida Lizier, Pamiers, 1320

AUTHOR'S NOTE

BETWEEN THE YEARS 1318 and 1325, in what is now the south of France, one hundred fourteen men and women from the diocese of Pamiers were tried for heresy, many from the village of Montaillou. This novel has been inspired by their depositions. While many of the characters and events are based on real people and the occurrences of their time, I have not hesitated to change history—both personal and communal—for the sake of narrative drama. This novel should thus be read as a work of the imagination.

1265 — 1300

Part I

ONE

LONG BEFORE a woman called Echo was tried for the crimes of heresy and incest, before even her mother was born a bastard, the boy Pierre Clergue looked out his window and decided to make the village Montaillou his own.

He had been woken that morning with the word that his brothers were to accompany their father down to the lowlands on a mission to purchase tools for autumn sowing. As Pierre was both sickly and gravely slight of stature for his seven years, he was to remain at home. His brothers made a great show of bundling themselves into their breeches and woolen tunics and hooded coats, taunting him with tales of adventure he would never know. Pierre pretended to sleep as they prepared, and covered his ears with the rough edge of his serge blanket. When his brothers left, he rose, climbed up onto the small beech-wood chest he kept propped at the foot of his window, and thrust open the leaves of the shutter. It had rained through the night, and a heavy mist lay over the village, which clung to the slope of a steep knoll on a plateau high in the Pyrenees. He spotted his brothers and father, riding mules down the winding village road. They disappeared into the shroud of mist, and he felt as if he had never been so alone.

Then dawn shone, and yellow light sifted through the mist, gilding the wet wood-shingled roofs of the village houses, and the sodden hillocks, stubble fields, and plowlands of the valley below. Pierre told himself he did not need his brothers' freedom. Montaillou contained as much of the world as he wanted to know, as much of the world worth claiming as his own.

THAT EVENING, as every evening, he and his mother attended Mass in the chapel to pray he would strengthen and grow. The rector was a tall, good-looking man with kind gray eyes and a voice as fluid as running water. After vespers were sung, he called Pierre up to the altar, and then pressed his hand down firmly on Pierre's shoulder, speaking a solemn prayer. "Lord, let this boy grow."

Pierre looked out at the grim faces of the villagers sitting on the straw-covered floor. Candles sputtered on the altar, filling the chapel with smoke and casting flickering light over the villagers. "Let this boy grow," they chanted mournfully with the rector, and Pierre's heart leaped up in exaltation.

Later, as he and his mother passed the crosses on the graves in the churchyard, he gazed up toward the summit of the knoll, at the moonlit towers of the stone fortress inhabited by the overseer of the village, an appointee of the Comte de Foix. He made out the dark, craggy peaks of the mountains rising above the fortress in the distance, and the mystery of the prayers that had been uttered on his behalf mingled with the mystery of the earth and the mystery of the Comte's greatness, and it seemed to him that he might indeed sleep and wake to find himself grown.

God did not answer his prayers. In the years that followed, Pierre grew very little, and then, when he was eleven, his hip began to deteriorate. For months, he tried to ignore the throbbing in his side, walking without limping in the presence of his brothers and staying in his room when the pain was too severe. One morning, he was making his way to the beech-wood chest by the window when his mother caught him limping. "Pierre," she said from the door. He turned and saw her quivering mouth, her blue eyes filling with tears. "Why has God not spared you?"

That afternoon, the healer Na Roqua paid him a visit, telling him to remove his linen undergarment and lie upon his bed. She was a lean, unmarried woman, with a head as bony as that of a corpse, and when she put her long, cold fingers to his hip, he gasped. "There are herbs for the pain," she said in a strained whisper. "Root of peony mixed with oil of roses. But herbs will not make this hip well." She squinted at his mother, standing near. "Perhaps the soul of this boy is eating away his flesh, trying to escape his body," she said. "Flesh is a prison of temptation. Unbearable for the soul that is pure." Pierre was at once frightened and thrilled by the mystery of her words.

That evening, his mother carried him against the softness of her body to the chapel for vespers. When the rector called him up for the prayer, he stood but did not approach the altar. If the healer had been correct and his soul was so pure it was trying to escape his body, then praying for his body to grow, for his hip to become strong, was praying for his soul to be further imprisoned. He glanced at the villagers sitting on the floor. A young, tender-eyed woman blinked at him with pity; her little boy hid his nose in her dress; a toothless shepherd sucked on his bottom lip, staring.

"Pierre," he heard the rector sigh. "Come up for your prayer."

He glimpsed the statue of the Virgin by the altar, and noticed her eyes gazing down at him with care. Her lips were pursed shyly, as if she were smiling at him, and he thought perhaps God had never intended him to grow. Perhaps growing was against the nature of his soul. He cleared his throat, looking to the rector, whose eyes narrowed with concern.

"I suppose, Domine," Pierre said in near whisper, "I would like to stay small."

A trembling smile played at the corners of the rector's lips. He nodded and Pierre sat, pretending not to notice his mother's furrowed brow. All his life, he would remember that moment as the first time he had attempted to abandon the misery of his body for the mercies of his soul.

HE DECIDED he wanted to follow the Virgin, and asked the rector if he might be his pupil, "so that one day, I might be priest," he said. For three years, he studied Latin, making letters first with a stylus on wax tablets, then with a quill on parchment. He learned rhetoric, logic, arithmetic, geometry, astronomy, and music. He memorized passages by Virgil and Ovid, from *The Moral Sayings* by Cato. Hymns and psalms played in his sleep.

In the daylight, he endured the taunts of his brothers and fellow boys. "Vechs Petitz!" they snickered. Little Penis! Or sometimes, if they caught him reading under the elm in the square, "Evesques Petitz!" Little Bishop! The latter was particularly painful for him, in that it mocked what he had begun to want most privately for himself—to be not only the rector of Montaillou, but also the bishop of his diocese, and thus more sweepingly important than any villager had been. He knew the boys must have seen a glimmer of self-satisfaction in his eyes when he translated a difficult passage. He thought, in some way, he deserved their mocking—they had caught him feeling reverence, not for God, but for his own burgeoning Godliness.

When he was fourteen, the rector named him the official curate of the chapel, and he performed his duties with vigor, lighting and extinguishing candles for the Mass, preparing incense in the thurible, and collecting oblations from parishioners—eggs at Easter, yarn at Whitsuntide, candles at Christmas, and loaves of bread at the Feast of the Virgin in September. As he worked, he believed his soul was growing stronger. But at home, in the company of his brothers, he felt invaded by the talk that spread between them, and by the force of their deepening desire for fleshly pleasure.

One evening at dusk, his mother asked him to fetch straw from the stable to sprinkle over the kitchen floor. As he approached the stable, he heard the mare making the sounds of mating. He entered, and stopped when he saw his older brother Guillaume standing in a shaft of orange light that fell from a hole in the roof. Guillaume had his trousers down around his ankles. In his hand, he held his member, visibly thick and firm. He was watching the mare kick away from the donkey trying to mount her. As the donkey thrust forward, Guillaume moved his hand quickly over his member, opening his mouth and tipping his head back, as if to drink the orange light.

Pierre crouched down in a shadowy corner behind a spiderweb, feeling his heart pound in his head. He stayed there until the mare stopped bawling and Guillaume passed by, wiping his hands on his trousers. When darkness settled all around, he walked home, hoping his mother would have already turned in for bed.

The summer after, he and his brothers were herding the family pigs through the forest so that the pigs might forage on fallen acorns and chestnuts and crabapples, when he overheard Guillaume describing how he had taken a girl named Marquise in a field. She was from the nearby village of Prades d'Aillon; Pierre had seen her before, seen her dark hair and one mysteriously narrow eye—an eye some said she had inherited not from her Aragonese blood, but from a race of people far across the sea. Her eye, Pierre thought, resembled both eyes of the Virgin.

"She was like lips down there," said Guillaume, pointing to his groin. He lifted his hands and made the shape of a woman's bottom in the air. "Warm and slippery," he said.

Pierre kicked a crabapple at a pig and his brothers broke out in laughter.

"Putana!" Pierre muttered, stomping off into the forest brush.

It would be more than forty years before he used the word "whore" again. Then, he would understand why.

THE BODY OF MARQUISE began to haunt Pierre. Alone in his room at night, he shut his ears and shut his eyes and tried to imagine the purity of his soul cleansing him of desire. But Guillaume's words played in his mind: *warm and slippery, like lips down there.* He saw Marquise, saw her bottom in the air, and his member reached out to her. There she was, standing by the bed, getting into bed, moving beneath him, her strange eye below him, staring up at him and then closing.

When he was eighteen, he learned that not even the priesthood smothered fleshly desire. He was polishing the darkened candlesticks on the altar, when the rector tapped him gently on the shoulder, asking him to join him in the vestry. In a moment, the rector confessed to having put his seed into a village woman. "Vows of chastity," he said, "are not as solid among mountain priests."

Pierre stared into the rector's untroubled eyes. He imagined his own member becoming stiff inside a woman, and then he pushed the image from his mind. "What will others say?" he asked.

The rector studied him, clasping and unclasping his whiskered chin. "They will say a priest should not take a woman. Or they will say it is the way of the priests of Montaillou."

Pierre felt the vein in his forehead pulse.

"You may judge me, Pierre," the rector said. "But you may also come to see it as I do." He paused. "Making love is not only the way of priests here. It is the way of humankind."

. . .

SINCE DECIDING to become a priest, Pierre had believed he would be celibate. As a celibate, his flesh would be all but dead, and he would be more God-like than common men. Now it seemed he was becoming a small organ in a sinful body, the very body of Christ he had hoped would purify him and make him spiritually tall.

One night, after a dream of Marquise, he woke to wet spots on his sheet and wanted, achingly, to abandon his path toward the priesthood. He wondered if Marquise would have him as a man. He limped from his bed to the room in which his parents slept. Pushing open the door, he saw the shape of his father nestled up against the body of his mother. He entered the room and heard their steady breathing. He knelt by his father to wake him.

"Papa," he said. "I need you now."

His father looked at him for a moment, dazed. Without speaking a word, he nodded and followed Pierre outside. They sat on a bench in the garden, the smell of lilacs sweetening the air, the moon casting light on his father's crooked nose.

"Papa," Pierre whispered. His voice was breaking, and he knew he was on the verge of tears. He tried to swallow. "Papa," he said again. "Would a woman have me?"

Still sleep-heavy, his father wiped sand from the corners of his eyes. His lips parted, and then closed. For a long while he sat thinking. When he was done, he shook his head. His nose moved in and out of the light.

"Anyhow," his father croaked, "it is better to stay away from female parts. Even if you were tall, a woman would be a burden. With a pretty woman, there are always other men to keep your eye on. And with a plain woman, there are always other women to lead your eye away." He cleared his throat. "Better to be a good chaste priest."

PIERRE TOOK THE VOW of chastity at twenty-three and told himself there would be no more dreams of Marquise.

Early that autumn, a little girl he recognized as the illegitimate daughter of the rector came knocking at his family's door. She was a brown-eyed, plump little thing, with dimpled cheeks, and she held her hand out to him wordlessly. He felt his heart skip a beat as he took it, feeling its damp warmth. He could not remember having touched a child since he had been a child himself. For what seemed like a lifetime, he had suspected he would never father children, and he had found himself sometimes feeling repulsed by their presence. They seemed to him to be a reminder of the baseness of humankind—spawn of flesh to flesh, spirits captured and tied to the earth because of sin.

Without explanation, the girl led him through the chill of evening down the road toward the rector's house. As they walked hand in hand, Pierre felt a tenderness such as he had never known. For a moment, he allowed himself to pretend he was her father, and it was as if something inside him lifted. All the torment of trying to be pure, trying to be right-eous, evaporated into the air, and here he was with his little girl, walk-ing under the wide twilight sky, the vastness of life quietly spreading before them.

The rector's house was comprised of a single room of wood and daub. A fire roared in the stone hearth and the rector lay under a heap of shabby, fur-lined blankets, his head sunken in a feather pillow. He was breathing heavily, his eyes half-open. He was dying, Pierre understood.

On a stool beside him sat the girl's mother. When she saw Pierre, she looked up at him anxiously and then burst out sobbing, holding a coarse cloth to her eyes. Pierre noticed that she was wearing mittens, worn out at the fingers and muddy, as though she had just returned from sowing winter wheat in the fields. The girl whimpered, ran to her mother, and buried her face in her dress.

Pierre, too, shed tears for a time, unable to speak. "Yes," he said at last. He did not know what else to say. No one, not even the rector, had prepared him for how to console. He thought of his hip, of how he had lost much of it when he was young, and how his faith in his own soul had made the loss less grievous.

The woman's sobbing subsided. She looked up from her cloth, waiting for his words, her face swollen. When he said nothing, she burst out crying again and pressed the cloth back to her eyes.

"His soul," Pierre mumbled. Then, more loudly, "His soul."

The woman's eyes lifted from the cloth again.

"His soul will be free," he said.

She wiped her nose, nodding, and smiled vaguely in appreciation.

He gave the rector his last communion, feeling what it was to feed a person the body and blood of Christ. He wondered why Christ had wanted to feed the apostles flesh. As he pushed the host between the rector's lips, he imagined that what he was giving was not flesh itself, but the illusion of flesh, all light and purity and spirit.

That night, he watched the rector draw his last breath. He fell asleep on the floorboards beside the rector's bed and dreamed of Marquise, dreamed of her eye blinking, dreamed of his own blood filling his member and spilling forth like milk.

In the morning, the girl's mother woke him. He stood from the floor, and she stared at him with red-rimmed eyes, as if to convey that she meant to tell him something significant. She held out her hand, unmittened now, and chapped though delicate. In her palm lay a tiny linen pouch—no bigger than a joint in her little finger. A slender cord, tied to the pouch, dangled from her hand to the floor.

"The rector's herb," she said. She pulled the cord up through her fingers and looped it around her soft white neck, so that one end fell between her breasts, and the pouch with the herb fell over the place between her legs. "The rector told me to show you," she said. "So the man's milk will not curdle."

Man's milk curdled to become a fetus—Pierre had heard that before. He realized she was offering him something to prevent the conception of a child. He felt himself redden, and drew away from her.

The woman slipped the cord from around her neck. He heard it hiss across her skin. She held the pouch out to him. "For you," she said.

He shook his head, shook away the thought of Marquise, but the woman pressed the herb into his hand, an expression of sadness and fondness in her eyes. "The rector said so," she said. "'The priests' amulet,' he called it. For the priests of Montaillou."

He wrapped the cord around the linen pouch and left quickly, limping down the road to the chapel—his chapel now. He hid the amulet under a stone behind the statue of the Virgin, where he could stare up at her long nose and curved mouth and remind himself of the dignity of chaste living. If every other priest of Montaillou had fallen into the clutches of the flesh, he would prove his spiritual fortitude by never succumbing.

THAT NOON, he delivered his first Sunday Mass.

"The rector is gone," he explained, gazing out at the long faces of the parishioners. After all the years of lighting and extinguishing candles, preparing incense and collecting oblations, he had never stood at the altar before the parish without the rector standing above him. He felt beads of sweat break across his forehead. "Loss of flesh is birth of spirit," he murmured, too quietly.

Some of the women began to weep for the rector, their lips stretching open with the shrill sounds of lamentation. Other parishioners looked at him restlessly, their eyes searching for his command.

"Loss of flesh is freedom from temptation," his voice cracked. The weeping continued. He saw his brother Guillaume frown.

"Loss of flesh," he said, but a young man began to wail loudly. And then an old man joined in. And then the tanner, and the village weaver, and their wives. Children howled. Babies wailed. Pierre felt sure the parish of Prades d'Aillon would come running to see what was wrong.

On and on the parishioners wept, and it seemed to him they were crying not only for the passing of the rector, but for every heartache they had endured—for all the difficulty of toiling in the fields daily and surviving droughts that left stalks scorched; for every animal that had perished or been stolen; for their fathers' spitting blood, their children's seizures, their wives' deaths in childbearing; for their fear of leprosy and its spread throughout the region; for the endless shortage of money and tithes to be paid; for their infidelities and the gossip against them; for the times they had felt unloved and their uncertainty as to whether or not they would be saved.

All this fear, this collective hurt, was suddenly unharnessed in the absence of a strong rector to hold it in and promise a good day coming. Pierre felt his own sadnesses surge up from beneath the surface of his spiritual well-being. How he hated his little body! Evesques Petitz! Little Bishop, indeed! His brothers had been correct. He was a small man greedy for righteousness. He felt his body shudder, and though he told his eyes to remain dry, tears sprang to them.

He saw an old woman stand from the floor and make her way through the parishioners. His mother, he recognized. Why had he never noticed how old she had become? Curls of white hair fell around the linen wimple framing her face. Her smooth skin had fallen, and her cheeks, once full, had hollowed. He wiped tears from his eyes and saw she was carrying a chest—the same small beech-wood chest on which he had stood as a child, looking out his window, surveying the land he had thought someday he would make his own.

His mother shuffled to the altar and put the chest down by his feet. She patted his hand. "Good boy," she said, smiling at him tenderly. She shuffled back to her place on the floor.

He stared at the chest, its wood darker now, its top scarred by a long scratch. He remembered how unworthy he had felt while standing on the floor with his brothers, and how limitless his future had seemed while standing upon the chest.

He turned to the altar and picked up the silver-gilt chalice and the ciborium with consecrated bread. Facing the congregation, he stepped up onto the chest. The parishioners had fallen quiet, and he could almost see himself through their eyes. Cloaked in holy vestments, holding the chalice in one hand and the ciborium in the other, the smell of holy oil issuing from the chrismatory, incense smoking so the church was all a haze, he was exalted, swept up to the highest of planes. God was nearby.

"*Domine Iesu Christe, Fili Dei vivi,*" he began.

All eyes looked to him as he offered forth the body and blood of Christ, as he read the words and order of the Mass from the missal, as he translated lessons from the Scripture, as he gave the Kiss of Peace and sang from the gradual in homage to the rector. And the words, the words of consolation, flowed from him.

THE RECTOR HAD HEARD confession and given Communion every year before Easter, and Pierre thought he would do the same. But four months after he delivered his first sermon, when the harvest was under shelter, the mountain passes choked with ice, and all the villagers closed cozily inside, his brother Guillaume came to him at the hour of prime, brushing the snow from the sleeve of his coat and quietly asking to make confession. He could not wait until Easter to do penance.

Pierre saw the haunted paleness webbing beneath Guillaume's skin and told him to kneel by the altar. He pulled a stool up to the altar for himself so he could look Guillaume in the eye. He wanted his brother to trust in his spiritual leadership, and thus to feel fully purged of his sin.

He began with the first question in the *Instructions.* "Believest thou in Father and Son and Holy Ghost?"

"Not that, Pierre," said Guillaume. He clenched one hand in the other and shut his eyes. "I've got something in here." One of his hands lifted and clutched at his chest, like an animal pawing. "Help me get it out."

Pierre's hip felt as if it were burrowing out his side. "You had better tell me, Guillaume," he said.

Guillaume opened his eyes. "A girl," he said. "But not just that. Marquise."

Pierre felt his chest tighten. "You have lain with her again?" he said.

"Yes."

"Have you made her pregnant?"

"Yes."

Pierre braced himself against the altar. He had been able to push Marquise from most waking thoughts. But still some mornings, the sheet would be wet and he would know he had dreamed of her and wanted her as his own. "And do you marry her?" he said. "And how do you tell Papa?"

Guillaume's eyes widened and he frowned with disgust. "I'm not going to marry that bitch," he whispered. "She can't do anything for the family."

Their father had always said Pierre would not bring in any land with a woman, and so Guillaume would have to bring in twice as much. "But Marquise," Pierre said. "The child."

Guillaume shoved himself from the altar and stood, his hands in fists beside him. "What do you understand?" he said, his voice quivering. "I ask for penance from you and you know nothing."

Pierre studied the pointed chin of his brother, the chin he had measured his height against as a boy. He knew it was his obligation to absolve Guillaume. "Say twenty-five Aves and twenty-five Paters," he said, calmly. "One for each of the years you have lived. Make a pilgrimage to the Blessed Virgin of Montgauzy and pray to her for forgiveness. And try to be kind, Guillaume. Kind to Marquise."

Guillaume's fists relaxed. He wiped his nose with the back of one hand. He bowed his head and left. Pierre imagined him walking past the crosses in the churchyard and into the square, leaning into the falling snow, the cold sweep of mountain wind stinging the length of his body—his thighs, his healthy hips, his groin. Guillaume had made flesh with the only woman Pierre yearned to be flesh with, a woman who wanted Guillaume's body, who wanted to open her body to his largeness. Marquise.

. . .

SEASONS PASSED and Pierre heard that Marquise was making her way as a maidservant in Prades d'Aillon. When winter returned with its cold, gray light, he knew she should have already borne her child, and he prayed she had survived. He imagined her, binding her baby in swaddling clothes. Yes, she had sinned. She had sinned with his brother. Still, he could not think of her as anything but pure.

One windy night that winter after the evensong service, he was extinguishing candles by the altar when he saw her standing in the chapel door. He nearly shouted and held the snuffer out in front of him, warding her off.

"Domine?" she said. Her voice echoed on the chapel walls.

He set the snuffer down and looked at her. She was draped in a heavy coat, her cheeks wind-scoured. In her arms she held a baby wrapped in cloth. Tiredness reached under her eyes and through the lines of her forehead.

"Come rest," he whispered. He extended his hand, but the chill of night on his fingertips made him feel exposed, and he dropped his hand to his side.

She walked toward him, rocking the baby.

"Have you been traveling?" he said.

She nodded and searched around. He grabbed the stool he kept by the altar and set it down. She took her time sitting, and he watched her snow-dotted lashes blink down at the baby, her eye more sad, more lovely than he remembered. The scent of horse and hay was on her clothes, and he knew she must have taken shelter in a grange along the way from Prades. Surely the path over the Col des Abeillanous had been almost impenetrable with ice.

"This baby is heavier and heavier," she said.

He glanced down at the raven-haired, sleeping child. In the dim light he saw nothing of his brother Guillaume.

"A girl," she said.

"A girl," he said.

"She is a bastard," she said. "You know that, I am sure." She looked up at him with dark, desperate eyes. "Tell me," she said. "Can a bastard be baptized?"

In the year he had been rector, he had never refused to wash away sin from a child by water, nor had the old rector instructed him to exclude babies born out of sin. Still, he had never baptized a baby more than a week old, a baby so in danger of dying in a state of original sin.

"Has she not been baptized already?" he whispered.

She stared up at him, her forehead tense with worry. "The rector of Prades would not have her," she said.

"And the midwife?" he asked. Midwives were advised to christen a child if no priest was nearby or willing.

"No midwife," she said. "I birthed her alone."

"Alone," he said, imagining her in a field as she had been with Guillaume, opening her body to the clenching pain of matter.

"Yes," he said. "This child can be baptized. And should."

Her forehead relaxed and she pressed the baby to her breast, smiling. The baby whined and she unwrapped it, revealing the clothes of christening—a long robe of cream-colored silk, hemmed with lace. He realized she wanted her daughter to be baptized now.

"Marquise," he said, and blushed for having spoken her name aloud. "Any baptism needs a godparent. At least one. For the rite to be real. Is there someone in the village?"

She fingered the silk robe, and he knew there was no one she could call upon. Not even the father of her child.

"You," she said, turning her eye his way.

"I am the rector," he said.

"The uncle," she said.

He breathed. "The uncle, yes."

She had been a lover in his dream life, but never a sister, never the mother of his niece.

As Marquise placed the screaming child on the floor and removed her coat, he unlocked the stone font and took salt and the vessel of holy water from the altar. When he turned back, he saw she was wearing a pale blue tunic, trimmed with fur and ornamented with thread the color of eggshells. There was a purse hanging from her belt. She opened it and took out a christening bonnet for the child and a little veil for herself, which she fixed to her hair with a band.

"Wedding clothes," she said when she saw him looking at her. "Mine. If I had been married."

New mothers usually missed the baptism of their child, as they were considered unclean in the month after they delivered. When they first set foot in the church again, they wore their wedding clothes. He wondered if Marquise had not entered a church since the baby was born. He looked down and noticed the soaked tips of her shoes peeking out from under her gown. They were of leather, worked thin and soft. It pained him to imagine how hard she had worked to accumulate such finery.

"Come," he said. He did not touch her, but stood by her as she picked up the whimpering child. Together, they walked to the chapel door, which was shuddering back and forth with the wind. He pushed the door open. "Stand outside," he said. "So that you may make a proper procession in."

She held the baby close for warmth and stepped out into the moonlit night. Carefully, he made the sign of the cross in front of their sweet, attentive faces. He sprinkled Marquise with holy water, and put salt in the mouth of the child so that one day she might enjoy the food of divine wisdom.

"Enter the temple of God," he said, walking backward into the chapel. "Adore the son of the holy Virgin Mary, who has given you the blessing of motherhood."

Marquise stumbled over the threshold, and he caught her elbow before she fell.

He walked to the font, where he waited, listening to the sound of her steps on the chapel floor. When she had made her procession back into the church, he turned to her and bowed his head. "Almighty and everlasting God," he said. "Who of thy great mercy didst save Noah and his family in the ark from perishing by water; and also didst safely lead the children of Israel thy people through the Red Sea; and by the baptism of thy well-beloved son Jesus Christ, in the River Jordan, didst sanctify water to the mystical washing away of sin."

The baby quieted with the steadiness of his voice, and Marquise kissed her forehead.

"We beseech thee," he continued, "that thou wilt mercifully look upon this child. Wash her and sanctify her with the Holy Ghost, that she may so pass the waves of this troublesome world and finally come to the land of everlasting life, there to reign with thee without end. Through Jesus Christ our Lord. Amen."

He looked at Marquise, her mouth held against her child. "Beloved," he said to her. "Ye have brought this child here to be baptized. I demand, therefore, dost thou, in the name of this child, renounce the devil and all works, the vain pomp and glory of the world, with all covetous desires of the same, and the carnal desires of the flesh, so that thou wilt not follow, nor be led by them?"

Her eyes gleamed. "Yes," she said, crying softly.

He wanted to hold her face in his hands. "The child," he whispered. "She has to be undressed."

Marquise held the baby out to him, and he took the baby and leaned her against his shoulder and kept her there for a moment, feeling her tiny movements, her warmth. Marquise lifted the robe off the baby while he held her.

When the baby was all pink and naked, he cradled her in his arms and stared down into her face. Her eyes, he thought, were like Marquise's. "Her name?" he whispered.

"Fabrisse," she said.

"Fabrisse," he said. He held Fabrisse over the font and dipped her body into the water until she screamed out. He said, "I baptize thee in the Name of the Father, and of the Son, and of the Holy Ghost. Amen."

He dried Fabrisse with his robe, caressing the back of her head. "We receive this child into the congregation of Christ's flock," he said. He dipped his finger into the chrismatory on the altar and crossed Fabrisse's forehead with holy oil. "And do sign her with the sign of the Cross, in token that hereafter she shall not be ashamed to confess the faith of Christ crucified."

He wrote the name of the child and the date of her baptism into his Book of Hours, his manual of prayer. As he knelt with Marquise for the Pater Noster, he looked up at the stone face of the Virgin and had the feeling that despite his station as priest, the Virgin was blessing him with Marquise, blessing Marquise as his bride, blessing this bastard baby as their child together.

T w o

MARQUISE NEVER RETURNED to his chapel, and he vowed never to seek her out. Occasionally, he traveled to Prades d'Aillon for counsel with the parish priest, but he avoided the house in which he knew she lived, telling himself that if he came across her in his path, it would be due to the will of One greater than he.

Through the years, his longing for her increased, encompassing him like vines curling branching stems around his body—his arms and legs and stunted torso heavy with the weight of so much Marquise.

He could have lifted the weight, eased the burden of his un-clenched yearning. He could have had other women. His father had been wrong. In the early Easter seasons of his priesthood, he learned confessing female parishioners were more comfortable when he showed signs of well-being with them. If he looked these women directly in the eye, if he placed his hands over theirs on the altar, if he squeezed their hands with compassion, they relaxed, cried more freely, and all the tension of their bound-in sin was released into the air. Protected by his verdant love for Marquise, he experienced no illicit thrill from such touching, could not imagine the warmth of his own skin kindling the flames of another's desire. He was stunned when a woman clung to him instead of leaving the stool after confession, pressing her forehead down onto his hands, brushing her lips across his knuckles. Then, and only then, would a dark place within him know he could have his pleasure if he wished. And sometimes he wished. Or almost wished. But he would remember kneeling with Marquise in her wedding dress, and he could not betray her.

FIVE YEARS AFTER the winter baptism of the bastard child, Guillaume died. A rash known as the fire of Saint Anthony consumed his leg, moving from his toes up to his hip, until the leg fell off and disease infected his opened body.

"Fungus on rye flour," the healer Na Roqua said. "Rye flour spoiled over winter."

Pierre tried to console his mother, taking her hand in his, smoothing down the spotted skin of her thumb. "Guillaume did not deserve this death," he told her. But in his heart, he felt justice had been served. Guillaume had never bothered to master his body, and now his body had walked away from him.

EIGHT YEARS LATER, when Pierre was thirty-seven, he ventured to Prades as he often did to discuss dues owed to the diocese with the parish priest. It was after Easter and spring was in the air, the valley damp with the rushing water of the Hers River. As he walked along the riverbank, passing water mills where grain was rendered flour, he glanced up at the sky, intensely blue, and he had the sense that he might be coming into a season of peace and new beginnings in his life.

He approached Prades, and stopped short when he spotted Marquise drawing water from a spring below the church. He did not trust she was herself at first. She was bent over a jug, her body heavier than he remembered, rounding out her dim blue dress. The jug overfilled, and she struggled to lift it up onto her head, where she balanced it with one hand.

He wanted to run to her, to lift the weight of water from her head. He wanted to offer her his life. But he did not. He had no courage. He watched her turn up the hill, never moving her sad eye in his direction.

THREE YEARS LATER, he was eating supper with the priest of Prades, cutting cheese from a wheel, when he asked a question he had never dared. "There is a young woman named Marquise in your parish," he said. "How does she fare?"

The priest bit into his cheese, his thin mouth glistening with moisture. "Young woman?" he scowled. "She is old enough. And dead, too. Just last autumn she passed."

Pierre set the cheese knife down on the table.

"Disease of the gums," the priest said. "Where the teeth had fallen out."

Pierre watched him chewing blandly.

"She died slowly," the priest said. "With much pain."

The priest licked his thumb, and Pierre felt his hand curl around the base of the knife. He wanted to stop the priest's tongue from flapping, to slice the look of indifference off his face.

"No need to worry yourself," the priest said, smiling wryly, as if he sensed Pierre's rising fury and enjoyed it somehow. "I gave the woman last rites."

"But her baby!" said Pierre. "Her child!"

The priest laughed. "Baby?" he said. "She is no baby anymore." He sniffed. "A strange girl, she is. Keeps to herself. A bastard, unfortunately. And she is quite alone now."

THE NEXT MORNING Pierre woke, saw the cat on the windowsill, and felt like a widower. His bride was gone. His bride. All this time, though her body had not been his, he had felt her presence, known she was somewhere breathing in the world. Now, his devotion to the priesthood and celibacy seemed less like steadfastness than sin. He had sinned against Marquise, left her alone to defend herself and her child. Worst of all, he had never told her she was loved.

Any possibility of honest living seemed to have passed him by, and his body somehow knew it, and threatened to stop. Every night, as he reached the cusp of dreams, his throat closed and he found he could not breathe, could not move or scream. He thought death had come for him, and he surrendered to it, hoping for stillness. But then his throat let loose and air filled his body and he fell again toward dreams.

When he woke each morning and remembered Marquise was gone, he tried to believe he would find her someday in Paradise. In his anguish, he could not believe. He had lost his beloved, and that was all.

GRIEVING AT THE LIMITS of grief, he knelt at the altar of the Virgin
one evening. Dark rain clouds had blown over the valley earlier in the
day, and rain had fallen in violent torrents, wind howling through the
apertures of the chapel walls and extinguishing the candles on the altar.

He lit a single candle and studied the face of the Virgin. In the
dim glow of the light, he saw her eyebrows, lifted in a manner he had
not noticed before—as if she were about to cry. A long, curved mark ran
from the side of her nose to the corner of her mouth, and it occurred to
him that while he had thought the mark was a crease in her skin, it was
more likely the flow of tears.

He hid his eyes in his hands, listening to the crackle of incense
burning in the thurible. How mistaken he had been as a boy, when he
had thought the Virgin was smiling for him, smiling for the greatness of
his spirit. That simple misreading had changed the course of his life. He
had shunned his body and learned how to read, following the Virgin instead of pursuing womankind.

He heard footsteps on the chapel floor, and he crossed himself,
standing. A young woman, no more than seventeen or eighteen, stopped
in the center of the floor. She clutched an unlit yellow candle to her
chest, and held a lantern at her side, light spreading out from her in a
half-moon. She was dressed in a cloak and what looked like a dark blue
gown, and she wore a wimple, a cloth wound around her head and chin,
masking her neck and hair. He could not recall having seen her before,
but she was familiar to him. He recognized the particular tilt of her head,
the way her eyes moved from his down to the floor. He limped toward
her and saw that her lips were chapped and bleeding. If it was confession
she had come to make, he did not want to force it from her.

"For the Virgin," she said, holding out the candle.

He reached to take it, but she clutched it back to her chest.

"The Châtelaine made it with her own hands," she said, bowing
her head.

He realized she was likely the maidservant of the Châtelaine, wife
of the Comte de Foix's military agent and appointee to the village. The
Châtelaine lived with her husband and two young daughters in the
fortress on top of the knoll.

"She needs you to come to the fortress," the maidservant said,
glancing up at him.

He knew the Châtelaine only distantly. Her visits to the chapel were infrequent, and each year in confession she grew hesitant when his questions moved to the subject of her bed. On several occasions, she had told him that her husband did not care to know her as a wife, and then she had fallen entirely silent. Rather than asserting his spiritual power over her and insisting she answer all his questions, he, too, grew hesitant, shy—as if, in her presence, he was a small boy again, and not even the beech-wood chest could raise him above her.

"Please," the maidservant said, gazing at him with a suffering expression now. She held the candle out from her chest. He took it and felt warmth where her hand had been.

"Is the Châtelaine ill?" he said. He could not remember having seen her in recent months, and thought perhaps she had requested his presence for fear she might die.

"She needs you," the maidservant said, shrinking away from him.

He watched her draw the cloak around her middle and walk to the opening of the chapel. She leaned into the doorway, staring back at him without a smile, the underside of her chin glowing in the lantern light. There was something about her that he found haunting. Something he could not place.

WITH THE CHALICE and the ciborium in hand for last rites, he followed the girl on a route he had never taken—around the back side of a dark cluster of houses, up a steep goat trail, through a horse stable, and down a rocky path along the back rampart of the fortress. A little faraway moon brooded in the sky, bathing poplars on the uninhabited slope of the knoll in an eerie evening light.

He ran his fingers against the stones of the rampart to keep his balance. He had been to the fortress for suppers and prayer services and the handing over of tithes, but he had always entered through the gate beneath the barbican that faced the village and the meadows below. He had thought the gate was the only entrance.

The girl ducked beneath a low opening in the wall, and he pushed his fingers into a moldy groove and crouched down to the damp ground, his hip throbbing. On the other side of the wall, the girl stood waiting for him, her dark eyebrows lifted like those of the Virgin. She looked away and he followed her lamplight through the dark.

He heard the clucking of chickens, the grunting of pigs, and knew he was passing by coops and pens. The smell of dog excrement and sulfur filled the air, and he imagined bombards all around. The girl disappeared into the mouth of a tower, and when he approached, he saw that she was descending the stairs.

"But the Châtelaine," he said, sure that the noblewoman and her husband slept among the respectable rooms above, where fires blazed and banquets were held.

The girl held a finger to her lips. "She is here," she whispered, her finger dropping. "Just down. Down." She turned and descended.

They were going to the dungeons, he knew, to the place where sinners against the Court were held in chambers as lightless and suffocating as Hell. He told himself that if the maidservant was leading him to the underworld, he would follow. Too weak to resist, he would take what the Devil delivered, take what he deserved for having done nothing while his beloved walked alone on earth until she fell.

THE CHÂTELAINE was sitting on a bench in a cell empty of prisoners, a lighted oil lamp by her feet. She was a handsome, tall woman, with a dark mole on the side of her chin and an imposing stare. When she saw Pierre in the doorway with the girl, she stood, the sleeves of her brown dress billowing out around her shoulders.

"I am glad you came," she said, in a slow, deliberate manner. "I will speak openly. Quickly." She glanced at the wooden planks of the ceiling, toward where he knew her husband would be. He shifted the chalice and the ciborium in his hands.

"The Good Men did not ask me to call upon you," she said.

"Good men?" he said.

"Yes," she said, her eyes flitting down over the length of his body. "They do not even know they have my sympathy. Although they may suspect."

"Please," he said. "I do not understand."

"That I am like you," she said. "That I know about their presence in the village, and choose to look the other way." She crossed toward him, pressing her palms together and holding them under her chin. "I told the maidservant to bring you here because I wanted to ask you if the bishop of the diocese is aware."

"The Bishop?" he said, utterly confused. "Is the Bishop aware of what?"

"Of the heresy," she said. "The heresy in Montaillou."

He had heard of heresy in the past, of crusades and inquisitions waged against it. When he had been small, his brothers had told him of the desolate, sacked heretic fortresses they had passed on journeys throughout the region with their father. But heresy in his parish? In the midst of his flock? Heresy now? He knelt down to relieve the pain in his hip. He smelled decay, human feces, the muck of prisoners over years and years.

"Heresy?" he said. "In Montaillou?" He looked up at the Châtelaine, at her dark eyes fixed on his.

"I thought you knew," she said, an expression of both pity and dread on her brow.

It occurred to him that he had been so deep within despair over the death of Marquise, he had gone through rituals of the Mass—prayers and orations—without even seeing the parishioners he was addressing, without recognizing they were straying from the true faith.

The Châtelaine knelt down beside him, her moist lips parted. Before he understood what was happening, she leaned her mouth against his, and he tasted her lips, the salt on her skin, the warm bitterness of her tongue. It was as if everything familiar to him had vanished, and the world were beginning again in one breath.

"You are like the old rector," she said, drawing back. "With just the same look of hunger."

THE NEXT EVENING, he limped alone up the goat path toward the fortress, carrying the amulet behind his back, trying to get the eyes of the Virgin out of his head. He sneaked up to the stables on top of the hill, telling himself the rector had been a good man, a good priest, a good priest with a woman, and he, too, could be a good priest with a woman. A woman had nothing to do with his power to hold the village from heresy.

He walked past the dung in the stable to a straw pile where the maidservant was waiting. She had hung her lantern from a nail in the wall, and when she took it, he could see strands of her hair falling from beneath her wimple, strands so black they were almost blue.

She led him through the gloom of the night down into the underground, the flame in her lamp sputtering with every step. Instead of leaving him alone in the dungeon, she leaned into the doorframe and set her lantern on the floor, her wimple hanging mournfully about her face and shoulders.

"I tell her to stay," the Châtelaine said. She was standing by the bench, clothed in a linen tunic that fell in gathers down to her toes. Her hair was unbraided, and it stuck out from her face like scrub, wild and full.

He glanced at the maidservant, staring down at the lantern, her shoulders curved toward her feet, her breath barely hushing through her lips, as if she were trying to make herself invisible. Her eyebrows were lifted like the Virgin's again.

"Pierre," he heard the Châtelaine say.

He crossed toward her, hiding the amulet in his hand, trying to forget the girl behind him. The Châtelaine looked at him with calm assurance and lifted the hem of her dress. He saw the ovals of her knees, tense and glowing. He could not bring himself to show her the amulet with the maidservant looking on. He squeezed it and knelt down, wanting to humble himself as he did before the statue of the Virgin.

"No," he heard the Châtelaine say. "Please stand."

He pushed himself up and stumbled forward. He smelled lavender and dampness, saw the softness of the Châtelaine's breasts pushing out from beneath her nightdress.

"It is good for a priest to love," she said. "Priests are the most ardent of lovers." She stepped back and raised the hem of her dress above the curling reach of hair between her thighs. She lifted the dress over her head and her breasts hung free, lit up in the lantern light over the slope of her belly. She spread the dress over the floor and he held the amulet out to her. She took it without pause, wrapped the cord around her neck, and drew the herb between her breasts and down. She had used the amulet before, he saw. The priests' amulet. For the priests of Montaillou. If making love to her was his fate, all he had to do now was give in to it.

She held her hand out to him, and when he took it, she pulled him down to the floor, heavy with prison stink. She leaned back onto her dress and raised her knees and then her calves up into the air. She was long, long, longer than he had imagined. He was overwhelmed by the way her thighs opened out like white trees, the amulet slipping so easily within her.

He untied the breeches beneath his priestly vestments and pulled them down. As he crawled over her and pressed against her thighs, the thought came to him that the Virgin was seeing him through the eyes of the maidservant now. She was seeing him, like an animal in the shit, sinning against Marquise.

THROUGH THE WEEKS that followed, he spent nearly every midnight in the dungeon with the Châtelaine, and though he reminded himself that the old rector had done the same, he felt his hold over the spiritual wellness of the village diminishing. He descended into the earth, and violated his commitment to the Church, to the Virgin, to Marquise. With every thrust, he killed his father in his mind—his father who had told him a woman would never be his. He killed his brothers, who had called him "Vechs Petitz," Little Penis—little penis that could satisfy no desire. It seemed to him that while Marquise had been alive, while he had been chaste, the village had been spiritually strong. When Marquise had died, he had fallen into heartache, into the void of doubt, and the serpent had crept in. Now anything could happen.

One night after he and the Châtelaine had made love by the low light of the maidservant's lantern, the Châtelaine said the time had come for him to know about the heresy and its presence in Montaillou. He hid his face in her breasts, longing for silence.

"You must be prepared to defend us," she said. "Word will spread, and the bishop of the diocese will come asking, and you alone will have the power to save us from inquisition."

She told him that during the previous season of Lent, she had gone to visit her ailing father in Varilhes, the village in which she had been born. She had found her father in a miserable state, no longer able to speak or swallow. Attending to him were two holy men, each pallid and gaunt and dressed in a modest black robe. As she came to learn, they were practicing heretics—Good Men—and brothers by the name of Authié. The elder had been a notary in Ax-les-Thermes before being converted to the faith of the Good Christians, as he called it, in Lombardy—where the heretics of old had fled during the Crusades. Both had sworn to renounce the pleasures of the flesh—the eating of meat, the drinking of wine, marriage, and reproduction—and traveled about the countryside on foot, preaching discreetly from a book called

The Text, and living on alms they received from those who believed in their ways.

As she waited by her father's bedside, the Good Men began to question her. They asked if she knew where human bodies went after death, and she responded that she thought they went to Paradise after being resurrected from the grave. "The Church is wrong in teaching you such lies," the elder told her. He explained that bodies were like cobwebs, grabbing at matter to feed on, but breaking apart with the sweep of a hand. Bodies dissolved into the ground after death, or into ashes when they were burned. Bodies were never resurrected. "Your father is not a body, but a soul," the elder said, "and only his soul will be saved."

She wept then for the loss of her father's body, and the elder told her to dry her eyes. He said that Christ Himself was not a body—no Godliness could be contained in matter. Rather Christ was an illusion of a body. And He came not to suffer for our sins, but to give forth the Word. And the Word was that Satan had created the earth and all things of the earth—mountains and bodies and rain and birds. If people believed their parish priests, their souls would be born again and again into the prison of matter, flesh and blood on earth. But if they were baptized by a Good Man and renounced the pleasures of the flesh, their souls would be saved, carried back up to their Maker. "Before your father ceased to speak, he asked to be baptized into our faith," the elder said. "He will join his Maker in no time."

She told the Good Men that she, too, wanted to be saved, to be with her father one day, and they replied that unless she intended to be a Good Woman for the remainder of her life, she should be a Believer— a follower of the Good Christians. "Believe in our Word through your life," the elder said, "and, like your father, on your deathbed ask to be baptized. Then you will be ready to renounce the flesh, and the vulgar practices of common men."

After her father died, the Good Men told her that they had visited Montaillou on several occasions. A villager had come across them in Ax-les-Thermes and had invited them up to his home. Already six families in Montaillou believed. . . .

Pierre drew away from the Châtelaine's breasts, overcome with fear and recognition. He wanted to hate the heretics—the men who threatened the Church and thus his power as parish priest. Their notion that Satan had created the earth was shocking, blasphemous. Still, he could not help but feel strangely comforted by their abhorrence of the flesh, by their conviction that the soul, rather than the body, was essentially eternal. It seemed to him that no creed of the Church had settled as easily in his mind.

"The Believers in the village want to be saved, Pierre," the Châtelaine whispered. "I want to be saved. But what is true?"

He saw her dark eyes searching his. In the underground, where the rules of light and the Church had no home, he could not answer.

A *FORTNIGHT LATER*, he was reciting the Quicumque Vult to a small group of parishioners at the Mass following terce. He stood on the beech-wood chest, smelling myrrh and cloves burning in the thurible, the glimmer of morning filtering through the apertures of the chapel walls.

"*Est ergo fides recta ut credamus et confiteamur, quia Dominus noster Iesus Christus, Dei Filius, Deus et homo est,*" he said. The true faith is: we believe and profess that our Lord Jesus Christ, the Son of God, is both God and man. "*Deus est ex substantia Patris ante saecula genitus: et homo est ex substantia matris in saeculo natus.*" As God He was begotten of the substance of the Father before time; as man He was born in time of the substance of His Mother. "*Perfectus Deus, perfectus homo: ex anima rationali et humana carne subsistens.*" He is perfect God; and He is perfect man, with a rational soul and human flesh.

Perfect God, perfect man. Although Pierre had said the Quicumque Vult more than a thousand times, he realized he had never fully given himself over to its words. As a boy, he had been necessarily committed to the notion of spirit as pure and flesh as corrupt. He remembered what the healer Na Roqua had told his mother when his hip had begun to deteriorate. *Flesh is a prison of temptation. Unbearable for the soul that is pure.* He had believed his soul was eating away his flesh—his crippled body was a testament to it. Even now, when he imagined himself in Paradise, what he saw was not a stunted man, but a surging spirit. A bodiless emanation of light.

"*Ad cuius adventum omnes homines resurgere habent cum corporibus suis: et reddituri sunt de factis propriis rationem,*" he continued. At His coming, all men are to arise with their own bodies; and they are to give an account of their lives.

No, he had not become a priest to save his flesh. He had become a priest to enlarge his already flesh-despising soul. And in the bottom of his heart he had never believed—or wanted to believe—that he would rise from death with his crippled body. His heart pounded and the faces before him blurred in the haze of smoke and light. If the Good Men were heretics because they believed that God by nature could not be made flesh, and that the body by nature could not rise up to God, how was he any different?

ON SEVERAL OCCASIONS, the Châtelaine tried to persuade him to meet the Good Men, but he knew if he revealed himself to be sympathetic to their faith, he would lose any power he had over them. Inquisition could start again in the region, and the Good Men could be apprehended and tried. They could speak against him. No, he must not present himself to them unless he was willing to risk everything—his position as spiritual leader in the village, his safety, his freedom, his life.

Easter came quickly, and with it the seasonal confessors. If any parishioner avowed heresy, thus bringing it into the light, he would be obligated to take a stand against it, and ultimately to inform the Bishop of its presence in the village. Not wanting to threaten the faith he had only just discovered, he tried to prevent confessing parishioners from divulging heresy of any kind. He spoke to them in starts, sometimes retracting a question before fully forming it in his mind. Sensing his frustration, parishioners grew silent after admitting small transgressions, causing him to lose his temper and inflict far heavier penances on them than they deserved—penances he knew they could never carry out; so he had the added burden of having prevented them from fully liberating themselves from sin.

During the Easter Mass, he scolded parishioners before he could stop himself, interrupting his reading and pointing at children slumped on the floor. "When the Gospel is read, stand!" he hollered. "When the bell rings at the Elevation, kneel and pray!"

After the service, he walked to the fortress, the amulet in his fist. The Châtelaine had told him to come after Mass; her husband was at the Court in Foix, and they would be able to make love in the light. Instead of taking his usual midnight path, he limped up the village road.

The day was crisp and bright, and he passed village women weeding in their gardens and washing clothes in buckets of lye, village men resting on benches outside and exchanging words as they watched their children play. A few parishioners nodded to him, but none stopped to question where he was headed. They trusted him implicitly.

Rounding the side rampart of the fortress, he tried to ease his shame with the thought that it was not *he* but *his body* that was driving him back. He waited in the stable for the maidservant to appear. Instead, a flaxen-haired girl he recognized as the youngest daughter of the Châtelaine poked her head in the door. "Do you want to see Mama, Domine?" she said. He stepped toward her and she spun around, her braids bumping against her backside.

She led him to the same tower, and up the spiral staircase to the second floor. They passed through a hall lined with tapestries, down a narrow corridor, to the great chamber where, she said, her mother and father slept. The Châtelaine was sitting before a mirror of polished metal, an enormous fire blazing in the hearth behind her.

The girl ran off, and the Châtelaine held her hand out to him. Without a word, he untied his breeches, stepped forward, and dropped the amulet. His body raged to have her whole.

"Pierre," she said, scowling at him.

He held her by the waist and pulled her down to the floor.

"You will rip my dress," she said.

He pushed her onto all fours.

"Pierre!" she cried, reaching for the amulet. "Wait!"

He lifted the back of her skirt and watched as she pushed the amulet into the opening between her thighs. Her head relaxed, falling toward the floor, and he forced his mind away from the thought that she was surrendering against her will.

When he finished, she collapsed and dragged herself away from him, like a snake on the ground, he thought. She pulled up her linens and stood, glaring down at him, her face red and angry. "The Good Men are coming today," she said. "And villagers who believe. They are coming to the fortress for a baptism. I thought you would want to meet them."

He felt his heart leap up in fear. The Good Men. Here in the fortress. No, no, he was not ready. He stood, pulling up his breeches, and limped past her toward the door.

She caught him by the elbow, gazing at him with desperate eyes. "Hide from them if you will," she said. "But see them at the very least." She stroked his sleeve. "See them, Pierre. And you will know how good they are."

SHE HID HIM in the shadows behind a coffer near the entrance to the hall, where, she said, the Good Men and the villagers would congregate. As he crouched waiting, his hip racked with pain, he peered into the dark recesses of the hall, lit up now and again by the roaring flames in the hearth. He heard an ominous shuffling—footsteps, he realized. A man he recognized as Raymond Belot and his wife, Guillemette, appeared by the door to the hall, their faces somber and yet betraying a gleam of excitement. They stopped to wash their hands in a large bowl of water that the Châtelaine had placed on a bench outside the hall.

Other villagers followed soon after—the family Maurs, Jean Marty and his wife, Philippe Guilhabert, the family Benet, the wife of the late Bernard Rives and her grown son Pons, all dimly clad and reverent. Pierre's heart skipped a beat when he saw the maidservant enter the hall. Could it be that the girl with the eyes of the Virgin was a Believer? She stood in shadow close to Pons Rives, as if she were intimate with him.

The room became very still, except for the shifting shadows spreading from the hearth. Then a man Pierre recognized as the weaver from Prades d'Aillon entered, followed by two men in black habits—the brothers Authié. They were pallid and emaciated, just as the Châtelaine had described them, both with dark, sunken eyes. Perhaps it was the play of firelight behind them, but they seemed to exude holiness, their gazes at once serene and penetrating, their movements unhurried and yet imbued with near Godly assurance.

The brother who looked to be the elder held a black book in his hands, and the other carried a folded white cloth under his arm. They stood before a large trestle table in the center of the room, the villagers clustering around them.

"Has each here washed his hands so that nothing should sully this sacred baptismal rite?" said the younger brother, in a steady bass voice.

"Yes," the villagers murmured collectively.

The brother took the cloth from beneath his arm, unfolded it, held one edge between his hands, and flapped it up into the air. It floated down over the table like a white ghost, then collapsed in creases that he straightened out with his fingers. He looked up at the villagers, his eyes severe. "Prades Tavernier?" he said.

The weaver from Prades came forward. He was a stocky man with a puffy face, and his steps resounded in the hall. He bent one knee and bowed awkwardly to the brothers, his thick hands clasped together. *"Benedicite,"* he said, his voice gruff. He bowed again and rose. *"Benedicite."* He bowed a third time. "Good Christians," he said on rising. "I ask for the blessing of God. And for your own blessing. Pray to the Lord for us. Pray that He protect us from an unworthy death. And lead us to a good end among the Good Christians."

Pierre shivered. The words were so noble, so foreign and yet familiar.

The younger brother nodded to the weaver. "Receive from God and from ourselves the blessing you besought."

The elder brother held up his book, a fearsome expression on his face. "Prades Tavernier," he said softly, almost singing. "Do you wish to receive the spiritual baptism through which the Holy Spirit is given in the Church of God with the holy prayer and the laying on of hands by the Good Men?"

"I do," said Prades Tavernier. "Yes."

"The Church of God has preserved this holy baptism by which the Holy Spirit is given from the time of the apostles to this day," the elder said. "It is passed from Good Men to Good Men until now, and the Church will continue to confer it until the end of the world."

Prades Tavernier bowed down on one knee, his head disappearing into shadow.

"You should understand, Prades Tavernier," the elder said, "that a Good Man has the power to bind and to loose, to forgive sins and to fix them on men, as Christ said in the Gospel of Saint John, 'Receive the Holy Spirit. If you forgive the sins of any men, they are forgiven them. And if you fix the sins of any men upon them, they shall remain fixed.'"

The elder was discrediting the authority of the Church, Pierre realized, and claiming the power of a priest himself. Pierre watched with a racing heart as the elder lowered his book and set it on the white cloth over the table.

"Prades Tavernier," he said. "If you wish to receive this power to forgive sins and to fix them on men, you must keep all the command-

ments of Christ and the New Testament to the utmost of your ability.
Know that He forbade men to commit adultery, and any act of coitus is
adultery. He forbade men to kill, to lie, to swear oaths, to steal, to do
unto others what they would not have done to themselves. He commanded them to forgive those who do evil to them. To love their enemies. To pray for and bless those who denounce and accuse them. To
turn the other cheek to those who smite them. To give up their cloaks
to them who take their cloaks away. He forbade them to judge and to
condemn." He paused, his eyes flashing. "Most importantly, you must
hate this world, Prades Tavernier."

The floorboards creaked as the villagers shifted. Prades Tavernier
fidgeted on the floor, and Pierre saw his head bob up and down in the
shadows before he broke out in loud sobs, gasping greedily for air. How
Pierre longed to release himself so fully!

"You must hate this world and its works and all things which are
of this world," the elder went on. "In his First Epistle, Saint John says,
'Beloved, do not love the world, nor the things that are in this world. If
anyone loves the world, there is no love for the Father in his heart. For
all that is in the world is lust of the flesh, desire of the eyes and pride in
life—things that come not from the Father but from the world. And the
world and its desires shall pass away, but he who does the will of God
shall endure forever.'"

The elder looked from villager to villager, and Pierre felt as
though he were being drawn forward, as though he himself were being
baptized into the heresy.

"You must keep the commandments of God and hate this world,"
the elder said. "And if you do these things well until the end of your
days, your soul will have eternal life."

"I have the will," said Prades Tavernier, clasping his hands together. He raised his head from the shadows and his eyes cast back and
forth about the room, as if he were possessed. "Pray God to give me the
strength to fulfill it!" he cried out.

"Do you renounce the cross made with oil and chrism by the
priest at your baptism?" the elder said.

"I renounce it!"

"My brother, do you give yourself to God and the Gospel?"

"I do!" Prades Tavernier kissed his fisted hands.

"Do you promise that henceforth you will eat neither meat, nor
eggs, nor cheese, nor fat, but will nourish yourself only with fish and oil?"

"Yes!"

"That henceforth you will not tell lies, nor take oaths, nor lend your body to any indulgence, nor walk alone when you could have a companion, nor sleep without breeches and vest, nor forswear your faith for fear of water, fire, or any other death?"

"Yes! Yes!"

The brothers blessed and forgave the weaver, and welcomed him into their midst with the Kiss of Peace. As the villagers moved to embrace one another, Pierre noticed the maidservant look back over her shoulder, directly into the shadows where he hid. It was as if she could hear his thoughts unraveling. . . . He had found kindred spirits—men who distrusted the flesh as much as he had since he was a boy. He felt terrified, elated, sick with apprehension and awareness. Everything was clear to him suddenly. He was a heretic. He was sure of it. And either he had to join the Good Men or join the efforts to rid them from the land.

THREE

THE MAIDSERVANT did not know for certain that Pierre was hiding in the shadows behind her, but she sensed he was not far. She had become familiar with his scent, dark and sweetly pungent, like the smoke of ripened leaves burning—a scent she could never entirely separate from the image of him making love to the Châtelaine in the dungeon, the low orange light of the lantern flickering across their bodies. She never imagined Pierre was her uncle, the man who had baptized her and blessed her mother Marquise seventeen years before. She would learn of their blood relation only after her own daughter had become his lover, and then the truth would be heavier than her heart could bear.

As a child, she had been reminded of her bastard station in life almost daily. She had no paternal surname because her mother refused to reveal the identity of her father to anyone—"Knowing his name can only bring you sadness," her mother said. They lived as servants in the house of a wealthy peasant in Prades d'Aillon. When the children of the house received whiter bread to eat or warmer cloaks for winter, her mother looked her in the eye and told her to stop her tears. "Fabrisse," her mother said. "You were baptized, yes. Your sins were forgiven. But the reputation of your mother can never be regained. You are a bastard in the village, if not in Heaven. It is best not to wish it otherwise." Her mother kissed her hair. "Hold on to your vergonha," she whispered. "You have so little to spare."

Vergonha, Fabrisse understood, was modesty, decency, honor—

the right to wear the name of a proud father, to be a bride. Once ver-gonha was squandered, it could never be regained. Her mother had squandered vergonha by birthing her without a husband, and now Fab-risse had no family clan to attach herself to, no prospects of a marriage of any kind. Still, because her mother had not sold any part of her own body—breast milk or the opening between her thighs, Fabrisse was not without a measure of vergonha, and from the age of eleven, she com-mitted herself fervently to preserving what remained.

She and her mother shared a room in the back of the house, and every night, after her mother fell asleep, Fabrisse would push back the woolen blanket, walk to the window, and crack the shutters open so she could see the starry night sky. There was no one to look upon her then, to see her hands folded together in a fist, pressed to her mouth, to see her tears. There was no one but God, and she prayed He make her stronger than her mother. She did not want to fall into the pit of even greater shame.

WHEN SHE WAS THIRTEEN, it seemed God delivered her a miracle. She had always been marked with peculiar hair—wild and kinked, holding on to knots and nettles and burrs, and of a blacker shade than that of other village girls, whose braids were earth- or nut- or wheat-colored, blending into the mountainside as easily as air. Fabrisse re-garded her hair as a sign of her cursedness, the legacy of having been born outside a family line. Still, to those children who gossiped about her—saying her hair had sprung from the same far-off land whence the tilted eye of her mother had come, "a land of pygmies and cyclopeans and snakes as ugly as Satan"—Fabrisse was defiant. "My mother and I, we come from the Garden of Eden," she said. "There, every sort of goodness grows. Trees with flowers in colors you have never seen. Scents, more scents than you can count. And when you breathe them in, it is like dreaming. All your pain, your sadness, disappears."

It was as if God listened to her story and decided to prove it true. One night, her mother discovered the sweet scent of honeyed almonds clinging to the bedsheets. She tracked the scent to Fabrisse's pillow, and buried her nose in her hair. "I am breathing Heaven," her mother mur-mured.

Soon village women were stopping Fabrisse in the street, taking deep whiffs of the scent they called medicinal, and asking to touch her softening hair. Fabrisse worked her fingers through its snarls, separating out strands from nettles and burrs. She borrowed a boar-bristle brush from the mistress of her house and brushed until her hair shone like the gauzy fine fabric of cobwebs caught on early morning grass. "Like halos around the apostles of our Lord after he was raised to Paradise," said one villager. "Like cloves, like anise," said another. "Like the scent of holy oil in the chrismatory."

Word spread as far as the villages of Limoux and Lordat, and more than a few peasants journeying across the region stopped in Prades d'Aillon to see her. An old shepherd came down with his flock of sheep during the summer transhumance, asking for her prayers for bestial fertility, and two monks from Toulouse made a pilgrimage to the village in order to evaluate her hair for holy quality. "A blessing of great beauty," they said. Fabrisse prayed to God that her hair would bring a husband before her bastard self curled and kinked its way to the surface again.

WHEN SHE WAS FOURTEEN, she was sitting in Mass, listening to a sermon about Adam and Eve. "Eve was made of Adam," the priest said. "Her body was opposite his, her organs more open, corruptible." Fabrisse saw his eyes turn to her, moving from her hair, to her lips, to her breasts. His eyes lifted and caught her gaze. "Take care to guard your organs," he said, scowling down at her, as if the very sight of her repulsed him. "Imitate the suffering of Christ. Flagellate your body into submission."

Though she did not have the words to describe how the priest's admonitions planted themselves in her mind, deep within her she sensed a connection between the wonderment her hair inspired and the wretched temptation female organs presented to men. When she arrived home after Mass, she stole a stretch of linen from the cellar. She braided her hair and wound the cloth around her head and neck and cheeks in the style of an old woman, so that no part of her hair showed. It was the practice for girls to wear their hair loose until they experienced the first change in life, and then to indicate their modesty with a simple linen band or bonnet. Fabrisse had not yet bled, but she felt her womanhood seeping from her, and wanted to gird it in. She would not have a man thinking her corruptible.

That night, as she lay waiting for her mother to dream, she thought of the priest staring at her body. She thought of Christ, and how he had battled for purity in the wilderness of temptation. She thought of the suffering He had endured. She pictured His head, pierced bloody by the crown of thorns. She pictured His hands and feet, crushed by nails and hammered into the cross. When her mother was asleep, she walked to the window, pushed the shutters open, and stood naked in the moonlight. Soft hairs had begun to grow over the place between her legs, and she reached down and plucked them out, one at a time, holding herself from crying with the words of the Pater. "Our Father, who art in Heaven, hallowed be thy name."

WITH HER HAIR BOUND in the linen wimple, village talk about her diminished, and though she sometimes missed the adoration of others, she was glad to have held on to her vergonha, glad never to have allowed her organs to deprive her of her honor.

When she was fifteen, her mother died. For the first time in her life she felt fully alone. The man of the house in which she lived and worked began to pay her certain attention, swatting her bottom as she ladled soup for dinner, or sometimes pausing by her door at night. She wrapped the wimple tighter around her head and plucked the hairs growing between her legs more fiercely, pulling each from the end rather than the root to induce more pain.

That winter, a messenger from the fortress at Montaillou arrived in the village. The messenger stood on the steps before the chapel, calling for all people to gather around. Fabrisse huddled close to the other villagers in the churchyard, breathing heat into her hands as she stared up at the messenger—glorious, he seemed to her. Nearly as tall as the chapel doorway and broad-shouldered, with black eyes, dark curly hair, and a pale coat dotted with flakes of snow, he looked like an angel of the Lord.

"I come for the girl with the hair," he said aloud, surveying the crowd. "The Châtelaine wants her for a maid."

Without thinking, Fabrisse stepped forward and the white smoke of her breath pushed out from her as if it were leading the way. The villagers parted and let her pass. The messenger descended the chapel stairs. Not knowing how to address him, Fabrisse bowed her head, pulling her wimple tight with one hand and wrapping her cloak around her body with the other. She turned and walked back through the parted crowd, looking over her shoulder now and then to be sure the messenger was following. He stared at her, his dark eyes calm and almost shy. She led him through village alleyways to the house in which she lived. As he waited outside by the frozen-over vegetable beds, she gathered objects she did not want to live without: the sun-bleached sheets on which she and her mother had slept, the tiny christening clothes that proved she had been baptized, and the wedding dress of her mother. Though she had come to accept that as a bastard she would never be a bride, having the dress was a consolation, a reminder that marriage might have been part of her history and fate.

She followed the messenger into the woods without ever stopping to look back at the village. The cool, dry air stung her face, and the silence of the snow absorbed her. For the first time in so long, her mind felt light and free. It was almost as if there were no sin in the world, no shadowy wantonness to steal away her vergonha. She watched the pale, broad back of the messenger gathering snow, and the shapes of the birch trees ahead, their lonely trunks reaching patiently toward the sky.

THEY ARRIVED in Montaillou when the moon was high, and its silvery light reflected off the snow-lined roofs of the houses clinging to the hillside. The fortress appeared massive in the moonlight, with four mighty stone towers, and a soaring barbican, fringed with snow. As she and the messenger mounted the icy village road, she shivered with sudden apprehension.

They entered the fortress through the gate beneath the barbican, a guard permitting them to pass, and then the messenger led her up a flight of stairs, down a series of frigid passages, to a room with a fire so bright and large and giving off such heat, she felt instantly comforted. The Châtelaine lay in a sumptuous bed of ermine-furred blankets and quilted serge coverlets. Her hair was loose, and she was wearing a tunic of deep red linen, her sleeves laced tautly from wrist to elbow. When she saw Fabrisse and the messenger enter, she pushed herself up to sit, staring at them with steady attention.

"Is it you?" she said.

Fabrisse turned back to the messenger, but found he had disappeared.

"You," the Châtelaine said. She held out her hand, with something of familiarity and care. "Come here." She dropped her hand and patted the bed beside her.

Fabrisse stepped forward, allowing her cloak to part. She sat down on the edge of the bed, so soft she smiled in spite of herself. She felt her face become hot, and she pulled the cloak up over her lap.

"Show me your hair," the Châtelaine said.

Fabrisse hesitated for a moment. She had not released her hair in front of anyone other than her mother since the rector of Prades d'Aillon had shamed her into girding it away. She reached behind her neck and untucked the folded wimple.

"Go on now," the Châtelaine prodded her, smiling with her eyes.

Fabrisse began to unwind the wimple from around her face and neck. She felt her ears come uncovered, and then the coolness of air touch the top of her head. She set the wimple in her lap and drew her long, heavy braid forward, pulling the twine off the end and pushing her fingers into the grooves—like so many hidden organs coming undone. She reminded herself that the Châtelaine was the only person in sight, but still she had the sense that she was undressing for a man now, opening herself to corruption once again. She unbraided, unbraided, and when she was through, she sat with her head bowed, her hair falling all around her.

"Good God," she heard the Châtelaine murmur, and saw that the Châtelaine's face had become pale. A shadow appeared on the wall behind the bed. As the Châtelaine reached out to touch her hair, Fabrisse moved her gaze in the direction of the shadow's source.

Beyond the doorway, in the corridor, she saw the messenger standing watch. His mouth opened when his eyes caught hers, but he did not turn away. His pale coat was gone now, and she could see the contours of his body—sturdier than it had seemed when he had been standing on the chapel steps. His shoulders and neck and leather-clad calves were as thick as those of a man who worked daily in the fields.

"Good God," the Châtelaine said again. "It does glow, your hair."

Fabrisse bowed her head toward the Châtelaine in a gesture of humility. After a moment, she looked back to the corridor, but the messenger was gone.

. . .

THAT NIGHT, the Châtelaine explained why she had called Fabrisse to
the fortress. "Beauty is like pestilence," she said. "It can be caught, inhaled, absorbed through the pores of the skin. My own beauty has
started to wither, and I want to be infected once more." She assigned
Fabrisse the role of guarding her body and all its manifestations. Among
the more basic tasks, Fabrisse was to massage the Châtelaine, sprinkle
her garments with iris-scented water, brush olive oil and cardamom
through her hair, inspect her skin for lice and ticks, and anoint her
breasts with pomades made from garden lavender and pork fat melted
over the kitchen fire.

At first, Fabrisse found these obligations to be agonizing. She had
come to regard her own body as something against which her vergonha
battled—its blood and smells threatening to soil the cleanliness of her
prayer. When the Châtelaine stripped before her, asking her to examine
her carefully, Fabrisse saw the awkward droop of her breasts—one hanging lower than the other—and the thin, translucent lines veining down
each breast to the nipple, and she tasted bile in the back of her throat.

With time, however, she overcame this weakness. She told herself
the Châtelaine was like a small child—incapable of doing her own
washing and changing—and this made her tasks more bearable. She began to look at the body of the Châtelaine as a thing unto itself, something akin to an animal or a plant that needed to be tended in particular
ways in order to flourish, and she memorized its most subtle fluctuations
to serve it better. She learned the translucent lines on the Châtelaine's
breasts diminished at the half-moon and grew longer when the moon
disappeared. She learned her nipples became more supple when massaged with calves' foot marrow, and took on a pinker hue in the early
light of morning, when the rays of day pierced the apertures of her
chamber wall. She learned her stools hardened with her monthly blood,
which began with the new moon and lasted nearly six days, requiring at
least two changes of linen. She learned only clysters made from the liquid of sheep head and violet oil softened the stools, whereas milder
remedies of leeks, senna leaves, and brews from borage did nothing but
lodge them in. She learned musk made her skin smell sour, while anise
made her breath sweeter, and applying pressure to the base of her
thumb could quiet even her wildest tears.

By summer, with the leagues of golden wheat stretching through the fields below and the buzz of hatching gadflies ever present in the warm air, Fabrisse had come to look upon her own body with a kind of gentleness. She shared a room with the cooks, and one wall was pierced by a slit through which she could see the village and the forests and the plots of sown land of the Pays d'Aillon below. Every night, when the cooks were sleeping, she would stand from her bed and go to the opening in the wall, to the calm moonlight. She would lift her nightdress and, instead of plucking out the hairs between her legs, she would regard them with pity. It was not their fault, after all, that they grew. Nor was it her fault. Had not God created the world and everything in it? She wondered if the organs folded within her were not, in some small way, blessed because they, too, had been formed by the hand of God.

Through the summer and into the crisp nights of fall, she allowed the hair between her legs to sprout and spread and curl, like the hair on her bastard head once had. She remembered how the messenger had spied on her the first night in the fortress, and though she had not seen him since, she imagined him watching her, admiring her body as something almost divine.

ONE EVENING, the Châtelaine asked her to bind her breasts tightly and braid her hair with an ivory ribbon. When the Châtelaine had been prepared, she gave Fabrisse a colored candle and a lantern, led her by the hand through the cellars and granaries on the ground floor, and showed her a hole low in the fortress rampart wall through which a person could easily pass. She guided her down a spiral staircase to the dungeons below.

"I will wait for you here," she said, pointing to a bench in one of the small chambers. "Go to the chapel at the end of the road. Find the rector, and give him the candle. Tell him it was made with my own hands."

The Châtelaine said that she wanted Fabrisse to lead him back unseen—up the goat path to the stables, along the back rampart, through the wall, and down the spiral staircase to the chamber. "Whatever happens, stay by the door," she said. "Listen for the sounds of impostors. Listen for my husband. Never leave me alone."

The cooks with whom Fabrisse shared a room often referred to the dungeons as "the privates" of the fortress, and smelling the underground, she understood why. The dungeons smelled of sweat and sputum and pus. Of menstrual blood and human excrement. Fabrisse did not know why the Châtelaine wanted the rector in the dungeons, but as she walked down the rocky slope of the knoll, holding her lantern out in front of her to watch for tree roots and snakes, she feared no good was coming.

The chapel door was parted slightly, and she gazed inside and saw the rector kneeling before the statue of the Virgin in the dim light. His head was bowed down, his hair dark, wavy. She pulled her wimple tighter and tucked it in behind her neck before entering.

The rector glanced back at her, and then stood with a start, crossing himself. She froze in the center of the chapel, waiting for him to approach. His expression was far gentler than she had expected, sad even, though the manner in which he held his arms out from his sides spoke of tension, fear. He was small but stocky, with short, thick arms and a heavy jaw. He stared at her, waiting for her to speak, and she found it impossible not to lower her gaze to the floor. She touched the wimple covering her head to be sure it was still there. It was not that he reminded her of the priest of Prades d'Aillon; there was nothing angry or violent in his gaze. But, in an instant, she had felt as if he had moved within her, resting inside her eyes. She held the candle out. "For the Virgin," she said.

He stepped toward her, and as he neared, she caught his smell—sharp and rich as soil. She had heard once that the stronger the stench of a man, the greater his virility. The rector reached for the candle, and she clutched it back to her chest in sudden fear. "The Châtelaine made it with her own hands," she said. "She needs you to come to the fortress." She pushed the candle out again. "Please."

He took the candle from her. "Is the Châtelaine ill?" he said.

"She needs you," she said, withdrawing from him.

At the chapel door, she turned and saw him peering back at her, his forehead furrowed, as if he were trying to recognize her. Perhaps he had passed her in Prades d'Aillon, she thought. Perhaps he had seen her mother.

SHE LED HIM up the goat path, through the stables, and under the wall. In the dungeon, she leaned into the doorway, staring at the lantern by her feet. The Châtelaine greeted him with a voice far breathier and higher in pitch than usual, and Fabrisse wondered if she, too, smelled his vigor.

Words moved through the air and Fabrisse tried to catch them. *Good men,* she heard. *Bishop. Heresy.* It seemed to her the words were like mirrors, reflecting each other back and forth so that nothing was perceptible. When the words stopped, she glanced inside the chamber and saw the rector on the ground. The Châtelaine moved toward him and knelt down, her face less than an arm's length from his. The Châtelaine opened her mouth, but said nothing.

Fabrisse lowered her eyes to the lantern again. The body of the Châtelaine was not a child's, she thought. It was the body of a woman. A body that Fabrisse herself had been preparing to be corrupted.

NIGHT AFTER NIGHT, she led the rector to the Châtelaine and felt her own vergonha slipping from her. Standing by the door, she came to think of herself as the guardian of sin—keeping out the forces of village and Godly law. Even worse, she came to need the adulterous lovemaking as if it were her own. When the Châtelaine informed her that the rector would not be coming on a particular night, she found herself becoming angry, and she had to bite her tongue so not to reveal her frustration. On nights the rector was there, she waited through their conversation, catching phrases here and there, like so many veils before the sounds she longed to hear—the sounds of mingling flesh and deep respiration, sounds that made her heart beat low, that made her have to grip the side of the door. She smelled leather, dampness, the rector's sweat. She heard lips, saliva, whispered sighs. She stole glimpses of the rector—the bottom of his spine, the mounds of his rear. She watched his hands fold into the Châtelaine's, and imagined her own hands clasping his.

After he had gone and she had retreated to her room, she looked out the slit in the wall at the expanse of the moonlit Pays d'Aillon, at the poplars sighing with the breath of night, and she found she could think her way beneath the rector. Feel *her* mouth kissing his, *her* crease being pressed into, *her* calves high above him in the air. Her body would be his, until the face of the messenger would flare up in her mind, his sweet eyes stunned to find what evils she had allowed in. Even her thoughts, her innermost self, had turned impure.

. . .

EARLY THAT SPRING, the Châtelaine called her to her room, and Fabrisse stood before the great, raging fire, basking in its hot goodness.

"Come," the Châtelaine said. She was sprawled out over the ermine blankets on her bed, wearing nothing but a thin linen chemise, and she held up her hand—just as she had on the first day Fabrisse had come to the fortress. She patted the bed, and Fabrisse sat beside her.

"Do you remember the man who brought you to the fortress?" the Châtelaine said.

Fabrisse nodded. She remembered the broad back of the messenger plodding before her through the mountainside, the snowy limbs of the beech trees twinkling in the gathering moonlight.

"His name is Pons Rives," the Châtelaine said.

Pons Rives. How startling it was to know his name.

The Châtelaine explained that he was not a part of the fortress household, but rather a village peasant of adequate means whom—because of his noble beauty—she had employed as a messenger from time to time. After he had brought Fabrisse to the fortress, however, he had asked to be relieved of this duty. His father had died recently and he had become so occupied with labor on the small square of land his family tended, he had even neglected his obligation to marry—or so his mother said. Only this past Sunday, Old Woman Rives had approached the Châtelaine in the square with words of concern about the future of her family line. Pons, she said, had refused each and every one of her suggestions for a wife. The only woman of whom he spoke admiringly was "the girl with the hair." When Old Woman Rives had asked Pons who this girl might be, he had said she was an attendant to the Châtelaine, to which she had responded that it would be better to have a servant wife than none at all. He had looked at her, stunned. "Wife?" he had said. "But she is not a girl to be a wife, Mother. She is like an angel." The Châtelaine said Old Woman Rives had clasped her hands together, begging her—for the love of her family line—to make a marriage happen between the young people.

"Do you understand?" the Châtelaine said, her eyes bright. "Pons admires you. A beautiful man admires you. And he wants you to be his wife."

Fabrisse shook her head in disbelief. "He does not want a wife," she said.

The Châtelaine smiled, stroked her cheek. "He is only shy," she said.

Fabrisse glanced through the doorway of the room and could almost see the messenger as he had been on that first day—leaning against the wall, waiting timidly for her to unbind herself. Her throat was suddenly tight and tears came to her eyes. Through one of the apertures in the wall, she saw a piece of sky, thick with mist, and the green tops of poplars giving way to the wind. This was, she thought, the moment she had always waited for—a moment, perhaps, that was always meant to be. The messenger was her chance for a surname, a clan to cling to, a family life. Her chance to want someone in the light. But she was a bastard. A bastard, and marriage had no place for her.

"A woman weds in the name of her father," she said. "I have no father, no name to offer up."

The Châtelaine moaned. "Fabrisse," she said, scowling with impatience, her cheeks flushed with emotion. "You speak like a girl who thinks the rules of the Church are always right. Hold your tongue, and you will find no one cares about your tainted birthright."

It was the most stunning and blasphemous statement Fabrisse had ever heard. She could have allowed her mind to spin webs of questions, webs of doubt, but instead she bent down and kissed the moist palm of the Châtelaine, demonstrating her gratitude, her assent.

IN ALL THE TIME she had lived in Montaillou, she had ventured outdoors only to gather herbs from the garden, or to meet the rector at the stables and lead him safely back to the dungeon. She had avoided Sunday Mass, occupying herself instead with preparing the Châtelaine and her daughters; she could not find it in herself to imagine sitting through a service conducted by a man whom she had watched making love, a man whom she had imagined moving into her.

The first thing she did when the Châtelaine excused her from her room on the day she consented to be married was to leave the fortress. She walked through the front fortified gate, passing the guard and breathing in the freshness of earth and air and mist. Half running down the stone steps that zigzagged down the bracken-covered hill to the head of the village road, she caught herself twice from falling. At the bottom of the steps, she bent down to remove her shoes, leather slippers inherited from the Châtelaine—so tight they cut into her heels.

Carrying the shoes in one hand, she walked a few steps down the road, the delicious coolness of the earth pressing up between her toes. She breathed deeply and swallowed in the new green growth of spring. A wild sprawl of violets clinging to the hillside rock caught her eye. She crouched by the blooms and leaned her back against the rock.

Still above the mist, she could see none of the houses below, and the guard standing by the fortress gate had retreated within. She felt, for the first time in so long, at ease. Why had she never come outside like this before? Why had she been, she realized now, so unhappy? She felt as if she had been holding her happiness within and all she had to do was release it. She looked up into the sky, beyond the clouds. *Mama,* she whispered, *I am going to be married.*

She closed her eyes and pushed her fingertips into the earth, and soon she found that she was laughing.

THE MARRIAGE was to take place on the evening before Easter, and one week before the event, Fabrisse learned from the Châtelaine that it would not be performed in the chapel by the rector, but in the home of Pons and his mother. At first, Fabrisse had been relieved—she had worried that standing before the rector during the ceremony, she would catch his scent and be plagued by lustful thoughts. But then the Châtelaine had said the wedding would be presided over by two brothers called Good Men, and Fabrisse had felt dread fan up between her eyes. She remembered how, over and over, the Châtelaine had spoken of Good Men to the rector in the dungeon, and how he had spoken of them back. *Good Men. Two brothers called Good Men. Heretics.* She had the dim sense that the Châtelaine and the rector not only were concerned for these Good Men, but harbored belief in their ways.

For days, she remained up in the bedroom she shared with the cooks, pretending to have fallen ill and pulling the stained sheets she had once shared with her mother up over her eyes. She remembered stories her mother had told her as a child about the heretics from long ago—heretics burned at the stake, heretic babies slaughtered in piles, heretic villages destroyed house by house. Heresy was sin, her mother had told her. And yet, and yet, she could not remember either the Châtelaine or the rector speaking of it so.

Two days before the wedding, when she had still not risen from bed, the Châtelaine came to see her and Fabrisse could restrain herself no more.

"What is a Good Man?" she asked.

The Châtelaine took time considering the question. "A perfect one," she said. "One who has received the spiritual baptism of the Good Christians." She paused, then added, "One who tries to live without sinning. The Good Men are celibate. They do not argue, do not take oaths or eat meat. They pass their days in prayer and preaching."

"And are they heretics? Is Pons a heretic?"

The Châtelaine hesitated. "He is a Believer," she said. "One who leads a secular life, and does not try to imitate the life of the Good Men, but hopes to be saved by the Church of the Good Christians in the end." She lay down by Fabrisse on the bed, and for a long moment they were silent, staring up at the worm-eaten planks of the ceiling. "Before he dies," the Châtelaine said, "a Believer asks for the same spiritual baptism the Good Men receive. He promises celibacy. Not to eat meat. And then. Then they say he dies free."

She closed her eyes and was so still, Fabrisse thought for a moment she had died. She wanted to ask the Châtelaine if she, too, was a Believer, but the question, it seemed to her, was indiscreet.

ON THE AFTERNOON before Easter, Fabrisse dressed in the wedding tunic of her mother. She fingered the pale blue silk, the softness of fur lining the collar, aching for her mother.

The Châtelaine came to her room, carrying a flat piece of blood-red glass. The glass had come from Toulouse, the Châtelaine said, and she had pressed it to her own lips, speaking into its dark color all the secrets Fabrisse had seen her commit—dungeon secrets too black for a new bride. "Now put what passed out of your mind," the Châtelaine said, giving her the glass. "Put it out of your mind and be a wife. It is nothing more to you now than a pretty thing to hide."

Fabrisse tucked the glass into the sack of her belongings and followed the Châtelaine down the knoll, toward the house in which she was to be married, the chapel bells clanging as if to mark her procession with significance. The house was larger than most in the village. As she approached, she made out a rose-hedged garden, a yard for chickens, a courtyard with a dung heap and a threshing floor, and a small stable beside the house. The wind had gusted down all the plums from a tree by the garden, and they lay like little succulent eggs among the vegetable beds and bushes of flowers. Around one bush puckered with pink color stood a group of women, silently staring up the road toward her. Fabrisse had worn her hair loose, as was the custom for brides in the region, and she felt more naked than if the place between her legs had been bare.

When she was near, a full-bodied woman with a rosy dimpled chin and warm eyes stepped forth. "Your new mother," the Châtelaine said, and the woman opened her arms to her, beaming with happiness.

"Mother Rives, you call me, dear," she said, pressing Fabrisse close. "And how your hair does smell lovely." She took the sack from Fabrisse and led her to the doorway of the house, which entered onto the kitchen, a wide room with a raised stone hearth, decorated by hanging earthenware pots and cauldrons and iron spoons. From the rafters hung bunches of drying rosemary and basil, smoked hams, and wicker baskets, and beside the hearth stood a cupboard swollen with eggs and dried fruits, bowls and tankards. The floor was strewn with sweet mountain grasses, mint, gladioli, and verbena, and the fragrance of the fresh greens and flowers mingled with that of the drying herbs, and of the wood burning in the hearth, and of the damp fug of the beasts that the family sheltered in the house when the stable was overfull. It was a good, full-bodied smell, the smell of life and hope and continuance, and Fabrisse inhaled it with more joy than reservation.

Pons was sitting on a skin-covered bench by the fire, his chin resting on his hand as he stared into the flames, his face so pale he could not have seen the sun for weeks. He was thinner than she remembered, wearing a bleak, gray-belted tunic, and she feared he was unhappy. Mother Rives pushed her forward, and Pons glanced up at her, standing suddenly. His eyes swept over her hair, and then he stared at her with a look of effort, as though he knew he ought to greet her but could not find the words. She was at once disappointed by his silence, fearful that she was a disappointment to him, and excited to be in his presence again.

In a shadowy corner of the room, by the trestle table, sat two men in black habits—the Good Men, she supposed. They were looking down at books in their hands, straining to read in the dim light. In all her life, she had never seen anyone read outside the Mass and a shiver passed through her.

Guests streamed into the kitchen, and then the Good Men stood before the glow of the fire. The elder raised his spindly fingers, asking Pons and Fabrisse to kneel down before him. Not a hush could be heard as they moved together and bent down, crushing the grasses and gladioli beneath their wedding clothes. Out of the corner of her eye, she looked at Pons, whose profile seemed to radiate warmth and goodness in the firelight.

"Do you want to be married?" the Good Man asked loudly.

She saw Pons speak the word yes, but no sound came from him. He cleared his throat. "Yes," he said.

"And you?" the Good Man said to her.

The muscles around Pons's eye twitched slightly.

"And you?" the Good Man said again.

"Yes," she whispered.

"Then it is done," the Good Man said. He sighed, moving through the crowd to his brother without a single blessing or prayer for beatitude.

THE WEDDING was accompanied by no music, no flowers, no feasting or dancing bliss. Only the service followed by a simple passing of the cup. Cup of water, not cup of wine. Good Christians, the Good Men said, fought against its soft seduction.

The room Fabrisse and Pons would share was on one side of the kitchen, and when they first entered it together that night, he quietly moved away from her until she could not see him in the dark and had to feel her way against the walls to the window, which she pushed open to have some light.

"Fabrissa," she heard his voice in the darkness.

She wrapped her arms around her body, listening to him step toward her. When he was an arm's reach away, he stopped, tall and almost blue in the moonlight. His eyes were dark, sorrowful, it seemed to her. She smelled his breath, sweet and smooth as milk. "What do I do?" she whispered.

He held his hand out as if to touch her cheek. "I have something for you," he said. He drew his other hand from behind his back, and she felt dizzy, suddenly sure he would present her with an amulet. "A brush," he said.

She reached down and took the object from him. Even in the moonlight, she could see that it was almost exactly like the boar-bristle brush she had borrowed from the mistress of her house in Prades d'Aillon when she was young—the bristles sewn onto a square of linen tied to a flat wooden paddle.

"From the fair in Ax," Pons said. "Do you have one?"

"No," she said, trying to mask her disappointment. "Thank you."

She held the brush up into the light and stared at it, not knowing what he wanted from her now. She remembered how the Châtelaine sometimes untied the rector's breeches before speaking a word to him.

"May I try?" she heard Pons whisper.

She swallowed, nodding, thinking he wanted to make love to her. Then he reached forward and took the brush, and she realized he meant to use it on her hair. She turned her back to him, so the fullness of her hair faced the room and she could hide her embarrassment in the night sky. She saw the massive shape of the fortress on the summit of the knoll, and the impression of angry mountains receding in the distance.

Pons touched the top of her head with the brush, then moved the bristles down until they caught a snag and he apologized. He began again, placing the brush on the top of her head and dragging it so that her scalp tingled and the skin on her arms went prickly warm. It was as if the most private and hidden part of her were being pulled out into the night. He brushed, he brushed, and a new calm washed through her. She felt shy and weak and opened at the same time. And never for an instant corrupted.

THE NEXT DAY was Easter Sunday. Instead of attending Mass and confession in the chapel, Fabrisse accompanied Pons and Mother Rives to the fortress for a secret baptism. Only now did she grasp absolutely that she had married away from the law of the Church by marrying into the faith of the Good Men.

As the brothers preached, she listened carefully to absorb their meanings. "You must hate this world, Prades Tavernier," she heard one say to the postulant. The phrase struck her like a burning arrow, and she shuddered, looking to Pons. She saw the corner of his eye close and open quickly, as if a small animal were traveling from his temple to the top of his cheek and he were trying to bat it away with his lashes. It was a twitch of torment, she thought, like the twitching of his eye at their wedding.

"You must hate this world and its works and all things which are of this world," the Good Man continued, in a breathy, singing voice. She caught the scent of something familiar in the room—a dark, autumnal sweetness that thickened the air all around. The scent seemed to spread out from behind her, and she felt her neck and shoulders stiffen. The rector was somewhere near—hiding, she realized. She wondered if he was on the verge of revealing himself to the brothers.

"Our Father, receive thy servant in thy justice and send thy grace and thy Holy Spirit upon him," the Good Man said. She saw villagers lean in to one another to give the kiss of peace, but she could give no kiss now. She had no peace in her. She imagined the rector's eyes on the back of her wimple, and she forced her mind to bend away from impure thoughts of him naked on the dungeon floor.

Slowly, she looked over her shoulder, into the shadows beyond the door. The rector had brought his wild scent up from the dungeon into the light of the hall, into the domain of the Châtelaine's husband, and she feared tragedy would follow.

FOUR

T HE FOLLOWING DAY, the husband of the Châtelaine was found dead beneath his covers, his body already swollen from the blazing heat of the chamber fire. He had returned from the Court in Foix late the preceding night, and the Châtelaine— or so the rumor went—had feigned sleep, listening to him crawl into bed beside her and toss until stillness took him. In the morning, she had left him in bed without a thought, the fire in the hearth raging at full force. It was not until the cook mentioned that he had not come to table all day that the Châtelaine returned to the chamber and found the room hot, the air heavy with the sickly smell of death.

A fortnight later, the Lord Comte de Foix came to the village and introduced the new overseer who would be moving into the fortress. Fabrisse stood in the square with a crowd of villagers, waiting to see the Châtelaine and her two daughters leave for Varilhes. It was a parching midday, uncommon for the spring season, and Fabrisse batted the flies away from her face, trying to find the rector in the crowd. She saw the village healer, with her bony long head, and children whom she recognized as friends of the Châtelaine's daughters. Try as she might, she could not find the rector. She wondered if he had been too grief-stricken to watch the Châtelaine go.

From around the bend in the road emerged the Châtelaine and her daughters, dressed in black and riding horses laden with bulging sacks. As they approached, Fabrisse saw the Châtelaine gazing toward the valley below with bland eyes, as if she neither heard her daughters weeping, nor saw the crowd assembled to wish her well. Fabrisse wanted to go to her, to take her hand and massage the soft flesh beneath her thumb to soothe her. "He will visit you," she wanted to say. "The rector will visit you, Madame." But in her heart, she knew what had passed between the rector and her mistress was over.

WITH THE CHÂTELAINE GONE, there was no one to protect the Good Men in the village and they fled. Fabrisse would come to think of the months following their departure as the season of happiness in her life, a period when Pons's eye was as calm and untroubled as that of a suckling child. There was much to be done in the fields, and she and Pons worked side by side for their shared sustenance. They hitched oxen to his plow and turned under weeds and residue crop in his few, small fields. They plowed again, encouraging the soil to breathe, and when the soil was warm they planted peas and beans in furrows, and oats and barley on the ridges between. They mowed and tedded grasses for storage, then harvested the winter wheat with sickles, slicing the stalks a hand's width beneath the ear. They gathered, bound, stacked, carried, and gleaned, laughing and enjoying each other throughout.

When she was not working by his side, she was taking joy in thoughts of him. Her laughter came in waves, surging up from her liquid center as she remembered how he sometimes stopped to kiss her cheek as they sowed the fields, how they often sat in the garden eating berries from the bush until their mouths were purple and delicious. All of life—the planting and harvesting and milking and spinning, the sleeping and cooking and gathering water from the spring—became for her a continuity of experiences that seemed new. How wonderfully soft the coat of a baby lamb was, she thought, as she sat shearing its mother. How wrenching the cramps that kept her indoors with monthly bleeding were, a blessed wrenching that meant she was alive and fertile.

She took to studying the body of Pons as she had studied the body of the Châtelaine—but how much more joyous the process was to her. When Pons drank from the family cup after dinner, she was sure to drink next from it, placing her mouth over the smooth wooden lip of the cup just where his had been, and tasting the bland bitterness he had left behind. When he brushed her hair at night, she would sit on his lap, feeling the muscles of his thighs and watching his eyes move gently over her. He was careful, so careful with her, making love to her with the shutters cracked open so that he could better see her body. She thought every goodness was hers; her soul, it seemed, had found its place of rest.

ONE SULTRY DAY in summer she returned from the little orchard behind the stable with a basket of fruit she meant to preserve in honey for winter. As she leaned against the door of the house to push it open, she heard a deep voice issuing from within. "When all the creatures of God the Father, that is to say, all the spirits, have been recuperated by him," the voice said, "wheat will burst forth, grow and flower, but will not have grain."

She peered into the smoky kitchen, buzzing with flies and gnats, and saw Pons and the Good Men—the same thin, sunken-eyed brothers who had wed them—sitting at the trestle table, an open book before them. The younger of the two brothers was reading aloud, and Pons was leaning toward him, as if to follow the words of the text himself. "Vines will have branches, but no grapes," the Good Man read. "Trees will have leaves and flowers, but no fruits."

She entered the kitchen, lugging the basket with her. She wanted Pons to give her a smile. Instead, he looked up from the book and glared at her.

"Go, Fabrisse," he said, waving her away with his gnat-bitten hand.

"Pons," she said. She stepped closer and set the basket down by the foot of the table. "I gathered fruit for winter. I will honey it this evening. Make you a sweet stew if you want."

"Go away and leave us be," he told her, his eye twitching angrily.

As if she had already disappeared from view, the Good Man commenced reading again, and she left for the open air, wounded by Pons's sudden rejection of her.

BEFORE DINNER that evening, Pons stood in front of the table in silence, his eyes shut. Mother Rives asked what he was doing. "Reciting the Pater," he whispered.

"A long Pater," Mother Rives said, breaking the bread.

"*Benedicite,*" said Pons, his hands on the table. "*Kyrie Eleison. Christe Eleison.* We must bless the table before we begin. . . . God, Who blessed the five loaves and two fishes in the wilderness for His disciples, bless this table and the things that are on it and shall be placed upon it." He made the sign of the cross in the air, saying, "In the Name of the Father, Son, and Holy Spirit." He sat, and broke a piece of bread for himself.

"There is goat meat," said Fabrisse. Mother Rives had killed the goat—too old to produce milk or babies, and she and Fabrisse had taken special care to tenderize the meat with herbs and oil.

"No meat," Pons said, biting into his crust of bread.

"You must eat meat for strength, Pons," said Mother Rives.

"Yes, for strength," said Fabrisse.

Pons took a long drink of water and said he was going to bed.

When Fabrisse had finished washing the supper pot and bowls, she lit a candle, and—protecting its flame with her hand—she crept to their room. She could see Pons on one side of the bed, lying on his back, his eyes closed. His breathing was unsteady, and she knew he was not yet asleep.

"Pons," she said.

He did not move.

"Are you hungry? Are you ill?"

He said nothing. She knelt down by the straw pallet on the floor and pushed her fingers through his thick hair. He rolled onto his side, facing away from her. As candle wax gathered in hot drips on her hand, she stared at his back, longing for a word from him. Finally, when the candle was no longer than her thumb, she blew out its flame and undressed in the dark, telling herself not to cry like a girl.

FOR A REASON Fabrisse could not yet understand, Pons had a deep-seated loathing for his pleasure-loving flesh; he wanted to be desireless, to be pure of physical yearning, and the Good Men sensed as much about him and narrowed in on him as an aspiring Good Christian, spending long hours with him in the house when he should have been in the fields, reading to him from their text and teaching him to read for himself. Some nights, Pons and the brothers read together past the supper hour, banning the women from the kitchen. When they were finished, Fabrisse and Mother Rives would have to scurry to cook a meal appropriate for the Good Men. "No meat no cheese no eggs no wine," Fabrisse reminded herself as she chopped leeks and chives and cabbage. On several occasions, Pons suggested the Good Men be served salted fish, and Fabrisse and Mother Rives gave up their own monthly rations to make Pons happy.

But happy he was not. Many nights, after listening to the Good Men, he would emerge from the kitchen with eyes red-rimmed, as if he had been crying. The twitching at the corner of his eye returned with new vigor, and he lost his temper with Fabrisse more and more often, fixing his gaze upon her so firmly that his pupil became narrow and hard.

One evening, long after the Good Men had left, she rushed from their room to the kitchen in order to keep a pot from boiling over. "What are you doing with a bare head?" he yelled.

She covered her hair with her hands, despondent, and he shook a spasm from his face, as if shaking the anger out of him. He pressed his palms to his eyes. "I am sorry," he said quietly. "You are so lovely, I cannot see to see when your hair is loose."

One day soon after, she returned from the woods with a bucketful of crabapples. She sat on a bench in front of the house, shining the apples and tasting their tart sweetness. Before she had seen Pons coming, he was standing over her, his hands on his hips. Without a word, he took the bucket from her lap and dumped the apples onto the ground.

"Pons!" she cried. "What are you doing?"

"What are *you* doing?"

"Eating," she said. "Shining the apples so we can eat them together."

He reached forward and pulled her wimple down farther over her forehead. "Keep yourself covered," he said. "You do not have to enjoy your food so much."

She wiped bits of apple from her lips, suddenly angry. She started to cry.

"Fabrissa," he said slowly.

"Don't apologize," she snapped.

He bent down and gathered the apples one at a time, putting

them back in the bucket. When he was done, he held the bucket up. "I am going to wash these in the spring," he said. "Will you come with me?"

She wanted to refuse, but she nodded. He pulled her close and kissed her forehead. She tried to kiss his lips, but he turned away, already moving down the road to the spring.

SLEEP BECAME IMPOSSIBLE. Pons ate less and less, sometimes fasting for three days or more, and at night his stomach growled with anger. He tossed and turned, and Fabrisse often found herself ready to scream. "Can I just get you a bite?" she whispered to him one evening. "Just a little scrap of bread, Pons. Just a little something." He refused, told her the hunger would pass. She searched for his hand, wanting to touch him, but he pulled it away without speaking a word to her.

Sleep-ruined, she worried through the night. She went over everything she had heard about the Good Men, every word they had spoken that had found a place in her mind. She remembered that the healer Na Roqua had told Mother Rives one day while spinning in the house that before the weaver Prades Tavernier had been spiritually baptized, he had demonstrated his moral ardor for a full year. He had committed himself to the rules of conduct by which the Good Men lived—excising his wife from his house; eating only bread, fish, and oil; and saying the Pater before any act of danger—mounting a horse, for instance, or passing on a plank over a body of water. Lastly, he had been instructed in the doctrine of the Good Christians and had memorized long passages of their text, passages he could recite aloud without a moment of hesitation.

As Fabrisse waited for the sun to break through the leaves of the shutter, she braced herself to be excised. She was a bastard, and to be excised was almost part of her legacy. The previous joyousness of her marriage, the hope she had found in her betrothal, seemed nothing but an illusion, a false promise of change—just as the transformation of her hair had been. Though she tried to reassure herself with the thought that Pons still made love to her, in her heart she knew his movements were loveless. He was a mouth and a member and a weight pressing down on her. And she, she was a vessel empty of sense.

. . .

SHE WORKED WITHOUT PONS in late summer, hiring plowhands to replace him and draining their resources. She flailed the wheat and barley, steeped the flax and hemp, pulled peas and gathered chestnuts for oil, anger gathering in her. Then one evening in early autumn, after Mother Rives left to salt a ham with a neighbor, she faced Pons in the kitchen, preparing to ask him if he was planning to excise her. *Are you going to become a Good Man, Pons? Are you going to make me leave?* She said the words in her mind as she watched him at the table, sipping water from a cup and staring severely into the fire.

"And do you think," he suddenly stammered, as if they had been in long conversation. "Do you really think that after all this sinning a man can be saved?"

She felt heat rise up between her eyes. "What sinning, Pons?"

He looked at her with an expression of surprise and despair. "What sinning?" he said. "What sinning?" A spasm shook his face pitifully. "Why, the sinning we do in bed at night!" He slammed his cup down on the table and water splashed onto the half-eaten loaf of bread nearby.

"Enough!" she shouted. She stormed to the table, picked up the loaf, and dried it with her skirt. "You are not a Good Man yet, Pons. You are married. We are not sinning."

He gazed at her unblinkingly, stunned to silence by her insight, she thought. *You are not a Good Man yet, yet.* She turned from him and heard him clomp away and out of the house. After a moment, she heard the steady *smack, smack, smack* of wood breaking under a hatchet outside.

WHEN HE DID NOT RETURN for bed that night, she lay down and fell hungrily into sleep. Somewhere in her dreams, the thought passed through her mind that a stranger was in the room, and then she opened her eyes and saw Pons over her. He grabbed her hair, pulling her head to one side.

"Fabrissa," she heard his muffled cry. He forced her thighs apart and buried his mouth in her neck.

She tried not to resist him, but still her legs had a will of their own, and they jerked together under his force. "Gently," she said.

"Fabrissa," he moaned.

She knew he was crying, because her neck was wet and his forehead slipped up and down as he tried to move to her. She wanted to help him, but he was thrashing and she could not take hold of him. She reached for his buttocks and held him forcefully so that he would be still.

"No!" he cried. He pushed away from her and stood from the bed. The shutters were cracked open and she saw his body in the moonlight, curved over and thin. His arms were wrapped around his middle, hiding his groin.

"Pons," she said.

"Be quiet."

She knew he was ashamed in his nakedness, and she pulled the sheet up and offered it to him. He yanked it away, burning her fingertips.

"I am the man," he said, his voice shaking. "What do you think you are? The man? I am the man! I know what I am doing. What are you? I know what you are."

"Pons."

"One of those women who has fucked before!"

"No," she breathed.

"What do you think I am? Stupid? Stiff forever? You think I can just tell it to be stiff and stay stiff? It is not going to stay stiff if it thinks you are a whore."

She pulled herself away from him and wrapped the blanket around her body. Her teeth ground into one another. "Not a whore," she said slowly.

"Your body is ugly," he said, walking out the door. "Disgusting to me."

She wanted to lunge at him, to push him down onto the floor, to make his forehead slap down on the ground so hard it would be bruised for weeks. She shook with cold. She was becoming a beast, she thought. A beast like him.

THE FOLLOWING EVENING, she was spinning thread by the fire with Mother Rives when she asked a question she had never dared. "For the Believers," she said, "for the Good Men, is the body the Devil?"

The old woman stared up from her distaff and squinted. Her lips were wet, glistening, and she wiped them with the back of her hand. "No," she said, exhaling heavily. Fabrisse smelled the sour air of her breath.

"Almost?" asked Fabrisse.

Mother Rives hesitated. "The Devil is the father of the body, just as God is the Father of the Spirit," she said.

"And who is the mother of the Spirit?"

Mother Rives shook her head. "No mother," she said. "No mothers. No wives. God does not have a wife."

Fabrisse watched her loop new thread around her palm. "But the Virgin."

"That was later," said Mother Rives with a smile. "Much, much later." She pushed the thread from her palm and placed it on the bench. Then she held up one hand and spread apart her short fingers. "One, God." She pointed to her thumb. "Two, God created Heaven." She wriggled her index finger back and forth. "Heaven was full of Spirits without flesh, Spirits created by God. But then the Devil came along, Three. The Devil created earth and bodies on earth. Bodies without souls, Four. But then he crept into Heaven and convinced the Spirits to come down to earth. And so, Five, the Spirits became souls trapped in bodies." Mother Rives pointed to her. "You are Five. I am Five."

"Pons is Five."

Mother Rives laughed. "Pons is Five but he wants to be Six—a soul that is saved, made a Spirit with no flesh again in Heaven. He wants to be Six now. His father used to tell him, 'Before you die, you will be baptized into the faith. Then you will take the vow of chastity. For now, have babies and be at peace.'" She sighed. "The family line needs Pons."

FABRISSE WANTED A BABY—not just in the obscurity of tomorrow, but today, now, as soon as Pons could plant one inside her. She tried to seduce him at night, stroking his member, kissing his neck. He would take her violently, sometimes pulling her hair as he thrust as if to kill the root of his desire. She wanted to scream out in pain, but she did not. *A baby*, she told herself. *A child.*

Sometimes in the early morning, after he had pulled her hair and her scalp was aching so that she could not sleep, she would stand from bed, passing fingers through her hair. She would watch as strands fell from her in the dim light—the same hair talked about from Limoux to Lordat, scattered now in pieces across the floor.

She was afraid she might hate Pons. The room they shared seemed stifling, and she would have to go outside in order to breathe. There was a ladder propped by the front door, and she crawled up it onto the flat, shingled roof of the house. Looking out at the distant hillocks and green pastures coming to light, inhaling the fresh air blowing gustily, she tried to conjure up the happiness that had sprung from her like a fountain when she had first learned she was to be married. She stared at the fortress above the village and remembered how dark and hopeless her world had seemed before that day. Dead as a corpse, she had been dead inside, and now she was dying again. *A baby,* she breathed, looking back to the sunrise. *A baby, a baby, a child for me.*

She began to pull her own hair on the rooftop—this time, the hair on her head. At first, she was almost kind to herself, gliding her fingers down to the root, plucking one hair at a time so that its small white bud popped out of the scalp clean. She developed the idea that, like the root of a plant, she was taking out her hair's seed. One less hair was one less hair for Pons to hate. But she lost patience and started twisting clusters of three or four strands between her fingers. Yanking them out suddenly. The small, sharp pain numbing her like an herb.

If Pons noticed the bald patch slowly emerging on the crown of her head—where the skull of a baby is still soft at birth—he did not tell her.

INTO THE QUIET of deep autumn, with its turning colors and slow surrender of leaves, she found solace in the companionship of Mother Rives. There was no longer enough money to hire hands to help plant winter wheat, but the old woman had faith Pons would return to farming in the spring. Though Mother Rives called herself a Believer, Fabrisse learned she cared as much for the goodness of flesh and food and laughter, and was always patient when Fabrisse ate twice her share at meals, compensating for the fasting Pons.

At night, as they sat spinning until the fire waned, Fabrisse gave voice to her fears about Pons's heresy. "They are teaching him to read," she said, speaking of the Good Men and their visits with Pons each day.

"They are teaching him to read, and words are filling the place where meat should be and hurting him on the inside."

Mother Rives sighed, her hands moving over the distaff slowly. "It will pass," she said. "Daughter, it will pass. When he sees the little creature that you bring forth into this world, he will love the earth again. He will become strong of body. You will see."

ONE MORNING, before dawn had broken, Fabrisse woke thinking of the piece of red glass the Châtelaine had given her as a present. She had hidden the glass inside the sleeve of her wedding dress, which she kept folded neatly in a chest in the bedroom. She crept to the chest, opened it carefully so not to wake Pons, and felt her way inside the sleeve of the dress. The glass was there—smooth and weighty as a small stone. She held it in her palm, absorbing its coolness. For a moment she imagined she could smell the rector. How well he had treated the Châtelaine, she thought. How loving he had been toward her—he who had taken a vow never to make love to a woman in his life. She squeezed the glass and pictured the rector in the room with her. He was holding his finger over his lips, telling her to keep quiet, then opening his arms to her. And she was falling, falling into his comforting clasp.

THE FOLLOWING MORNING, as she crawled up the ladder to the roof, she felt a strange sensation in her side—a pinching, like the small throb she had with every full moon. She clung to a splintery wooden rung to keep from falling and vomited off to one side.

When she returned indoors, Mother Rives was waiting for her in the kitchen. "I heard you," she said. She patted Fabrisse on the back so firmly, she gagged again. "Now, now," said Mother Rives. She guided Fabrisse to the bench by the table, on which she had already placed a steaming cup of clear broth and a crust of dry bread. "You must keep your food for the baby," she said. "Go on, now. Eat. Eat."

That afternoon, Fabrisse returned home tired from milking. She heard Pons in the kitchen, and prepared herself for the reading voices of the Good Men. "*So, frir,*" she heard. It was Pons speaking, and his sounds made a word. *"So, frir. Sofrir."* To suffer, to bear, to endure. A wave of sickness passed through her.

She peered into the kitchen and saw Pons sitting alone at the table, stooped over a book, tension in his shoulders. His skin had a yellow cast to it, and he looked exhausted, frighteningly undernourished. His finger moved on the page and he spoke the word again and again. *"Sofrir. Sofrir."*

"Pons," she said from the door.

He gasped with surprise, looking up at her. A spasm lurched across his features.

"Pons," she said again, seized with pity. She wanted to take his face between her hands and press him to her breast. She wanted to tell him she was sorry—for the temptation she knew her hair presented to him, for the shortness of her temper, for everything. They were man and wife and would have a child now.

"I am trying to read," he said. "Go away."

She stared into his eyes, seeking warmth in them. "You are going to be a father," she said. "A papa. We are having a baby, Pons."

His hands lifted from the book and his eyes, instead of melting, became hard. It was the same look that pointed out from him before his fury rained down on her in pieces.

"I am happy," she said, her teeth clenched shut. She saw him squint and she left the kitchen before he could harm her with fist or words.

FROM THAT DAY FORTH, he kept his anger within himself. His eyes became soft and unfocused, spasms afflicted him almost without cease, and deep lines etched their way in jags and darts across his face.

He read more and more, but seemed to make no progress. The Good Men came to the house once a fortnight—not every few days as they once had, and rather than engaging him with passion, they listened in silence as he stuttered the words he read.

"Veire!" Pons said to them one day. Glass. "You see? *Veire!* Just there! *Veire!"* Fabrisse saw Pons point to a word on the page, and the Good Men eyed each other wearily. Without waiting a moment more, she raced to the chest, her heart beating quickly. The glass, her glass, was her last piece of privacy, a small, smooth thing unbroken. She felt it in

the sleeve of her wedding dress, and clutched its redness in her fist until she could not feel her heart in her body.

ON THE EVE of Christmas that winter, when the Good Men happened to be visiting, the village healer, Na Roqua, came to the house. She had looked everywhere for the Good Men, she said. The wife of Jean Marty, Bernadette, had just given birth to a deformed boy, and both mother and child were on the cusp of death and needed the Good Men immediately.

In order to help, Fabrisse, Pons, and Mother Rives accompanied the Good Men up the frozen slope, wind lashing at their faces. When they arrived at the house, Jean Marty greeted them in tears. "Thanks be to God!" he said. "The blessed ones are here at last!"

The kitchen had been cleared of all furniture, and Bernadette—so pale she was almost gray—was lying on a pile of straw before the roaring hearth, bloodstained blankets and sheets around her. She whimpered softly, staring down at the newborn whose face was hidden underneath a square of linen draped over her breast. Even from the kitchen door, Fabrisse could see the twisted leg of the child, blue and kicking angrily into the air, exposing tiny, misshapen genitals.

"Do you not want to save that child, woman!" the elder Good Man exclaimed. He raced to her and snatched the baby from her arms, exposing her breast.

"Give him back!" Bernadette cried. The baby wailed and Bernadette began to weep, her mouth stretched open and watery.

"What are you doing?" said Mother Rives to the Good Man. He flushed crimson, astonished, as if in questioning his authority she had blasphemed God.

"Mother," said Pons with a whine.

"Give the child back," Mother Rives continued. "The boy needs milk now. And Bernadette needs to give him suck."

"Mother!" said Pons.

The Good Man pressed the wailing child to his chest. "This boy," he said. "This little creature of the Lord, would have been entirely pure if his mother had not given him suck. . . . That taste of milk, of her body, was the taste of sin itself." He bounced the baby up and down. "If the mother and father want their child to be saved, they should let him go without milk. He is almost bodiless now, and his soul is sure to go straight to Heaven."

Bernadette gagged on her tears. She coughed harshly, deeply. "Give him back!" she cried.

"Now, Bernadette," said Jean, standing in a corner, as if afraid to come any closer to his wife. "You hear what the Good Men say about the boy. He is sure to be saved if you keep your breast from him."

"That is correct," said the Good Man.

"Correct," said his brother.

"No!" cried Bernadette. A deep, growling noise came from within her and she tried to push herself up from the blankets.

"You stay there," Mother Rives commanded. She crossed to the Good Man and held out her arms. "Give him to me," she said slowly.

The Good Man grimaced and then his face went calm. "Very well," he said. He held the baby out and Mother Rives took him carefully, supporting his head in the crook of her arm. She knelt by Bernadette and passed the child to her. Bernadette put the baby to her breast. When he did not turn his mouth to her, she pressed her breast against his cheek, opened his lips with a finger, then pushed her nipple inside.

Fabrisse watched aghast. She kneeled down by Bernadette, shedding tears on her behalf.

By the time night had fallen, the baby was dead. Bernadette finally let her husband take him from her. She had lost so much blood, she had no strength left to hold him.

The Good Men stood over her and performed a spiritual baptism, laying their hands on her head and cleaning her of all impurity. "It is time to make your decision," said the elder to Bernadette. "Will you be a martyr or a confessor?"

"Martyr?" asked Jean from his corner. He was bobbing the child up and down as if it were still alive.

The Good Man explained that if Bernadette chose to be a martyr, a pillow would be held over her head for a long while. If she chose to be a confessor, she would have to fast for three days without food or water. In either case, whether she lived or died, she would be saved.

For the first time, Fabrisse was aware of the hatred for the Good Men that had been mounting in her. They hated life, it seemed. In the name of salvation, they destroyed.

"A martyr," Bernadette said.

"Now, Bernadette," said Jean, his voice rising to a high pitch. "You may live yet. You do not need to be a martyr."

The Good Man turned to the hearth, holding his hands over the orange flames. Fabrisse could see that his hands were trembling.

"I want to be a martyr," whispered Bernadette.

"I will not let you," said Jean. "You will not leave me. I will not be left."

Mother Rives stroked Bernadette's damp hair. "You do not have to decide now," she said softly. "You have time to think it over."

"A martyr," Bernadette whispered again.

Fabrisse glanced at Pons, who was crouched by the door, his knuckles between his teeth. She stood and went to him, took his hand from his mouth. Instead of drawing away from her, he allowed her to hold his hand between her own. "Let us go," she whispered into his ear. "Please, let us go."

He did not resist her. She led him from the house, out into the open, frosty air. As they walked side by side, she turned her eyes from him to the moon, which was shining hopefully in the night sky. Perhaps, someday, peace would be theirs.

BERNADETTE DIED A MARTYR, the winter ice melted, and new green shoots budded up from the earth and onto the branches of alders and beech trees. Geese grew fat with their goslings in the poultry yard, and Fabrisse felt her child swimming within her. If it had not been for the dead look in Pons's eye, she might have been able to convince herself that happiness was indeed around the corner.

One evening at dusk, she was walking to the house from the stable, a heavy bucket of goat milk balanced on her head. She wanted to heat a cup of the milk mixed with honey for Pons to entice him to take nourishment—so thin was he becoming. Before she had even reached the garden in front of the house, she heard Mother Rives screaming within. She let the bucket drop to the ground and ran with all her might toward the door.

In the kitchen, in front of the fire, Mother Rives was kneeling before Pons, grabbing at his mouth. Her fingers were inside his mouth, pulling apart his lips, and Pons was shaking back and forth, shaking the way a wolf shakes its kill before it eats. "Let me inside!" Mother Rives screamed.

Pons gripped the legs of the bench, thrashing and biting and gagging, and then his head fell back and his eyes rolled into his head. Blood pooled around the corners of his lips and Mother Rives pulled her fingers out. Whimpering, she covered her eyes with her hands, and the blood on her fingers smeared across her brow. Pons started howling like a beast. He bared his teeth and gripped his throat and low animal sounds curled out from him.

"What is it?" Fabrisse screamed. Mother Rives turned her blood-smeared face toward her, and then her face contorted and she began to sob.

Pons moaned and doubled over. Blood spilled from him onto the floor. Fabrisse ran to him and supported his forehead with her palm. She did not know whether to pound on his back to help the blood up, or to force him to sit erect to stop the blood from coming. This was not spitting blood, she knew. This was something she had never seen before.

"He did it to himself," cried Mother Rives from the floor.

Pons began to vomit, and a bright red paste splattered onto the ground. He moaned between heaves.

"What did you do, Pons?" said Fabrisse. She stared at the vomit, so strangely brilliant.

He heaved again and wiped his mouth with the back of his hand.

"It is in the book," cried Mother Rives. "He said it is written in the book what he has done."

The trestle table had been pushed beneath the window, and upon it, illuminated by the golden light of spring flooding through the parted shutters, Fabrisse saw a thin book lying open—the same black, leather-bound book Pons had borrowed from the Good Men. She recognized its small shape, no bigger than the palm of a man's hand.

She approached the table, took the book in her hands, and stared down at the marks on its open page. She had never looked inside it before, afraid the marks would carve their hatred for earthly things into her. She carried the book to Pons and thrust it under his eyes.

"Show me," she said to him.

He clutched his belly with one hand, writhing in pain. He squinted at the book, then opened his mouth as if to vomit. Nothing came out, and he began to cry softly—tears streaming down his cheeks, clinging to his chin and jaw and ears.

She set the book on the bench, ran to the bedroom, and dragged the pallet to the kitchen, cursing when it caught on the frame of the door. She threw the pallet on the ground, wrapped her arm around Pons, lifted him onto the pallet, and threw her coat over his body. Finally, she took the book from the bench and closed it over her thumb to keep the page. "I am going for the healer," she said to Mother Rives, still sobbing into her hands on the floor. "And I am going to find out what this book has done to Pons."

THE HEALER SCREAMED when she saw the blood on Fabrisse, then told her the Good Men had been at the house of Jean Marty earlier that afternoon. "If God is merciful, they will still be there," the healer said, taking up her sack of ointments and herbs.

Fabrisse ran up the dark road to the house in which she had seen Bernadette ask to die. She stormed into the kitchen without announcing herself. The Good Men were eating supper with Jean at the table, and she held the book out, open to the page her thumb had kept. "Pons has done something," she said, slapping the book down by a plate of fish.

The elder Good Man turned his lean, cheerless face down to the book's open page. He slid the book his way, reading with a listless expression.

"What have the words told him to do?" she said.

The younger brother pulled the book close, breathing heavily as he read.

"What have they told him?" she said again.

"There is no time," the elder Good Man said, and in his somber, even tone, she heard a note of terror.

THE BROTHERS FOLLOWED her home in haste, and when they arrived Mother Rives was holding Pons like a child, rocking him back and forth. Pale and still as death itself, he was wrapped in the coat like a swaddled baby, blood dribbling from the corner of his mouth. Na Roqua was squatting at his side, trying to tie a goat to the pallet with a blanket for heat. The goat kicked away from her, as if it sensed death nearby.

"Woman," the elder Good Man said to Mother Rives, "let your son go." He approached, and Mother Rives pressed Pons to her breast.

"He is dying," she said in a shrill voice. "Leave him be."

"Let him die in peace, woman," said the Good Man.

"Peace?" said Mother Rives bitterly. She rocked Pons back and forth and Na Roqua held the goat still, tying the blanket around its legs.

"Let him go," said the Good Man to Mother Rives.

She rocked, pretending not to hear, gazing down at Pons with loving eyes.

"Let me," Pons whispered. He looked steadily up at his mother, imploring her with his eyes.

Mother Rives shook her head. Then, with a gasp, she lowered him down onto the pallet and drew away from his body. The Good Men gathered around. Fabrisse knelt by Mother Rives.

"Do you surrender yourself wholly to God and the Gospel?" the elder said.

Pons spit blood to the side. He bent his head as if to nod. "Yes," he said softly.

"Do you promise never again to eat meat, eggs, cheese, or venison, never to lie, swear, indulge any lust, sleep unclothed, or kill?"

"Yes," Pons said, and his features pinched together as though the act of speaking caused him great suffering.

"Do you promise, Pons," said the Good Man, "never again to touch a woman?"

Fabrisse shook her head as if to answer for him. Never to touch him again or be touched by him . . . *No.* Pons shifted to look at her, his thin, wan hand extending toward her. She took it, so very cold, and pressed it against her cheek. *Do not promise,* she wanted to say, hot tears coming. She bent down and kissed his lips. She smelled blood on his breath, saw his eyes, warm and kind as they had been on their wedding day. He moved his hand down and touched the fabric of her dress over her belly. She felt the weight of his finger press against her, against their child within her. He drew his hand away.

"Do you promise never again to touch a woman?" the Good Man repeated.

Pons closed his eyes, nodding slowly.

"Say '*Benedicite*' if you can," said the Good Man.

"*Benedicite,*" Pons whispered, his voice thinner than air.

"*Deus vos benedicat,*" said the Good Man. "We pray to God that He may keep you, Pons Rives, from a bad death, and bring you to a good end." The Good Man opened his cloak and pulled a small book from his pocket. He kissed the book and placed it on Pons's head. "We worship Thee, Father, Son, and Holy Ghost. May the Holy Ghost the Consolator descend upon us now." He shut the book and slipped it into his pocket again. "Let us say the Pater all together," he said, closing his eyes. "Our Father, who art in Heaven . . ."

Fabrisse felt Mother Rives begin to quake. There was so much blood everywhere, so much flesh wasted all over the ground—tears and vomit and strands of hair, her hair in the bedroom and on the roof, and what was it all for?

"Forgive us our daily trespasses," Fabrisse said with the others. *Forgive us, God, now.*

The Good Man kissed Pons on the forehead. His brother did the same, and then they kissed each other. Fabrisse saw that Pons had become very calm, his face radiant, his eyes open and staring up at the ceiling.

"Do not give your son any food or drink, even if he pleads for it," said the Good Man to Mother Rives.

Her eyes flashed with anger. "If my son wants food or drink, I will give it to him," she said.

"Then you will be depriving his soul of salvation," he replied.

"I will give it to him," said Mother Rives.

Fabrisse watched the Good Man stand and walk to the fire. He stared down at his hands, as if he did not know them, and then he rubbed them together and held them out over the flames. "Some say death by illness is not the same as taking one's own life," he said. "Some say Satan is the master of death by illness. He can send the soul of a man dead by illness back into another body, keeping him from Heaven."

Fabrisse looked at Pons, still gazing at the ceiling, a slight smile on his lips, as if he were already seeing the face of God.

"There is a recipe in the book for taking one's own life," continued the Good Man, glancing back at her. "A drink of the juice of wild cucumbers mixed with powdered glass. The recipe was on the page you showed me." He paused. "But how did he find glass? There is not a glassblower in all the region outside Toulouse."

The goat tied to the pallet began to bleat, and Mother Rives screamed. Na Roqua prayed aloud and Fabrisse knew Pons was leaving. She leaned in to take hold of his hand, but stopped herself in mid-gesture. He had vowed never again to touch her. Her husband was here, just here, still here, but going, and she could not touch him to feel the presence of his last breath.

FIVE

AFTER PONS PASSED, she gathered sheepskins and pots of olive oil as alms for the Good Men, and tucked Mother Rives into bed with a lighted candle by her side. Alone with the body in the dim light, she unwound the wimple from her head and tried to indulge her sadness with the sounds of lamentation. Her grief was of the kind that would not let her weep. She raised her fingers to her head and pulled out strands of hair until her eyes watered at the corners. With every yank, she imagined Pons becoming again incarnate. There he was, *yank*. Just there, *yank*. Pulling her hair as was his way.

She knew well enough that the glass by which he had taken his life was in all likelihood her own small, red secret, though she did not know how he could have found it—so carefully had she hidden it away. She could not bear to open the chest and push her hand up the wedding-dress sleeve. If the glass was gone, so, too, was her own place inviolate. She felt she would shatter under the weight of knowing not only that her last good thing was gone, but that it had not been good after all—like other blessings come her way, too lovely, too captivating simply to be admired.

Neither she nor Mother Rives spoke of the reason Pons had taken his life. They had no need to speak of it. Though the Good Men would have them believe he had died a brave man, Fabrisse and Mother Rives had seen Pons become more childlike and broken with every asceticism he took on. Fabrisse knew her own presence in his life, in his bed, by his side, had plunged him into despair; and the word that a child would be coming—had she not known, in the vagueness of her heart, that such news would kill him in the end? *I cannot see to see,* she remembered him telling her when she had emerged from the bedroom wearing loose hair. *I cannot live to live,* she almost heard him say. Pons had wanted to walk in the ways of the Perfect Ones, and her body had presented too much temptation, too much wretched femininity for him to live a life of the senses restrained.

She held her culpability in her throat, wanting neither to spit it out nor to swallow it down. As if to torment both herself and Pons, she tended to his body with hair uncovered and brushed to a silken sheen. She wanted him to raise his fist up in anger, but he did nothing. Without a soul, he was a body at peace—a slight smile on full lips, half-opened eyes with lashes long and curling. She had forgotten how beautiful he was of the flesh. She undressed him and was moved to pity by the hair above his groin, rough and dark—hair that she had never fully seen. She had heard it said that if one took bits of hair and nail from a corpse, it would not carry away the family's fortune in farming. She cut clippings of the locks on his head and then parings of his toenails, which she wrapped in a piece of linen to be saved for Mother Rives. Although the Good Men had said not to preserve any part of the body, she could not bring herself to throw all of Pons away.

He was buried under a twisted elm below the village, next to Bernadette and her baby boy—all three graves unmarked. Because the Good Men paid no heed to the body, they did not attend the ceremony, and as Jean Marty lowered Pons into the ground, Mother Rives said again and again, "But where have the Good Men gone? Where are they?" Fabrisse looked up the hillside, flattened by the weight of the gray, lowering sky. Beside a boulder in the distance, she saw the figure of a man—the rector, she knew by his smallness of stature. He was perfectly still, his arms held slightly out from his sides, as if he could neither approach nor withdraw—caught between his parish and the gathering of Believers. For a moment, everything but his figure disappeared for Fabrisse. Though she did not have the words to explain the feeling that came over her, she was aware of being yoked together with him—yoked together by urgings neither of them dared name. She was the widow of a Believer, but loved the earth with all her might; he was a priest of the Church who had broken his vow of chastity, but believed in the ways of the Good Christians all the same. She heard Jean Marty call her name, and she stooped to gather a fistful of wet earth. As she opened her hand over the mouth of the grave, scattering away another body, she thought how unbearable all this was, this endless suffering, this waste.

EVEN WITH PONS UNDERGROUND, she felt no relief. Though his body had at last found peace, his soul, it seemed to her, was restless. She caught glimpses of him everywhere—on the violent surface of water boiling in the pot, on the rough underleaf of wild hillside sage slashing against the wind. At dawn one morning, trying to sleep against the coarseness of her sheets, she opened her eyes and saw Pons slinking against the light, passing beams of morning cut through shutter cracks. He held something in his fist, something as smooth as glass. She sat up, about to scream, but found she could make no noise. She shut her eyes, holding her hand to her belly, afraid this haunting would scare her child away.

Mother Rives, too, had become a ghost, it seemed. With the struggle against the death of Pons, she had lost the vital force that kept her living. She had no remaining strength to fight against her own demise, and she sat from dawn to dusk on a bench in her room, staring at the line on her palm that led down to the unmarked place where death was said to come finally. When Fabrisse tried to feed her spoonfuls of cabbage or salt-pork broth, Mother Rives held the food in her mouth, shifting it from cheek to cheek, as if she found the food as foreign and bland as stiff clumps of sheared wool stealing moisture from her tongue.

Without Mother Rives to help, the burden of familial survival was on Fabrisse alone. She had no hope of remarrying, as the flesh of a widow was thought more unclean than even that of a bastard girl. She resumed her old habit of being untouchable with a numb heart, and immersed herself in the work her hands could do—bolting flour, spinning thread, gathering kindling, weaving wattles to replace a collapsed fence, tending to the animals and the poultry, cultivating vegetables in the garden, haying meadows, turning under the residue of old crop in a fallow field to prepare it for spring planting. She was tired beyond feeling, her fingers blistery and bloody, her back hunched and dimly aching.

Only in the darkness of night—when she could not see to milk or spin or lose herself in endless furrows to be planted with seed—would the numbness within her begin to fade. Then, the shock of Pons's death would strike her so forcibly, she felt she would die. She saw life stretching insufferably out before her; never again would she be held or claimed as a wife. Even the thought of the child, beating to life within her center, tormented her rather than bringing her light; fatherless, the baby would be scorned as if it had been conceived a bastard. Rather than sleeping, Fabrisse would throw off the sheet suffocating her swelling body and open herself to the elements of the room. Voices, male and female, groaned out from the chest by the door—the same chest in which she had hidden the glass the Châtelaine had given her. She covered her ears and tried to pray the voices away. In her heart, she knew they would haunt her forever. Pons had broken the glass, releasing the dungeon secrets within, and now they would burrow under her skin like pests, never to leave her.

"Go away!" She hissed into the darkness, as Pons had commanded her to do before.

THE BABY began to show through her dress and in her lumbering, and the village clattered with gossip about what was inside her. Some said the baby was the spirit of Pons come again incarnate. Others spoke of the shame the child would inherit, born into the wake of suicide.

One wet evening at dusk, on her way home from the fields, she paused in a grove of dripping plane trees to forage for mushrooms and pick snails for supper soup. The grove was thick with evening fog, and she had to strain to see the tawny caps of the mushrooms by her feet.

"Your baby needs out!" she heard a hoarse voice call to her. In the gloom of the evening, among a cluster of far trees, she saw Na Roqua kicking up her chin like a pony. The healer approached, holding her coat closed around her thin neck.

"No," said Fabrisse, feeling suddenly vulnerable. "No, thank you."

"You are carrying the baby of a dead man," said the healer. She stopped an arm's length from Fabrisse. "A man who has gone up to the Lord. He wants his baby with him." She pointed to the fog-covered sky. "You know," she said, "some babies are bad babies. With evil spirits sent from the Devil. Sent to torment good people and bring nothing but grief." She squinted, as if trying to divine the future in Fabrisse's eyes.

"This could be a bad baby. If you allow it to live, Pons will be angry. He will haunt your house and your mind and your body. And your baby. He will haunt your baby. If you allow the baby to live, he may kill your baby. Make your baby very, very sick."

She reached under her coat, and from a sack hanging from her belt she withdrew a small package wrapped in twine, which she dropped into Fabrisse's basket. "When you swallow the herb, the baby will go away," she said. "The haunting will go away. Pons will be at peace." She bowed, then walked away.

"I do not want the herb!" Fabrisse called after her.

"Evil baby!" the healer shouted.

Fabrisse cast the package by the base of a tree, suddenly sick to her stomach and shivering.

THERE WAS no one left for Fabrisse in the village, it seemed—no one but the half-dead Mother Rives and the rector, caught, too, between the judgment of parishioners and Believers alike. When the soil turned warm, Fabrisse planted peas and beans and barley, and at night, she slept with her arms wrapped around her belly. Precious things were taken when left unguarded, and she would not fully rest to let her baby be plucked from her womb.

On the first day of May, when all the village usually proceeded across the fields to bless the fruits of the earth, a sharp frost blew in from across the mountains, followed by a heavy rain. The spring crops were destroyed, and Fabrisse became despondent. As Pons had been too pre-occupied with the Good Men to plant winter wheat the preceding autumn, two crops had been as good as ruined.

Soon she was forced to sell off one animal at a time for grain. No amount of bread seemed to satisfy the child forever pushing out in a point from her navel, and Fabrisse's arms and legs and neck grew gaunt, the flesh over her cheeks and eye sockets sinking beneath the bones. She was sure she could hear the baby inside her howl with hunger. By late summer, when not a pinch of flour was left in the kitchen and Mother Rives had refused to allow any of the family fields to be sold, Fabrisse knew she would have to sell something of herself.

All her life, she had known that only women without vergonha sold pieces of their bodies. Her mother had told her that those women had lost pride in themselves; they had lost the will to preserve their honor, or the hope in a future of better times. Fabrisse had tried to keep what vergonha she could, but little by little it had fallen to the wayside. She did not lack for will to save herself from scorn, and still sometimes she dreamed the sweet, misty dream of future joy, but now necessity beckoned her. She must keep herself and her family alive. Her hair, once sold, would allow them to eat for a time.

One morning, in a kind of waking daze, she left the village, the distant greystone peaks of the Pyrenees peeping over the early mist as if to watch her descent into shame. She followed a rocky path at the base of the knoll over the Col de Pichacca and the Col du Chioula, then plunged down a steep slope into the town of Ax-les-Thermes. The narrow, hot streets of Ax were full of townspeople and merchants pushing carts loaded with smelly meats and fish for market, with blades for sale—sickles and scythes and felling axes. Artisans roamed with wares on their backs, wine criers promoted taverns in which to drink and whore, hens pecked at muddy puddles by the side of the road, children screamed by, nearly knocking Fabrisse over.

After wandering into the early evening, she found on a signboard the symbol she had come looking for: scissors and a blade, the sign of the barber. In the light of several oil lamps within the door, she saw a fat old man snoring on a chair, and behind him an equally corpulent old woman, bending over a basin of water, washing her hands. When the woman saw Fabrisse, she scowled and wiped her thick hands on her skirt.

"Someone at the door!" she shouted.

The man shot up from his chair. "A cut? A shave?" he stuttered, and then his features bunched up in confusion when he glimpsed Fabrisse in the door.

"A cut," said Fabrisse, entering.

"You mean to sell it?" the woman said curtly, cruelly.

Fabrisse unwound the wimple from her unbraided hair. As the man and woman stared at her in bewilderment, she approached and sat in the chair.

"Christ the Lord," the barber whispered. He took a candle from a nearby table and held it up to her hair. "Come look," he said to his wife. "She does have some of the Lord in her."

The woman neared, the flickering flame of the candle casting angry shadows across her brow. "Something is wrong with her," she said. She gestured toward the crown of Fabrisse's head, patchy from plucking.

"Is this disease, woman?" the husband said in a breathless whisper.

"No," she responded. "No." How could she explain the violence she had committed against herself?

"Not one for words, is she?" the woman muttered.

Fabrisse smelled the woman's hot, onion breath, and realized with a stinging shock that the woman had named a truth about her. From the beginning of her life, she had been taught that words could wound—the name of her father, her mother had said, could only bring vexation; the words of other village children could make her want to hide in the dark. Later, the words of her parish priest taught her shame; the words of the Good Men taught her heresy; and the words of a book killed her husband. No, she was not one for words; indeed, she was tired of so many tongues flapping. "A cut for money," she said, without an inflection of humility. *Go on, go on,* she thought. *Let it be gone with. Let it be over.*

The man grunted, set the candle on the table, and took up a rusted set of scissors, slicing the air. "Worth less than it would have been had it all been there," he said, and then he gathered one side of her hair in his fist and she felt the cold instrument pressing against the top of her ear. In no time, a piece of her womanhood was cut away.

SHE LEFT THE SHOP shaking, gripping the change she had been paid. Her womb cramped and she feared if she did not satisfy the baby with a meal soon it would force its way out of her. Down a dark alley, she heard the sound of uproarious laughter and found a tavern, tucked behind a stone wall, the smell of fried garlic and sour wine issuing from the door. She knew this was not the kind of place meant for decent women, but rather for men seeking whores; still she was so desperate with hunger and pain, she entered. She was not a decent woman, she reminded herself. She had just lost what decency in her remained.

She sat at a table, at the other end of which a group of men were playing noisily at dice. In the shadowy depths of the tavern, she saw women, loose-haired and sitting on stools or leaning against the wall, waiting—it seemed to her—for the men to be done with one another. The tavern keeper, a man of no more than twenty or thirty years with a long, thin body like that of a young oak, brought a jug and a tankard to her. "Wine?" he said. She nodded and he poured.

Three tankards' worth of wine later, she remembered she had come to feed the child. "Soup, I think," she mumbled. The tavern keeper snickered, demanding that she pay for the wine before she ate. She opened her fist, filled with sous and deniers, and allowed him to take what he would from her.

How much time passed after that she did not know. The dice-playing men disappeared one by one into a room at the back of the tavern. She slept and woke at the table, drank, slept, and woke, and then raised her eyes with the sound of the creaking door and saw a man whom she recognized enter—the rector. He was gazing into the depths of the tavern, as if he meant to solicit the pleasures of a whore. Before she could straighten her wimple, which she had wound carelessly around her head after the cut, the rector spotted her. His mouth opened and closed as if he were trying to find words to speak, and she realized by the shamed, stunned expression in his eyes that he not only regretted being seen by her, but imagined she had come to the tavern to whore herself.

"No," she said, wiping her mouth, but could not seem to say more.

He bowed, blinked at her as if with remorse, and departed as quickly as he had entered.

IN THE EARLY LIGHT of dawn, she trudged up the mountainside toward Montaillou, her remaining change clenched in her fist. As she reached the cusp of the Col de Pichacca, nearly impassable for all the holm oak and prickly broom that clung tenaciously to the rocky path, the sack of her baby's waters broke from her in a warm spout. Later, she would think that God had been with her then, for as much as her body was wrenched by spasms so intense she vomited up all the wine she had drunk, the baby stayed safe inside her, and she was able to walk until the moment she reached home.

In the kitchen, she let the coins drop to the floor, untied her cloak, removed her wimple, stripped off her dress, and struggled to unwind the linen bandage wrapped under the roundness of her belly. Mother

Rives stood watching her, pale and distant in the eye, as if she were already far away from the earth and the agony of changing matter. "You have no hair left on your head," she said.

A deep spasm took hold of Fabrisse. "Help me, please," she cried, collapsing to the floor. The old woman scurried out of the house and returned with a bundle of straw. She scattered it over the floor before the hearth, then went about closing all the shutters and stopping up the door. "You must not catch a shiver," she said, building up the fire. "All evil spirits must be kept out until the child is safely born."

When the room was hot, Mother Rives pushed a bench toward Fabrisse and told her to lean her back against it and spread her legs so that she might see if the baby was soon coming. Fabrisse writhed with pain. It seemed to her the baby could not break through her as much as it tried.

"Good God," said Mother Rives, peering between her legs. "It is here. I see it. Keep pushing, daughter." Fabrisse bore down and saw the old woman glance up at her, a look of wonderment spreading over her features, as though she had returned to the realm of the living.

"Again!" said Mother Rives. "Nothing is so painful that it cannot be borne."

THE BABY was delivered a girl, and Fabrisse took one look at her and wept bitterly. Her arms were covered with purple puckered rings, and her face was so red and swollen she looked as if she had been battered into life.

"Pons has hurt her," she cried.

Mother Rives was silent.

"He has shaped her badly."

"No," said Mother Rives.

"Look at her skin. It is overcooked."

Mother Rives fingered the womb wounds on the child and traced the bottoms of her little lined feet. "This is a good baby," she said. "She has only fought to get out into the world." She held the cut cord up in the air. "Watch," she said, stroking the end of the cord across each of the baby's cheeks. "For a clear complexion," she said. She rubbed the cord three times over each eye. "For better eyesight. We want her to see everything." She smiled at Fabrisse. "Now give her suck. She must be hungry."

Fabrisse wanted to fold the child back into the nest of her body, to shield her from the torment of the world. Instead, she held her to her breast, and the little girl found her nipple and sucked forcefully.

"But what shall her name be?" said Mother Rives.

Fabrisse had thought that if the baby was a girl she might call her after her own mother, but now—just now—the name Marquise wearied her. There was too much sadness sewn into that sound. She rocked the child, gazing down at her, and the sensation of feeding her from her own body struck her as one of the most pleasant and poignant she had experienced in life. The girl, too, was pleasant—hardly beautiful, but sweet.

"Grazida," she said, the word in their mountain language for pleasant.

"Grazida," the old woman said to the child, "and so you are named."

WHAT ARDOR Grazida had for things of the earth. She attached her-self passionately to Fabrisse's breast and soon began to smile whenever she was stroked. Fabrisse caught her gazing at every finger, every form that passed her eyes, as though she could not get enough sight of matter.

In tending to Grazida, Fabrisse found a purpose she had never known. It was as if she had finally become the person God intended her to be—not a bastard, but a nurturer. She abandoned the torment of worrying about what she would do for food when the money from the sale of her hair was gone. She left her thoughts of Pons and the rector and the haunting voices in the chest, and rested in the mercies of mother-hood. For the first time, she saw a glimmer of a world outside herself, outside the laws of vergonha—a world guided not by the morality of the Church, but by the morality of nature, of feeding and of growth, of the need to stay alive. All the animals and plants of the wild seemed more kindred to her. And when her breasts were sucked dry, and Grazida howled as if her very life were being drained away, Fabrisse cried. Deep in her heart, she knew she loved her child more than was healthy for any soul to love another, but she did not care. Grazida had become the very soil of her life.

. . .

SEVERAL MONTHS AFTER Grazida was born, when Fabrisse was feeding her in the kitchen and Mother Rives was warming her old hands
over the flames in the hearth, Na Roqua came rushing in unannounced.
"There has been a murder," she said. "A Good Man is dead. And Esclarmonde d'Argelliers has confessed to the crime."

Fabrisse had never seen Esclarmonde—said by some to be a sorceress and lover of Satan—but she had often passed her house, which
stood decrepit and lonely, below the other houses on the knoll, just
above the square. Fabrisse had heard rumors that Esclarmonde lived by
herself, her husband having abandoned her decades before. Though
many curious children had tried to taunt her to the window or the door,
it was said that Esclarmonde only made herself seen when her grown
daughter came bearing goods for her.

Na Roqua explained that a Good Man from Lombardy had traveled to the region. Despite his obligation never to go about without a
companion, he had wandered alone to Montaillou, asking for alms and
spreading his word. A heavy rain had begun to fall when he arrived at
the house of Esclarmonde. He knocked once, twice, not realizing that
Esclarmonde was a recluse within and would never answer. Finally, he
decided to take refuge inside. He pushed against the door, then pushed
more violently, then hurled his body with all its weight upon the wood.

Imagining her husband had come back for her, Esclarmonde had
taken an old, rusted sword off a shelf in the kitchen and walked to the
door, anger boiling through her bones. After all the years of loneliness
she had endured, she did not want to let her husband live and she held
the sword out in front of her. Not a moment passed before the door
gave way and she was knocked to the ground, the Good Man skewered
on top of her like a pork loin roast over a fire.

"She screamed like a bloody devil," said Na Roqua. "Screamed and
screamed, but not a word for the Good Man. Just tears for her husband
still missing and the many bones broken in her body and the lump on
the back of her head and the mess of so much blood upon her."

Fabrisse pictured the Good Man poked through by the wrath of
Esclarmonde. How feeble human promises were, she thought—there
the Good Man had promised never to touch a woman again, and yet
had tasted life for the last time while pressed against a woman aching
from abandonment, from an endless lack of touching or being touched.

. . .

WITHIN A RISING and setting of the sun, Esclarmonde was pardoned by the new overseer in the fortress—who made a public statement in the square that the killing had been a mischance and thus not worthy of punishment under the law. It was said by some in the village that whereas the Châtelaine had been sympathetic to the Good Men and the Believers, the new overseer regarded them as poison in the clear water of his terrain, and wanted to drain them away. The wind of suspicion gusted down the hillside, and though the overseer remained silent in the rock of his fortress, villagers began to fling threats at their neighbors like spears, charging one another of heresy in order to demonstrate fidelity to the Church. Soon, Na Roqua prophesied another murder to come.

As Fabrisse nursed Grazida on the rooftop in the early morning, breathing in the breaking light of day, she saw men leaving their houses with not only spades and scythes, but also swords—as if frightened that the very neighbors whom they had breathed beside all their lives would pounce upon them unexpectedly. It seemed to Fabrisse the village would never recover from Esclarmonde's mistake. All trust had been torn from its center.

ONE DAMP SUNDAY MORNING in early autumn, when Mother Rives was still sleeping and Fabrisse was changing Grazida's linens on a sheep fleece before the fire, there was a knock at the door. She left Grazida and went to see who had come selling.

The rector stood beyond the threshold in the lightly falling rain, a sleeping newborn child in his arms. For a long moment, she simply stared at the pair, so awkwardly matched in appearance. The rector was graying, and his skin had the powdery look of someone blood-deprived; even his eyes, once so brightly green, looked worn. He held the child out from his body, as if it were as unnatural to him as holding the soiled linens of a woman. She pushed the door open wide, and the rector held the baby farther out. She took it wordlessly.

"You need work," he muttered, a hint of color washing up under his eyes.

She remembered their encounter at the tavern, and realized that he had indeed assumed she had gone there to sell the place between her thighs. She felt herself flush with shame.

He gestured toward the child. "His mother was a peasant of Prades. She died yesterday. This morning his father came to Mass asking if there was not a wet nurse in the village. I thought of you." He paused, a strained expression in his eyes. "Not that you are a wet nurse of practice. But you could feed the child. . . . You did give birth recently, did you not? The child lived, I hope."

She nodded, embarrassed for not yet having brought Grazida to him to be baptized. She had been afraid Believers in the village would turn their swords against her if she did. "Born a girl," she said.

He smiled halfheartedly. "I will pay you a wage, of course. The father will pay."

Again she flushed, understanding that he hoped to save her from the tavern by offering her work less degrading. Much as the prospect of earning money by selling yet another piece of herself did not offend her now, she knew she could not accept the rector's offer.

The rain began to fall vigorously outside. She heard Grazida whining. "Please," she said, not wanting just yet to turn the rector away. "Come inside. I fear the fire may be waning, and I hear my daughter's cry."

He obeyed her, wiping the wetness from his face with his thumb as he entered. She set the sleeping, swaddled child down on the fleece, and Grazida began to wail more loudly, as if sensing what the boy threatened to steal from her. The rector prodded the fire with a stick, and she rocked Grazida, the familiar ache of longing for the rector spreading up through her body. Enclosed in the heat and glow of the room, she could almost pretend he was her husband, almost pretend the babies were their very own.

"You will be good for the boy," the rector said, turning to her with sympathetic eyes.

She glanced down at the sweet face of the sleeping child. "I am sorry," she said. "But you must find another to feed him." Her throat became hot and she lowered her eyes. "I have lost my husband, you know," she said. "And I am a bastard. I would be no good for the boy." She looked up at him quickly, and he frowned, less in judgment, she thought, than in concern for her.

He limped toward her and stooped down, taking Grazida from

her, supporting the child's head with his hand. "Wheat has been raised on stormy ground before," he said. "You are a good mother. And the money from the boy will feed you well."

Grazida gazed up at him, her mouth open in wide joy. Perhaps now was the time for her to be baptized. "Will you christen her?" Fabrisse whispered.

Again the rector frowned. A shadow seemed to pass over his eyes. "God will have her or He will not," he muttered.

Fabrisse wanted to tell him she knew he had been at the fortress on the day Prades Tavernier had been made a Good Man; she knew he had watched Pons being buried. He was a Believer in his heart, but she did not care. She only wanted him to speak the words of baptism on behalf of her daughter, who had inherited so little in the way of vergonha. "Baptize her, please," she said. "I can get Mother Rives to witness the rite."

He closed his eyes for a long moment, then opened them and sighed. "There is no need," he said. He touched the girl's forehead with his finger. "What is her name?"

"Grazida," she said.

"Grazida." He made the sign of the cross on her skin. "I baptize thee in the Name of the Father, and of the Son, and of the Holy Ghost." The child smiled at him, and he chuckled. "Grazida," he murmured, grinning up at Fabrisse. "But what is your name? I do not know."

"Fabrisse," she said, smiling.

An expression of dread drained his features of all joy. He held Grazida out, as if he could not stand to touch her anymore. When Fabrisse took the child, he stood quickly and limped to the door, pausing with his hand on the latch.

"You are a child of the Lord," he said without meeting Fabrisse's eyes. "God is your Father, and you are his creation. You do not have to call yourself a bastard anymore."

SIX

I T *HAD BEEN* twenty years since Pierre had heard the name Fabrisse, and then it had passed from the lips of the only woman he had
thought of as his bride. *"Fabrisse,"* Marquise had whispered when he
asked the name of her child to be baptized. He had been holding the
little girl naked in his arms, and when Marquise spoke her name, he repeated it, *"Fabrisse,"* and then dipped the child into the still, cool water
of the font so that she screamed aloud. He remembered her scream. It
was a cry of life, filled with the same urgency and longing and bitterness
he felt churning in his chest now, twenty years later, after having heard
the name for the second time. Fabrisse. He left her house and limped
out under the flatness of the gray sky. Rain drizzled down onto his forehead and nose, and as he wiped it away with his sleeve, he thought if
only he could scream loudly enough, he could forget the look of Marquise in Fabrisse's eyes. He could forget the way she had leaned into the
doorway of the dungeon, tilting her chin down as he took the Châtelaine like an animal, with neither discretion nor pride.

He shuddered to think to what depths he had fallen—and fallen
further still since the Châtelaine had left Montaillou for Varilhes a widow.
If he had not been heart-stricken with her departure, he had been sick
with physical deprivation—feverish, nauseated, aching in the loins. At
the same time, he had been tormented with memories of the Good
Men's words at the heretic baptism of Prades Tavernier in the fortress.
*"You must hate this world. For all that is in the world is lust of the flesh, desire of the
eyes and pride in life—"* Yes, yes, he had believed in those words, and yet a

hunger had been awakened in him, and without the Châtelaine to satisfy it, he could not stop his body from hunting for more of the same.

ONLY A FORTNIGHT after the Châtelaine had left the village, he seized upon his first victim. She was a pale, fine-boned woman named Rixende, whom he had heard his brother gossiping about one night. "That woman," his brother had muttered. "She doesn't even bother to turn her bottom away from the road when pulling up beets from her garden." Oh, how Pierre longed to see that bottom high in the air. He walked up and down the dusty road, waiting for Rixende to emerge from her dust-covered house, and when she did not, he knocked upon her door.

"You did not come to Easter confession," he said to her wide, deferential eyes.

She blushed deeply. "It is true, Domine," she said.

"Come with me," he said, touching the little bones of her wrist. He led her down to the chapel, and in the perfect, hot stillness of their solitude, he told her to kneel by the altar. He sat on a stool, watching as she silently folded her hands together. A candle burning on the altar lit up her lips, the tip of her nose. He asked her all the questions the *Instructions* required him to, speaking in a low half-whisper. Had she performed any sorcery or wished her neighbor ill?

"No," she said. "No, Domine." Her eyes lifted to meet his.

"And have you sinned in lechery?" he asked her.

The flap of her ear turned pink and bright and he knew that if he touched it with his finger, he would feel heat. "No," she said. "Not in deed, Domine."

"And in thought," he said.

"Only in thought," she whispered.

Her eyes blinked back tears, and as they blinked, she said that her husband gave her what he could, but what he could was not enough for her, so she got more in her mind. More from other village men. She unclasped her hands and rubbed her tears away with her fingers. He wanted to touch her, to caress her. "Forgive me, Domine," she said.

Moved to pity, he blessed her, gave her what she needed. "Say fifteen Paters and twenty Aves," he told her. "My daughter, you have not sinned so gravely."

HE HAD REDEEMED himself then, but just as soon fell into even greater acts of lechery. One Sunday in early summer, he was delivering a sermon in Mass, when a young red-haired woman entered his chapel for the first time. He saw her through the haze of burning incense. She was the smallest, most delicate creature he had ever seen in his life. All through the Mass, he found himself nearly unable to hear his own chanting in his ear, so transfixed was he by her beauty. At the end of the Mass, he stepped off the beech-wood chest and proceeded through the standing parishioners, his heart beating quickly. When he brushed past her—so close he thought he could smell her skin—he realized the top of her head was lower than the bottom of his chin. How easily her body would fall and fold around his . . .

He squandered no time. By nightfall, he learned that her name was Jacotte, and that she had come from Lordat as the new bride of a villager by the name of Gérard Den Baille. The following morning, when the light was soft and blue, he crouched behind a barrel not far from their house and gazed through the parted shutters of the kitchen window at the gleaming fire in her hearth. When he saw Gérard leave with a sickle over his shoulder, he crept out from behind the barrel and approached the house. Jacotte came to the door, shyly tucking the tips of her red hair under the cloth covering her head. He smelled oak logs burning within. "Tithes," he sputtered.

"Excuse me, Domine?" she said.

He coughed into his palm. "Tithes," he said again. "I have come to discuss tithes with your husband."

"With my husband," she said. She smiled. "But he is not here. And he will not return for a long while." She stepped back from the door. "Come in for a bite."

He hesitated, felt the warm wind of early summer on his side. "New parishioners must confess to their priests," he murmured, backing away from the door.

Her expression grew solemn. He saw her frown, and her eyes moved down to his toes. "Confess," she whispered. "Yes. Of course."

"Tomorrow at sundown," he said, limping away. "At sundown in the chapel."

"At sundown," he heard her say.

Sure enough, the following evening, she arrived in a dark dress just as the sun was slipping behind the mountains, fanning shades of red over the sky. She crossed herself and studied her hands, folding them together. On the stool, he was two heads above her eyes.

"Believest thou in Father and Son and Holy Ghost, Three Persons in Trinity, and in God, swear thou to me?" he began. He noticed her little finger. Such a tiny finger. He felt a rush of pity for it.

"Yes, Domine," she whispered.

"Believest thou that God's son mankind took in maid Maria as saith the Book, and of that maid was born?"

"Yes, Domine." Her bottom lip sank as she spoke, uncovering teeth, tiny and yellow, twisting into one another. He felt sorry for those teeth, sorry for the way they must be aching, just like his hip, throbbing beneath him. "I am not of the Devil," she said. "I believe."

"And believest thou in Christ's passion and in His resurrection?"

"Yes."

"That He shall come with wounds red to judge the quick and the dead?"

"Yes."

"That we shall rise at the day of Doom and be ready when we come?"

"Yes, yes."

He did not even hear the words he was saying, words he now believed to be false. He saw nothing but the thin, blond fur above her lip, fur that reminded him of an animal that needed to be stroked, made to feel not small. She deserved to feel not small. Before he could think what it was he was supposed to ask next, he had his mouth on her fur, his tongue against her teeth, ridged and cool and slippery.

She did not move, did not make the slightest motion to stop him. Just waited and waited with her mouth held open as he petted her throat and then the skin under her collar, and when he moved his hand over the fabric of her chest and held one covered breast in his palm, she brushed her tongue against his.

"Domine?" she said, drawing away from him. When he did not answer, she covered her mouth with her hand, her little finger poised in the air. "Domine?" she said again.

It was a question, he realized, and he did not know how to answer. Had she moved the inside part of her mouth because of his position in the Church, or because somehow she had desired him, too? He glanced up and saw the Virgin looming over them. Her stone lips seemed to be turned down in disappointment.

"I—" he said.

Jacotte stood from the altar and shook her head. "It is forgotten," she said. "Forgotten." She moved her hand out over his head, as if she were going to bless him, and then she hastened out of the chapel.

Alone, he looked to the Virgin, to the eyes so much like the one narrow eye of Marquise. He covered his face with his sleeve. *You have failed me*, he imagined the voice of a woman saying—but was it the voice of the Virgin or Marquise he heard? Perhaps all of womankind. *You have failed me*. He covered his ears. *You have failed me. You have failed me.* In a mad frenzy, he stood, picked up the stool on which he had been sitting, and threw it to the ground. He saw that it had not broken and took it by a leg, striking it against the wall until it did.

THE FOLLOWING AUTUMN, when the leaves had already darkened but not yet fallen to the ground, he was alone in the vestry of the chapel, trying to write a lesson on the seven deadly sins to deliver at Mass the next morning. He often wrote in the vestry, where he had set a narrow table next to the coffer containing the vestments he wore on festival days. From the table, he could glance up from his parchment page and meditate on the cross hanging above the shelf of sacred vessels, gleaming in the candlelight. Often, he would burn myrrh in the thurible, and—like a trick—the sweet scent would stir his soul, spilling forth words for him to write. On this autumn day, however, even the myrrh choked his faith. What was myrrh, in fact, but a resin of a plant, a material thing? No, myrrh had nothing in common with the spirit. He dipped his quill into a shallow jar of ink and made a brown dot on the corner of the parchment, listing the seven deadly sins in his mind— pride, covetousness, wrath, gluttony, envy, sloth, lust. *Lust.*

He dropped the quill, walked to a cupboard by the window, and opened a chest in which he kept scrolls of old sermons and lessons he had delivered. Opening scroll after scroll, he found a lesson he had written several years before on mortal sin. He carried the scroll back to the table and held it under the candle's flame as he read:

OF MORTAL SIN

We are all sinners in this world, sometimes in ignorance and so in bliss. When Grace allows us to name a sin we have committed, we see in the dark alleyways of our soul a wretched temptress, trying to thwart our union with God. We may repent of our sin then, and so accept the mercy of God and be forgiven. If we persist in our sin, however, and deliberately decide to commit an act contrary to divine law, we reject the salvation offered by the Holy Spirit. Unrepented, our sin destroys in us the possibility of eternal beatitude, bringing eternal death instead.

He released the scroll, and it fell onto the table, curling into itself and rolling until it bumped against the candlestick. He held his hand up to the flame of the candle and pinched the wick so that it smoked up from his skin. *"Can a man take fire in his bosom and his clothes not be burned?"* he thought, Proverbs VI, xxvii. He was burning from within, burning from without, and soon his whole parish would see Hell flames rising from him. He had to have a woman. He had to quench his desire.

Quickly he turned away from the table, knocking over the jar of ink so that it made a deep brown blot on the page. From the sack of tithes, money to be handed over to the bishop of the diocese, he withdrew two handfuls of coins—which he stuffed into his pocket—and then took up his cloak and walked from the vestry to the altar, careful to avoid the gaze of the Virgin overhead. He knelt by her feet and lifted the stone under which he had hidden the amulet when the Châtelaine had left for Varilhes. He pushed the amulet into his pocket with the coins and backed away from the Virgin like a boy—afraid that if he turned from her now, she would suspect him of naughtiness, of mortal wrongdoing.

He wanted to fly down the road to Ax-les-Thermes, but trudged through the thickness of broom and scrub on the uninhabited slope of the knoll to avoid being seen, and then made his way to the path that led to the Col de Pichacca. As he walked, he tried to convince himself that the needs of his parish justified his taking a woman—a woman would suck the desire out of him so he could write and preach once more. *Write and preach lies,* he thought, remembering the Good Men and their hatred for the Church. All his life had become deception.

When at last he descended into Ax, his hip aching intolerably, he did not hesitate, but walked directly to a tavern he had passed before and hungered to enter. As the night was still early and there was no fair in town, the tavern was nearly empty, except for a cluster of men playing at dice around a table, and a girl—no more than eleven or twelve—standing alone by a small flaming hearth. Her brown hair was braided with a yellow ribbon and tied up on her head, and her throat was pale as milk.

"Wine?" he heard. It was the tavern keeper, a tall youth, come around with a flagon and a cup. He smiled at Pierre, surveying his holy vestments, and then cocked his head slightly and squinted. "Or women?"

Pierre sat down and reached into his pocket—his hand brushing against the amulet within. He withdrew a denier and tossed it onto the table before him, indicating that it was drink he wanted. The keeper set the cup down and poured. Pierre eyed the girl again.

Her fingers were tiny, and they played over the surface of her skirt, smoothing the fabric down and then crinkling it up, before smoothing it down again. Pierre took the cup and drank the wine without pause.

"Keep paying, keep drinking," he heard the keeper mutter. He reached into his pocket and threw down more change. In the light issuing from the hearth, the girl's eyes appeared golden brown, and she flicked them from him to the keeper and back down to her skirt. Pierre drank another cup.

"Another?" said the keeper.

Pierre tossed down a sous. The girl licked her lips quickly, and they glistened with her moisture. Pierre drank again. "Vows of chastity," he muttered.

"What vows!" the keeper said.

Pierre turned to the keeper. He hated the snide smirk pinching the keeper's lips together. "Vows of chastity," he said again, "are not as solid among mountain priests." He remembered the old rector of Montaillou telling him that. How disturbed he had been by the profession. He had been pure then. Good then. He grumbled and drank.

"Ten for the girl," the keeper said. "Mondinette!" he shouted.

Pierre looked up at the keeper, then at the girl. He had never said he wanted her, had not in fact admitted to himself he did. Still, he felt his member stirring as she approached one tentative step at a time. He saw her wipe the wetness from her mouth, and he felt as if he were looking at the mournful ghost of someone he had just murdered.

"You are lucky tonight," said the keeper. "She is fresh. Not new, but fresh. Well worth ten. She's no hag, Domine."

The back of Pierre's neck prickled with the appellation. The girl was only an arm's length away, and he could smell her cleanness, see the smoothness of her skin, the freckles dotting the bridge of her nose. Even more, she was just his height—he knew absolutely, although he was still sitting. He pulled a handful of sous and deniers from his pocket and scattered them like rain onto the table.

The keeper counted out ten sous, scooped them into his hand, and stared at the remaining coins. He took another sou and held it up in his palm like a relic. "For good luck," he said with a smile. He turned and disappeared into the back of the tavern, leaving Pierre and the girl alone.

"Come on now!" the keeper shouted. Pierre moved to pick up the coins, but saw the girl gazing at them longingly. He pushed the coins toward her. Without once looking up into his eyes, she swept them jingling into the pocket of her skirt.

"Mondinette!" the keeper shouted. Pierre stood and limped toward the darkness of the back, listening for the jingle of the girl behind him. He found the keeper in a small room, barren except for a pallet on the floor and a thin gray cat suckling a pile of kittens on a pillow. The keeper carried a short lit candle between his fingers, and when he saw Pierre, he held it up to him. "When the candle is out, you're through with her," he said, and he inserted the candle into a holder on the wall. "Mondinette!" he shouted again, and then batted the cat and her kittens off the pillow with the heel of his boot. The cat moaned and sulked from the pillow to a corner of the room hidden in shadow, her kittens scurrying behind her.

The girl appeared in the door, pulling her skirt around her legs, as if to wrap them shut forever. The keeper took her by the shoulder and shoved her jingling into the room. "What do you have there, little thief?" he spat, and then felt her up and down, stopping at the bulk of coins in her pocket. He shoveled them out into a makeshift pocket of his own. "That'll teach you," he muttered.

"They are mine," the girl whispered.

The keeper barged out of the room and shut the door behind him. For a moment, Pierre and the girl simply stared at each other. His hand began to shake by his side, and she glanced down at it, an expression of horror passing over her face—as if she were witnessing the weapon that would soon be used against her. She let out a little whimper. Pierre stepped toward her, wanting to comfort her, but she whimpered again. He reached into his pocket for the amulet, and then untied his holy cloak and let it drop to the floor. She began to cry.

When he was close enough to her to feel her breath on his face, he touched the freckles on her nose and stroked away her tears with the tip of his thumb. She closed her eyes, and he knew there was nothing left to do but seal his fate. In one quick movement, he grabbed her by the back and the thighs and carried her down to the pallet. He pushed up her skirt and pried apart her legs and tried to force the amulet inside her. She screamed fiercely, and he let the amulet fall to the side. He untied his breeches, leaning in over her, and despite her stiffness, despite her tears, despite his horror at his crime, he entered her then, entered into a bliss deeper and fuller and sweeter than any Paradise he could imagine. It was as if he were making love to Marquise, his spiritual bride. This girl was so new, so fresh, she was almost disembodied.

ALL THROUGH THE WINTER and the following spring, he returned to the tavern, looking for Mondinette. He never found her there, shyly smoothing down her skirt by the heat of the hearth. Some nights, he feared he had killed her with his strong, urgent love. He took refuge in the whores who clustered around the gaming table, or hovered in the depths of the tavern, carrying their well-used bodies like sacks of hay to be sold at the fair. Between their breasts, he felt almost freed to be a flawed man of the flesh. But when he left their bodies, left the tavern each night and entered into the clean night air, he felt himself a smaller man, and further still from God.

That spring, he was journeying down the hillside toward the woods and the tavern, when he caught sight of a small congregation of villagers gathered in the distance beneath a twisted elm. It was a gray, windless day, and through the gloom he recognized Jean Marty, Old Woman Rives, and Fabrisse—whom he knew then only as the Châtelaine's former maidservant. There were mounds of dirt circling an open grave between them, and a shovel leaning against the trunk of the elm. He remembered having spied on all three villagers at the baptism of Prades Tavernier, and he realized suddenly that he was witnessing the burial of a heretic. Though he knew he should either pounce upon the villagers in the name of the Church or flee quickly—and so escape unseen—he could do neither. The maidservant turned her gaze in his direction, and he felt pinned to the earth by her eyes. For a long moment, they stared at each other. Then she turned her gaze away, and he fled.

He managed to hide from the heretics and the maidservant for a time, and even to push them from the front of his mind. He carried on with his dual life, delivering proper Masses to his parish by day and hiding within the bodies of whores by night. Then, sometime in late August, he made haste for the tavern and found the maidservant sitting at the foot of a gaming table. Her face was flushed, her cheek creased and wet, as if she had been dozing on the table, drooling as she slept. Her belly, he noticed, was full with child. Had she come to the tavern to whore herself? She would know—surely she would know—that he himself had come for more than drink.

"No," she said, wiping her cheek, her mouth. Her chin quivered and her eyes became moist.

He bowed to her, unable to speak, trying in a moment to convey his shame.

SOMETHING BROKE in him after that night. If he had hated himself already, he hated himself even more after having seen the maidservant—in all her pregnant vulnerability—trying to sell herself by the tavern door. Not a single woman seemed unconquerable to him anymore.

On the day of the Assumption of the Virgin, he was delivering a bidding prayer in Mass, looking out at the grim faces of the villagers seated on the straw before him, at the faces of women whose bodies he might as well have known.

"Almighty God," he said, feeling dizzy, as if the taste and odor and smoothness of each of these women were buzzing inside his brain at once. "Almighty God," he said again. "To whose power and goodness infinite all creatures are subject, at the beseeching of thy Glorious Mother . . ."

He gripped the side of the altar to steady himself. "Thy Glorious Mother, Gracious Lady, and of all thy saints, help our feebleness . . ."

The altar slipped from his grasp. He teetered. "Help our feebleness with thy power, our ignorance with thy wisdom, our frailty . . ."

Feebleness. Frailty. He closed his eyes, and the thought came to him that the Glorious Mother, Sancta Maria, was a woman. A woman of the flesh, like any woman in his parish, who walked and urinated and bled so that her baby could be born. She was a woman, and he could no longer believe her body had contained the pure spirit of the Lord.

HE KNEW IT was only a matter of time before he proceeded to the heretics. When the Châtelaine had lived in Montaillou, and they had been making love underground, she had told him that the Good Men did not value the virginity of Sancta Maria because they did not view her as having given birth to Jesus in the flesh. Rather, they considered Christ to be the illusion of a man—a pure spirit—and they preached that Sancta Maria had thus never tainted Him with flesh and blood, but "shadowed Him forth." Pierre latched on to that phrase now—*shadowed Him forth*. How else could he raise his eyes to the figure above the altar and not imagine the long cord of his amulet wrapped around her neck, draped between her breasts and down?

Only a fortnight after the Assumption of the Virgin, he blew out the candle beneath the altar, left the chapel, and walked up the road to the small house of Na Roqua, whom he remembered seeing at the baptism of Prades Tavernier in the fortress. It was she who had put her hands on his aching hip when he was a boy, telling him the words he still clung to—*"Flesh is a prison of temptation. Unbearable for the soul that is pure."* Without much deliberation, he decided that it would be she who would lead him to his fate now.

He entered her house without knocking and found her sitting on a bench in front of the kitchen fire, kneading the joints of her fingers. She smiled at him as if she had expected him all along.

"Yes," she said simply. "I do not imagine it is herbs you want now."

He hung his head, ashamed at his weakness, and walked toward her.

"Your limp is better," she said.

He coughed into his hand. "Not worse."

He sat on one end of the bench, gazing into the fire. They were quiet together, and then she patted the bench with her hand and said, "Come closer."

He slid over and she put her old hand in his lap. "You are sad," she said. "But there is no reason to be. There is goodness in our village now." She held his hand up and put it in her own lap, patting it again and again. "Would you like to see the goodness, Pierre?"

He let his head fall on her shoulder.

"Yes," she said. "That's right, my boy."

When the moon was high, she led him by the elbow to the house of Jean Marty, where she said the Good Men were staying for the night.

She told him to wait in the garden while she went inside the house, and he stood among the pigs and listened to their grunts and groans and wanted suddenly to hide.

Soon enough, she came out for him, saying it would take some coaxing for the Good Men to believe he was not a spy. She cocked her head and raised her thin eyebrow. "You are not a spy, are you, boy?"

Pierre shook his head. "No," he said, as much to himself as to her.

Inside, the two brothers in black habits were sitting at the kitchen table, several empty bowls and a cup before them. Jean Marty was on a bench by the wall, and his mother, Old Woman Marty, was standing by the fire, wiping her hands in her apron. They all eyed Pierre, and when neither of the Good Men greeted him in any way, Old Woman Marty proceeded to talk as if Pierre had never entered.

"I am afraid you did not like the bread I prepared," she said to the Good Men.

There was a long pause.

"I liked it very much," said the elder brother.

Old Woman Marty took a jug from a shelf by the hearth and walked to the table, pouring water from the jug into the empty cup before them. "Fine sieves are not to be found in our mountains," she said. She finished pouring and wiped droplets of water from the edge of the jug with her apron. "The bread that we knead is coarse."

There was another pause.

"It was delicious," said the elder.

Old Woman Marty walked the jug back to the shelf, set it down, and smiled.

Jean glanced at Pierre, still in the doorway of the kitchen. He seemed to want to say something to Pierre, but turned back to the Good Men. "My mother is pleased you enjoyed her bread," he told them.

"Yes," said Old Woman Marty. "Pleased." Her eyes slid to Pierre, then quickly back to the Good Men. "And the fish," she said to them. "How did you find it?"

"Also delicious," said the elder.

"Delicious," said his brother.

"Pleased you enjoyed it," said Old Woman Marty.

The room went quiet and all was still, save for the crackling dance of the fire. The elder held the cup to his lips and drank slowly, his eyes falling into shadow. When he was through, he tapped the cup against the tabletop.

"Are you sure you will not have some cheese?" Old Woman Marty asked.

The elder set the cup down and stood, facing Pierre. His hand clutched the table, though there was nothing of anger in his eyes, nothing of accusation. Rather, he had the aspect of a loving father, quietly waiting for his son to make the decision that would turn him into a man.

Pierre sank to his knees. "I have been a deceiving hypocrite," he said.

The Good Man walked toward him and Pierre closed his eyes. After a moment, Pierre felt the warmth and weight of hands on his head. "Go on, brother," said the Good Man.

"I spied on you in the fortress," said Pierre. "But I believed you. I believe in what you said. I hate the world. Hate my body. Hate the way it hurts."

"Yes," said the Good Man.

"Still, I cannot stop myself," cried Pierre. "Cannot stop myself from wanting. Wanting women." He groaned. "Whores."

The Good Man sighed. "You must walk away from the Devil," he said.

"Walk away," said the younger brother.

"Walk away," said Na Roqua. She knelt beside Pierre, her healing hands on his back.

"Help me," cried Pierre.

The Good Man bent down and touched Pierre on the knee. "You will help yourself by helping us," he whispered.

Pierre felt as if he had just been given penance after confession. "I will, Father," he said, gazing up into the Good Man's fierce, fire-warmed eyes. He had been told what he must do, and what he must do would save him.

THE FOLLOWING SUNDAY, he delivered Mass to a large group of parishioners, stealing creeds that were his no longer. After the Mass, a humble peasant from the parish of Prades approached him with a pale-faced babe in arms. The child's mother had died the previous evening, and the peasant had no means of paying for a wet nurse, he explained. He had come seeking charity, as the priest of Prades had none to offer. Pierre almost turned the peasant away before he remembered the maidservant, and how pregnant she had been only two months before. If he compensated her for nursing this baby along with her own, she would have no reason to return to the tavern for a time. He took the baby into the cradle of his arms, telling the peasant he would return it to Prades when it was weaned. Yes, he owed this small thing and more to the maidservant, who had seen him fall so far and looked upon him compassionately nevertheless.

Outside, clouds clustered in the sky, and within moments the wind came carrying the scent of pine, and then a sprinkling rain. Pierre carried the child through the rain toward the house of Old Woman Rives, whom he remembered standing by the maidservant during the secret burial under the twisted elm. When he arrived at the house, he knocked upon the door, his heart thumping. He had not in fact conversed with the maidservant since she had appeared in the chapel announcing that the Châtelaine needed him in the fortress. How long ago that had been . . . He did not know how he would speak to her now—there had been so much silence between them.

It was she who came to the door, fresh-faced, as if light were radiating from beneath her skin. She looked at him in astonishment, her dark eyebrows lifted, an expression of both fear and entreaty in her gaze, and then she glimpsed the baby in his arms and slowly her eyes became tender. He held the baby out in silent appeal, and she smiled slightly, taking the child from him.

He would never fully remember what was said between them then, but he would remember how their conversation ended: with her name, with the memory of Marquise and the silent vow he had spoken to be her spiritual husband, the spiritual father of her child. What a wretched father he had been. . . .

He left the house and struggled down the road, wanting to lose himself again inside the bodies of whores in the tavern. He would have gone that far, to Ax and farther—so much did he long to unclench himself of all pretense of being a good man, a holy man—but something of a miracle and a tragedy happened then. He rounded the bend leading to the square, and saw—gathered beneath the elm by the churchyard— a crowd of villagers standing silently before a preaching man. The man was dressed in the clothes of a friar, and when Pierre approached, he saw that the top of the man's head was shaven in a perfect circle. A Dominican had come to Montaillou. The inquisition of the village had begun.

1300 — 1308

Part II

SEVEN

THE FRIAR in the square was a man of thirty-eight named Bernard, who had entered the order of the Dominicans as the result of an event directed—he had chosen to believe for most of his life—by the hand of God. As an infant, before he even had teeth to chew, he had been left on the bank of the River Vienne, wrapped in a mat of straw. The Dominican prior of Limoges at the time—an old, white-bearded man named Grégoire—had been walking by the river when he heard a helpless cry and saw a baby planted among the reeds. Grégoire took him back to the monastery, named him after the great Saint Bernard de Clairvaux, and suckled him on warm goat milk until his teeth budded out from his gums. Though in practice the friars raised Bernard collectively, it was Grégoire whom he loved as his only earthly father. He slept on a mat by Grégoire each night and prayed the old man would never leave him for Heaven.

One evening, when Bernard had been at the monastery for seven years, he asked Grégoire a question he had never before dared. "Father?" he whispered. He heard Grégoire wet his lips, then inhale forcefully, as though the room were empty of air and he had to take great gulps of it to be replenished.

"Yes, my boy."

"Did you have a mother?" For as long as he could remember, Bernard had tried to imagine Grégoire as a boy, with a mother, a real mother. He had found the image almost impossible to conjure up, and had hoped, secretly, that Grégoire had also been left without a sign of fleshly provenance.

"A mother?" he heard Grégoire croak. "Yes. I did."

Bernard's heart sank.

"A good woman," Grégoire continued. "She had brown hair." He paused. "She didn't like it when my father spat in his hand."

Bernard had seen his share of females in Mass and during funerals at the cemetery. He pictured one woman whom he had noticed on several occasions. She had a broad, red mouth, brown hair that fell in strands around her face, and a bottom that jiggled when she walked. He felt his eyes pinch together, and he realized he had started to cry.

"Now, now," said Grégoire. He coughed, and then coughed again, and then coughed as if he would never stop. When he was through, he breathed for a long moment. "What do you need a mother for? You have more than twenty fathers here in the monastery, where most boys have only one."

"Only one," whispered Bernard. In his heart, he knew he, too, had only one, and that was Grégoire, and Grégoire was dying from age. Bernard pulled his wool blanket up over his chin and curled his knees against his chest. He thought he might cry some more, and squeezed his eyes shut to stop the tears from coming. When his throat had loosened, he opened his eyes. "Tell me about Moses," he whispered, "when he was a baby."

"Again?" moaned Grégoire. He sighed. "But just this once, you hear?" He coughed, and then grumbled and spat, and Bernard waited for the story to begin of the blessed boy left among the reeds at the brink of a river, in a basket made of bulrushes and daubed with bitumen and pitch.

WHEN BERNARD had been at the monastery for nearly ten years, Grégoire breathed, then breathed no more. Bernard had been standing by his bed, helping him drink water from a long wooden spoon, when Grégoire shut his lips and fell back on the pillow, looking with wide eyes up at the ceiling. The air within him crackled from the corners of his lips, and Bernard dropped the spoon so that it clattered onto the floor. He ran through the monastery, shouting for help, and then, too frightened to follow the others back to Grégoire, he escaped out into the rainy courtyard. He crouched beneath a pruned cherry tree and wiped rain from his face again and again.

With Grégoire gone, Bernard turned his heart away from human-kind. It seemed to him—though not entirely clearly—that the precious things in his own small life, the woman who had borne him and the man who had taken him in, were like shoots on the spring branches. The winter of death had frozen them away, and he did not want to mourn for yet another passing. Only God was like the rock beneath the soil, without beginning or end and thus steadfast in His presence. Two months after Grégoire was put in the ground, Bernard asked the friars to be tonsured as a sign of both his devotion to God and his intention to take the habit of the Dominicans when he was old enough one day. The Bishop of Périgueux performed the ceremony, shaving a circle on the top of Bernard's head. "The Church is your mother now," the Bishop muttered as he dipped the razor into clear water. "Love her, and she will suckle the stomach of your mind." Bernard watched the hair on the razor's edge float over the surface of the water. Slowly, he raised his hand to his head and felt the smooth, wet circle of skin there. Yes, his mind had been scrubbed clean—clean enough to be suckled by the bride of Christ.

For three years, he threw himself into the study of grammar, learning letters that made words that made sentences of Scripture on which he fed. He progressed with ease, proving his facility for language and giving the friars every opportunity to show him favor. By his thirteenth year in the monastery, he had nearly forgotten his loneliness and bore the affect of an age-old man of wisdom. Only occasionally would he return to the mat on which he had slept by Grégoire and be overcome by fear. In the blackness of night, he saw—or thought he saw—a vision of the world deprived of the Church, his only mother now, and again, he was like a baby left in the reeds—his heart beating as if at any moment it would stop. He would have to feel quickly for the chamber pot on the floor, so he would not wet himself. Lying down, he would curl his knees to his chest, pull the blanket over his chin, and pray, pray to God the Church would never leave him.

IT WAS AROUND THIS TIME that he began to take long walks by the bank of the River Vienne, dipping his bare feet into the water to be cooled, and searching the reedy shore for a scrap of the mat in which he had been wrapped as a baby. He wanted to know just where his mother had stood when she abandoned him. He wanted to stand in her place and feel her in the ground.

Increasingly, he thought of his own life in light of that of Moses, and he longed for the gift Moses had received from God in the burning bush: a sign, an appearance, a pronouncement as to how he was to live according to the path of righteousness. Walking through the densely leafed forest by the river, he played the scene out in his mind: "It is I," he would hear from within a flaming tree. He would be told to remove his sandals, just as Moses had been told, for the place whereupon he stood would be holy ground. He would hide his face, never daring to put his eyes on God. And then God would tell him, "I will be with thee." The great question of his life would be solved, for he would have discovered the person God wished him to be.

Half-listening for the rumor of God in the breeze, he took long walks deep into the forest. Each bud, each silver-skinned branch of a birch seemed to quiver with mystery and meaning. For the first time in his life, he recognized the overwhelming gift God had made in nature: the wet leaves of so many greens, the muddy footprints of the forest foxes, the red-bellied robins with their beaks agape—even the sodden roots beneath the trees seemed clean.

In the winter, he ventured out into dry snow flurries and admired the way snow stuck to the earth and muted sound. For days, he waited on the covered-over crabgrass, more sure than ever that—in this resplendent field of white—God would smile at him from the vantage point of the earth. He waited, waited, thought if he were to give himself a new name, it would be "He Who Waits." The drizzle of spring turned the snow to slush, and he crafted phrases in his mind: *At the end of my anticipation, there is the face of God . . . Who is my ancestor? One who is surer than all.*

IN HIS FIFTEENTH YEAR at the monastery, he received what he believed to be the sign from God he had been waiting for. It came not in the form of a burning bush or a flaming tree—indeed, it came not in nature, but on the pages of a ledger he found hidden beneath the straw pallet on which Grégoire had slept. Until that time, the pallet had been kept like a sacred altar—untouched, undefiled by another's sleeping body, and so unexorcised of the spirit of Grégoire, whom Bernard sometimes sensed drifting by him in the night. A new prior entered the monastery that spring, however, bringing with him an aesthetic of efficiency—"What we pluck, we use," he said when he saw the pallet gathering sunlight from a window in the corner. The prior assigned the pallet to an incoming novitiate and asked Bernard to dust it thoroughly for mites.

How redeemed Bernard felt when he found the ledger flattened onto the floor beneath the pallet! He hid it under his shirt and took it out to the riverbank. Sitting with the tips of his toes in the cold water, he opened the ledger and smelled the smooth surface of the parchment page, bitter enough to make his mouth water. Though his reading skills were still green, he managed to comprehend the scrawl that bumped across the top of the page. "A History of the Order of Preachers," it read, "from Grégoire to his son Bernard." As if he were holding the book of his life in his hands, he felt a wave of panic pass through him and he wanted to slap the ledger shut to hide his eyes from the blinding light of his future. He breathed, and when his heart was no longer in his throat, he read on:

> I will take no time to embrace you with words, my son, as I am with you in the flesh still as I write, and feel my spirit tied to yours now and evermore. Do not feel me gone when you hold this book in your hands. I write for you, that you might understand my failings as a friar in the Order of Preachers, and so, by example, not repeat my mistakes.
>
> I was a young man of seventeen, living in Belpech, when the canon of Osma—in the Kingdom of Aragon—delivered a sermon to our small parish. In spirit, I had already given my life over to the priesthood, though I had not yet taken the habit. My father had seen both of my older brothers killed as soldiers, you see, and so had taken great care with my education that I might become a high-ranking man of peace.
>
> Barefooted and unadorned, the canon of Osma, Father Dominic de Guzuran by name, was the very model of humility, and my heart gave way to him as he spoke of the heresy spreading throughout our region. At that time, men and women calling themselves Good Christians lived like monks and nuns in convents throughout the provinces, and were often protected by their Lords, who built great fortresses high above the

ground to defend them. Father Dominic argued that the heresy had begun
in part as a reaction against the immoderation of the Church, and said
that an order of mendicant friars—humble in dress and possessions as
Christ—was needed to wean the people of the region back to the true faith.

How could I look the other way? It seemed to me then that if
Christ had seen the wealth local bishops were amassing at the cost of the
peasants, He too would have taken to the road, to the open field, to the
people, that is, with a message of humility. I swore an oath of obedience
to Father Dominic and, with a flock of legates of Pope Innocent III—
who supported our mission—spread throughout the region, preaching
the modesty we practiced.

There were those who warmed to us and fed us graciously, and
for the most part those were girls, too young to have lost much in the
form of tithes and penances. We brought some of them with us to the
countryside near Fanjeaux—a stronghold of the heretics—where we
formed the Convent of Prouille.

Soon thereafter, one of the papal legates was murdered along the
banks of the Rhone. As we later learned, the legate, Brother Pierre de
Castelnau, had excommunicated the Count of Toulouse—the most
powerful lord in all the region. The Count had tried to make amends by
vowing to obey the legate, but nevertheless had resolutely refused to
chase the heretics from his land. It was said that during a session of
heated negotiation the Count had threatened the legate, telling him that
his watchful eye would be upon him wherever he might go. The following day, the legate was murdered. Although it was not at all clear that
the Count was responsible for the assassination, Pope Innocent III accused him of collusion, pronounced him again excommunicate, and
called for a crusade against the entire region of the south. Some of us retreated to the Convent of Prouille with Father Dominic, but almost all
of the remaining legates returned to their former posts discouraged.

The King of France at the time was Philippe-Auguste. Though he
did not take up the cross himself, a group of northern nobles—hungry
to conquer territory of infidel lords—marched south with their battalions.
On the twenty-second of July, in the year twelve hundred and nine, an
army of faith surrounded the fortified city of Béziers—known to be diseased with heresy. We heard word that the legate leading the war had
commanded the battalions at the gates to the city, "Kill them all; God
will know his own!" Not one pair of eyes was left blinking in Béziers,
my son. Though Father Dominic never spoke a word of reproach as to

the siege, I saw him shrink into his body then. His mission had been one of humility, and I think he felt he had betrayed those heretics to whom he had promised a Church of mercy.

For the next twenty years, we of Father Dominic peacefully preached and prayed, while holy war ravaged the land. By the year twelve hundred and twenty-eight, Father Dominic had passed from the earth, the Toulousan countryside had been burned to the ground, the vines slashed, and the cattle slaughtered. The Count of Toulouse begged the Pope for negotiation and, according to the Treaty of Meaux, was made not only to abjure persecution of the heretics, but also to promise his only daughter in marriage to the brother of the King of France, and thus to concede Toulouse and its diocese to the powers of the north after his death. As a man of the Church, I rejoiced enough, but as a man of the region—whose ancestors had worked the hot soil for centuries—I regretted the treaty as I had regretted no written word before.

The crusade was over, but heresy breathed still in the land, and we of the Order of Preachers were called upon to lead the efforts against it once more. As it was, long before the crusade began, Pope Innocent III had decreed heresy to be treason under law. He had revived an ancient inquisitorial procedure once employed in the imperial courts of Rome. Under this procedure, a judge could initiate an investigation against a suspect of his own accord; whereas in the former accusatorial procedure, the judge had been made to wait for a minimum of two accusers before opening trial. Pope Innocent III had held first local bishops and then local lords responsible for the inquisition of the heretics, but neither had proceeded with much vigor. In the year twelve hundred and thirty-three, with the crusade over, Pope Gregory IX wrote an encyclical letter to the priors and friars of our order, calling upon us to lead a general inquisition in the south. He charged our highest prior to name two inquisitors, and one of those chosen was me. I was a man of forty-three then, and peace-loving, and unprepared for much more than humble preaching, though I had studied some Roman and canonical law before taking the habit as a young man. With the authority of the Holy See and the King of France behind me, I was sent to Toulouse, and it was there that I fell into the failures I have already alluded to, my son. Take heed. Take heed and learn from the example of your father.

At the Cathedral Saint-Étienne—where both Father Dominic and your namesake, Bernard de Clairvaux, had preached their Word—I addressed a crowd of townspeople resentful of my presence. There was to be a period of grace, I announced, during which all who were guilty of betraying the True Faith should come forth and confess, and they would be looked upon mercifully. After seven days, however, I would instruct the clergy of Toulouse to issue citations to those suspected of heresy. Informers would not be named to those they accused, and thus should come forth willingly, however carefully—lest they be caught in the sin of false accusation. Each suspect would be investigated and interrogated, and then imprisoned in the church dungeons while awaiting trial. I said all this— I did, but my words were not where I failed, Bernard. Where I failed was in how I spoke them—that is, in a trembling voice, with such trepidation, I thought at any moment I might stop breathing. I am sure my habit was soaked through, and my face was wet with perspiration. And worst, worst of all for our Mother Church, I had no fire in my eyes, no fire of conviction—how could I have, when I did not believe myself capable of carrying out such actions. I had never imagined that my calling as one of Father Dominic's order would be not only to preach, but also to investigate, to imprison. All my eyes could have conveyed was melancholy, and a strange faithlessness, and a desire to say the Pater in solitude again.

More than a few confessors and informers came forth that first week, but I was slow in carrying out the investigations of those accused. I dawdled, sometimes suspecting false accusation, never certain that I had amassed enough evidence to open a trial. In truth, I believe now that I was frightened of passing sentence on a man. I had been instructed to relax to the secular arm all heretics beyond hope of conversion, as we of the Church were barred from administering any penitential punishment ending in bloodshed or death. You understand my dilemma, Bernard, do you not? Our Lord Jesus Christ called upon us to turn the other cheek, yet I was being asked to strike a retaliatory blow—more than that, I was being asked to send men to prison, if not to death, and pretend my hands were clean.

As I dawdled in Toulouse, my fellow inquisitor in Albi, Brother Arnaud Catalan, held a trial against a dead heretic woman, and—as she had been buried on consecrated ground—ordered her body exhumed and burned. The people of Albi revolted, beating Brother Catalan and dragging him through the streets to the River Tarn as they shouted, "Away, rid the earth of this fellow! He has no right to live!" I do not need to tell you how this incident affected me in Toulouse, my son: Not only was I plunged into an even deeper fear of taking action, but also the people of Toulouse began to sniff the possibility of resistance in the air.

Sure enough, in October of the year twelve hundred and thirty-five, as soon as I had finally found the courage to summon twelve prominent Toulousan citizens, a squall of opposition rained down on me. The consuls of the city commanded me to leave, and when I dawdled in this, I was physically torn away by the hair that remained on my head. I will confess to you now, as I have confessed to God before, I did not resist the men who ejected me. I walked willingly beside them as they pulled my hair and tore my ear, and though my heart was heavy with defeat, I felt the peace of an ending near—the ending, that is, of my own term of influence as a man. I hid for a time in Carcassonne, from which I unenergetically sent word to the clergy of Toulouse to issue a second citation to the suspects. Without a strong inquisitor to defend them there, the clergy too were ejected. Soon the consuls of Toulouse ordered its citizens to refuse to engage with the lot of us, including the Bishop and his canons. The Order of Preachers was officially expelled from the city in November, and the humiliation of that public defeat was nothing in comparison to the humiliation I felt before God. If I had known then that my failure in Toulouse would inspire a rash of riots against future inquisitors over the next decade, I might have committed a great and unspeakable crime against myself and God. Blessed is our lack of foresight when we take a wrong path among those that are presented to us, Bernard. May you not take the wrong path for having read this caution here.

Upon reading this letter, you may ask yourself why—in all the years your father spent with you in the flesh—he never spoke of inquisition, nor of his personal responsibility for the violence too often committed against his future fellow inquisitors. In truth, I found no reason to worry you about heresy, as—since the middle of the century—it has been, if not a corpse, a dying thing in our region. There is yet another reason why I remained silent. Bernard, you are the one thing about which I never hesitated. When I found you by the river's brink, I did not have to pause before taking you up in my arms. As you grew, I talked with you and taught you according to my heart—nothing more or less. Sweet boy, you never caused me any trouble. If I could not bring myself to tell you of my failings, it was because I wanted you to believe your father was good and devout and strong, and moreover, contented with his life. I wanted you to see beyond me, to have a time of knowing nothing about persecution, nothing about the calling of the men you lived among to investigate and interrogate and sentence if need be.

I do pray that by the time you read these words, heresy will have *long been a thing of the past. But if it should not be, my son, and if you have chosen to take the habit and are called forth as an inquisitor some-day, I tell you now to be the arm of justice your earthly father had not the courage to be. Would Father Dominic have approved of sentencing a heretic to prison or to the stake? It was a question I asked myself too often. Here, now, at the end of my life, I tell you that you must believe he would have, son. You may feel yourself a hypocrite and worse, but you must always remember that it is sometimes necessary for a man to fall, that others might not fall lower still. Look to the prophet Moses as you did when you were a child. Let him be your example. He was the first inquisitor, and he was unflinching. I have always thought you would walk in the way of his ardor.*

Farewell in Christ, my son. How else should I leave you? A boy by the river, you were. In Christ, farewell.

Bernard read the words of the letter, his heart beating with their thrum, until the wolves began to howl and the moon fell asleep, low in the blue-black sky. He stood from the bank of the river and loped through the chill of night to the monastery, wondering what Grégoire had meant by calling Moses the first inquisitor. He tucked the ledger under his shirt and pressed it, burning, to the skin of his belly. If he could have pushed it inside himself, he would have then. Though he had not fully understood its contents, he knew they were as vital to him as the blood coursing through his body.

From that day forth, Bernard pursued his studies with the singular purpose of preparing to be an inquisitor. By the time he was seventeen, he had interviewed nearly every friar in the monastery about the history of the Inquisition. At eighteen, he took the habit as another man might take a first lover—that is, passionately, with awe and trepidation at what divine mystery was opening before him. After a one-year novitiate, he stood before the head prior of all Dominicans and solemnly swore, "I, Bernard, make profession and promise obedience to God, and to the blessed Maria, and to the blessed Dominic. And I pledge to be obedient to you, Brother, master of the Order of the Preaching Brothers, and to your successors until death." The question of his heritage passed into oblivion as the ecstasy of becoming one with the Order of Preachers flooded his mind.

He was sent to Figeac to study logic for one year, and then to Bordeaux to study philosophy: Aristotle, Albert the Great, Thomas

Aquinas—thinkers whose words he stored mentally by the ledger under his habit, like so many arrows he would take to the bow one day. After a two-year appointment at the school of his vicariate in Brive teaching logic, he returned to Limoges to study theology, and his soul thrilled in anticipation. It was then that he read the Old Books of Scripture for himself and listened to long lectures on the lives of the great patriarchs—Abraham, Isaac, Jacob, Moses.

Moses. He devoured the books of that prophet like fresh meat. In Exodus, he read of how Moses had turned the sword against his own people when they had made a molten calf of gold and worshipped it instead of the Lord. *"Thus says the Lord God of Israel,"* Moses told the sons of Levi. *"Put every man his sword on his side, and go to and fro from gate to gate throughout the camp, and slay every man his brother, and every man his companion, and every man his neighbor."* Three and twenty thousand Jews were slain on that day alone. Bernard wrote the number on a scrap of parchment he kept folded inside the ledger. Beside the number, he wrote the word "unflinching."

In Leviticus, he read the decrees of Moses to the sons of Levi— marked to assist the Jewish priests. If a man were to curse his father or mother, he should be put to death. If a man were to commit adultery with the wife of his neighbor, both he and the adulteress should be put to death. If a man were to lie with the wife of his father, both he and the wife should be put to death. If a man were to lie with his daughter-in-law, both should be put to death. If a man were to lie with a man as with a woman, both men should be put to death. If a man were to take a wife and her mother also, all should be burned with fire. If a man were to lie with a beast, both should be slaughtered. And if a man were to perform fortune telling or magic, he should be stoned to death, his blood put upon him.

Finally, in reading Deuteronomy, Bernard understood at last why Grégoire had called Moses the first inquisitor. According to the law Moses set forth for the people, they—like an inquisitorial tribunal— were to "inquire diligently" when a man or woman was suspected of transgressing God's covenant. On the evidence of at least two witnesses, the suspect was to be stoned. *"The hands of the witnesses shall be first upon him to put him to death,"* said Moses, *"and afterward the hands of all the people."* Bernard shuddered, trying not to picture Mary Magdalene, hounded by a circle of townsfolk ready to stone her. No, he could not let his mind settle on the image of her frightened face, nor on the sound of Jesus' injunction that those among them who had not sinned cast the first stone. Moses had set down the law for a reason, he told himself, and the firmness of that law had saved the people—the people of *Jesus*—from wiping all goodness from the land.

WHEN BERNARD WAS THIRTY, he was assigned the position of assistant lector at Limoges, and in the fall of that year, he heard word that heresy had reared its head in the region once more. He was in the refectory of the monastery, drinking water from a bucket with a spoon, his eyes closed so that he would not have to peer into his own reflection, when he heard a friar speaking in a high pitch behind him. "It is back," the friar said. "I heard in Albi. There are fistfuls of heretic men there." Bernard let the spoon sink into the water. He swallowed and turned to the man who had spoken, one of the novitiates—a short, tubby youth, recently returned from a pilgrimage to the south. Bernard held a finger up to his lips, silently commanding the youth to quiet his tone. As he turned back to the bucket, all the tension in his body drained into the ground. What he had been waiting for had shown its face at last, and he was poised to fight it as no other young friar in the order.

Within days, a high-ranking friar by the name of Nicholas d'Abbeville was appointed Inquisitor of Carcassonne, from which the efforts against heresy in the region were to be based. Bernard immediately went to the prior of Limoges and asked to be relieved of his duties as assistant lector. "Father," he said, bending down at the feet of the prior—a spindly old man with patient, clever eyes, who was writing a letter at his desk. Bernard lowered his gaze in a sign of humility. "My apprenticeship here is no longer in the interest of the monastery."

The prior was silent. Bernard glanced up at him. The prior set his quill down and clasped his hands together. "It is true," he said, "that your sermons to the young novitiates are not of the most inspired." He paused, as if considering this last statement. "Though nobody has complained to me of boredom."

"Father," said Bernard.

The prior held up a thin finger. "It is also true that you have proceeded remarkably well in your studies. . . . Though a scholar does not a preacher make."

"Father," said Bernard.

The prior held up his finger once more. "Now, now," he said. "This may be just your problem." He nodded to himself. "Lack of patience. Too much inside your mind." He tapped his head. "If you want to be of more use in your preaching, you must leave your mind now and then. Open yourself to be moved by the Spirit."

Bernard felt his breath come quickly. He watched the prior pick up his quill. "I have been moved, Father," he said.

The prior looked from his page, smiling slightly.

"The Inquisition," said Bernard. "It is so much . . ." He meant to say it was so much on his mind, in his thoughts, but he felt his hands gripping his chest, the place over his heart.

"You want to go to Carcassonne," said the prior, turning to his page again. He dipped his quill into a jar of ink. "You are relieved, then. Go."

CARCASSONNE STOOD MIGHTILY, overlooking the River Aude. From the distance, its turrets and castellations appeared so numerous Bernard feared he would be swallowed whole in his approach. He had learned that at the time of the crusades, Carcassonne had served as a refuge for the heretics. So many of them had crowded within its ramparts that the heat and stench had become unbearable. Food had fallen short; disease spread rapidly. When the crusaders reached Carcassonne after the massacre of Béziers, they doubted their capacity to take the city by force and proposed an accord: The heretics would be permitted to live if they left bearing only their sins. Bernard held his breath as he passed through one of the gates to the city, half-expecting a disease-ridden heretic to barrel him down.

The Inquisitor, Nicholas d'Abbeville, was wary of Bernard from the start, and refused to allow him to attend the trials already being held against several accused heretics. Determined to apprentice to the Inquisitor nevertheless, Bernard spent long hours in the tower among the inquisitorial records that had been amassed over the century. These records became his education in methods of inquisitio, and moreover in the forms and variations of heresy itself. Upon examining the collection of books in the tower—among them the very useful *De auctoritate et forma inquisitionis*, on inquisitorial practice and pilgrimages imposed on penitents—Bernard realized that none had been written as yet that out-lined the heresies themselves. Without quite understanding what he was embarking upon, he began to plod systematically through the records with quill in hand.

Aside from the sorcerers, diviners, and Jews who had converted to Christianity and then relapsed, the heretics whom Bernard studied tended to cluster in one of three categories. Firstly, there were those who called themselves the Poor Men of Lyons. They had a grim con-tempt for ecclesiastical authority, and considered themselves to be the true successors of the apostles, claiming direct communication with God. They were enchanted by the state of poverty and preached chastity to their followers; yet they advocated marriage to those burn-ing with lust.

Secondly, there were those whom previous inquisitors had re-ferred to as "False Apostles." These heretics followed a doctrine con-trived by one Gerard Segarelli of Parma, who advised his disciples to live in obedience to no one but God. The power that Christ be-queathed to the apostles, they believed, had been transferred to this Gerard Segarelli, not to the Catholic Church—which they called "the great whore of Babylon." Only they had the authority to nullify con-tracts of marriage, they preached, and none outside their sect could hope to achieve salvation. Though they went about pretending to be as innocent as saints—singing on the byways and reciting the Pater Noster, the Ave Maria, and the Credo—they traveled with women whom they called *"sorores in Christo."* "These wretches," wrote Bernard in his ledger, "sleep in beds with their 'sisters in Christ,' asserting men-daciously and falsely that they are troubled by no temptations of the flesh."

Finally, the most prominently represented heretics in the archives referred to themselves—when they did confess—as Good Men or Good Women, or more commonly, as Good Christians. In order to be-gin to describe methodically the tenets of their ideology, Bernard made a list of practices particular to them: "They observe Lent more than once a year. They refrain from eating anything produced by animal re-production. Those who are men do not allow themselves to touch women. They have a curious practice of bowing repeatedly and utter-ing such words as *'Benedicite!* Good Christians pray God keep us from a bad death and lead us to a good end.' They adamantly refuse to take oaths. They claim to be the successors of Christ's apostles. They make a mockery of the Sacraments of the Church—in particular the Holy Eucharist, which they deny could be the body of Christ because, they say, 'even if it were as big as one very large mountain, the Christians would already have eaten it all up.' They believe in an original creation of everything immaterial and spiritual by God, and a secondary creation of everything material and base by Satan. They claim Christ was never incarnated, and thus neither perished on the cross nor rose from the dead. They refer to the Catholic Church as 'the whore and the church of the Devil.' Lastly, they choose to identify their sect as the veritable Sancta Maria, birthing spiritual children." These heretics, Bernard knew, were the men and women who had hounded Grégoire in Toulouse sixty years before, and thus the heretics whom he hated more than any other.

When he had finished an eighty-page draft of the treatise on heresy in its manifold forms, he turned it over to Nicholas d'Abbeville, hoping in this way to gain the confidence of the Inquisitor. He was nevertheless condescended to just as he had been upon arriving in Carcassonne. The Inquisitor confiscated the manuscript and commanded Bernard to cease all activities of research, calling him "nearly a novitiate," with none of the scholarly refinement to accomplish such a holy charge as the differentiation of true faith from blasphemy. "My good boy," the Inquisitor said with the manuscript tucked under his arm and a smile upon his face. "You have a very lofty impression of yourself." He turned to go, but stopped himself, glancing back at Bernard. "If you want to be helpful," he said, "go underground. It is too dark to read and write there, and you might talk some sense into the heretics." He chuckled. "Jean Maulen is particularly difficult. He even refuses to confess."

That afternoon, Bernard followed the jailer into the underground, black and air-deprived as a tomb. As they proceeded down a narrow corridor, he heard a sound that made his heart nearly leap out of his chest. It was a human sound, the sound of voices, moaning and weeping and crying out. He wanted to turn back, felt he could not breathe. "Please," he said to the jailer, "I am ill."

The jailer held his oil lamp up to look Bernard in the eye. "Seem well enough to me," he said after a moment, then he plodded on toward the darkness ahead.

They passed several doors, and the human sounds were so loud and close, Bernard felt them vibrating off his skin like flies. His whole body prickled. "Here he is," said the jailer, stopping in front of a door. He took a ring of keys from his pocket and inserted one into the lock. Bernard felt liquid gathering on the back of his tongue. He swallowed.

"I'll wait here," said the jailer. He handed Bernard the oil lamp and pushed open the door. "Don't you worry. He can't move."

Bernard held the oil lamp out in front of him and proceeded into the tiny, narrow cell. Immediately, he was so overwhelmed by the stench of human feces and urine, of bile, mold, and death, he had to stop and wipe his mouth. He heard liquid dripping, as if from the boards of the ceiling above. He turned back to the door, holding the lamp up to be sure the jailer was still there.

"Please," he heard coming from behind. "Please. Now. Please." He held the lamp in the direction of the voice, and against the far wall of the cell, he saw a man in ragged, threadbare clothes lying on the floor. Jean Maulen. Emaciated and exhausted, he was squinting into the light of the lamp, an expression of despair on his open mouth, his hands and bare feet in iron shackles. There was filthy muck all around him. His own waste, Bernard realized. "Please," the man moaned. "Please. Now."

Bernard stepped closer, the stench consuming him. He held the lamp over the man's dark whiskered face, and saw that one of his eyes was clouded with infection, that what teeth remained in his mouth were no more than rotten stumps. There were scabs on his face, and dried blood at the corners of his lips. "What is it you want?" Bernard whispered.

Jean Maulen raised his head slightly from the floor, his eyes widening with surprise, as if he had not yet realized that someone he had never encountered had entered the cell. He let his head fall back onto the floor. "To die," he cried softly. "They keep me alive in here and I've begged them. I beg you. Please, please, now."

Bernard knelt down. "I do not want you to suffer," he said.

The man cried more freely. "Thank you," he said, his breath foul.

"But you must confess your fault."

The man moaned and his face rolled into shadow.

"Confess and your suffering will end," said Bernard. "The Church is your mother. Merciful and kind."

Jean Maulen's face rolled toward Bernard. "You are just like the rest of them," he said. "You have no mercy at all."

. . .

FOR MORE THAN A WEEK, Bernard returned every day to the cell of Jean Maulen, trying with all his mind and heart to move the man toward confession and conversion. At first, he relied upon the logic he had learned in Figeac, and when that had no effect, he drew upon the more subtle philosophical arguments he had learned in Bordeaux. Finally, he threatened the man with the laws of Moses, claiming that Moses would have had him stoned for his sins—but that method was less effectual still, as Jean Maulen accused Bernard himself of not following the laws in allowing a sinner to live.

One night, in the privacy of his own room, Bernard reread the letter Grégoire had written to him. He found the old man's lack of conviction in the face of heresy to be so repugnant to him now, his bowels would not rest to let him sleep. At daybreak, he ordered the jailer to deprive Jean Maulen of water for two days. At the end of the second day, he entered the cell and shook Jean Maulen awake with the heel of his sandal. "Repent," he said firmly. "Repent and your body will know thirst no longer."

Jean Maulen peered up at him. He licked his dry lips, then turned his face toward the wall. He did not even ask for water, and Bernard knew he was trying to ease his way into death.

"Get him water!" Bernard shouted to the corridor. When the jailer brought in a bucket, Bernard spooned the water into Jean Maulen's mouth himself. "You will drink," he said again and again. He was going to save the soul of this man one way or another.

The following morning, the jailer led Bernard to an empty cell before taking him to Jean Maulen. In the center of the cell stood a complicated piece of machinery, which—the jailer said—the inquisitors of old had employed in order to coerce heretics into confession. The contraption consisted of a triangular framework with a roller at each end. The jailer explained that the heretic in question was fastened to the rollers by his wrists and ankles, and the joints of his limbs stretched until he indicated a willingness to confess. "It causes intense suffering, brother," said the jailer. "No other form of torture has quite the effect."

Together, Bernard and the jailer went to Jean Maulen, unshackled him, and carried him back to the cell with the contraption. They set him on the structure and tied his wrists and ankles to the rollers.

"You will repent," said Bernard, "or every bone in your body will betray your will."

Jean Maulen did not so much as whimper.

Bernard instructed the jailer to stretch the man's arms back. The jailer did as he was told, forcing Jean Maulen's chest to arch upward.

"What is your faith?" said Bernard to him.

Jean Maulen was silent.

Bernard instructed the jailer to stretch the man's legs. Jean Maulen's hips lurched up, as if his back had snapped.

"What do you consider to be a good Christian?" said Bernard.

Jean Maulen did not answer. He bit his lip, and Bernard pulled the ropes by the man's wrists. Jean Maulen began to shake, his face red and perspiring. Bernard saw blood pooling over his teeth, bearing down on his lower lip.

"Repent," said Bernard. He tried to stretch the man's legs further, and burned his fingers on the ropes. "Repent!" he shouted again like a curse. He clenched the rope more firmly and wrenched it down.

Jean Maulen made a moaning sound. It issued not from his mouth, but from somewhere within his body, like a scream held in the chest. Bernard realized that the prisoner would not even grant him the pleasure of hearing his cry of anguish. He released the rope and almost kicked Jean Maulen.

"Release him," he murmured to the jailer, retreating into the infernal blackness of the corridor.

EACH DAY that he had left Jean Maulen without saving him, Bernard had felt his own heart bleeding. Now he felt the wound in his heart was too deep to heal. There was no hope of converting the prisoner, no reason to keep him alive. The next day, he went to see him in the cell, but his own heart was so hard he could not utter a word. He stared into the squinting eyes of Jean Maulen and felt as if he were looking at a dead man—someone he had already sent to Hell.

That same day, he approached the Inquisitor in his private room of study and said he believed Jean Maulen was beyond hope of being saved. For the first time, the Inquisitor beheld him without a smirk of ridicule. "You believe he should be relaxed to the secular arm?" he said.

Bernard remembered Deuteronomy, and the law Moses had set forth. "You must give the people an example of how justice will be served," he said to the Inquisitor. "You must prove a point."

The Inquisitor paled and Bernard realized that, in an instant, he had become this man's authority. He had the courage of conviction, the courage to kill, whereas the Inquisitor had not.

TWO DAYS LATER, Jean Maulen was relaxed to the secular arm. The morning after, Bernard watched a scaffold being erected in the square. Jean Maulen was brought out in the fading light of dusk. He looked exhausted, but at ease, as he was led to a fat stake at the center of the scaffold, and made to face the west, rather than the more holy east. His ankles, knees, groin, waist, and chest were secured to the stake with ropes. Then his neck was fixed with a chain, and fagots were heaped up to his chin. It was merciful, Bernard thought, that his body had been hidden from the throng of people gathered around, a throng eerily still and silent for its mass.

The Count, who was overseeing the burning, advanced and asked loudly, "For the last time, man, will you repent?"

Jean Maulen stared out from behind the fagots. He seemed to be looking beyond the crowd, and did not even blink in response to the Count, who retreated and clapped his hands together. The people in the crowd gasped collectively, and the executioners, who had been standing aside with their torches, approached the scaffold. They held their fire to the base of the fagots, and quickly a blaze spread. Jean Maulen gazed out peacefully. For a moment, Bernard wondered if he had mistaken a saint for a heretic. He remembered the words of Christ on the cross, "Forgive them, Father, for they know not what they do." He clenched his own hands together and pressed them to his lips. *Forgive me, Father, for I know not. I know not.*

Jean Maulen closed his eyes. His features squeezed together, and then he opened his lips in a silent howl until the flames took him and there were no lips of his left to see. The people in the crowd began to shout in protest, and Bernard turned his gaze to the smoke-choked sky above them all. For the first time in his life, it seemed to him, God was nowhere near.

HE KNEW he had to reach the heretics before they had been incarcerated, before even they had committed themselves to heresy with their blasphemous rites. He told Nicholas d'Abbeville he needed his manuscript, and the Inquisitor yielded it without question. Early one spring morning, before the sun had spread its light, Bernard tied the manuscript and the ledger of Grégoire to his body and set off from Carcassonne. He was going to make a journey in homage to Saint Dominic, he told himself, a journey of simple preaching to the men and women who needed to hear the word of God most.

For six years, he walked the dusty roads between Limoges, the coastal vineyards of Bordeaux, and the Pyrenees. For six years, he preached peacefully and listened for the whisper of heresy in the air. Then, in his seventh year, he was circling the Comté de Foix, when he came upon a terrain freshly sown with heretical ideas. Preaching in the square of Ax-les-Thermes on the resurrection of the body, he was interrupted by a sallow-skinned, red-haired man who stepped forward from the crowd.

"If you don't mind, Brother," the man said. "You've got my head in a terrible muddle." The man gripped his chin in his hand.

"What has confused you?" Bernard said.

The man made a little humming sound

"Something I have said about the resurrection of the body, perhaps," Bernard prompted.

The man nodded. He released his chin, pointed a finger at Bernard, and opened his mouth as if to speak. Then he dropped his finger and shook his head. "Something about that," he muttered. He gripped his chin again.

"Perhaps you have heard that only the soul is resurrected," Bernard said.

The man made the humming sound again. "According to you," he said, "the soul is the body. Because it doesn't leave the body after death."

Bernard bit his tongue so not to correct the man. He wanted him to continue.

"But that's not what I've heard from others." The man shook his head. "No, no. They have lots of ideas about the soul and what happens to it in death, but none like that."

"And who are *they*?" said Bernard.

"They?" said the man. He held out his arms. "Some here, some there. No one in particular. Everyone has his own ideas." Whispers passed through the crowd behind him and several villagers left. The man looked over his shoulder at the villagers who remained, and then back to Bernard. "Mind you," he said, his eyes wider. "Every man's ideas aren't *mine*."

"Yes," said Bernard. "Of course they are not."

Several more villagers left, so that only five or six remained, including the man, who was still standing at the front. He glanced down at his shoe and kicked a pebble to the side. "If I tell you," he said, "no harm will come to me, will it?"

Bernard thought for a moment. "Why should harm come?" he said at last.

The man stuffed his hands into his pockets. "Some say the soul is like a kitchen fire," he began, "escaping like smoke when the body dies. Through the chimney of the throat and out into the sky."

Bernard nodded.

The man went on. "Some say the soul is simply blood. If you chop off the head of a goose"—he illustrated with his hands—"blood sprays out and the life drains away. The soul leaves and that is all. No resurrection of any kind."

Bernard nodded once more.

"Some say a dying man's final exhale is the soul escaping," said the man. He spoke the words "soul escaping" in a slow, breathy manner, as if he were telling a tale of phantasms. "This soul flies through the night until it finds some new body to enter."

"A new body," said Bernard.

"That's right," said the man. He scratched his cheek. "A wheat farmer told me that a soul without bread is no soul at all. . . . Souls die as supplies of bread die. Which is why farmers of cereals are harvesters of souls, nearly as holy as friars." The man looked pained suddenly. His forehead creased. "Mind you, this isn't my idea."

"Of course not," said Bernard.

The man scratched his cheek again. He seemed to want to say more.

"Is there something else?" asked Bernard.

The man chewed on the bulbous tips of his fingers. "There is just one thing," he said.

"Yes?"

"Though it is so awful, I wouldn't think to say it before you."

Bernard felt the base of his neck prickle. "It will cleanse you to relieve yourself of it," he said.

The man nodded, then stared down at the toe of his shoe again. "They say that every body, every *single* body, is made by—" He could not go on.

Bernard waited.

The man winced. "By fucking," he said. "That's what they say. By bodies fucking and shitting. They say Christ wasn't resurrected in the body, because he didn't have a body, because he couldn't have been created as all bodies are created." He winced again. "By fucking, that is," he whispered. "By bodies that shit and then fuck."

No one made a sound. Bernard felt his stomach turn, as if he would be sick.

"How could the soul be the body," said the man, "if Christ was pure soul and had no body?" He shook his head and gripped his chin again. "No, no. You have me all in a muddle."

AFTER CONVINCING the man and his fellows that the soul was not the body, but that God had created humankind in the flesh and in His own divine image, Bernard took the man aside. In the name of Jesus Christ and His most holy Roman Catholic Church, he persuaded him to reveal the names of those who had spread false rumors about the soul. Though he had never intended, in his travels, to amass a list of suspects to be interrogated one day, he felt as if he were being guided now to do so, much as once he had been guided to discover the ledger that would determine his fate.

As Bernard interviewed the people of Ax-les-Thermes, the name that came up again and again was Authié. "The brothers Authié." It seemed that the elder of the two brothers, a former notary from Ax and so an educated man, had traveled to Lombardy, where he was converted by heretics in exile. He in turn had converted his brother, and the two of them went about from village to village throughout the mountain region, preaching the word of Satan in the guise of humility.

One day, Bernard was questioning a group of villagers in Ax-les-Thermes outside the tavern. He asked if any had seen the brothers Authié of late, and he was answered with a resounding "No, Brother!" When all the villagers had scattered, he noticed a girl standing near the cart of a spice vendor. She was eleven or twelve at most, with shy brown eyes and milk-white skin. Her hair was done up as that of a whore, though she did not carry herself as if she were selling her body. After staring at Bernard for a long moment, she cautiously stepped toward him.

"They say those brothers have gone to Montaillou," she said.

Bernard was so stunned that she had spoken, a moment passed before he understood what she had said. "Montaillou?" he repeated.

She nodded slightly. "Montaillou," she said again. She flushed. "A bad rector lives there."

Bernard approached her and she seemed to become tense. "Tell me of the rector," he said slowly.

"He," she said. She looked down and shook her head. "He is little." She held her hand up to the top of her head. "Little for a man. And he does what priests are not supposed to."

Bernard wanted to ask if the rector had been unchaste, but he feared offending the girl.

"He takes girls," she said. "Women, I mean. Whores. He takes them in the tavern. And rectors are not supposed to do that at all." She looked Bernard's habit up and down. "Are they, Father?"

Bernard shook his head. "No," he said. "No, child. They are not."

He thought he saw tears bud up in the corners of her eyes. She nodded, then turned from him and walked away.

"Wait," he said to her.

She glanced back at him.

"Does this rector protect the heretics? The brothers Authié."

She shrugged, walking on.

"Your name!" Bernard shouted after her. If someday he were to bring the rector to trial, he could rely on this girl as a witness, or else ply her for the names of witnessing others.

She glanced back at him again, but remained silent.

"I will say a prayer for you," he said. "But I need your name for that."

She seemed frozen in thought, and then she nodded to him. "Mondinette," she said. "Mondinette of Ax-les-Thermes."

THE NEXT DAY, Bernard paid a local boy to guide him up the mountain until Montaillou was in sight. It was a hazy blue Sunday, and as he climbed the steep footpath, passing through forests of firs and oaks, he breathed in the breath of coming rain and tried to calm himself. The rain arrived in torrents, and he and his guide took shelter under a dripping pine. When at last it left off, they proceeded over a brushy pass and then entered onto a cool, still plateau. Beyond a stretch of sodden wheat fields, through the white haze of the day, he saw a fortress high on a green knoll, and beneath it, a mosaic of huddled houses.

Alone, he made for the empty village road, noticing the chimneys puffing innocently on the slope. He rounded a corner by the chapel and entered into a desolate square. A woman worked on hands and knees in a nearby garden, a dog yapping by her ear. She batted the dog away, and it ran in small circles before catching sight of him. The dog bounded toward him, barking as it jumped up onto his habit. Gently, he pushed its forelegs to the ground. The woman in the garden glanced up at him, wiping her nose with the back of a soiled hand. He nodded to her, then noticed another woman peering out at him from within an adjacent house. Soon, he found he was being observed from all around.

With the dog at his heels, he walked toward the elm in the center of the square. Its branches fanned out all around, creating a natural cathedral. He waited, and before long, several villagers came out to bid him well. Two women brought loaves of bread as alms, and he blessed them in gratitude. If he had not preached from the heart to novitiates as a young assistant lector in Limoges, he would preach from the heart now. His Mother Church depended on his preaching. He would not forsake her, nor would he leave this village alone until the crimes of its people had been revealed and atoned for.

EIGHT

FABRISSE DID NOT COME across Bernard until his second visit to Montaillou, on Christmas Eve. Before that time, she was sunken within the den of her kitchen, slave to the needs of the weakening Mother Rives, Grazida, and the baby boy. Whereas once Fabrisse had found merciful respite in motherhood, the demands of two infants sucked all joy out of her and she was plagued by memories of Pons dying, plagued by the fear that her red glass had torn all life from him in the end. She tried to forget what secrets the glass had hidden, tried to forget the moist sounds of dungeon pleasure that had once shaken her to the stem. A baby at each breast, she smelled the smoky sweetness of the rector, tasted the thickness of his scent in the air. Her heart beat quickly with old shame and fresh desire. Her blood grew hot and she pulled the sucking mouths of the infants from her nipples, fearful her milk would blister their soft new bodies with sin.

Every new moon, the rector left her a small pouch of change by the threshold, knocking and then retreating without pause. When she went to the door, she saw him hunching away down the road, past village women working in their gardens and children laughing carelessly in packs. The pouch lay dimly in the dirt, and, as she bent to pick it up, she felt the weight of village scorn pressing down on her. She stood and shut herself again behind the door, imagining the pitying tones of women outside gossiping about the hair cut from her head, the milk drained from her breasts, the daughter birthed from her only to receive less than her share.

Grazida had been hungry since she had first sprouted in Fabrisse's womb, and now—though her little thighs and arms were plump with fat—her hunger consumed her like madness. While the boy was content with what milk he received, falling asleep at the breast without fail, Grazida fed with eyes wide open and focused on the task before her. Long after a breast had been drained, she held fast to the nipple, refusing to unclench her gums and pushing her fists into the soft flesh of the breast. If the boy awoke and cried when she was feeding, she sucked more fiercely and kicked the heel of her foot against the opposite nipple, hoarding the milk for herself. And when Fabrisse carried her over her shoulder, Grazida's lips felt for the lobe of her ear and sucked that, as if what she were hungry for was not milk itself but the body of her mother.

Some nights, Fabrisse could no longer bear Grazida's clutching mouth and hands. In that rampant need for more, she saw the reflection of her own desire for touch, for love—a desire she had tried to pluck away, to bind and to temper. Even more, in her daughter's hunger she saw the reflection of Pons's buried desire, so furious when it flared it had hurt her and frightened him. She remembered the words of the healer Na Roqua during her pregnancy after Pons had died: *If you allow this baby to live, Pons will be angry. He will haunt your house and your mind and your body. And your baby. He will haunt your baby.* Fabrisse left Grazida and the boy by the bedside of the sleeping Mother Rives and crawled up onto the roof outside. Feeling her body as her own in the clean, dark air, she plucked herself calm hair by hair.

WINTER CAME, and her milk seemed to freeze inside her. For a full day, she held her withering breasts to the flames of the fire, squeezing her nipples and praying for her milk to come. Then, after dusk, the babies screaming, she stood from the fire as if in a trance, picked up an empty jug on the shelf by the hearth, and walked from the house into the cold. Snow was falling and she stepped into the deep icy wet feeling nothing, her breath pushing out from between her lips in clouds that lit up the way to the neighbor's stable. She unlatched the wide wooden door of the stable and walked to the only goat within—a spotted brown female eating from a trough. She petted the goat and took hold of one of her teats, squeezing a warm stream of milk from her into the jug. The goat raised her head from the trough and eyed Fabrisse, letting her milk go patiently. When the jug was filled, Fabrisse set it down on the straw by her feet and returned the goat's gentle stare. She had not felt so provided for since she had been a girl, near to her mother. With one hand on a teat, she pressed her forehead against the fur, afraid to let go, to leave the goat and be motherless once more.

The boy accepted the milk graciously, drinking it down in spoonfuls until he fell into a fast sleep. Grazida, however, wrinkled her nose and batted the spoon away. All that night, she sucked at Fabrisse's barren nipple, straining to find the sustenance she craved there. Finally in the morning, she took the milk and vomited unhappily. Fabrisse glanced into her weak eyes and saw how much Grazida had lost already—a father, a place alone by the breast, and now the only thing that yoked her firmly to her mother.

For weeks, Fabrisse crept into the neighbor's stable at night and stole milk from the goat, which gave it to her willingly. It was not for want of money, nor for fear of shame that she held onto the boy rather than returning him weaned to the rector. Instead, she was afraid of being left alone with Grazida, of feeling the fullness of pain behind her eyes—as brown and sorrowful as those of her father. Often Fabrisse chose to take the boy in her arms when both babies were crying. His pale, wide features had a calming effect on her, and when she kissed the soft bottoms of his feet, pretending for a moment that it was *he* who was hers, she felt a surge of joy, a delirious freedom from the aching presence of her history.

It was on such a night, in the depths of winter, when Fabrisse was holding the boy in her arms by the fire, that Grazida sat up for the first time. As in a feat of acrobatics, she was lying belly down on the sheep fleece in one instant, and sitting with legs extended in front of her the next. From the vantage point of her new, upright position, she stared at Fabrisse and the boy, taking a moment, it seemed, to recognize the maternal affection that was not hers alone. She gripped the fleece in her fists, bobbing back and forth for balance, and Fabrisse felt that she had just been caught committing a crime. She saw herself through Grazida's eyes—ever more remote, ever more uncaring.

"Mother Rives!" she called.

After a moment, the old woman appeared in the kitchen doorway, rubbing her thigh through her dress with the base of her palm.

"Look after her, please," said Fabrisse. "I am taking back the boy."

· · ·

AS SHE PREPARED to leave the house, she noticed how torn her dress had become around the sleeves and the neckline, how scarred her hands were from baby nails always scratching. She covered her dress with a cloak and hid her hair in a wimple. Though she knew she had no beauty, no pride left to protect, she could not summon the strength to forsake convention. She swaddled the boy in a sheep fleece and walked into the night, the silence of the snow absorbing her. Like a dark shadow, she passed down the road, noticing neither its curious emptiness nor the lack of light behind the cracked window shutters of neighboring houses. At the bend in the road, she saw the chapel, decorated with garlands of ivy around the door. The sound of chanting issued from within, and she made out the words—"*Quem quaeritis in praesepe?*" She had sung those words in her youth. *Quem quaeritis in praesepe?* Whom do you seek in the manger? It was Christmas Eve, she realized. She had been too deep within the cave of motherhood to see the holy night drawing near.

She approached the chapel, shining in the light of the moon. The last time she had entered within was the first time she had set eyes on the rector—the evening the Châtelaine had sent her to fetch him. She walked through the graveyard of crosses to the chapel door, opening it slightly. Inside, villagers sat silently on the floor, holding candles flickering with yellow light. Among them, Fabrisse recognized Na Roqua, Old Woman Belot, and Jean Marty—husband of the late Bernadette. How strange, she thought, that such Believers in the Good Men were worshipping here, paying homage to the rector in his chapel, and to the virgin birth of a Christ they believed to be bodiless.

The rector stood on a small chest in front of the altar, pale, wild-eyed, and silent, as if waiting for some other authority to lead him in the Mass. After a moment, he wiped his brow and glanced to his side at a man sitting on a bench by the door to the vestry. The man was dressed in black and white robes, and the top of his head was shaved. He was a friar, she realized. She had seen such men as a girl in Prades d'Aillon.

"*Credo in unum Deum,*" said the rector, his voice thin. I believe in One God.

"*Credo in unum Deum,*" the villagers repeated. "*Patrem omnipotentem, factorem caeli et terrae, visibilium omnium et invisibilium.*" I believe in One God, the Father almighty, maker of heaven and earth, and of all things visible and invisible.

Even the Believers moved their lips to the creed, as if in the glow of this holy night they, too, had faith in a singular creator. "*Et unam, sanctam, catholicam et apostolicam Ecclesiam,*" they said. And I believe in one holy, catholic, and apostolic Church. "*Confiteor unum baptisma in remissionem peccatorum. Et expecto resurrectionem mortuorum, et vitam venturi saeculi.*" I confess one baptism for the remission of sins. And I look for the resurrection of the dead, and the life of the world to come.

"Amen," said the rector and the villagers together.

"Amen," whispered Fabrisse.

As if the rector had recognized the particular timbre of her voice by the door, he looked up from the crowd, directly at her. His face flooded with warm color and one corner of his mouth turned up in a smile. Fabrisse could not help but smile in return. How good it was to see him again, to see his eyes reaching across the room to rest in hers. It was as if she were his beloved, home from a long journey. Yes, in that moment, she felt in her place in life.

The friar rose from his bench and approached the rector. He faced the villagers, a grave, almost wrathful expression in his eyes. "I have asked the priest of this parish to make a list of the wayfarers among you," he said.

The rector shifted on the chest, and she knew by the manner in which his shoulders shrugged that he meant to speak.

"Let it be known," the friar continued, "that if any of you confess your sins or the sins of others to me, I will look mercifully upon you, as will your mother Church. But if you do not confess, and if your name should arise on such a list—"

"There is no one to list," sputtered the rector.

"If your name should arise on such a list," the friar said, as if he had not heard, "you will be turned over to the Inquisitor of Carcassonne. God help you then, for the Inquisitor is not a merciful man by nature."

"No one to list," the rector repeated.

The friar returned to the bench by the vestry, and the rector looked to Fabrisse with suffering eyes. She knew that there were villagers to list, and that he knew as much. She tried to comfort him silently, but his eyes closed and he began to pray.

. . .

WHEN THE MASS was over, she stood to the side of the door as villagers streamed out of the chapel. The friar was the last to leave, and as he passed, he glanced from her face to the child in her arms, and back to the rector at the altar—drawing them together with his hawkish gaze.

The rector was extinguishing candles around the statue of the Virgin, and when the friar left, he turned to Fabrisse, snuffer in hand, a look of dread suddenly taking hold of his features.

"My milk," she said.

He waved the smoke of the extinguished candles from his eyes. "Milk?" he said. "I am certain that your milk is good."

"No," she said, stepping toward him. "It is dry. And the boy . . ." She paused in the center of the chapel and looked down at the quiet face of the child. Even in this moment, he was untroubled. "Please take him," she said, holding him out.

The rector squinted at her, as if asking silently what she would do now for work. Finally, he set the snuffer down and approached. She lowered her eyes, shy suddenly. His hands brushed against her torn sleeve. She felt the pressure of him pulling the boy away, and for a moment she resisted.

"Do you want to hold the boy for a time?" he asked her.

"No," she said, letting the boy go.

At the chapel door, she hesitated. She wanted to thank the rector for taking the boy without reproach, for providing her with winter work, for trusting her during the Mass with his eyes. She knew such loving glances could not be expected in her life.

"No," she said again, and stepped into the snowy night.

BY CANDLEMAS in February, nothing remained of the rector's final payment to her but a few deniers and near worthless half-obules. There was little in the house in the way of goods. Even the sack of millet for which Mother Rives had bartered a cooking pot had been depleted. Whereas other women might have tried to persuade a neighbor to lend supplies of grain, Fabrisse prepared herself to sell yet another piece of her body—a thought more natural to her now than asking for aid.

One gray, wintry morning, after an evening supper of stolen goat milk, she threw her cloak over her shoulders and left Grazida in the care of Mother Rives. She did not take time to cover her hair. With a combination of pride and self-loathing, she no longer wanted to pretend to walk in the way of respectability. She was a widow, a bastard, a seller of her own milk. She was the subject of public scorn. Why contrive the appearance of honor anymore?

As she walked down the road through a stream of gawking villagers, she fixed her gaze on the sorrowful, dark fields below the village, avoiding every eye. When she passed the chapel, rain began to fall, and by the time she reached Ax-les-Thermes late that afternoon, her short crop of hair—too meager to sell—was a tangled, dripping mane.

Her feet led her through a web of alleys to the tavern, and she stood outside it, peering in through the open door. She saw a cluster of men gaming at a table and a child whore standing stiffly beside the smoky hearth. She felt a rush of tenderness for the girl. What man, what mother, had abandoned this child so that she had no vergonha to keep her from such vileness? Fabrisse's chest suddenly became tight. How she hated the men inside, hated what had become of her life! Of her own will, she had come to deliver herself to the men like a lamb at slaughter, like a dupe. She was revoltingly weak, undeserved of mercy, nothing like the proud girl she had once been. The tavern keeper gestured to her at the door, his jug of wine held high. She drew away, and ran down the alley as appalled as she was ashamed.

DARKNESS WAS GATHERING and she meant to leave for Montaillou at once, but on a crowded street behind the church she heard the cries of a wine seller and yearned to forget her shame in the comforting warmth of drink. She had only a few deniers in her purse—the only deniers that remained to her. But she cast about for the crier, and spotted a young, plain woman pushing a cart along the swampy edge of the street, amid a flock of hens foraging in the puddles for grain. "Wine!" the woman cried. "Wine!"

Fabrisse ran to her, and then withdrew her remaining deniers. Without a word, the woman took a coin and poured her a cup. She watched with narrowed eyes as Fabrisse drank quickly. "From the look of you, dear," the woman said in a gentle, almost motherly voice, "you'd be better off selling than drinking."

Fabrisse opened her fist, holding up her last two coins.

"You aren't from Ax, are you, dear?" said the woman.

"Another, please," said Fabrisse.

"From a mountain village, then?"

Fabrisse closed her fist.

"Is there a tavern keeper in your village?"

"No," said Fabrisse. "No tavern. No keeper."

The woman's eyes twinkled. "Selling," she said, "can be a blessed thing."

Rather than pour Fabrisse another drink, she suggested a business exchange: she would provide Fabrisse with a jug of wine, which Fabrisse would carry back to Montaillou and sell cup by cup at the rate of two deniers. When the jug was depleted, Fabrisse was to return on muleback to the woman and pay her half of what she had earned. If it appeared that there was thirst for wine in the village, the woman would supply Fabrisse at that time with three or four jugs instead of one, and on and on they would proceed—both making money.

"You will return," the woman said as Fabrisse strapped the jug onto her back with twine. "I can see you need this more than I do."

THE NEXT MORNING, Fabrisse set off to sell wine door-to-door in Montaillou, a cup in one hand and a leather flagon in the other. She tried not to notice the sad eyes of Grazida as she left. "I will buy you a goat with the money I gather," she said before kissing her goodbye.

She decided to visit the houses of the Believers first. Though the Good Men preached that wine inspired Devil's work, the Believers were the folk she had come to know best through her marriage into the family Rives. At the house of Old Woman Belot, she held her breath and knocked on the door several times. The woman came to the door at last, cracking it open slightly.

"Madame Belot," said Fabrisse. She held up a cup of deep red. "Can I offer you some wine?"

The old woman scowled in dismay. "You should not do that, Fabrisse Rives," she said. "Sell wine about the village." She craned her thick neck, looking up and down the road. "You should not do that," she said again, glancing back into her house. "Just a little one, then."

Fabrisse lowered the cup. "Two deniers."

The woman grumbled. "All right, then, all right," she said. She disappeared into the house, and returned moments later with the money. She took the cup brusquely and drank. When she was done, she smacked her lips together. "Go on, then," she said, waving Fabrisse away. "And if you must come, this would be the time of day."

FABRISSE SOLD EVERY DROP of wine within the week. When she returned to Ax on muleback, the woman was there with her cart on the same street, ready to provide her with four jugs. By the end of three months, Fabrisse had enough deniers to buy a pair of pigs, a rooster and a hen, and a lactating goat. The constant flow of milk eased Grazida's hunger for her, and she was able to spend a greater portion of the day selling wine—a practice she learned to enjoy for more than its mercenary value. There were many villagers who drew comfort from her wine, and from the ear she offered as they sat drinking; she heard herself in some of their stories, and so found solace, too, in the wine they drank.

One woman with whom she developed a friendship was named Ava. Tall, slight, and warm-eyed, she had a daughter several years older than Grazida and a husband named Philippe no gentler than Pons had been. Like Pons, Philippe had come to be a Believer, and no longer regarded his marriage to Ava as legitimate because it had been consecrated by the rector rather than the Good Men. Whenever Ava questioned the Good Men's creeds, many a bitter word and wallop followed from Philippe.

One day in early summer, when Fabrisse came wine-selling, Ava appeared at her door with a purple bruise on her forehead. She led Fabrisse by the shoulder to a shadowy bench in the courtyard, passed her a needle and accepted a cup of wine as trade. When she was finished, she touched the bruise and winced. "There are rumors," she said. "Rumors that Philippe has another wife in Catalonia. A wife and three children. A family. He says the rumors are lies. . . . But I cannot believe him."

Her bruise showed like a weeping third eye. "Every day," she said, "thoughts grow in my mind. Thoughts of him hitching this woman, this wife, in Catalonia. Hitching women here in Montaillou. I close my eyes and see him hunting bottoms and breasts and thighs. . . . I tell myself he is a good man. But thoughts grow in my mind. Thoughts that he is a bad man, only concerned with himself and his pleasures. . . . And when he comes to me at night—" She shook her head. "When he comes to me at night, I cannot look at him. He says he will not do it that way, thinking I don't want him. And I say he has no power as a man. It is cruel, I say, to start and stop and start and stop and start and stop."

Tears streamed steadily from her eyes. "But I am the cruel one, Fabrisse. I am the one who is lying. Saying I've done nothing by staring at the ceiling instead of him at night. Because I want him to feel what he's done to me. Made me a slave. A slave to his thing. And I don't want to be a slave like every other wife of his. I want him to feel what he makes me feel. Coming apart, dying."

COMING APART, DYING. The phrase was like a mirror in which Fabrisse recognized her own unraveling. Though she was working more honorably than she might have been, and though she had found female friendship for the first time, she was restless inside, desperately lonely, and suffocating under the ever more clutching neediness of her daughter.

At only eleven months, Grazida had begun to walk—as if she could no longer bear being walked away from. She followed Fabrisse everywhere when she was not wine-selling—to the stable to milk the goat, to the threshing floor to beat the grain, to the garden to water and pull the vegetables, and back inside to tend to the fire.

"Leave me," Fabrisse would say to her, staring into her dark brown eyes. "Please. Leave me." Grazida would blink up at her, without the words yet to refuse or to comply.

Soon enough, Fabrisse took to hiding from her—under a bench, under the covers of the bed, even outside. Once, kneeling behind a bush of pink blooms in the neighbor's garden, she heard Grazida's cries coming thick and wild. "Mama! Mama!"

Suddenly, the neighbor appeared over her, threatening the air with a soup spoon. "Fabrisse Rives!" she hissed, with her small, red mouth. "I have less than a breath to spare! Come out now and shut up your daughter!"

Fabrisse slunk out from behind the bush and saw Grazida standing no more than five steps away, her little grubby shift falling from her shoulders, her hair in wild ringlets. She hiccuped with one finger in her mouth, staring at Fabrisse. After a moment, she pulled her finger from between her lips and opened her hand, holding it out. Slowly, Fabrisse went and took her hand, ashamed.

WHEN GRAZIDA WAS TWO, she began to echo for the first time. Fabrisse had been hiding in the neighbor's stable, when all at once the neighbor barged in.

"Fabrisse Rives," she said, her fat hands on her hips. "If I catch you in here once more, I'll chop your daughter into my supper."

Fabrisse brushed past the neighbor on her way to the door. "Don't you want her?" she heard the neighbor say. "I have four sons, and two more that died, but never a daughter. Not so much as one."

Fabrisse glanced over her shoulder and saw that the neighbor's hands were folded together under her chin, and that her eyes had become kind. "A daughter is a blessing from God," the neighbor said. "If you don't want her, somebody else will."

Fabrisse found Grazida outside, tears caught in the hollows under her eyes. "You forget," said Fabrisse, taking Grazida in her arms.

"You forget," said Grazida.

"Mama needs to be alone."

"Mama needs to be alone."

"Leave Mama alone. Don't tell the neighbor. Don't cry."

"You don't cry."

Grazida reached out and stroked the hollows under Fabrisse's eyes, as if tears were caught under her eyes.

"I won't cry," said Fabrisse. "And no more echo. Be a little girl, not a little echo."

"Little Echo," Grazida replied.

From that day forth, Little Echo was her name.

BY AGE THREE, Little Echo refused to be left alone with Mother Rives, who had become so tired of life that she tried to sleep all day, hoping sleep would swallow her alive.

"I am going," Fabrisse would say on her way out the door for wine-selling.

"I am going," said Echo.

"No, you are staying."

"You are staying."

Fabrisse felt heat rise from her chest to her cheeks. She raised a finger. "If you echo me, I'll slap you now. I have to go and sell for food— Don't echo me! I'll bring you if you don't echo me!"

Echo smiled and nodded, eager. If Fabrisse could have looked into her heart then, she would have seen that Echo hungered to be near her not because she wanted to consume more of her still, but because she believed Fabrisse's body was her own. Being without Fabrisse was being without all of herself. Being with her was being.

At night, Echo slept curled around Fabrisse's thigh, and woke when Fabrisse drew away. In the morning, she watched as Fabrisse dressed in the dark, her heavy breasts disappearing beneath the dim, blue cloth of her shift. When Fabrisse went outside to the ladder, she followed, crawled behind her up onto the roof and nuzzled against her hip like a cat. She reached to pull on the soft flesh of Fabrisse's ear and listened to the sounds of Fabrisse's body—the streams of breath whispering through her nostrils, the grumblings in her throat becoming soft words.

"Time for work," Fabrisse would say, nudging her away.

"Work?"

"Please, Echo. Let me be."

"Let me be," said Echo, clinging ever faster to Fabrisse's thigh.

ONE AFTERNOON in the biting cold of February, when Echo was six, she trailed behind Fabrisse to Ava's door. Echo knocked and Fabrisse filled her cup with wine. After several moments, Ava appeared at the door, ashen and with a small blue bruise on her cheek. Rather than accept the cup, she stared out with eyes so flat and lifeless, she seemed not to be seeing Fabrisse at all. She turned without a greeting and disappeared inside.

"Ava?" Fabrisse called after her.

"Ava?" said Echo.

Together, they entered the kitchen. Ava was sitting on the floor in one corner, her nine-year-old daughter, Béatrice, whimpering softly by her side. The fire had almost died, and one of the shutters had torn loose from its hinges. Wind gusted inside.

"Did you forget your fire, Ava?" said Fabrisse, setting her flagon and cup on the floor. She made for the window, pulled in the shutter, and latched it closed. Then she crossed to the hearth and raked the lifeless fire with a stick. A few glowing embers remained, and she threw kindling and heather upon them, building the fire up slowly before laying in a few good oak logs.

When the fire was raging, she turned to Ava. "Have you gone mad?" she said to her. "You and your daughter could die in this cold."

Béatrice began to sob loudly. "Papa!" she cried.

Echo raced to Fabrisse's side.

"Where is your husband, Ava?" said Fabrisse.

"Gone away!" Béatrice cried. "The rector said bad men are coming to get him. So he went away. Far away."

Fabrisse sat on a bench by the fire. Echo sat beside her. "Is it true?" Fabrisse asked.

Ava nodded absently. "Do you remember," she said, "that friar who came to Montaillou?"

"Friar?"

"The Dominican," said Ava.

Fabrisse had thought of the friar from time to time since she had seen him at the Mass on Christmas Eve more than five years before. While wine-selling, she had heard gossip that certain villagers—no one knew who—had told him the names of Believing families. It was said that the rector had denied the presence of heresy in the village again and again, and that the friar had trusted him finally. Indeed, the friar had not reappeared in Montaillou to act on his threat that he would put all those unrepentant and accused at the mercy of the Inquisitor of Carcassonne. Fabrisse had felt her devotion to the rector deepen with the thought that he had forsaken his calling to the Church to defend the village.

"I know what man you speak of," said Fabrisse.

"He is an inquisitor now," said Ava.

"Inquisitor?"

Ava nodded. "Inquisitor of Toulouse. And Montaillou is within his province."

"But there is no Inquisitor of Toulouse," said Fabrisse. She did not know if this was true, but she had not heard of an inquisitor based in a town other than Carcassonne.

"There is an Inquisitor of Toulouse now," said Ava. "And it is he.

That friar. Cruel man." Her mouth curled. "Who can you trust in this village? Talk here. Talk there. Fingers pointing. Swords sticking out from men's groins. I don't trust a soul."

"But the rector came to warn you," said Fabrisse. "And Philippe will be safe."

Ava's eyebrows pinched together. "He came. Yes, he came." Her words pointed to darkness beneath their simple meaning. "Béatrice," she said, turning to her daughter, "take Echo to the cellar. Go and play with her there."

Echo frowned up at Fabrisse. "Go, Echo," Fabrisse told her.

Reluctantly, the girls left the kitchen, disappearing down a narrow flight of stairs into a half-underground room where Béatrice slept among casks of grain.

"What did the rector say?" asked Fabrisse quietly.

Ava twisted her fingers. "I cannot speak of it," she said.

"When did he come?"

Ava bit her fingers one by one. "Yesterday," she said in a whisper. "Béatrice was out milking, and Philippe was out reaping, and so I was alone when he knocked at the door. He asked if Philippe was home. I told him he was not, and without a word more, he entered. . . . He went to the room Philippe and I share."

Fabrisse felt her heart begin to race.

"He stood in the doorway of the room, and he said in four days' time, henchmen will come. Henchmen of the Inquisitor of Toulouse. He told me that the friar was the Inquisitor now, and that the friar knew Philippe had housed the Good Men from time to time. I denied it, but he stopped me. He said all the village knew Philippe was a Believer, and worse than that, an adulterer. Not an adulterer, I said. But he said yes."

Ava touched the bruise on her cheek. "He asked who had struck me, and when I did not answer, he said Philippe. I told him no. But he said yes. And then he touched me. Gently." She stroked the bruise. "He touched me with the tips of his fingers. I was shaking. I told him to stop. But I did not want him to stop. Stop, I kept saying."

"And he stopped," said Fabrisse.

"He didn't," said Ava. "He kept touching, and then he moved toward the bed, cornering me. I didn't try to run away. We were at the edge of the bed, and I said, 'You must go. At once. Now.' But he only smiled and drew me down. And then he kissed me on the cheek." She touched the bruise again. "Here. Kissed me."

She looked at Fabrisse, her eyes bright. "He was so gentle. Even doing what a man does. He was different, careful. He asked what would please me." She flushed deeply, blinking. "I didn't tell him. I was quiet. But I wished Philippe were gone already. I wished he were dead and would never come back."

The room seemed to be stifling suddenly. Fabrisse thought if she did not soon escape, she would be sick.

"When it was over," Ava said, "he told me which mountain pass Philippe should take to escape to Catalonia and avoid the henchmen. He said when the henchmen arrive, in three days' time now, I should tell them Philippe has been dead for more than a day. Killed by bandits on a mountain pass."

Fabrisse spotted her flagon and cup on the floor. The cup was filled with wine already, as if awaiting her. She went and drank down the acrid sweetness, then glanced at Ava, whose eyes flashed back at her, anguished, alive. In the distance, the iron bells of the chapel clanged.

"What am I to do?" Ava cried. "How was I to know he would be so gentle, so fine?"

NINE

I T HAD BEEN more than six years since the friar Bernard had stood
under the arching elm in the square of Montaillou, determined to
root out heresy from the village. That day, his first in Montaillou,
he had preached to a gathering of villagers that had soon become a
crowd, and he had felt an intoxicating warmth spread through him. How
open the faces of the villagers were, like sunflowers, turning toward his
heat and light. They were a simple folk—honest, trusting, in desperate
need of an honest priest, not one whose loins had led him away from
celibacy.

Bernard had tried to reason with the villagers of Montaillou by
comparing the well-trodden path of the Church with the traditional
techniques of sowing seed—"Old paths are always the safest, the soundest," he said. Out of the corner of his eye, he noticed a man limping
down the dusty, winding road toward the square, and almost simultane-
ously, the man stopped in his tracks, returning Bernard's gaze with eyes
at once fiery and frightened, and a crease of torment on his brow. Bernard
recognized the man as the rector: he wore the vestments of a village priest,
and was disturbingly small of stature—just as the young Mondinette
had described. He appeared to be a few years Bernard's senior—forty,
perhaps, or a bit older. They stared at each other in silence, and the
faces of the villagers turned from one of them to the other.

After a moment, the rector nodded to his parishioners, then
quickly to Bernard. "In God's name, continue, Brother," he said, without
approaching.

Bernard looked back to the villagers. When he had their attention, he began where he had left off. "Old paths," he said, "are the safest, the soundest. Outside the old path of the Church, the only Church, there is neither true penitence nor salvation."

He glanced at the rector to see his reaction, but the road was empty, the rector nowhere in sight.

THAT EVENING, as the dying sun flooded the plateau with golden light, the villagers scattered from the square. The overseer of Montaillou approached Bernard on his horse, inviting him to supper in the fortress—where, he said, Bernard was welcome to stay if he needed lodging.

Supper was served in a small banquet room. Except for the young servant who brought out dishes of broad beans, roasted chicken, and fish, no one was present at the meal but the two of them. Bernard spoke a prayer of blessing, and the overseer announced in a casual manner that it appeared as if the Dominicans in Albi were up for a battle. When Bernard asked why the overseer supposed this, the overseer looked at him with a puzzled expression and said, "You don't mean to tell me you haven't heard about the riots."

During Bernard's travels throughout the region over the previous six years, he had encountered the occasional fellow Dominican on the road or stopped in a monastery for a meal and a pallet to sleep on, but he had been so driven to quell heresy at its source, he had not concerned himself with how the inquisitorial efforts of the Church at large were proceeding. The thought struck him now that although he had maintained the appearance of a friar of the order and always preached according to the teachings of Saint Dominic, he had wandered away from his brotherhood, and away from the example of Grégoire.

"Has there been rioting in Albi?" he said, with only a shade of surprise in his voice. He remembered the riots in Albi of which Grégoire had written—riots against the Dominican Inquisitor.

The overseer speared a leg of chicken with a fork. "There has been rioting for some time now," he said, biting into the leg.

Through the course of the meal, Bernard learned that the present Bishop of Albi, a man named Castanet, was—in the overseer's words— "hungry for influence," eager to name consuls and act as the single judge of town affairs. "Castanet wants to be king," said the overseer. "And the townsmen hate him for it. They nearly appealed to the King of France himself before Castanet squelched them like flies under his thumb."

The outbreak of riots had started when Castanet arrested twenty-five of the leading citizens of Albi and accused them of heresy. They had been tried quickly by both Castanet and the Inquisitor of Carcassonne, Nicholas d'Abbeville, and all but one had been found guilty. Their property had been turned over to the Church, and they had been sentenced to long terms of imprisonment.

"They say prison in Carcassonne is worse than Hell," said the overseer, peering at Bernard. "Do you imagine there is any truth to that?"

Bernard understood that the overseer suspected the imprisoned citizens of Albi had been tried unfairly. Very likely, he thought, the overseer was a Believer himself. Bernard stood from the table, holding up his hand in a sign of peace. "Do not those who have sinned against God deserve punishment worse than Hell?" he said, doubting his words even as he spoke them. "I must be leaving. Thank you for supper. God be with you."

At the door to the banquet room, he turned back. "They say the rector of this village is harboring heretics," he said. "Brothers by the name of Authié who are corrupting the villagers, preying upon their innocence."

The overseer wiped his glistening lips with a cloth and frowned. "You'd best talk to the rector, Pierre Clergue," he said. "From where I sit, the people of this village are a tithe-paying, sturdy lot."

As Bernard descended from the fortress down the dark, steep road, he knew he would have to leave for Albi immediately. If the people of Albi succeeded in seizing all power from the Church, the entire region would be torn from the breast of Rome. With fewer mouths to suckle, the Church would diminish in spiritual influence, and her message of redemption would be put at risk. Albi needed him, and he would go there and stand by his Dominican brothers. But first, he would present himself to Pierre Clergue.

ON THE VILLAGE ROAD, he met a woodcutter returning from the forest with a heavy pack on his back. Even in the moonlight, he saw that the man wore a friendly, toothless grin, and he asked if he might take shelter with him until daybreak, when it would be safe to travel. Before following the man to his home, Bernard told him he had need of speaking to the rector. With a look of worry, the woodcutter led him back up the road a ways, to a barn behind a two-story house which, he explained, had belonged to the rector's father before he had died, and was now inhabited by the rector's two living brothers and their wives. "They say the stench of so many women in one house troubles the rector," the woodcutter said, with something of pity in his voice, "and so he makes his sleeping quarters in the barn." Indeed, Bernard saw light issuing from a high window on one side of the barn. He thanked the woodcutter, asked him if he would not mind waiting for him on the road, and then knocked on the barn door.

After several moments, the rector came to the door with a candle in his hand. His hair was in disarray, and his vestments hung crookedly on his shoulders, as if he had been naked and reclining, and had thrown the vestments over his body in haste. "Yes," the rector said when he saw Bernard, and then looked past him into the night. "But who has brought you here? One of my brothers?"

"No," said Bernard.

The rector peered at him. "Shelter," he said. "You have come for shelter, of course." He pushed the door open and beckoned Bernard inside.

Bernard entered. There were stacks of straw everywhere, several goats with their kids huddled in a corner, and a host of chickens pecking at seed on the ground. A narrow ladder led up to a loft, where, Bernard imagined, the rector slept at night.

"I have not come for shelter," he said to the rector, who was forking straw from a tall heap in order to make a bed for him on the ground.

The rector stopped his activity and leaned against the fork. "If you have come for food," he said, "I am afraid I have no kitchen here. But my brothers' wives are skilled with their hands, and their bread is as good as any in the region. I will take you there." He let the fork drop into the heap of straw, stepping over the bed on his way to the door.

"I have not come for supper either," said Bernard. He saw the back of the rector's shoulders stiffen. "You saw me preach to your people today."

The rector turned to him, stony-eyed.

"They are a good people, your people," said Bernard.

"A good people, yes."

"But that is not the word in the region. It is said that they make a home for two heretic brothers named Authié. That they are sympathetic to the brothers' wayfaring ways."

The rector frowned. "I do not know—" he said, but then he seemed to grow confused and he shook his head. "Brothers. Authié, you say."

"Do you know them? Have you come across them before?"

One of the goats bleated loudly and the rector limped over to her and took the kid from her teat. He lifted a leather bottle from a hook on the wall, held the kicking kid, and stuck the nipple in its mouth.

"Nature is a poor teacher," Bernard said when he could not bear to watch the rector gazing down at the kid any longer. "We are hungry for the milk of our mothers, but only the milk of our Mother Church can save us in the end."

The rector pulled the nipple from the kid's mouth and set the kid on the ground by his feet. "I have not come across these brothers you speak of," he said. "I have neither seen them nor heard of them, and I can assure you that the people of my parish are innocent of all wayfaring."

Bernard felt anger surge through him. "Innocent as little Mondinette of Ax, no?" He had not meant to speak of the girl—not yet. He had wanted to appear compassionate, to *be* compassionate, until compassion no longer served the ends of saving the village from heresy. He looked into the rector's large eyes and said quietly, "I would like a list of the wayfarers in the village. I am on my way to Albi now to fight against the heretics there, but I will return for the list. I will expect it." He bowed slightly. "God be with you."

He walked to the door and as the freshness of the night air stung his cheeks, he heard the rector's words, "And also with you."

BY THE TIME Bernard reached Albi, the city was nearly in a state of civil war. The townsmen were convinced that the allegations against their fellow citizens had been devised fraudulently, and the Dominican friars knew that their convent could be besieged at any moment. While the friars in the convent tried to keep their private peace, to be forever patient with one another, their voices were of a strained pitch when they spoke, their prayers too often fervent—as if fear were spreading like disease beneath their skin.

In the second month that Bernard was in Albi, a delegation of townsmen traveled north to Senalis to meet with the King of France— Philip IV, or Philip the Fair, as he was called, the grandson of Saint Louis. The King was in the throes of a dispute with Pope Boniface VIII, who insisted upon maintaining his position as leader and arbiter of all realms of the Christian world. As the King was finding the Pope's power over the Church in France to be ever more insufferable, he eagerly met with the delegation, levied Bishop Castanet with a heavy fine, and restricted the powers of the inquisitors in the region, such that they were no longer permitted to summon a suspect solely on the basis of public rumor, and were prevented from taking an active role in seeking witnesses or other proof of culpability.

Some of the friars in Albi, attempting to boost the morale of the others, pointed to the inquisitorial difficulties of old and preached that struggle was a part of what made the Dominicans strong as an order. Bernard was among them, and he told stories before supper in the refectory of how Grégoire had been ordered to leave Toulouse by the consuls of the city, and how he had been pulled from his inquisitorial seat by the very hair on his head. The friars listened quietly as Bernard spoke. What none of them said was that it was not merely the consuls battling against them now, but the King of France himself. Gloom settled over the refectory as the friars bowed their heads in prayer and took their food. What had animated their every action, their every prayer, was the urge to convert, to restore, to bring heretics back into the fold, and without the freedom to work as they might, they were not serving God as they yearned to. They ate, and Bernard ate with them, and even the summer pears were heavy and tasteless on his tongue. He swallowed, and listened to the others sipping, swallowing, sustaining themselves because they were obliged to.

It was a time of silence in the convent, of sleeplessness, when— because the friars were prevented from converting others—they were forced to look within. When Bernard looked within, what he saw increasingly was the face of Pierre Clergue. He saw him just as he had been in his barn, his hair in disarray, his eyes at once large and strangely placid. He remembered the words of the young Mondinette—that Clergue did what priests were not supposed to do: took girls, women, whores—and indiscrete images of bodies pressing together flared in his mind. Despite his efforts to turn his mind elsewhere, he wondered whether or not the rector gazed at the girls he pressed into with the same easy placidity. Hadn't every priest been taught—he thought angrily— that the greatest threat to the love of God was the love of another with a beating heart? Throughout his own life, he had avoided the temptation to seek out human touch, and he had shuddered at the thought of fornication, which had seemed to him a meager and perverse attempt to forget a loneliness that only God could dispel. Now the purity of his anticipation of the face of God seemed to him defiled in the face of Clergue's lust.

One night, he dreamed that he inhabited Clergue. There was a girl—Mondinette?—stepping toward him in a church, her young body bending into him, as if to kiss him on the mouth. Suddenly he was within her, breathing, reaching, expanding to fill her very core. Contained by her, he felt he could not contain his joy. She was everything: the reedy shore, the water rushing by his ear, the mountaintops he had yearned toward on his journeys, the winter ice in the forest of his youth, God. She, this sleeping beauty in him in Clergue, was every beauty that had quickened his heart.

He woke with wetness on his sheets and a feeling of loathing for Clergue. He had worked all his life—without even knowing he was working—to keep his mind clean, his every thought chaste, his body a vessel for the divine only; and Clergue was skinning his goodness away like bark.

The summer passed and the nobles of Albi began seizing tithes they said Castanet had stolen from them. Autumn came, and with its falling leaves Bernard felt ever more tormented. In the early mornings, he lay on his pallet, watching the dormitory come uncertainly to light, and it seemed to him that he was a boy again, in the recent chill of knowing and almost understanding that he had been abandoned by his mother. His commitment to the Church had kept that chill away, but now he was shivering, and his solitude looked him in the eye. He longed to be made pure of heart and mind again; he longed to be made One with God.

When winter came and he could no longer support his thoughts and dreams, he packed a satchel and left the convent early one morning, headed for Montaillou. He was determined to save the villagers whose fall away from the Church he saw now—more clearly than ever—as the failure of Pierre Clergue.

AFTER A NEARLY impossible journey through snow and wind and ice, his fingers and toes and eardrums throbbing, he arrived in the night on Christmas Eve. The village was white—white ground, white roofs, and beyond it, white peaks retreating range upon range. He mounted the slick, hard road, listening to the wolves howling nearby. Light issued from the apertures in the chapel walls, and he heard the sound of chanting from inside. *"Quem quaeritis in praesepe?"* Whom do you seek in the manger? The holy service had already begun.

Inside the chapel, he saw the rector standing on a wooden chest before the altar. When the rector caught sight of him, he stopped singing, and the villagers sitting before him turned their candlelit faces toward Bernard.

"Quem quaeritis in praesepe?" Bernard chanted, encouraging them to continue with the Christmas hymn.

The villagers sang, and as they sang Bernard proceeded through them toward the rector, whose features, he observed, were not as fine as he had remembered. Indeed, as he neared the rector, he was increasingly repulsed by the roundness of the tip of his nose, by the moisture that glistened on the skin of his brow, at the corners of his lips, even in the whites of his eyes. Bernard felt that he would be infected with this effusion of liquid if he came too near, and he bowed slightly to the rector and sat on a bench by the door to the vestry until the hymn was over and the Symbolum Nicaenum had been said.

When he finally stood to address the congregation, he noticed a young woman standing by the door to the chapel, carrying a swaddled baby in her arms. Though she was dressed in a torn cloak, there was something of grandeur about her. She did not lower her eyes when he looked her way, but instead stared fiercely in the direction of the rector. Bernard approached the rector, wanting to steal away her gaze and the gaze of the others in the congregation.

"I have asked the priest of this parish to make a list of the wayfarers among you," he began in a voice at once firm and calm—a voice he knew Grégoire would have been proud of. "Let it be known that if any of you confess your sins or the sins of others to me, I will look mercifully upon you, as will your Mother Church. But if you do not confess, and if your name should arise on such a list—"

"There is no one to list," sputtered the rector.

Something about the look in his eye—a look of both weakness and enduring vigor—reminded Bernard of Jean Maulen, and an image of the rector strapped into a device of torture branded itself into his mind.

AFTER THE MASS, he stood in the cold among the crosses in the churchyard, watching the villagers disperse and waiting for signs of repentance among them. A sign did come, in the form of a sharp thwack to his calf. An old man passing by struck him with the end of a walking stick and then was gone. Bernard watched the old man hobble out of the churchyard and glance back, as if to gesture that he should follow at a distance.

When nearly all of the villagers had left the square, Bernard walked briskly in the direction of the old man, who disappeared into a small house off the road. The door to the house opened before Bernard had a chance to knock upon it. The old man grabbed him by the sleeve, pulled him in, and shut the door quickly.

By the light of the fire in the kitchen, Bernard saw how gaunt the man was, his bright blue eyes bulging out from their sockets like enormous gems. He pointed Bernard in the direction of the table, hobbled to the hearth, and stooped to pick up a thin log, which he threw into the sputtering fire. The deep smell of burning oak filled the room. From a shelf by the hearth, the old man took down a jug. He poured some goat milk from it into the pot hanging over the fire and watched the milk in the pot until it came to a boil. Then he poured the milk into a wooden cup and presented it to Bernard.

"You're the friar," he said.

Bernard murmured a prayer and sipped the milk, so sweet it tasted sugared. "Yes," he said.

"The one who came before."

"Yes."

"You were standing under the elm. You talked about seed. Sowing seed. That's all I know about, sowing seed and reaping. The harvest. That's all I'm good for."

Bernard searched the kitchen. "You live here alone?"

The old man appeared suddenly pained, his blue eyes collapsing beneath their lids. "I had a wife," he said. "But she's dead now. Wasn't the prettiest in Montaillou, but she was kind. Never a harsh word for me, I tell you. That was my wife. My girl."

"And children?" said Bernard.

"Yes, children," said the old man. "But they're also gone. One at birth, two in childhood, and the fourth, my Bernadette—" He heaved a sigh. "Now, she was pretty." He pointed to the cup in Bernard's hand. "Drink," he said. "It'll warm you."

Bernard finished off the milk. "Have you asked me to come so that you can confess your crimes against the Church?" he said.

"My crimes?" said the old man, his blue eyes wide. "My crimes? No." He pressed a thin knuckle to his lips. "Bernadette was pretty, she was," he whispered. "Three men in the village wanted her, and I had so little to offer. That's how pretty she was. 'Papa, can I marry Jean?' she asked me. What judgment did I have? My wife was dead already. I said Bernadette could choose her husband for herself. . . . Jean Marty was his name. Why she wanted him, I don't know. But they were married and soon a baby was growing in her and all the while she was speaking about things I wish I'd never heard."

"Things?" said Bernard.

The old man moaned. "No, my wife wouldn't have stood for it. Talk of Jesus Christ being a spirit without a body. 'He didn't have a body, Papa,' Bernadette said. 'He was too good for a body.' And the Good Men, she never stopped talking about the Good Men. 'Meet them, Papa. You must meet them. How good they are!'"

"Good Men by the name of Authié," said Bernard.

"Yes, yes," said the old man. "And another one, too. Prades Tavernier, he was called."

"Prades Tavernier?"

"He wore the habit and bowed and prayed just like the brothers. Jean Marty invited them into his home and gave them alms as if they were real friars. But they weren't real. No. Real friars speak of truth—Jesus on the cross, sowing seed. Like you." He pointed to the cup on the table. "More milk?"

"No," said Bernard. "Thank you." He paused, wanting at once to spare the man more agony and to pry from him all his knowledge of heresy and its propagators. "Were there others?" said Bernard at last. "Other Good Men besides the brothers and Prades Tavernier?"

"Others?" said the old man. "I don't know. All their bowing and praying and whispering words. No, I don't remember seeing others in habits like theirs."

"And other Believers, besides your daughter and her husband?"

"He was no kind of husband! He corrupted my daughter! 'You must save yourself, Papa,' she told me. 'Before you die, you must be saved.' She died after childbirth because of him. Saved by the Good Men. And her son 'saved,' too, without a hope of holy baptism." The old man shook his head. "I never got to see my grandson. Never got to comfort my Bernadette as she died. . . . I was with my brother in Saverdun for the winter."

Bernard reached out and took the man's cold hand in his own. Wind cried through the throat of the chimney, and the fire in the hearth spread flickering tongues of light and shadow over the old man's face. "Where are these Good Men now?" Bernard whispered. "Where is the man who called himself your daughter's husband?"

"Gone, gone!" the old man cried. "He's a dead man to me. Though I've heard it said that he travels about the region with them as they preach their heresy. To Ax and Tarascon and through the mountain passes when they hear you Dominicans are about. Now and then they're in Montaillou, or so it's said, but I don't see them. Not the men who killed my daughter."

Bernard pressed the old man for the names of Believers, and the old man spoke of his longing for Bernadette. Bernard asked about the rector and his relationship to the Good Men, and the old man held up a knife and stabbed a side of ham hanging by the hearth. "That is what should be done to the Good Men!" he cried. "That is what should be done to Jean Marty!"

Bernard's eyes became so heavy he could no longer will them to remain open. He told the old man that he was needy of rest, and the old man made a bed for him in the room he said his young boys had shared. "I do like you, Brother," he said, "but I must ask that you leave before sunrise. I can't have the village knowing me for a gossip."

"I'll be gone long before," said Bernard. He thanked the old man and told him he had served the Lord greatly. The old man frowned and shut the bedroom door.

By the light of a candle, Bernard reached under his habit and withdrew the ledger of Grégoire. He took a jar of ink and a quill from within his satchel and opened the ledger to a blank page at the back, drawing a vertical line down the left side of the page and four horizontal lines spaced a hand's width apart.

Brothers Authié, he wrote on the first line.

Prades Tavernier, he wrote on the second.

Bernadette Marty, he wrote on the third.

Jean Marty, he wrote on the last.

Within the box beside each name, he transcribed the old man's testimony, and when he was done, he wrote a final name beneath the others: Pierre Clergue.

AS HE HAD PROMISED the old man, he left long before dawn, after a frenzied stretch of dreams of Clergue. He could not bring himself to confront the rector again, and told himself that once the Good Men and Jean Marty had been apprehended, evidence against the rector would emerge.

Back in Albi, he made haste to write Nicholas d'Abbeville, notifying him of the heresy spreading in the mountain region of the Sabarthès, and listing the heretics he had received testimony against. He urged the Inquisitor to send legates to apprehend the heretics—"three of them Good Men," he wrote. If legates were not to be had, he suggested, perhaps the Inquisitor could send a dictum to the priest of Montaillou—"one Pierre Clergue, a man guilty of easy living and fleshly sin"—to apprehend the men himself.

Within a fortnight, Nicholas d'Abbeville sent him a terse response, in which he reminded Bernard that the King of France himself had decreed that inquisitors were no longer to seek out witnesses or other proof of culpability, and that in doing as much, Bernard—although not an inquisitor—had as much as guaranteed the freedom of the heretics he had gathered evidence against. He wrote that he sincerely hoped Bernard would learn from his missteps and remain furthermore obediently in Albi. "The perpetuation of heretics in the cities of Albi and Carcassonne is the great threat against our Mother Church," he wrote. "Buzzing flies in the mountain region can be swatted out in a stroke. Your peasant heretics are no more than parasites, kept alive by the flames of those in the city. It is those in the city that we must crush, through conversion, of course." Bernard folded the letter into smaller and smaller rectangles, until he could not fold the letter anymore.

In truth, the situation in Albi was dire. Castanet, who had fled to Toulouse when the riots had begun, finally returned to Albi, and was met at the city gates by a swarm of seething citizens, shouting, "Death! Death! Death to the betrayer! Death!"

Until this time, the friars in the convent had collectively supported Castanet, and viewed the angry citizens as not merely ignorant, but on the side of sin. Soon after Castanet's return, however, the bayle of Albi—who had once assisted Castanet in the arrest and imprisonment of the suspected heretics—was mysteriously poisoned, and the priest Jean Fresqueti—who had tortured the accused by Castanet's side—was found murdered, his head sliced clean from his body. Upon hearing word of the murders, Bernard had assumed that the citizens were guilty of the crimes; but after listening to the friars' sometimes hushed, sometimes desperate talk, he came to understand that both the bayle and the priest had been spotted in the homes of angry citizens before their deaths. Though none in the convent explicitly said as much, it was understood that Castanet had arranged for the murders in order to eliminate evidence of his own wrongdoing. There was nothing to be done—it seemed to Bernard—but wait, and avoid Castanet, and pray for the merciful day when conversion could be pursued again.

Soon enough, the anger of the townsmen turned against the Dominicans. When the friars attempted to preach, they were driven from the lectern. Even those citizens who until now had remained loyal to them refused to give them alms or to bury their dead in the cemetery of the convent. Finally, on a balmy night, the convent was sieged.

Bernard was alone in the room of study at the time, reading from Grégoire's ledger, flipping back and forth from the history to the list of heretics he had written, as if to fortify himself for the fight against the enemy. He heard rioting outside, but rioting was common enough. He leaned farther over the ledger, and sweat dripped from his brow onto the page. Wiping it away, he smeared one of Grégoire's words, and bit his tongue so not to curse the men outside for making so much noise.

Suddenly, a crashing sound filled the air. He heard glass shattering, then the sounds of men—many, many—hurling their insults and bodies through the monastery. Bernard snatched the ledger and crouched down. He knew he should go and defend the monastery and his brothers, but he could not bring himself to move. He remained kneeling, one hand clutching a leg of the table, until the sounds of violence had ceased entirely.

Slowly, he stood and made his way to the refectory. Several benches had been split in pieces, tables gouged. He heard whispering in the dormitory and discovered two friars standing pale-faced before a row of pallets that had been split open.

"Where are the rest?" he asked them.

They shook their heads, and he understood that they also had been in hiding.

The three of them wandered through the wasted convent together. In the dim, hot chapel, they discovered the lectern overturned, the cross dismantled, all the stained-glass windows broken, and the candles on the altar split in two. Together, they lit the remains of a candle, raised the cross, knelt before it, and prayed. The flame of the candle sputtered and died.

Later, while they were praying in the darkness, the friars returned, some abused of body, all weary. They said they had been chased from the convent and down the streets, a mob of citizens squawking like crows behind them. They had been locked out of the city, until one of Castanet's men had opened the gates for them. By the time they had returned to the convent, the portraits of Saint Peter and Saint Dominic that hung over the gate had been dismantled, and renderings of leading citizens of Albi had been put in their place. "Heretics!" one friar yelled. "Sinners!"

"Albi," said another, "we've lost her."

No one asked Bernard where he had been, but as he lay on his split pallet later that night, the straw nipping at his skin like worms, he promised himself that he would never again shame his order.

THE UNREST PERSISTED, and Bernard eased his humiliation by setting out to write the authoritative history of the Dominicans. By day, he researched and wrote, and by night, he was haunted by Clergue. Why was he unable to shake off this fixation on a simple mountain priest? He implored his thinking mind to dream of something loftier, but too often his dreams led him to Clergue. There would be a road, a barren road, neither overgrown nor littered with leaves. As he walked on the road, he had the dawning sense that sickness was overtaking him, and he could do nothing to save himself from it. The road would turn, and suddenly, there would be Clergue—standing on his chest, or in a barn with a kid in his arms. Bernard wanted to kill him then, but instead he was compelled to follow him to a dim room with a girl, or a woman, or several at a time. He was compelled to watch as Clergue sullied himself without pause or remorse.

He would wake, make his way to the bucket where water was kept, and spoon himself a mouthful, wanting to rinse away the taste of torment and something worse. At the bottom of his heart, he knew that he and Clergue were wedded now. Without ever meaning to, without ever folding together his hands in sacred prayer, he had made a kind of vow to Clergue—a vow not only to catch him, but also to break him, to force him to turn on his own people, and to prevent him from having his pleasure evermore—and until that vow had been fulfilled, Clergue would be his failure, his greatest suffering, the wretched opening to his own desire.

The manuscript was completed within a year, and it represented for Bernard not only a history of the Dominicans, but a more personal history of his own battle against Clergue: every word had been written out of his own urgent need to demonstrate the honor of the Dominican life, as opposed to the squalor of the life of luxury and heresy and temptation. Bernard could not restrain himself from concluding the history with an argument against the notion that "buzzing flies in the mountain region" could be "swatted out in a stroke." The preoccupation of the inquisitors with the heretics in the major towns, he argued, allowed for the propagation of heresy in the more remote villages. Carcassonne was at too great a distance from the mountain villages to obliterate heresy there. The province of the current Inquisitor of Carcassonne, he suggested, should be split in two, and a new inquisitorial office should be established in Toulouse.

He bound the completed manuscript with twine and attached to it a letter, which he addressed to the head of the order: "As an obedient son, with due obedience, to the master of the Dominicans, so that the latter might examine, correct, and approve it."

By autumn, the manuscript had been declared authoritative, Pope Boniface had died, King Philip had called upon the Dominicans to restore order, and Bernard had been rewarded for his writing with an appointment to the priorship in Limoges. He returned to his home and his higher station with gladness.

. . .

IF HE HAD BEEN SPURRED to action under the shadow of Grégoire's defeat before, he was so now even more. Grégoire had been prior of Limoges and an already failed inquisitor when he had found Bernard by the bank of the river. As Grégoire's successor, Bernard was determined to use the priorship to attack heresy with ever greater vigor.

He decided to build a library dedicated to the dual subjects of heresy and inquisitio. The only other such library in the region was that in the inquisitorial office of Carcassonne, and, very discreetly, Bernard sent scribes to "study" the texts there—papal documents, doctrinal acts of church councils, decrees of the King of France and the Count of Toulouse, inquisitorial records, and treatises on inquisitorial practice. When the two hundred forty-seven leaves from Carcassonne had been copied, Bernard sent scouts to Florence and Rome to transcribe what historical records and treatises existed there. By the time three winters had come and gone, Bernard had amassed the largest monastic library in the region and had read more books on heresy and inquisitio than Nicholas d'Abbeville himself.

The successor to Pope Boniface, Pope Clément V, former archbishop of Bordeaux, was sufficiently impressed by the rumors of the library's breadth that he paid a visit to Limoges, bringing with him eight cardinals whom Bernard kissed one by one. The Pope wasted no time in asking to be shown the library, and when Bernard attempted to discuss the ideas he had put forth in his own history—a book he featured on a small table near the entrance to the library, along with his own manuscript of heresy in all its forms, Pope Clément held up his hand to indicate that he wanted silence, and set about reading.

All day, the Pope read and Bernard waited in frustration, thinking that as he had not only amassed the books, but also read them in their entirety, he was worthy of the Pope's hours.

At midnight, the Pope emerged from the library, his cheeks ruddy. He smiled at Bernard and patted him on the cheek. "You have read all these books, have you?" he said.

"Yes, Your Holiness."

"Good."

In the morning, Pope Clément and his cardinals left without a word.

Two months later, the province was split in two, and Bernard—at forty-four years of age—was named Inquisitor of Heretical Depravity for the new province of Toulouse.

ON A CRISP, WINDY DAY in February, flanked by twenty friars from the monastery in Limoges, Bernard set out to claim his power over the new province, which stretched down from Limoges as far south as the Pyrenees, as far west as Bordeaux, and as far east as Carcassonne. As he walked the roads that led to Toulouse, he saw the full expanse of his land in his mind's eye: from the river valleys deep with olive groves, to the rolling hills and vineyards by the Mediterranean shore.

Pausing at the banks of the River Garonne, where Caesar himself had encamped his battalions, he surveyed the frozen fields to the south. If Moses had been alive, he thought, he would have cautioned the people of the province that a drought was imminent. He heard the words of Deuteronomy XI as if Moses were speaking them in his ear: *"Take heed lest your heart be deceived, and you turn aside and serve other gods and worship them, and the anger of the Lord be kindled against you, and he shut up the heavens, so that there be no rain, and the land yield no fruit, and you perish quickly off the good land which the Lord gives you."*

A fortnight before, Bernard had sent both a warning and a summons to Pierre Clergue, requesting his presence at the first Sermo Generalis to be held in Toulouse and stating in no unclear terms that if the rector failed to present him with a list of wayfarers in Montaillou at that time, he would be suspected of collusion. Additionally, he wrote that the brothers Authié were being summoned to appear at the Sermo Generalis, and that the rector was to notify them of their summons if— at any time before then—they were to appear in Montaillou. Disobedience of the summons was punishable by imprisonment in the tower of Toulouse. He had meant to summon Prades Tavernier and Jean Marty as well, but in the end he determined to reserve those names for later use, when the need might arise to demonstrate his sources other than the rector. He wanted to frighten Clergue, to crush his flagging confidence little by little, and he knew that he must deploy evidence against him and his parish as carefully as final arrows.

As Bernard approached the gates of the red-bricked city, his heart beating loudly in his chest, he wondered if Pierre Clergue was already waiting for him there. He and the friars were met at the gates by a crowd of royal officials from Foix, town consuls, and common folk dressed in their brightest colors. A tenor standing on a scaffold by the gate began to sing a processional hymn, joined by a contralto beside him and a portative-organ player, and it was all Bernard could do to follow in step behind the officials, rather than searching the crowd for Pierre Clergue.

Though he had visited the Cathedral Saint-Étienne several times before, he gasped at the sight of it now. Wide as it was tall, with a rose window piercing its façade—dusky pink in the light of late afternoon—it seemed crafted by the powers of One greater than a league of men. A wave of dread passed through him. It was not that he doubted his knowledge of heresy or methods of inquisitio, but that, for a moment, he doubted that God would have chosen him—out of all men—for the task at hand.

Inside, he proceeded down the nave of the Cathedral, toward the pulpit, upon which not only Grégoire but also the most holy Saint Dominic and Saint Bernard had stood before. He listened to the sound of so much human noise filling the Cathedral behind him, and he breathed in the sour air.

A crowd of clergymen was gathered before the pulpit, and in an instant, Bernard spotted Clergue—standing a foot shorter than the others, and staring back at him feebly. As Bernard approached, Clergue stepped toward him, holding out a small scroll. Bernard took the scroll in hand and paused briefly to nod at Clergue.

Mounting the pulpit, he stumbled on his robe, and a friar caught him before he fell. The friar walked with him up the narrow steps and stood beside him at the pulpit, taking in the crowd. Though Bernard knew all of Toulouse was waiting for his words, he allowed the friar his moment and opened the scroll. There was no opening address, no closing signature, only:

> *Of the others you have summoned, I know nothing. I have neither seen them, nor been able to apprehend them. I have however identified a parishioner who has strayed, one Philippe Guilhabert. He is guilty, or so it is said in the village, of both adultery and sympathy with the heretics of whom I have no knowledge. Herein is your list.*

The word "list" maddened Bernard, but as the friar brushed past him and descended from the pulpit, leaving him alone to bask in the glory of his new position as Inquisitor, he told himself that the rector was weakening. Soon Bernard would have enough evidence against him to lock him in a putrid cell. Before taking away the rector's freedom, however, he would steal away everything else—his influence over his parish, his dignity, the women he so lewdly thrust his pleasure upon. Little by little, Clergue would be crushed.

Bernard cast his gaze over the sea of upturned faces below, and felt the dawning tranquillity of his new power. All sinners of the province were subject to his will now. They would repent, they would convert, or they would have their lives sucked dry.

"It is the will of Christ that all Christians be as one!" he shouted, in a voice so furious that he himself was awed.

TEN

AMONG THE GUILTY in the Cathedral was a man of twenty-two named Arnaud Lizier. Although he had never confessed his sins to an authority of the Church, he had lived in private repentance for years.

Long before he had understood the concept of remorse, Arnaud had grieved the life stolen from his mother. She had died after laboring for three days to give birth to him. His father, a prominent doctor in the town of Foix, had been too weak with sorrow to open her womb by force. He had wept on her pillow, paying no notice to the young midwife in attendance, who drew a scalpel from his medical bag, pulled the blanket away from his wife's bulging belly, and sliced an arc clear across her womb. Arnaud was brought into the world moments later. "A nonborn," the midwife called him, "dragged into life against every force of nature."

The midwife stayed on to raise Arnaud, and often she told him the story of his birth. Her face grew hot and animated as she spoke, and Arnaud found it impossible to turn his eyes away from her. "What a little frightened thing you were," she said. "All curled up in the red darkness of your mother. Looked like you wanted to stay in there for good. I pulled you out and patted you on the back. Would have taken you for dead if your eyes hadn't batted around. Not a peep you made. Didn't even want to share your voice with the world."

With all the primal wisdom of his early years, Arnaud knew he had been silent at his birth because he did not want to live without the woman whose life he had taken.

· · ·

HIS FATHER TALKED to him often of the many wonders of nature. Nowhere was God's glory more apparent, said his father, than in the natural function of reproduction.

One morning in the heat of summer, when Arnaud was nine, his father came to his room to bid him goodbye for the day, and told Arnaud to cover his nakedness with the sheet. When Arnaud was covered, his father sat on the bed beside him.

"Soon," his father said, "you will find your body changing. Growing."

"It is growing already, Papa," said Arnaud.

"It will grow even faster." His father gestured to Arnaud's groin. "Your member will grow," he said. "It is a gift of God, your member. Part of God's larger design."

"His design, Papa?"

"That we reproduce," said his father. "That we engage in our chiefest duty." His father's eyes softened. "There is nothing more necessary than bringing children into the world," he said quietly. "You must not forget that your member is there for that function alone. Do not abuse it, even as it grows. It grows toward life, not toward private pleasure."

SOON THEREAFTER, Arnaud began to accompany his father on visits to the bedsides of ailing patients, in order to initiate his own training in the medical arts. When his father was attending a woman, Arnaud waited outside the sickroom. In the treatment of men, however, he came to participate actively with his father, holding up the chamber pot when patients were too weak to stand to deliver a specimen, supporting their legs and arms for bloodletting, and sponging their hot skin with cool lavender water.

Often, his father would test his knowledge of the human body during such visits. "The stomach is a kettle," his father liked to say. "It is a kettle in which our food simmers. If we eat too much, the kettle will boil over, and then we will have digestive difficulty. And what heats this inner kettle, the stomach? Arnaud?"

"The liver, Papa."

"Yes, the liver. That is correct. The liver."

By the age of eleven, Arnaud could list the humors of the body and their characteristics, the names of the various forms of fever and their patterns of recurrence, and the phases of the moon and constellations of the stars on which the recovery of patients necessarily depended. He could detect an abundance of sugar in a specimen of urine, time a patient's pulse with a sandglass, and determine which kinds of wounds would benefit from a medicament of the liquid white of egg. He had not witnessed any kind of surgery, however. His father said a man needed to be the master of his temperament before he witnessed surgery, so not to risk turning his stomach away from the practice of medicine for good.

"Remember, Arnaud," his father said when patients wept at the prospect of impending surgery. "A good doctor does not feel the pain of his patient. A patient may weep, a patient may cry, but no life will be spared if the doctor hears."

ONE EVENING IN WINTER, Arnaud was accompanying his father through the snow-covered streets of Foix, when a young woman approached them. She was dressed shabbily, wrapped in an old cloak that was far too large for her. Her cheeks were pink and her lips were bright and cracked from the cold.

"Sir!" she said to his father. "I knew I could find you!" She was panting and clasping her hands together by her chest. "I went to your house and the lady there told me you had recently departed."

"I cannot help you," said his father abruptly. "I am on my way to see a patient now."

"But my sister," said the woman, beginning to cry. "She has been in labor for more than two days and nights, and the baby will not come."

"My fees," said his father. "They are much too high for you." He took Arnaud by the hand and squeezed his fingers together. "Come, Arnaud."

"But sir!" the woman cried as they turned to go. She caught Arnaud by the edge of his cloak. He looked back at her bright, weeping face, and his throat tightened with pity for her.

"Papa," he whispered. "The lady is crying."

"Not a lady," his father muttered.

"She is crying," said Arnaud.

His father coughed into his fist, then set his eyes on the woman. "I can promise nothing," he said to her. "Your sister will very likely die, and in agony at that. And if the baby lives it will grow without a mother."

The woman pressed her hands to her lips, as if she were saying a prayer. "Thank you, sir," she said. "God bless you. Anything."

THEY FOLLOWED HER to a small house by the bank of the river, where people of the lesser classes lived. The house was like none that Arnaud had entered before. It was only two stories in height, and hauntingly cold and drafty, without a single tapestry covering a wall. As soon as they had mounted the stairs within, Arnaud heard moaning. "You wait here," his father said, and proceeded with the woman up the stairs.

Arnaud followed their path to the landing, then walked to the door behind which his father and the woman had disappeared. Over the moaning, he heard his father shout for a bowl of wine and a bundle of cloth, and then the door opened and the woman who had come for them appeared. She seemed not to notice Arnaud, but hurried past him, leaving the door open behind her.

Inside, her pregnant sister was lying on a pallet on the floor. She was completely naked, her legs spread apart. Arnaud had never seen a woman naked before, and he felt his stomach contract with the sight of the glistening, dark red opening between her legs. The opening pulsed like the throat of a toad—*in, out, in, out.* Arnaud did not want to see it split open.

His father knelt by his medical bag, took out a scalpel, scissors, a needle and some thread, and set them down by a lit oil lamp on the floor. The woman returned with the bowl of wine and a square of folded cloth, and his father instructed her to dip a section of the cloth into the wine and wipe it over her sister's belly.

"Her belly, sir?"

"In God's name, hurry!" his father said, and picked up the needle and tried to thread it.

The woman sat by her sister and did as she was told. "Cold," her sister murmured.

Just then two men brushed by Arnaud and entered the room. Both were remarkably tall, with full heads of bristly, brown hair—brothers,

Arnaud supposed. They stood by the door, one staring with a pained expression at the pregnant woman being wiped with wine, the other looking down at the tips of his thumbs pressed together.

"I don't want to die," the pregnant woman said.

"Damn this needle!" his father cursed.

"You won't die," said the woman wiping wine. "No, no." She let the cloth fall on the pallet and held her sister's head and kissed her on the brow. "No," she said again.

"You thread it!" said his father to the woman wiping wine. "I must start. There is no time."

The woman left her sister's side and rushed to take the needle from between his fingers. She stooped by the lamp as his father picked up the scalpel and scanned the room. His eyes caught Arnaud's, and for a long moment Arnaud was sure he would be scolded. Then his father looked to the men by the door. "You must hold her," he said to them. "Be brave. Hold her now."

The pregnant woman began to whine as the men approached, knelt down, and took hold of her, one by her ankles, the other by her shoulders.

"Carefully," his father murmured. He leaned down over the roundness of the woman's belly, gripped her thigh for support, and pointed the scalpel at her womb.

Arnaud was not able to remain watching. He heard a cry and he backed onto the landing. He crouched down, his eyes shut, his ears covered with his hands. He hummed a tune his midwife had taught him when he was a little boy missing his mother. *Nonborn, nonborn,* he thought as he hummed. He had been born against nature, as if nature hadn't wanted him born. As if God hadn't wanted him living. And now another nonborn was being dragged into life, a nonborn whose mother was screaming, dying. He decided that he never wanted to father a child of his own, to kill another woman. But hadn't his father said reproduction would be his chiefest duty?

He fell asleep, mercifully, and when he awoke, his father was hovering over him, a worried look on his brow. "We can go now," his father said.

"But the nonborn," said Arnaud, still heavy from sleep.

His father frowned at him and held out his hand. "Up," he said. "You must have some supper and then bed for you."

They walked past the room where the pregnant woman had lain, but the door was shut. Arnaud heard no noise from within. He looked up at his father. "Did the sister die, Papa?"

His father walked more quickly as they descended the stairs.

"Did she die?" said Arnaud again.

"Not as yet, Arnaud," said his father.

"Will she die?"

"Very likely."

They walked outside, and even in the darkness, the street was bright with the moon on the snow. Arnaud nearly asked if the nonborn had lived, but then he thought he didn't want to know. It wasn't intended to live anyhow.

SOMETHING IN HIS CHEST began to ache after that night, and he found he could not accompany his father on visits to the ailing anymore. Every morning, his father would come to his room to wake him, and he would sit with a start, shouting.

"Hush, Arnaud!" his father scolded him.

When his father tried to touch him, he recoiled. He couldn't help himself. He cried.

"You are not a baby, Arnaud," his father told him.

"I know, Father," he said, and shut his eyes. He pressed his face down into the pillow and tried to imagine the darkness of his mother's womb all around, the peace of a time before he was a nonborn.

By springtime, his father had arranged for him to attend a school in the nearby town of Pamiers. On the afternoon he was to leave, the midwife tied his cloak tightly and kissed him goodbye. His father had left early that morning and did not return to bid him farewell. A servant from the school arrived on muleback, and Arnaud left with him, scanning the streets for his father until they passed through the walls of Foix into the countryside.

Pamiers was filthier than Foix, thicker with moving, breathing life. As he and the servant squeezed through the streets, people shouted over him and dogs barked at his feet, rubbing their gutter-grubby muzzles against his stockings.

The servant led him to a darkened quarter where no people roamed—the tanners' quarter. He recognized it by the rotten, fleshy smell that had made him want to choke in the tanners' quarter in Foix.

They drew up to the front of a small house, and the servant helped him dismount and strap his pack of clothes onto his back. Then the servant led him to the front door, shoved it open, and entered.

"Arnaud Lizier!" he heard after a moment. It was a man's voice, followed by an outbreak of cackles coming from deep within the house. "Arnaud Lizier!"

He moved toward the sound of hushed whispers—down a hall and then into a dark room, where he found a crowd of boys slapping at one another around a long trestle table. A candle burned on the table, casting shadows over the boys, and he could see that they were of various ages—one with an enormous Adam's apple flickering in the light, and one so fine-featured, with hair so long and curly, he could have been mistaken for a young girl.

"Arnaud Lizier." A man emerged from the dark. He was slight of stature, with small, irritable eyes, and a rod in hand.

"Yes, sir. My name is Arnaud Lizier."

"You are here."

"Yes, sir. I have been sent to study with Master de Massabuçu. To learn grammar. Are you Master de Massabuçu?"

The man's smile straightened. "Father de Massabuçu," he said. "Say Father de Massabuçu. Someday I am going to be a friar." He pointed with his rod to a seat next to a boy whose wide brown eyes reminded Arnaud of an owl. "Sit down. We are practicing table manners."

Arnaud dropped his pack and sat in front of a rusty knife. Other knives and spoons were strewn across the table, and he noticed that each of them was crudely made. Not silver, like his father's. And only one set for every three or four boys.

"We are having trouble with table manners," said the Master, "and so we are trying to make the trouble go away." He walked around the table and smiled at Arnaud. "What would you say is essential to good table manners, Arnaud?"

"Me, sir?"

"Father."

"Me, Father?"

"Yes." He paused. "One rule of good eating. Tell us one rule."

Arnaud did not want to embarrass himself by failing to come up with a rule. He looked around the table and caught sight of a cup, wooden and warped. "Father says not to drink with my mouth full," he said.

The boy with the Adam's apple snickered.

"Not to drink with your mouth full," said the Master. "Good. And what else?"

Arnaud touched the rusty knife. "Not to lick my knife with my tongue," he said. "Not to talk. I don't remember any more."

The Master turned to the boys. "Remind Arnaud," he said. "And slowly." He extended the rod in front of him and waved it about as if he were leading them in song.

"Eat without hurry," the boys began to chant. "Be moderate with the size of your bites . . . Eat soup without slurping . . . Never talk with a full mouth . . . Don't belch, stoop, blow on your bread, or bite into it without breaking it first . . ."

Arnaud noticed that the boy beside him was moving his lips without making any sound, and that some of the boys on the far side of the table seemed to be progressively cheering up, lifting their chins and elbows hopefully from the crusty tablecloth.

"Never pick your teeth or nails or *nose!*" A few boys broke into laughter.

"Enough!" said the Master, and beat the end of his rod against the ground.

WHEN THE MEAL was over, the Master asked Arnaud to clear the dishes with a boy named Vital, who had a scab on his eyelid. They made several trips between the table and the kitchen, balancing stacks of bowls between their hands and stopping at each corner so that Vital could readjust his bowls and pivot slowly before moving on.

"Is your father noble?" Vital asked him in the kitchen.

Arnaud wiped his hands down the front of his tunic and wondered how to answer best. Though his father had no land, he was of a noble birth, and he associated strictly with the nobles of the court in Foix. He shrugged.

"Is your father dead?" asked Vital.

"He's a doctor."

"Then he's noble."

"Yes." Arnaud set the bowls down.

"My father's noble," said Vital.

Arnaud nodded and turned to get more dishes.

"Did you see that weasel at the end of the table," said Vital. "That boy with the nose all bent up?"

Arnaud stood in the doorway. "Yes."

"His father's dead."

Arnaud remembered the pregnant woman with the nonborn inside her. Maybe they were both dead now.

"I said his father's dead," said Vital.

"Yes."

"But he was noble. And that's why the weasel's here."

They wandered back to the table—slowly, because, as Vital explained, as soon as they got back, they would have to take out their Latin grammars and practice their memorization. Arnaud told Vital that he did not know how to read Latin, let alone read their own language, but Vital just nodded and said Arnaud had better watch out about who he had to share a bed with. "You'll probably have to sleep with The Small."

"Small?"

"*The* Small."

"Which one is that?"

"The big boy."

"With the Adam's apple?"

"Yes."

"But he's not small."

"No, but he's smaller than his father. And he shaves."

AS VITAL HAD EXPECTED, he was made to sleep with The Small. There was only one dormitory for the Master and the students, and it was packed with a row of narrow beds. "Two boys to a bed," the Master told him after assigning him half the bed that would be his. "And let me assure you that if your body so much as touches the body of your companion, you will be stripped of the sheets and beaten naked for all to laugh at you." The Master raised his rod by way of example, and Arnaud nodded though he did not understand why touching was punishable as sin.

That first night, he watched the boys strip themselves down to their linens as the Master paced around looking them over, tapping the rod against his palm. When the Master extinguished the lamp, Arnaud heard the sound of the linens falling like sheets, and then he dropped his own drawers to the floor and felt for the cool edge of the bed. He tried not to imagine the body of The Small naked beside him, tried not to imagine The Small's Adam's apple moving up and down in the dark. He held himself against his side of the bed, gripping one corner of the cover as the sound of The Small's heavy breathing moved across his back. When he finally fell into the start of sleep, the thought passed through his mind that The Small wasn't even closing his eyes.

EACH DAY IN SCHOOL he learned more. He learned that he enjoyed sitting with the boys on the floor, listening to the Master read aloud or point out a craftily constructed turn of phrase. He learned that even though he could not understand Latin, he took pleasure in the experience of collective drill and memorization.

"*Sicut hic est fallacia . . .*" the Master read aloud.

"*Sicut hic est fallacia . . .*" Arnaud repeated with the other boys.

When Vital leaned over to him and translated the passage of the day—"Thus here there is a fallacy in a certain respect, simply, A is able to be created by God, therefore A exists; and similarly here, A does not exist, therefore A is not able to be created by God"—he learned he loved the language of logic, loved the trustworthiness of its simplicity.

Still, it was the business of forming letters that he loved most. He enjoyed the silent work of pressing the bone stylus into a wooden tablet coated with green wax, and making pale, almost white scratches that he would finger lovingly and then rub out with his thumb. He enjoyed the loneliness it allowed him. He would sit long after the other boys had gone out to play, pushing his stylus into the wax and imagining that his marks were sentences that made wonderful meaning.

Perhaps because of his determination, the Master began to take special interest in him. Three months after Arnaud had arrived, the Master came to him and commented on his nature. "You are not like the others," he said, gazing down at Arnaud, and then at his letter-covered tablet.

"No, Father?" said Arnaud.

The Master set his rod against the table. "Those boys," he said, "they are wild-tempered. Rough." He sat across from Arnaud. "But you?" He studied Arnaud for a long moment, and Arnaud felt himself begin to blush. He looked down at his tablet and busied himself with making more letters.

"Arnaud," said the Master.

Arnaud made the first letter, *A*, on the tablet.

"Your father is a doctor, is he not?"

"A doctor, yes, Father." Arnaud made the second letter, *B*.

"And would you like to be like him?"

Arnaud looked up and saw the Master's nostrils flare.

"Would you like to be like your fleshly father?" the Master said. "Or would you not rather be like your spiritual Father?"

Arnaud did not understand. "Do you mean God, Father?"

The Master laughed. "No, no, boy." His face became serious. He leaned toward Arnaud and took him by the hand. "Me," he whispered. "Your new Father in life. And a man of God." He paused. "Not that I am a friar yet. But I will be. Yes. Someday I will." He squeezed Arnaud's hand. "And you have the steadfastness of spirit to become a friar yourself. Perhaps even a bishop. Wouldn't you like to become a bishop?"

Arnaud's hand felt hot and sweaty, and he slid it out of the Master's grasp. "I want to be a doctor," he said. "Papa wants me to become a doctor."

The Master sighed. "A doctor," he said. "A doctor is useful. But how much more useful is a friar? A man who, in the name of God, captures sinners before they corrupt. Can your father do that? Can he save the innocent from sickness?" He shook his head, stood, and paced from the table, rapping the rod on the ground with every step. "Bedtime soon, Arnaud," he called from the doorway. "You must wash with the others."

"Yes, Father," said Arnaud, and even as he spoke, he thought, *No*, his father could not save the innocent from sickness. Too often, he could not even save the sick.

THROUGH THE MONTHS, Arnaud tried not to think of his father, tried not to miss him, to feel the shame of having disappointed him, to see him as a failed man. His friendship with Vital grew and proved to be a merciful distraction. Instead of working alone at his tablet in the evening, Arnaud chased Vital up and down the alleyway behind the school until he was exhausted. They sat together at meals and kicked each other under the table to make themselves snicker.

One afternoon in late summer, when the Master had gone to buy quills and all the students had been instructed to memorize a passage of Latin, Vital kicked him under the table and gestured for Arnaud to join him.

Together they sneaked to the window at the end of the hall. Vital pushed the shutters open and pulled himself up and outdoors. "Come on!" he said to Arnaud in a half-whisper.

When Arnaud had climbed over, Vital pushed the shutters closed and smiled broadly. He had never taken Arnaud to this secret place before, and Arnaud surveyed the surroundings carefully. It was a very narrow space—not an alley but a small rectangle between their school and the towering home of the tanner next door, whose black roof and sooty chimney pitched over as if about to collapse on them. There were bits of grass growing in the mucky ground, and the smell of rotting hides everywhere.

"No one knows about it but me," said Vital.

"It's good," said Arnaud. "But the Master. Won't he find out?"

"Not if you don't tell him."

"I won't."

"I didn't think so."

Arnaud paced around the space, making a small tour and trying not to inhale the stinky smell.

"You can do it here, you know," said Vital.

Arnaud was not sure what they could do here that they could not do elsewhere. He watched as Vital untied his trousers and pulled out his stubby member. "Oh," said Arnaud. He turned his back to Vital, untied his own trousers, pulled out his member, and began to urinate on the ground, aiming for a patch of grass several paces from the tips of his toes.

"Christ!" said Vital. "I'm trying to concentrate."

Arnaud looked back at Vital and saw that his hand was on his member, which was bigger than it had been before.

"I was only trying to do it," murmured Arnaud.

"Do it?" said Vital. Suddenly he was laughing, cackling like a rooster and falling down on the messy ground, his member no longer stiff at all. He covered his mouth as if to stop himself from making too much sound. Finally, he sat up, winded. "You don't know how to do it, do you?"

Arnaud was silent, humiliated. During Vital's laughing spell he had hidden his own member back in his trousers, and now he sat with his hands crossed over his groin.

"If I show you," said Vital, looking serious, "you must vow not to tell."

Arnaud considered. "I vow it," he said at last.

"Now abjure it."

"I abjure."

"In the name of God," said Vital.

"I abjure it in the name of God."

"And Christ."

"And Christ."

"And the life of your mother."

Arnaud frowned. He had never told Vital about his mother, and he wanted to sock him now—not nicely, not because he was his friend.

Vital held up his hands. "Not the life of your mother, then," he said. "God and Christ are enough."

Vital propped himself against the wall and stretched his legs out in front of him. "I have to pretend you aren't watching," he said. He closed his eyes and began to stroke his member, which grew and grew in his hand. "You have," he said as he stroked, "to think of something. A girl. A lady. The part between her legs."

Without wanting to, Arnaud pictured the red, toadlike opening of the pregnant woman struggling to give birth. His stomach tightened, and he tried to push the thought away. Vital was making strange sounds, moving his hand faster and faster, and Arnaud could not help but imagine Vital pressing into the woman, making another nonborn. Arnaud stood, afraid he would be sick. He lowered his eyes and hummed the tune his midwife had taught him.

After a moment, Vital knocked him on the shoulder. His trousers were up and tied. "I was trying to teach you," he said. "You could have watched."

"I did," said Arnaud.

"I pictured a good one," said Vital.

"Yes," said Arnaud. "Me, too."

WHEN VITAL INVITED HIM to the secret place over the months that followed, Arnaud found ways not to go—the Master had assigned him extra lessons, he said, or he could not finish his writing exercises as quickly as the others. Arnaud remembered the conversation he had had with his father long before, during which his father had warned him that his member would grow, and that he should preserve it for its true function. "Do not abuse it," his father had said, "even as it grows. It grows toward life, not toward private pleasure."

Arnaud's member did grow. As he lay naked by The Small at night, he noticed how large it was becoming, and with its largeness, its appetite increased also. Arnaud felt it tingling, wanting to be touched, stroked as Vital had stroked his member. Arnaud told himself that thinking of a woman while producing private pleasure was less of a sin than producing private pleasure alone—as a woman was necessary to reproduction. He tried to touch himself while imagining the pregnant woman, but his member's appetite diminished as soon as he started, and he did not go on.

One night, in the heart of winter, he was trying to sleep against his member's will, when he realized that The Small had stopped breathing. He turned to see if The Small's eyes were open, and he made out the impression of The Small's chin and strong nose, softened in the night's blackness. He knew The Small was not dead, because he felt the weight of his stare. In the distance, he heard the Master's snoring, and without another thought, he reached toward The Small's shoulder. He touched The Small's skin and heard his breathing begin. And then he heard The Small's breathing come more quickly.

Suddenly, there were hands on his stomach, hands on his thighs, on the member between his thighs, already stiff and aching. He thought of his father, thought he should turn away, somehow stop this touching, but he had been so lonely for touch, for closeness—all his life, it seemed, he had been lonely. The Small stroked his member, up, down, up, down, and he thought he wanted to reach closer, closer to The Small. Soon he was touching, touching The Small's largeness, his firmness. He was touching as he was shown, up, down, up, down, gently, gently so the bed didn't creak.

What happened then was a tremendous surprise—something inside him burst out and he moaned, and then wetness was on his hand

and The Small rolled away from him. The Master was still snoring, and Arnaud lay with his hand against his thigh, relieved, frightened, thinking he had truly disobeyed his father now.

He curled onto his side and listened to the sounds of the crickets beyond the walls. He listened to the breathing of the boys, and the beating of his own heart, and the silence between him and The Small. Silence, as if nothing had happened.

THE SEASONS TURNED, and Arnaud mastered his letters. Soon he could read sentences of Latin, then paragraphs; then he was being asked daily by the Master to read passages aloud.

All the while, he kept on with The Small, and in time The Small was good to him even in the light, saving him apples from dinner, and tussling with him during games of ball. When they passed in the hall during the day, The Small smiled at him as no one had ever smiled at him before—with lingering warmth and kindness. He imagined that his mother might have smiled at him that way.

Sometimes when The Small touched him at night, he panicked, remembering the Master's words of caution on his first day—that if he touched the body of his sleeping companion he would be stripped and beaten. He knew now what kind of touching the Master had been speaking of, and he understood that this touching—this boy-to-boy caressing—was not meant to be in the world. It was something to hide, and hiding transformed him. He found he could not play with Vital as he had before. He could not bear the thought of seeing his father. The Small was his broad, new world.

LATE ONE AFTERNOON, when the other boys were at play and the Master was snoring alone in the dormitory, he and The Small crept down the hall and out the window to the secret place Vital had shown him long before. Arnaud and The Small had come to the place several times, and now, in the chill of dusk, they huddled together against the wall. They embraced, and Arnaud felt engulfed by The Small. He pulled The Small's cloak, pulled him down to the ground and on top of himself. The Small kissed him with light, sweet kisses—on the lips, between the eyes, behind his ear so that it tickled. Arnaud tried to keep his laughter within. He squeezed his eyes shut and turned his head so that the other ear might be kissed. He tried not to think of Vital, of what Vital would do if he found them pressed together. The Small kissed the side of his neck, and Arnaud laughed aloud, his eyes opening.

In an instant, he saw the Master just above, leaning out the window with a wretched look on his mouth. Arnaud kicked against The Small to make him stop, but The Small only grabbed him more fiercely and thrust his hips closer. Arnaud fought against The Small, his feet and elbows clawing for space. He wanted to speak, to say something to warn The Small, but his voice failed him.

"Swine! Swine!" the Master snarled, and The Small looked back and jumped off Arnaud in one movement.

"I was only trying to teach him a lesson, Father," The Small stuttered.

"Sodomite swine," the Master said.

LATER, THEY WERE STRIPPED of their clothes and bound to a post. The other boys were made to stand in a circle around them as the Master prodded their penises with the tip of his rod, then smacked their sides, their bellies, their shoulders, their ears.

"Blessed Father!" the Master said. "Unknot the evil from their flesh!"

He whipped them until their heads hung and their penises bled. He whipped them until The Small began to vomit. He left them overnight to suffer on the pole for their sins.

"Bastard with his lying fucking mouth," said The Small. Arnaud heard him crying softly in the dark.

In the morning, the Master unbound them and told them they could remain in the school on the condition that they confess the full extent of their crimes. "I will listen to your confessions," said the Master. "I will administer penance, and judge if you are to be forgiven."

He set up his confessional among the supplies of food in the cellar. The Small was the first to visit him there, and Arnaud waited for his turn at the top of the stairs. When The Small appeared at the cellar door, he glared at Arnaud, and he would not touch him as they passed.

Inside the cellar, the Master sat on a stool, candles flickering on the tops of the barrels by his side. Arnaud had never been to confession, as he had still been too young to receive his First Communion when he left Foix. He stood by the door to the cellar, his hands clasped over his groin.

"Come closer," the Master said. His voice was deeper in the underground.

Arnaud stepped forward.

"Closer."

Arnaud saw the rod in the Master's hand, its tip resting on the ground in front of him. He walked until he could smell the Master's breath.

"Remove your clothes."

Arnaud felt a chill pass over his skin. He did not want to remove his clothes, to be whipped again. Already, he was bruised and in pain. "Must I?" he whispered.

"You will do as you are told," said the Master, "or your father will find out what you are."

Arnaud took off his shirt. He untied his trousers and pulled them down with his drawers.

"Now you will show me," said the Master. "Show me what you have done with The Small." He lifted the rod and pointed its tip at Arnaud's member. "Has he touched you there?"

Arnaud shivered. He nodded.

"Show me how."

Arnaud shook his head. "Please forgive me, Father."

"Show me."

Arnaud began to cry. He touched his member, held it in his hand, moved his hand lightly back and forth.

"Bad, bad boy," said the Master.

Arnaud wiped his eyes and stared at the ground. "Yes, Father," he said.

"On your knees," said the Master.

Arnaud looked up and saw the Master's nostrils flare.

"Turn around and get on your knees."

Arnaud turned and knelt down.

"Stop whimpering," said the Master.

Arnaud felt the tip of the rod brush the skin of his rear. "Did he touch you here?" said the Master.

The rod pressed against Arnaud's anus and he gasped. "Just once," he said.

"Sodomite," said the Master.

Suddenly, Arnaud felt a pain shooting up into him, and he let out a bloody cry, falling forward. The side of his head struck the ground, and he saw the Master standing behind him. The rod was in him, like a knife, cutting deeper and deeper, and all he wanted was for it to be out. *No*, he thought, but he was silent.

He took his penance and waited for it to be over.

HE BLED through the afternoon, and in the evening, he stuffed his tablet, stylus, and Latin grammar into his sack. He was assigned a new pallet on which to sleep, and that night, when he heard the Master begin to snore, he rose from the pallet, dressed, and crept to The Small, who was breathing steadily in sleep. As softly as he could, he touched The Small on the side of the cheek and left.

It was springtime, but still the night was wintry cold. As he stepped from the school into the open air, he held his sack against his chest for warmth. He walked and walked, and when his bottom began to bleed, he left the main street to hide behind a dung heap in an alley.

Lying on his back, he ignored the flies buzzing around him, and the stench of so much waste, and the throbbing in his body. He looked up at the houses on either side of the alley, and at the stars beyond—so many stars, he could not begin to count them if he tried. He remembered how his father had taught him to count when he was a young boy, and he realized he could never return to his father now. The Master would write his father and his father would be ashamed of him. He was alone.

THE NEXT MORNING, the owner of a nearby shop discovered him. The man had come out with a fresh bucket of dung to dump, when he saw a stream of dried blood leading out from behind the heap. He found Arnaud, bruised and asleep, and took him for murdered. "God Almighty!" he shouted at the top of his lungs, and Arnaud gasped and sat up, then yelped in pain.

"You're not dead?" said the man, staring at Arnaud as if at a ghost.

Arnaud shook his head. "No, sir," he said. He stood, wincing with the pain, and picked up his sack. "I am sorry to have troubled you."

"Troubled me?" said the man. "I'd say you're the one in trouble."

Arnaud did not know how to respond, and so he bowed his head slightly and stepped around the man. He walked several paces down the alley, then paused and turned around. "Excuse me, sir," he said. "Could you tell me, which way do I go to leave Pamiers?"

The man scratched his belly, which protruded out of the front of his cloak. "How old are you, boy?"

"Fourteen, I think," said Arnaud. "Yes, fourteen."

"And do you have a mother to nurse those wounds?"

Arnaud shook his head.

"I have a wife," said the man. "She's always trying to mother me, and I can't imagine she'd mind mothering another." He chuckled. Arnaud noticed how calm the man's face was. His forehead was as clear and unlined as Arnaud's father's was furrowed.

"You're not a thief, are you, boy?" said the man.

"No, sir."

"Not a killer?"

"No!"

The man sighed. "I can see by your eyes that you're speaking the truth. And since you're not a thief and not a killer, you have a home with me."

AS THE MAN led him through his shop, he told Arnaud that he was a cobbler named Jean—"Jean the Cobbler," he said. He led Arnaud up a flight of rickety stairs, calling, "Wife! Wife!"

A woman greeted them in a small room at the top of the stairs. She held a baby on her hip and her cheeks were as red as cherries. A little boy scurried about the room behind her, and when he saw Arnaud with his father, he stopped dead in his tracks and stared.

"You poor dear!" the woman exclaimed before Jean had introduced Arnaud to her. She gave the baby to her husband and brushed Arnaud's hair back from his brow, examining his face for cuts and bruises. "Who has done such a thing to you?"

Without waiting for an answer, she shooed her husband away from her. "You leave us be now," she told him. "I know how to fix him right." She took Arnaud by the arm and led him up a second flight of stairs, to a barren room with a dusty pallet on the floor.

"Used to be an apprentice lived here," she said. "But he's gone and left us now. All grown and joined the Guild. Started a shop of his own somewhere." She let go of Arnaud, stooped to pick up the pallet, and beat it vigorously. "He was a sweet boy," she said. Dust filled the air and she coughed. "A bit like you. With the same sad eyes." She let the pallet drop to the ground. "But we'll make you brighter." She held her hand out to Arnaud. "Come and sleep, dear."

Not long after, she brought up a bench and a bucket of steaming water. She undressed Arnaud, and he closed his eyes, allowing her to wipe his wounds. He thought of his father, of how he himself had once cleaned wounds and sponged bodies to cool them down. He wanted a compress of cold wine for his bottom; he wanted the liquid white of egg to apply to his wounds—but he feared having to explain his knowledge of such remedies. "Thank you," he said to the woman.

"Bertrande," she said. "Bertrande, you call me." She kissed him on the forehead. "Are you an orphan, child?"

Arnaud looked into her sweet, honey-colored eyes and nodded. When she left, he cried.

FOR DAYS, Bertrande attended to Arnaud. Sometimes he would wake and see her nursing her baby on the bench at his bedside. Sometimes she would sing to him and the children together. In the evenings, she would leave him for a time while she fed the children, and Jean would occupy him with talk.

"Orphans have a harder part in life," Jean would say. "You best watch out. Find a trade and a master before age catches up with you."

Some nights, Jean would joke about the pretty women who had visited his shop. He said that if Arnaud were to become his apprentice, and were to progress steadily in his craft, he would give him a stipend for monthly visits to the brothel. "Fourteen is old enough, if you ask me." Jean laughed.

By the time Arnaud was nearly healed, he had agreed to learn the trade of shoemaking under Jean's supervision. He knew that medical school was an impossibility without his father's name and support. In truth, he did not know if he wanted to become a doctor anymore.

On the evening he agreed to become Jean's apprentice, Jean disappeared downstairs, then returned with a miniature box in hand. He sat on the bench by the pallet, breathing heavily, and held the box up in the air.

"I don't imagine you'll be able to guess what's in this box," he said. He opened the lid and withdrew a tiny piece of bone, no bigger than a nail clipping. "Bone," he said. "And do you know whose?"

Arnaud squinted at the bone. "No, sir," he said finally. "I don't."

"The veritable bone of Saint Bernard."

"Saint Bernard, sir?"

"Saint Bernard! Veritable Saint Bernard! And I want you to swear on it. To swear on this piece of bone."

He held the bone in front of Arnaud's nose, and Arnaud examined it. "Sir," he said, "what do I swear?"

Jean leaned in toward him, and the bone shook in his hand, nearly dropping from his fingers. "That you will stay with me for no less than five years," he said.

"Five years?" said Arnaud.

"Five years. On each day of each of those years, from sunrise to sunset, you must work for me. Every moment of every hour, you must demonstrate prudence, loyalty, and a strong desire to master your craft." He sat back on the bench. "In return, I will pledge you food, lodging, and clothing. And shoes, of course." He smiled. "And I will always be respectful of you, Arnaud. As if you were the son of a nobleman."

Arnaud could not look at him anymore.

"Many cobblers are merchants of some status," said Jean. "And many have acquired modest wealth. Shoemaking is not a profession to be ashamed of."

"No, sir," said Arnaud. He placed his finger on the bone in front of his nose and swore.

HIS FIRST DUTY each day was to make the rounds to the leather suppliers in the tanners' quarter. While in the beginning he was afraid of being spotted by Master de Massabuçu or one of his former school fellows, in time he realized that he belonged to Jean now, and that the Master could no longer claim him as his own.

Each morning, as he neared the tanners' quarter, the pungent

scent of dying flesh overcame him, and his body was fooled into thinking that it was again in the secret place Vital had shown him, the place
he had shared with The Small. He lingered outside the various tanners'
shops, watching the masters and their apprentices bending over flattened tree trunks, scraping hair from animal skins and peeling away
flesh with sharp blades. He watched hides being rubbed with cold poultry and softened with warm pigeon dung, and he could almost feel
The Small enveloping him, could almost hear the scratching sound
of The Small's cheek bristling against his own.

Back in Jean's shop, he would sit at his workbench selecting and
cutting soft leathers for proper shoe uppers, and shaping and fastening
tough leathers for proper soles. He would think of The Small and what
they had done together, and when men and women came to purchase
shoes, he would wonder what secrets these people hid beneath their respectable linen tunics, trimmed and lined with respectable fur.

THREE YEARS came and went, and through them all, Arnaud worked for
Jean with the same discipline and vigor with which he would have worked
if he had truly wanted to become a cobbler. With time, he came to love
Jean, Bertrande, and their children, but he felt ever more estranged from
them. They were an honest, good people, with nothing of pain or shame
to hide, and the more he grew attached to them, the more he feared they
would discover him for what he truly was—a liar, a failure, a sinner.

In the evening, after he and Jean had dismantled the posts supporting the shutter that opened the shop onto the street, he ate with the
family, then excused himself for a long walk. Some nights, he thought
of The Small. Others, he did not think at all. He walked and walked.
He observed—boys playing chase, women bartering for goods, peddlers selling their wares. In the midst of strangers, he felt more himself
than he felt elsewhere. He did not pretend as he walked. He yearned.

One hot night in summer, he was walking by the light of the moon,
when he spotted a boy in a courtyard kicking a stone over one of the
heaps. He could see that the boy was not more than twelve or thirteen—
the same age he had been when he had started with The Small. He felt
compelled to speak to the boy, to at least move close to him and look
upon his face.

He walked toward the boy and saw that his skin was freckled, and that his eyes were dark. The boy smiled as he approached.

"Hello," he said to the boy.

"Hello," the boy said to him.

"Are you playing?"

The boy nodded. "Playing get the rock on top of the pile so it sticks."

The boy began to kick the rock, his tongue pressed between his lips in concentration. He seemed to forget that Arnaud was there.

"Do you like this place?" said Arnaud.

The boy looked up at him. "Rocks stick good on top. Better than dirt." He went back to kicking.

Arnaud imagined whispering into the boy's ear and the boy's returning his words with a long and curious gaze. He imagined pulling the boy up on top of the heap, trying to untie his pants. But in his mind, he was shaking. In his mind, he was shaking and he could hardly keep the boy in his arms.

"Good evening, then," he said, but the boy did not seem to hear. He stepped down from the heap, glad to be alone in his shame.

NOT LONG AFTER, he was walking at night along a route he knew well—down a web of alleys that curved from the tanners' quarter past a row of dung heaps to the Cathedral—when he noticed a man in a dark coat leaning against a wall. The man appeared to be about his age—a few years older, perhaps. They watched each other in silence, and Arnaud felt his heart pounding in his chest as he neared.

"Looking for a woman?" the man called out.

Arnaud stopped. "A woman?" he said.

"A whore."

"No, I—" Arnaud could not think of what else to say.

"Wouldn't be the place to find one," said the man.

Arnaud nodded. He continued to walk.

"What are you looking for then?" said the man.

Arnaud looked back at him. "Walking," he said. "I'm—nothing. I must be on my way."

The man stepped from the wall. "Seen you before," he said as he approached. "Always with a frown on your face. Never looking straight in front of you." He stood less than an arm's length from Arnaud. "I know what men who walk to think look like—look at the ground in front of their toes. But not you. You're looking."

Arnaud's heart beat wildly. He felt recognized.

"A little money, and I can ease you," said the man. "A little money, and you won't have to search at all."

IN TIME, Arnaud came to know the men who paid for the same kind of relief. They were there, slinking about the streets of Pamiers in common cloaks and common trousers, purchasing common shoes and practicing common trades.

At night, he would find one of them in the shadows. What drove him there was not lust, but the desire for an intimacy of the kind he had shared with The Small, a yearning to feel once again close, beloved. He would lose himself in the warmth of their skin, the smell of their sweat, the sound of their breathing in his ear. Even the wild, shamed look in their eyes comforted him. These men he encountered were alive, their hearts pumping blood through the veins he saw bulging from their skin, and he needed their aliveness desperately. The silence of his life was so cold.

Afterward, he would walk home, pulling his cloak around his shoulders, around his chin, watching the breath come from his body in short, smoky puffs. He would punish himself for the comfort he had found with thoughts that he had forsaken his father, and even worse, God's injunction that man use his seed to multiply. He began to conceive of the world in terms of light and shadow—everything of reproduction and women, he saw as bright and pure and Godly; everything of men like him, he saw as dark and evil, deathly.

One day, he caught a glimpse of himself in a mirror in the barber's shop, and he felt as if he were witnessing his own mortality. When he was a child, his midwife had told him that he was a beautiful boy. Now he was an ugly man with purplish-red rings under his eyes. An ugly man with ugly ways. Death was eating him alive. He knew he had to leave before Jean and Bertrande and the children saw death in his eyes.

When he had worked for Jean for five years to the day, he took the money he had saved from stipends, as well as several masterpiece shoes, and appealed to the Guild for membership. He proved that he had saved enough to establish his own business, and paid the induction fee, instantly becoming a master within the Guild.

The next morning, he began to pack, and found his old tablet, bone stylus, and Latin grammar at the bottom of his sack. Any excitement he had felt about becoming a master drained from him. He had been a boy of letters. Where was that boy now?

That afternoon, he bade the family goodbye. Bertrande fell against his chest and embraced him. "I love you as a son, child," she whispered into his ear. "Must you go?"

He hugged her back, but with reserve, afraid that on him she would smell the scent of crime. He pulled away from her.

"Where will we say you have gone if someone comes looking?" she called after him as he left the shop.

He paused, looking back at Bertrande and the children and Jean huddled together beside the bench on which he had sat every day for five years. He wanted to remember the family just as they were now, to preserve this image of their sweet, loving faces.

"Toulouse," he said. He bowed to them one at a time, and then struck out for the city.

HIS HEART was heavy, and yet he was almost exhilarated to be free. On foot, he followed a procession of merchants and caravans carrying sacks of what he imagined were silks and spices from the farthest reaches of the world. He heard the sounds of foreign curses and commands from merchants and realized that there must be a fair in Toulouse—a fair by which to pass into the city undetected.

He traced the curve of the River Garonne and saw rising before him the scorching red walls of Toulouse. For a moment, it seemed he was approaching the gates of Hell, but as he neared, the fields of fire became fields of brick, turning violet in the dying light.

He entered through the city gates and heard the humming sounds of celebration—hammers banging, children laughing, men singing to the music of lutes being plucked and viols being bowed.

In the distance, he heard the clapping of castanets. He knew very well that only lepers wore castanets. The clapping was mounting.

"Stay close!" he heard a woman call to her children.

The lutes and viols grew still. The crowd parted, and through the river of newly opened space, he saw a body of church and state officials leading a flock of lepers toward him. Flanked by henchmen, the lepers were shrouded in black. They held their gloved hands up in the air, clapping their castanets fiercely. "Christ is near!" they chanted, and the bishop before them shouted something Arnaud could not hear.

As they approached, one of the lepers, a tall man with a ravaged nose, lurched at the crowd and a henchman restrained him. Another leper held up his tiny boy, as sweet-faced as an angel, and set him on his shoulders.

"Will they burn the little one, too?" a woman cried out from the crowd.

The officials passed Arnaud, and he heard the words of the bishop. "Be dead to the world! Be alive again to God!"

He looked toward where the officials were headed, and saw—in the heart of the crowd—a large scaffold, supporting at least twenty fat posts. The celebration was not a fair, but a burning. The lepers were on their way to the stake.

AS A BOY, Arnaud had sometimes heard his father speak of the lepers of Foix, who were kept in an enclosed colony by the river. Before their separation from the townspeople, the lepers were brought before a church tribunal and examined by two or three leading physicians of the town, his father among them. The lepers were instructed to disrobe and display their bodies. If pronounced diseased, they were cloaked in a shroud, given a service of the dead, and carried through the town to the colony, where they were left to die. "Spiritual rot," Arnaud heard his father call them once. "If God wanted them restored, he would have infected them with a disease that could be cured."

As Arnaud wandered through the narrow, rubbish-lined streets of Toulouse, avoiding the dung and dogs at his feet and trying not to listen to the burning lepers screaming, he began to hate his father as he never had before. What authority his father claimed over the will of God, over disease itself! What if leprosy had a will of its own—directed not by the hand of God, but by its own internal force? What if those struck by the disease were not fallen, but saintly?

Over the months that followed, though the lepers were gone, talk of the disease spread through the city. Arnaud set up a shoemaking shop, and as he worked at his bench, he heard passersby discussing the manner in which leprosy spread. "Not by breath, not by touch," said some. "By touch alone," said others. "By breath. By water. By dust," thought Arnaud. "It is everywhere."

During the day, he worked in silence, and at night, he walked the city streets, telling himself that if leprosy wanted him, it would have him—just as the lust for men had taken hold of him, despite the nagging of his wounded, moral will. In time, he found the shadowy corners of the city where male prostitutes sold their mouths and anuses and members. He paid and consumed their parts without examining them in the slightest.

"Won't you tell me who you are?" asked one youth, blond and pretty, before pocketing Arnaud's money.

Arnaud held a finger over his lips.

"Won't you tell me what you do?"

Arnaud drew the boy toward him.

"Won't you tell me if you're diseased?"

"I'm not wearing castanets," said Arnaud. He backed away, unable to continue. The boy was filled with the faith that he could save himself from disease, protect his immunity, and Arnaud could not bring himself to sully him. He left, and found another who asked no questions.

If Arnaud was looking for an end to the emptiness he felt, to his shame and self-hatred, he did not acknowledge it.

AN END DID COME. Two years after he had arrived in Toulouse, he was urinating in the early morning when he noticed a blister on his member. It was painless, but large enough to frighten him—about the size of one of his fingernails. For a full week, he lived in agony and in celibacy, knowing leprosy might be upon him. Then the blister dried and disappeared, and again he gave way to recklessness of body.

A month later, he was with a man at midnight, down by the river, among the trees. The man was crouching before him, and in the light of the full moon, Arnaud could see the curve of the man's back. The man peered up at him, and then, suddenly, he gasped. He pointed to Arnaud's face and pulled away, scurrying to a standing position.

"You—your—" he stuttered.

Before Arnaud could stop him, the man was gone—ducking out from under the trees and running along the bank of the river to the road. As Arnaud watched, he began to feel a tingling sensation along his cheeks and chin and forehead—a prickling, then a swelling, as if his face were metamorphosing. As if leprosy were striking him now.

He stumbled out to the riverbank and knelt by a rotting log, with its fecund stench of dying life. He stared into the moonlit water and saw a version of his face that was terrible, unrecognizable—flickering and shifting and blistered and unclean. He touched his face and felt fields of tiny blisters covering his skin. He drew away from the river's edge and crouched into a ball.

The night was enormous around him—surging up, black and endless, the stars so high and far. He thought, if he cried out, no one would hear. A fly nipped at his ear. Rain would be coming—he smelled its nearness, and he was afraid of it somehow. Soon, he would die—sooner still if his disease was discovered. He heard crickets chirping, and even their modest sound chilled him to the core.

He remembered having heard the noise of the crickets after his first time with The Small. How innocent and yet already ashamed he had been then. He had felt apart from the boys breathing around him— normal boys, not motherless, not alone. Now, he felt a surge of pity for his young self, for all the loneliness he had endured since. He had become a man in hiding, and he did not want to hide anymore. He wanted to live, to live in the light. It seemed to him that his already rotting body was more fiercely alive than ever before.

For a moment, he thought he would go to his father and repent for having left him, for having sinned with The Small and become a lowly cobbler. Then he remembered his father's words, "spiritual rot," and he knew any hope of reunion was over.

The rain started coming and he gazed up into the wet sky, at the brightest star. He felt God watching and he clasped his hands together. He had not prayed in two years, but the words came quickly. "Dear Lord, forgive me. Forgive me. Forgive me."

He was drunk on the night, and the whole sky seemed to be contained in the brightest star, and he thought the star might be God. Though he was dark with mourning, though he knew he had already begun to die, to see the edges of his small, fleeting life, he wanted to cry out to Heaven, to spread his wings in uninhibited love for life, for loving.

He promised never again to soil himself with a man. If he was cured, he would do as God willed—he would marry, reproduce, lead the life intended for him from the beginning. He prayed until the moon was low, until the crickets stopped chirping and the rain died and the brightest star had disappeared into the sky.

By dawn, by God, the blisters were gone.

As THE DAY came pawing through the leaves onto the riverbank, he stared into the water and touched his face in disbelief. He wondered if he was lost now in dreams, or awake now and dreaming earlier.

Finally, he left the riverbank and walked home. He had lived a life contained by fear, by hiding—he had learned as much through the night, and now his life had opened immeasurably. God had forced his life open, and with God's eye upon him, there was nowhere to hide anymore.

He walked down the familiar streets of Toulouse, passing peddlers and children and men of the cloth, and it seemed to him that he could see the impenetrable sheaths that these people hid themselves within.

At home, he found that his senses were keener than he remembered them having been before. The garments on his skin felt achingly cold, the bare branches whacking against the shutters sent tingles up his spine, and the leather of his trade smelled almost unbearably pungent with taken life. He fingered the smoothness of his skin, the wondrous completeness of it, and he murmured his thanks to God.

Through the enormous summer with its dry leaves blowing, he waited restlessly, afraid the blisters would return, afraid he would forsake God by forsaking his vow to Him. He had promised to find a woman and make a life of reproduction with her, but every time one of the female sex entered his shop, he was so overcome, he could not look at her, but thrust shoes onto her feet and took her money quickly.

Instead of lurking about the streets at night, he studied from his Latin grammar and practiced writing. By the time winter came, he had memorized the grammar and saved enough money to purchase a slim volume of Ovid, from which he read nightly. In particular, he found that he was moved by the story of Narcissus, a beautiful youth filled with such pride he rejected the advances of all who sought his love. One of his admirers was the nymph Echo, who had previously used her wily tongue to trick the goddess Juno, and so had her powers of speech curtailed, such that she could only repeat the last of any words she heard. When Echo spied Narcissus in the woods, she was overcome with love and longed to steal close to him with seductive words. She heard him call, "Is anyone here?" and shouted, "Here!" But when she emerged from her place in hiding, Narcissus spurned her. "Hands off! Embrace me not! May I die before I give you power over me!" Shamed, Echo hid her face among the leaves and languished in lonely caves. She became gaunt and wrinkled, and all moisture faded from her body into the air. Only her voice and her bones remained; then only voice.

Arnaud did not want to spurn any womanly love that came his way—but how was he to open to it? He, a nonborn, afraid of hurting women, in love still—somehow—with The Small.

ONE MORNING in the chill of February, he woke to the sound of hammers banging, and he felt his face furiously, sure that lepers would be burning again soon in the square. His skin was still smooth, and he thanked God and dressed quickly.

Outside, the town was buzzing with activity. People of all ages—dressed in their finest—were cleaning the rubbish and muck from the streets, scattering grasses, and hanging florid festoons, tapestries, and brightly colored cloths over building façades. There were no stakes to be seen in the square, but, nearby, a throng of musicians tuned their instruments. Arnaud recognized one of them as a man to whom he had sold a pair of shoes, and he approached and asked the man what the excitement was about.

"A new Inquisitor," said the man, fingering his bow.

The musicians proceeded to the city gates and Arnaud followed. Although he had some knowledge of the Inquisition of the past, and of the heresy that was said to be spreading in the region, he had never seen an inquisitor. At the gates, he saw men he recognized from his youth—royal officials from Foix, men his father and he himself had treated. For a moment, he wanted to flee, but then he realized that he had been a boy of twelve when he had left his father and Foix, and now he was a man.

A tenor and a contralto began to sing high above him on the scaffold. "He's coming!" someone shouted, and the crowd roared.

When the Inquisitor arrived, Arnaud could not see him from behind the masses of people. Still, he followed the procession through the streets and into the Cathedral. Over the tops of the heads before him, he saw a man whom he assumed to be the Inquisitor mounting the pulpit to address them all. He was dark, forty, perhaps, or forty-five, with a capped head of curly, graying black hair, and a nose that looked like a beak. He seemed to stumble, and then a friar came to his aid, helping him up the final step to the pulpit. As the Inquisitor peered down at a scroll he opened, the friar paused to gaze at the crowd below. Arnaud froze: Master de Massabuçu had become a friar after all.

"It is the will of Christ that all Christians be as one!" the Inquisitor began as Master de Massabuçu descended the stairs. "For all those who have been beguiled by false shepherds and left the flock of Christ's goodness, there will be a period of grace. During three weeks, any Christian who has embraced heresy, or assisted, defended, or concealed heretics in any manner, may come forth to confess and abjure his sin. Such sinners will be redeemed in the Church through penance."

Murmurs rippled through the crowd. "For heretical thought held in secret," the Inquisitor continued, his voice a shade deeper, "the penance will be lighter than for open defiance of the Church. And for those crimes which insult the Benevolence of the Lord—adultery, incest, sodomy . . ."

Arnaud stopped listening. *Sodomy.* He had not realized that the Inquisition labored against that crime, too. *Sodomite swine,* Master de Massabuçu had called him, and Master de Massabuçu was serving in the name of the Inquisition now.

Slowly, Arnaud squeezed his way through the masses of people toward the portal of the Cathedral, wondering if God had accepted his vow and given him new life only to punish him more severely. He had heard the Inquisitor's promise of a period of grace, but he did not for a moment consider confessing. How could he believe in confessional mercy when his only confessor had abused him, violating his body with a rod?

ELEVEN

SIX DAYS AFTER the Sermo Generalis in Toulouse, four days after Pierre Clergue had entered Ava's home and made love to her, Bernard's henchmen came looking for Philippe Guilhabert. They arrived in Montaillou just after the evening sun had settled, when most villagers were seated snugly before the hearth, enjoying a winter supper of smoked ham and chitterlings.

Fabrisse had not yet finished her daily rounds of wine-selling, and was just about to knock upon the door of one of her frequent purchasers, when she caught sight of two men on horseback in the distance. Because Ava had told her that the henchmen were coming, and because these men rode at a pace faster than she had ever seen anyone travel uphill, she knew at once danger was near. She hitched up the hem of her dress and ran back home.

Mother Rives was asleep as she nearly always was, and Echo was attempting to chop a cabbage for their supper. Fabrisse took a warm loaf of bread from the sack of goods she had collected as barter, grabbed Echo by the hand, and led her to their bedroom.

"Quiet. We must be quiet now," Fabrisse said.

"Now, Mama," Echo said, holding out her hand for a piece of bread.

If the henchmen could come for Ava's husband, Fabrisse thought, they could certainly come for her—married into heresy by the Good Men; they could certainly come for Echo.

She waited until Echo had devoured the bread and fallen into a fast sleep. She listened, listened, and heard only Echo's steady breathing, and the low calls of a far-off owl, and a certain scuttling in the bushes outside her window.

When the moon was high, she wrapped her cloak around her body, left the house, and panted up the icy road to Ava. At the front door of Ava's house, she was suddenly afraid that the henchmen might still be there, and she ran around the side of the house and tapped quickly at Ava's bedroom window.

After a moment, the shutters cracked open. "Philippe?" she heard Ava's voice whisper.

"Me, Ava," said Fabrisse. Through the small slit between the shutters, she saw Ava—naked and shivering in the cold, her long braid twisting down over her shoulder and one of her small breasts. She was carrying a candle, and the shadows that flickered over her face made her seem now frightened, now sullen, now peaceful, beautiful. Fabrisse could not take her eyes away from Ava's long, slim form—what the rector had seen, had wanted. There was something about Ava's slenderness, about the way her braid curved over her shoulder, that made even Fabrisse want to adore her. *He* had adored her, held her, and even more.

"I was afraid they had taken you in Philippe's place," said Fabrisse.

Ava shook her head and her braid swung across her breast. "No," she said. She left the window for a time, then returned wrapped in a heavy serge blanket. She pushed the shutters open farther. "I told them Philippe was dead. They looked at me as if they didn't believe and said they would return with the Inquisitor's orders. . . . Go home, Fabrisse. It is no longer safe in this village."

THAT NIGHT, Fabrisse could not sleep for all the images that crowded her thoughts—images of the rector and Ava. In the dungeon of the fortress, she had seen him between the Châtelaine's legs, seen him in the lamplight glow. Now she saw the back of his neck, of his legs, the mounds of his rear. She saw the way he contracted until he fell, and she hated Ava for being another he fell upon.

She drank cup after cup of wine until her flagon was empty. "No food for Echo tomorrow," she chided herself, and then she took down the jug of wine—rationed for selling two days later—and began to drink from that.

She was startled when she looked past the rim of her empty cup and saw Echo standing naked not more than ten paces from her.

"Go to bed, Echo," she said, the words coming out in a thick slur. Echo held her hand out.

"Go to bed," said Fabrisse again. A wave of sickness swept through her. She wiped her lips and leaned over to lie on the bench.

"Bed, Mama," said Echo. She walked to Fabrisse and pulled on the sleeve of her shift.

Fabrisse hid her face in her arms. She felt fingers pinching at her skin. She was going to be sick. "Away, Echo," she said, and the girl grabbed at her breast, as if she were an infant and sucking were still native to her. "No," moaned Fabrisse. She was tired of her soul being sucked out like marrow. She wanted the rector to kiss her. "Away," she said, saliva filling her throat. She lowered her arm and caught a glimpse of the little girl's pale, frightened face, before she vomited wine all over her.

For a moment, Echo stood stunned, her arms held out from her sides. Slowly, she looked down at her body, dripping with the sickness—not a brilliant red, but the burnt shade of dried blood. She glanced up at Fabrisse's mouth, then her own mouth opened and she began to bawl.

"Echo," said Fabrisse, wiping her lips. "I told you to be gone. Look what you've done."

Through her drunkenness, Fabrisse struggled to heat a pot of water, which she carried to the barrel outside. She lifted Echo into the barrel and wiped her down in the steaming water. "Enough crying, Echo," she said. "You must forgive me. Tell me I am a good mother. Say it. You are good. You are a good mother."

Echo looked up at her and could barely see with all the tears in her eyes. She pursed her lips together and strained to reflect her mother's words, but as much as she tried, her voice was silent. For all her youth, she knew something of the way her father had stolen his life, of the way he had vomited blood out of his body, and when her mother had vomited on her, she had thought the vomit was blood, that her mother, too, was dying.

THE SEASON of seeding passed, the rain did not come, Fabrisse drank wine instead of selling, and Echo kept her silence. When it could not be denied that spring should have already arrived with its showers, drought was declared, and the people of the region prepared themselves for shortage.

In the place of water, henchmen soon flooded Montaillou. They announced in the square that Jean Marty, Prades Tavernier, and the Brothers Authié were being hunted. Those who had knowledge of the whereabouts of any of the four should come forward or else confess to the rector. Ava was summoned to testify against her missing husband. She would have to find her own way to Toulouse and her own lodging there, and if she did not appear on the date of her summons, she would be arrested.

After the henchmen left the village, Fabrisse sat in Ava's kitchen, watching as Ava paced back and forth in front of the fire, trying to determine a path of action. She could flee with her daughter, but if she was caught, she would be imprisoned forever. She could testify and persist in her lie that Philippe was dead, but if he was apprehended, she would be accused of swearing falsely. "The only path is confession," she reasoned. "Philippe may be found, he may be arrested, but if I confess the truth about him, they may have mercy on me."

Ava did not wait to consult the rector, and Fabrisse thought perhaps she was afraid he would make love to her again, afraid he would convince her to keep quiet about the lie he had constructed on her husband's behalf. Before the sun's first rays shone over the plateau the next morning, Ava was gone with her daughter.

AS FABRISSE LEARNED LATER, the Inquisitor found it in his heart to be merciful toward Ava, and instructed her to undertake a pilgrimage to the Cathedral of Chartres, to fast every Sunday, and to say the Pater thrice daily. Long before she had returned from her penitential pilgrimage, however, the henchmen had arrived again in Montaillou.

This time, they presented themselves at the house of the healer Na Roqua, and found her moaning in her bed, claiming to have fallen off a ladder and broken all her bones. They told her they would return with a summons for her in summer, and left for the house of Old Man Belot. There, they found the rooms empty of all people and food—not a ham hanging from the hearth. They charged down the road to the house of Esclarmonde d'Argelliers—the old recluse said to be a sorceress, who had killed the traveling Good Man by mistake. When Esclarmonde would not answer their knocks, the henchmen broke down her door and found her crouching in a dark corner with her sword. Misinterpreting her fear as resistance, they apprehended her at once and returned to Toulouse.

Rumors flew that the rector had known of the henchmen's coming, and that he had instructed the old healer to falsify an accident and assisted the family Belot in its escape to Catalonia. Some said he was using the Inquisition to his advantage with the women of Montaillou, and that he had taken many likely female suspects as lovers: Raymonde Gauilhou, Gaillarde Benet, Alissende Roussel . . . The list was long.

"The village will talk because the rector is on the side of the Church!" said one of Fabrisse's purchasers, and Fabrisse wanted to believe her. But when she sat on her roof at sunrise, watching the rector limp down the road to the chapel, she thought she recognized a look of madness on his distant face—the same madness she had seen as she led him from the dungeon and the Châtelaine. It was the madness of falling from the path of virtue, she thought now, the madness of fearing that he was falling further still.

THE DROUGHT WORE ON and villagers bickered in the streets, hurling accusations of heresy like stones. One morning in May, rain fell lightly and everyone ran outside, clapping and laughing in praise and prayer. Then the rain stopped, and villagers turned their backs on one another once more.

It was not long after the rain that Philippe Guilhabert was apprehended. He had attempted to steal a loaf of bread from a young shepherd in the mountains, or so the story went, and the shepherd tied him up and reported the crime to the bayle of Lordat, who pried Philippe's name from him and sent notice at once to the Inquisitor.

Two months later, when the earth was beginning to crack from lack of moisture, Jean Marty, Prades Tavernier, and the younger of the Authié brothers were seized on a pass from Cubières to Torroela de Montgri in Aragon. It was discovered after a time that the Inquisitor had promised Philippe freedom if he not only swore to convert back to the true faith, but also helped the henchmen to capture the men. Pretending to have lied his way out of a conviction, Philippe paid a visit in Foix to the Authiés' mother, who—having fed and housed Philippe on numerous occasions and having trusted him—told him that her sons were hiding with Jean Marty and Prades Tavernier in the house of a Believer in Arques. Philippe found the brothers and their two companions, and told them an elaborate lie, claiming to have overheard the Inquisitor scheming to surround the town with henchmen. He persuaded them to leave at once for Aragon, where he said his cousin, also a Believer, was hiding. Henchmen lay in wait for them near Torroela on the pass. If it had not been for the digestive difficulty that caused the elder brother to turn back at Cubières, all four men would have been snatched.

Fear in the village of Montaillou festered. No one knew whose names would emerge from the testimony of the men who had been apprehended, or who would be put on trial for heresy next. Without grain growing to reap, villagers stayed indoors—sheltered from the heat of the sun and prying eyes. When the body of Bernadette Marty's father was found dismembered and dumped outside the fortress walls soon after, no one was surprised. Na Roqua's prophecy of a murder had been accomplished, and talk traveled that the old man had entertained the Inquisitor with his words. It was understood that the murder was a warning to prattlers. Even the overseer of the fortress appeared too frightened to pursue suspects in the crime.

"An old man has died," he said nervously in the square. "He has lived a long life. Now let us be good to one another."

IT WAS NOT for lack of reason that Ava decided to flee. After her testimony and pilgrimage, many in the village had accused her of bearing false witness. Now that Philippe had been discovered for a traitor, Ava knew her life and the life of her daughter were in danger.

On the night before she was to leave, Fabrisse brought over her flagon and cup, and the two of them packed a bag of food for Ava's journey.

"I will tell you a secret," said Ava, her tongue loose from drinking. "Some nights ago, a messenger came to me. It was the middle of the night and he threw a pebble at my window and I thought it was you.

'Fabrisse?' I said. 'Is it you?' And he said, 'No, it is a messenger from your husband.'"

"And were you clothed?" said Fabrisse.

"Clothed?" said Ava. "I didn't let him see me, for fear he was a spy of the Inquisition or else a murderer. But I listened as he told me that Philippe was in the charge of the Inquisitor now, working for him. He could not say where Philippe was living, but he would take me to him. Philippe has forgiven me for confessing to the Inquisitor, and he wants me and Béatrice."

"You're not going, surely," said Fabrisse.

Ava nodded. "He wants me. Don't you see? I kept thinking, he'll go back to his wife in Catalonia, with his heaps of children. Or he'll find another woman to hitch. But no, he chose me."

"But you wish him dead, Ava."

"I wished him dead, yes, but things will be happier now that he wants me." Ava took the cup from Fabrisse's hand and drank. "The rector came last night," she said. "He's come since that first time, but last night was the first I told him to leave. 'Without a kiss?' he said, and I told him about Philippe—how he wanted me back and I was going. 'But I love you like no other,' the rector told me, and my heart nearly burst for loving him back. 'You're one to talk, with all your women,' I said."

"He has women then?" said Fabrisse.

Ava sighed. "Many!" A little smile played on her lips. "There is something he uses on me—a pouch he says will keep us safe. I've asked him to leave it. 'If you have no other women,' I say, 'it will be safe with me.' But he never leaves it. No . . . There are others. And I told him there was another for *me*, and that was my husband, the only man who had given me his seed."

Fabrisse remembered the madness she had seen on the rector's face, and she wondered if her own face bore that madness now—she, a woman who wanted a man in whose goodness she could no longer fully believe.

AVA LEFT AGAIN. Still the drought persisted, and the lack of wheat from lack of rain meant less surplus among villagers to barter for Fabrisse's wine. She demanded less in trade for a cup, and then even less, and when Echo cried into her empty bowl after a supper of watery soup one night, Fabrisse realized that the drought had only just begun to make itself felt. She had nothing of surplus to trade for more wine from her supplier; she realized that she would have to stop drinking if she wanted to keep her daughter alive.

Without wine, she became more bitter, more frustrated at Echo for her persistent silence, and more suspicious that Pons had stolen the girl's voice. One morning in late summer, she shook Echo awake with the announcement that the girl was seven years of age. In truth, she did not know the date on which Echo had been born, but she remembered laboring in the heat of summer—and she had never known heat as she did now.

The girl propped herself up on her elbows, smiling and happy.

"As a girl of seven," Fabrisse continued, "you must speak."

Echo's brow furrowed. She lay back on the bed and pursed her lips, her cheeks turning crimson as she strained to find voice. Finally she rolled onto her belly, pressing her face into the pillow in shame.

Fabrisse scowled at the ceiling. "Give it back, Pons!" she cried.

Just then, there was a violent thrashing at the door. Fabrisse jumped up, sure it was Pons coming for her in his rage. "By the order of the Inquisitor of Toulouse!" she heard. "Open this house!"

Henchmen.

She hid Echo with Mother Rives and went to the door, her heart pounding. Had someone testified against her? Why had the rector not warned her of the henchmen's coming as he had warned others before?

Beyond the threshold stood two men wearing strapped and buckled coats of armor. Behind them, in the new light of day, a crowd of villagers was gathered in her garden.

"Is this the house of Pons Rives?" one of the men said to her.

She shielded her eyes to make out his features. He had a thick neck, and a deep dimple in his chin, and he looked her over as if he were a wolf on the verge of pouncing.

"He is dead, my husband," she said. "And there is no heresy here now."

"Yes," said the other. He was a pockmarked boy with gentle eyes. "May we enter?"

She stepped back to allow them in and caught sight of the rector standing among a group of children to one side of the crowd. He flinched and lowered his eyes as she shut the door.

Inside, the henchmen sat at her kitchen table, and the gruffer of the two announced that Pons had been tried for heresy in the Inquisitorial Court and convicted. She asked if she might know who had spoken against her husband, and the gentle-eyed boy glanced at her hand plucking hair from her scalp. "No one has spoken a word against you, Madame," he said, "and you are not being summoned as yet."

The other grumbled, his eyes wandering from Fabrisse's throat down to her breasts. "Your husband has been convicted," he repeated. "And a sentence has been imposed on him by the Inquisitor." He leaned toward her, and the bench on which he was sitting creaked. "If you want to avoid suspicion," he said, "you will take us to the place he is said to be buried next to the heretic wife of Jean Marty."

AS THE MEN WAITED for her in the kitchen, Fabrisse went to the room of Mother Rives and found her crying softly in her bed, Echo curled in a ball beneath the covers beside her. "You have heard, then," said Fabrisse. The old woman pulled the sheet up to her chin. "I will help you out of bed," said Fabrisse. "If you want to come to his grave this last time. I will help you."

The old woman turned her miserable eyes toward her and said, "I will never leave this bed again. . . . My poor Pons . . . My poor Pons."

Although it had been years since Fabrisse had covered her hair, she wrapped her head carefully now, and draped a large, dark shawl of mourning around her dress. Leaving Echo with Mother Rives, she emerged with the henchmen into the crowd and noticed that many of the village men bore shovels in their hands. She shuddered looking into their expressionless faces. It was not that their eyes lacked pity for her, but that there seemed to be no presence of soul behind them—as if the spirits of these men had fled their bodies for the moment, so that their bodies might unfalteringly follow the henchmen's command.

All walked silently down the road, past the chapel, to the grassy hill and the twisted elm beneath which both Pons and Bernadette lay. "Under there," Fabrisse said, her voice cracking.

"Where is it, you say?" said the gruffer of the henchmen.

"There," said Fabrisse, pointing to the roots of the tree. "There!" She turned away and walked a short distance from the crowd, then gazed up the hillside at the boulder by which the rector had been standing during Pons's burial. It had been gray that day, and the sky had seemed to flatten the hillside down. Now, the sky was so blue it was almost blinding. The grass was yellow and she did not know whom to trust anymore. She heard the men grunting as they dug behind her, and she glanced around. A young village woman, who had previously been one of her occasional purchasers, was rooting through a mound of upturned earth, dark with hidden moisture. The woman pulled up worms and grubs and hid them in the pocket of her skirt, shamelessly. Fabrisse could not watch any longer. She turned around to face the boulder.

When the digging was finished, and the remains of the bodies had been pulled up from the ground, one of the women in the crowd tapped Fabrisse's shoulder. "It is done," she whispered, and cautiously Fabrisse looked around. Although she did not want to see what was left of her husband, she knew it was her obligation to support him even in death.

In front of the mounds of earth around the base of the tree, on the yellow grass, between the crowd of villagers on one side and the henchmen and the rector on the other, lay two piles of bones. Fabrisse had been prepared for something gruesome—flesh gouged out by worms, faces so badly decayed they were barely recognizable; but she had not been prepared for nothing. Not bones. Where had Pons gone?

"Gather them up, then!" the henchman called.

Without thinking, Fabrisse shouted out, "No!" The absent faces of the villagers turned toward her, and she silently approached the broken skeletons, looking from one to the other. "I will . . . I will carry my husband," she said. Surely she should know which pile was Pons— but she could not tell, she could not.

"He is on the left," the rector's voice sounded by the elm. She glanced at him, and he nodded to her when their eyes met. "There was a ring on the finger of the body to the right," he said. "A ring that has been removed. Bernadette wore a ring, I remember."

As the others picked up Bernadette's bones, Fabrisse spread her shawl out over the ground. She sat staring at the repose of Pons's bones. Fibers of earth hung from the skull, from the two holes where eyes had been. She wanted Pons's eyes, kind when they had first known her. She wanted his hands, stroking her calm. She wanted his sex, his pubic hair, as much him as his soul—she believed that now. He had killed a part of his essence in an effort to save another.

She touched the skull, cooler than she expected, and when she held it in her hands, lighter. She placed bone after bone onto the blackness of her shawl, and wondered at the completeness of each of them—there was no sign anywhere of the glass that had torn life from them more than seven years before.

She heard the gentler henchman tell the other to be still. "There is time," he said. "Give the woman a moment." She tied the ends of the scarf together, bundling the bones, and saw the roots of the elm greedily reaching toward her on the ground. When she had buried Pons, she had thought the elm was innocent, but she saw now that this obstinate tree had consumed him, silently, as life consumes life to go on.

WHEN THEY HAD CARRIED the remains to the square, and the henchmen had instructed the villagers to build up two pyres and the villagers had obliged them, the bones were burned. Fabrisse stood with the others in a ring around the flames, watching the black smoke soundlessly rising, and thought, *That is Pons, that smoke, making its pathless way into the sky, drifting, ascending like an angel, lifting then falling in pieces of ash to the ground.* Although she knew the occasion ought to have filled her with the kind of grief she had never known, she felt a strange elation growing in her bosom, and she could not believe that it mattered whether Pons was burned or buried whole in consecrated ground. Ashes and dust, was that not what Scripture said we were? And she had seen it—into the grave a man, exhumed a man no more. He was the elm now, he was the smoke. And every body that had been buried to lie in wait for the day of Judgment was the grass and the grain and the fruit, growing again and fading, feeding children so that they might grow. What God would keep a man from Heaven because he had tried to serve Him as well as he knew how?

Not even the children broke the silence as Pons and Bernadette burned, but stood in the circle with the others. Fabrisse felt their silence, and the thoughtfulness of her neighbors, and she thought that even if they all had been stretching their hands out to meet one another in prayer, they could not have been closer than they were. No woman wailed, no man shouted in protest, but she felt the force of their compassion. And as black as her life would be at times afterward, she would always have the memory of their unrequested love.

•   •   •

THE FIRE was put out when the sun was high at noon. Fabrisse has-tened to collect the ash, which had scattered like powder over the dry ground—but the gentler of the henchmen bent down over her and whispered that she should stop. "You wouldn't want to appear to be making a martyr of your husband," he said. He waited for her to dump the ash back onto the ground before retreating to where the other henchman stood near the smoldering pyre.

In a sweat from the heat, they announced that Jean Marty, hus-band of Bernadette, had converted back to the true faith on the eve of his conviction. As such, his house would remain standing, but the prop-erty of Pons Rives was to be confiscated to the Church, and in two days' time, at dawn, his house would be burned so that it might be a sign of the consequences of abandoning the flock without repentance. The gentler henchman turned his sad eyes to Fabrisse. "In two days' time, at dawn," he repeated, "so that the remaining family might have time to prepare."

Fabrisse wandered home in a daze, wondering what she and Mother Rives and Echo would do now. She had resisted turning to drink of late, but still she was bringing home barely enough in the way of goods to trade for foodstuff. She could never afford to pay for a house—however much that might cost. No. She would have to beg for shelter, and if that didn't work, she would have to return to Ax-les-Thermes.

At home, she found Echo circling Mother Rives's bed in a panic. The old woman was flushed and burning to the touch, and the girl was whining breathily like a wounded animal.

"What has happened?" asked Fabrisse. Her first thought was that Mother Rives had poisoned herself. She had not seen sickness come on so quickly since Pons's death. "Get a cloth and cool water," she said to Echo. When the girl was gone, she bent down over the old woman and examined her mouth for blood. "You have not hurt yourself, have you?" she whispered.

Without opening her eyes, the old woman shook her head, and a tear trickled down the side of her cheek. Fabrisse brushed the tear away and took the old woman's hand. "You must get well," she cooed. "I need you now."

Echo brought a bowl of water and a cloth, and perched at the foot of the bed as Fabrisse stripped the old woman of the bedcovers. Fabrisse dipped the cloth in the water, wrung it out, and wrapped the old woman's feet. "That will cool you," she murmured. Very quietly, she whispered that Pons was free and that they were being made to leave the house. "There has been so much sadness between these walls," she whispered. "It is best that we leave, and who am I in this village without you? Who is Echo?" She removed the cloth from the old woman's feet, dipped it again in the water, and wrung it out. She pushed up the old woman's nightdress and wiped her legs down.

"I will not leave this bed, I told you," the old woman spoke, her eyes still closed.

Fabrisse turned to Echo, who was cringing on the floor as if she smelled death in the air. "Pray," Fabrisse told her. "That He might show us mercy now."

BY NIGHTFALL, Mother Rives was so deeply in fever that her mind had begun to go. She saw Pons through the window—which Fabrisse had opened for air—and called to him. "Come nearer," she said. "Nearer."

Once, when Fabrisse had managed to get a spoonful of water in her mouth, the old woman raised her head and spit the water out, pointing a shaking finger to a black corner of the room. "Do you see him?" she whispered.

Fabrisse looked and saw nothing but Echo, curled up in a blanket and sleeping on the ground.

"My husband," said the old woman. "And he—" She strained forward, as if listening. "No!" She scowled at the corner. "I won't!" She fell back on the pillow and her gums began to chatter together. "Get a Good Man," she moaned. "Quickly, before I go."

SOON AFTER MIDNIGHT, Fabrisse went outdoors and crawled up the ladder to the roof for a breath of open air. Since she had returned from the burning, she had not had a moment to worry about having to leave the house. Mother Rives was dying, and it seemed to her that God might indeed be punishing them after all. She did not want the old woman to die without the consolation of a Good Man, but with the henchmen in the village, where was a Good Man to be found?

She remembered her own mother's dying day in Prades d'Aillon. Sensing that her mother's death was near, she had cried to the village priest until he accompanied her to her mother's bedside to administer extreme unction. She knelt by the door as the priest placed a cross in her mother's hands and dipped his thumb in the holy oil. He touched his thumb to her eyes, ears, nostrils, lips, and palms, uttering his prayers, and then he pulled the sheet back from her mother's body and lifted her skirt above her hips. As Fabrisse looked on, bewildered, the priest stroked her mother's loins with his oiled thumb. "Through this holy unction and His own most tender mercy may the Lord pardon thee the wretched sins thou hast committed by carnal delectation," he murmured. Fabrisse saw his hand pause for a moment over her mother's groin before pulling her skirt back down. When she went to her mother's side after the priest had left, her mother stared up at her—not with surprise, not with horror, but with sadness and concern.

On the roof now, in the quiet of night, Fabrisse gazed up at the little moon shining above the poplar and felt the presence of her mother. "Mama," she whispered. She heard footsteps on the road, and she made out the rector limping toward the house. He looked up at her, and it was as if every fear she had been sheltering evaporated into the night air. He had come at last to defend her, to make love to her. . . . Nothing would stop her from falling against him now.

They stared at each other in silence, he by the ladder, she near the roof's edge, until finally she crawled down the ladder, her body aching sweetly. He stepped back to allow her to pass to the door, and wordlessly they entered the house together. He watched as she uncovered and raked the fire. The flames flickered, blue and orange, and his eyes were brown in the light, not green, and his hair, she saw, was losing color. She realized he must be nearly fifty. They stood several arm spans away from each other, and she took a step toward him.

"I wanted to tell you—" he said suddenly.

"Yes," she said. "What?"

He wiped his mouth with his thumb and forefinger. "You will not be without a home after they take this from you."

She tried to focus on his words, but her mind slipped back to what would soon occur between them.

He drew away from her. "Esclarmonde d'Argelliers has served a short sentence for sorcery and has been pardoned," he said. "She is living with her daughter now in Prades d'Aillon, and I paid a small price for her property. It is yours."

She shook her head, not hearing.

"It is yours," he repeated. "I give the property to you. To you and your daughter. And to the mother of your late husband, of course."

As if the old woman had heard him from her room, she cried out, "I will not!"

The rector gasped and spun around.

"Mother Rives," Fabrisse explained. "She is in fever. Dying, I fear. She—" She stopped herself short. She had meant to say that the old woman was in desperate need of a Good Man, but then she realized that although she knew without a shadow of a doubt that the rector was sympathetic to the Believers, she had never heard him say as much— not even to the Châtelaine in the underground. "I did not come for you to administer extreme unction yet," she continued. "And I should have."

"But you did not," he said, and in the firelight she thought she saw his eyes say, I understand.

THE RECTOR ASKED to be taken to Mother Rives. When the old woman saw him standing in the doorway with a candle, she stopped rocking back and forth and said, "Has a Good Man finally come? Bring him to me."

Echo was sleeping soundly in the corner. As the rector entered the room, he glanced over at her before proceeding to the bedside. The old woman clasped his arm and gazed up into his eyes. Still, she did not seem to recognize him as the parish priest. "Save me," she cried. "Console me with the hope of salvation."

Fabrisse watched as he knelt by the bed and set the candle beside him. He touched the old woman's cheek with the back of his fingers, and brushed her hair from her brow. He stroked her eyelids, the folds of her ears, the openings of her nose, the chapped skin of her mouth. He took her hands in his, as if rubbing oil into their wrinkles. "I don't remember," he said at last. "Remind me how to give you consolation."

The old woman moved her head back and forth in her delirium. She began to whisper to herself. "You say," she said, "you say something . . ."

"What do I say?" the rector asked.

The old woman moaned, her eyes fiery in the candlelight. "Do you surrender to God and the Gospel, you say." She paused. "And I say, Yes."

"Do you surrender?" he said.

"Yes," she said.

"Good. And what else."

Her head moved back and forth as she thought. "Do you promise not to eat meat and such things, you say."

"Do you promise?" he said.

"I promise," she said. "And there is more . . ."

"What more?"

"Do I promise not to enjoy lust and to kill? Yes, I say."

"Good." He stroked her hands in his. "And more still?"

Again, her head moved back and forth. "Do I promise not to touch a man?" she said, pulling her hands from his. "Yes, I say, of course. And 'Benedicite,' you tell me to say."

"Say 'Benedicite.'"

"*Benedicite,*" she said. "I remember it now." She pressed her trembling hands together and held them to her forehead. "Pray," she said. "That God may keep me from a bad death."

"May God keep you from a bad death," he said, clasping his hands over the flickering flame.

"May the Holy Ghost descend upon me now," she whispered. "And the Pater."

He nodded and joined her with his words: "Our Father, who art in Heaven, hallowed be thy name . . ."

WHEN THE OLD WOMAN had closed her eyes in thankfulness and in rest, Fabrisse followed the rector from the room to the kitchen. "Thank you," she whispered to him, and he hung his head.

"She saved herself as we all might," he said. He turned to the door before stopping to glance back at her. "You are not frightened to be alone?"

"No," she said, but then she nodded yes.

Shadows of the flames in the hearth flickered over his cheek. He told her he would go to the chapel for candles and a cross and his vessels of oil and holy water in case the old woman did not live through the night. "If word spreads that she has passed, the Inquisitor's men may come looking," he said. And then, "There are laws of the Church regarding burial. If she does pass before the men depart, we must bury her in the churchyard."

He left, and Fabrisse could not bring herself to smooth her hair or wash her neck or rub lavender buds under her arms. She paced back and forth from the kitchen to her room, looking in on her bed, straightening the covers, crossing to look in on Echo sleeping on the floor. She prayed that the girl would not awaken and spoil the night she had always suspected would be hers. She pictured the rector cornering her by her bed, and felt the touch of his fingers on her navel, the slip of his palm between her thighs, the tickling whisper of his words in her ear—
I love you more than any other.

When she heard him at the door, she nearly raced to greet him. He was wearing a black stole, and carrying the vessels in one hand, and a cross and a clutch of candles in the other. She took the candles from him, and he brushed past her.

It was not to her room that he went, but to the side of Mother Rives, who lay perfectly still in her bed. Not even her breathing could be heard. The rector bent his ear down to the old woman's mouth and listened. After a moment, he stood and glanced at Fabrisse by the door. "Sleeping still," he said.

He asked for a stool to sit on, and when Fabrisse returned with it, she found him standing over Echo, gazing down at her. Fabrisse held the stool out to him, and he took it, distractedly, making a clunking sound as he set it down by the bed.

Echo woke with the noise. She raised her head from the ground, looking with dark, sleepy eyes first at him and then at her grandmother.

"Sleep," said Fabrisse to her. "Your grandmother has not left us yet."

As if Echo did not hear, she pushed back the blanket and stood, naked, her hair in thorny curls around her shoulders.

"Cover yourself," Fabrisse snapped, rushing to cover the girl herself. "There is a priest in the house. Aren't you ashamed?"

Echo ignored her. With the blanket wrapped around her body, she tiptoed to her grandmother's side, directly opposite the rector. She stared down at the old woman, a finger in her mouth. And the rector stared at her.

Fabrisse rounded the bed and stood by the girl, pulling her by the shoulders away from the rector's hungry eyes, which had the look at once of mystification and fright and something like desire. Echo wandered back to her place on the floor and lay down, falling asleep again quickly. Fabrisse wanted to ask the rector what he had seen in her daughter, but he went to the open window and kneeled before the blue-black sky in prayer.

ALL THAT NIGHT, the rector stayed at Mother Rives's side. He sat on the stool, his eyes sometimes on the old woman, sometimes closed in prayer. Once he seemed to be sleeping, but then he belched quietly and his eyes blinked open. He gazed over at the sleeping girl—her hair in disarray, one pale leg sticking out from beneath the blanket.

Fabrisse thought perhaps it was due to the presence of Echo that he did not come to make love to her, and she considered carrying the girl away from his sight and back to their room—but then where would love happen? She watched the flame by his elbow burning low until it burned out, and she walked heavily into the kitchen, hoping he would follow, but he did not. She comforted herself with the thought that it was far more sinful to engage in love with death near; and she waited for the moment when he would find her commiserating eyes in the dimness of the room and feel pardoned—if only for an interlude.

AT DAWN, the old woman sat up, said she wanted to leave the house, and fell back dead on her pillow. The rector examined her. "You must tend to this woman's body," he said finally. "I will wait in the kitchen as you do."

Mother Rives lay with her chin thrust up, her nostrils stiff, and her lips parted. As Fabrisse bent down to pull the covers back from her, she saw the shape of the old woman's skull through her thin flesh, under her iron-colored hair. Suddenly, she remembered Pons's bones, and she felt the full force of having lost the old woman. Where was Mother Rives's life now? It had deserted her body, as if her body were something foul. She could not bear the thought of Mother Rives as nothing but bones underground.

She lifted the nightdress off the old woman and sponged away the waste that had been expelled from her stale, dry flesh. She braided the old woman's hair, then dressed her in her only shift, made of smoky muslin and worn through under the arms from sweat. She pushed shoes over her feet, cracked and yellow from so many years of walking, working.

When she called to the rector that the body was prepared, Echo rolled over, covered her head with the blanket, and slept again. The rector returned and looked down at Echo—a bundle of blanket and hair. He smiled vaguely and walked to the bed. In the old woman's hands, he placed a small wooden cross. He lit several candles and told Fabrisse to say that he had sprinkled the old woman with holy oil and water if mourners came wanting to view her.

"Now I will see to the coffin," he said.

Again, Fabrisse followed him to the front door, searching for a way to keep him there. He had been too frightened to abandon himself to her as yet, but if he had a moment more . . .

"I have no money for a coffin," she said, eyeing his hand on the latch.

He turned to her. "Sleep if you can," he said calmly. "There is a long day ahead. For the heat, the woman should be buried by evening."

"Perhaps I am mad," she whispered.

He squinted at her, then shook his head. "No," he said. "No, you are only tired."

"Not tired," she said.

"Grief-stricken," he said.

"Not tired, not grief-stricken," she said. She saw his mouth open in surprise, a frown crease his forehead, and then her knees struck the floor and she embraced his legs with all the passion of her desire. "I know," she murmured, "and you do not have to be frightened."

She felt his legs pulling away from her grasp, and she gazed up into his large, bewildered eyes. "I know," she said again. "And I feel the same. Just the same." She pressed her cheek against his robe, over his thighs; she kissed his thighs. "You love me," she said. "You love me, you love me, and I love you despite the others. I love you and I am happy for your love."

His legs went suddenly still, and she gazed up at him again, sure he would confess himself to her. He was not frowning any longer, and her heart leaped up in gladness before she noticed that the new, calm wonder in his eyes was not for her. He was staring past her. She glanced

back over her shoulder and saw Echo standing naked by the door to
Mother Rives's room.

In the space of a moment, she understood what she had not before.

"Prepare yourself for the viewing," the rector stuttered, withdrawing from her clasp and unlatching the door, gone a moment later.

FOR A LONG TIME, Fabrisse sat curled on the floor, too humiliated to
cry, too stunned by the awful truth of the rector's hunger not for her, but
for her own young daughter. When she finally lifted her head, she saw
Echo crouched against the wall, peering at her with frightened eyes.
Fabrisse did not try to comfort her. She glared at Echo and crawled on
hands and knees away from her toward the smoldering hearth. She
stood and took the flagon down from the shelf, tipping its mouth into
her own as she collapsed back down onto the floor. A seed of hatred for
Echo had planted itself deep in her heart, and it would root itself firmly
there, never to leave her.

Through the morning, she wandered past Echo in the kitchen,
drinking and dripping with sweat, the heat boiling her from within.
Now and then, Echo tried to steal the flagon from her, but she slapped
the girl's hand away, cursing at her.

A man came bearing the coffin on his back. Fabrisse recognized
him as a woodcutter, and when she smiled at him, the flagon propped under her arm, he looked at her with an expression of pain and puzzlement,
saying the rector had instructed him there. He struggled to carry the coffin to the back of the house, and then lifted the old woman up gently,
pushing the cross between her fingers after it had fallen to the ground.

Later, the mourners arrived bearing flowers and eggs, nut-colored
roots and bits of ham. One brought a cup of milk for Echo, and she
greedily drank it down. Another brought scraps for the pigs. Echo ate
those, too, and Fabrisse did not correct her.

Old Woman Maurs closed the shutters, complaining that the heat
was turning the body sour. Fabrisse thought she would suffocate in the
smoky air, with the smell of death on her skin and the reek of ham gone
rancid. She thought she could smell her own blood, coming soon with
its scent of loneliness.

Old Woman Maurs began to wail, and the others joined in, the rotten stumps of their teeth showing, their features twisted in grief. Echo sobbed without sound and Fabrisse sobbed with her. She had lost the hope of love, and without that hope, what was she? A woman alone, trapped within the web of her own shame.

THE RECTOR RETURNED that afternoon in his black stole, carrying his vessels, and she stayed far from him. The henchmen also came—the pockmarked boy bearing a cross and a look of pity in his eye, and the other carrying a stoup of holy water. With the salt of sorrow still in her throat, she watched as the rector sprinkled water over the old woman's body in the coffin, reciting prayers. Several men among the mourners hoisted the coffin and followed the rector, who followed the henchmen from the house toward the chapel.

The heat was sweltering, the sighing of the poplars far above the only breeze. Fabrisse shaded her head with her hands and saw the pigs fenced in a corner of her yard, lying on their sides and panting. With Echo beside her, she followed the others, dragging her feet over the hardened ruts that wheels had furrowed in moister days, passing chickens squawking for want of grain and the dung heap, fuming. A mutt howled as they entered its shade under the arching elm, and then passed into the churchyard with a new grave dug from the grass, yellow as piss. They pushed through the narrow chapel door, toward the hint of coolness inside.

The coffin was placed in the center of the floor, and candles were lit all around. Fabrisse stood beside Echo, flies biting at the skin around her eyes as the rector said the vespers for the dead. "Requiem aeternam dona eis, Domine; et lux perpetua luceat eis . . ."

After the Mass the coffin was carried out to the grave, and Fabrisse listened to the soft noise of legs brushing cloth as mourners left the chapel, the noise of men breathing under the strain of the dead body's weight. The heat of the day pushed down from the dusky sky, and the coffin was set among the stones on one side of the grave. People chanted sluggishly. The rector sprinkled the coffin again with holy water, praying as it was lowered into the ground, "Grant this mercy, O Lord, we beseech Thee, to Thy servant departed, that she may not receive in punishment the requital of her deeds who in desire did keep

Thy will, and as the true faith here united her to the company of the faithful, so may Thy mercy unite her above to the choirs of angels."

The true faith, thought Fabrisse, *the company of the faithful* . . . How could the rector pray so falsely? Mother Rives had remained faithful indeed—but to a faith different from that of the Church. Where was Fabrisse to find faith among so much pretending, so much loss? Even life seemed nothing more to her now than a reverie, with bodies so feeble they slipped away as in dreams.

The rector sprinkled holy water on her face, and she lowered her eyes and would not look at him. He stooped in front of Echo, sprinkling her, and Echo clung to Fabrisse's thigh, surprised by the wetness. The rector murmured something to the girl that Fabrisse could not hear. He stood to leave and a light rain started falling.

Everyone was silent as they tilted their heads back, opening their faces to the wet, to the coolness descending from the darkening sky. Fabrisse felt her dress becoming heavy, clinging to her body like another child. She was glad Mother Rives would have a final drink. When the men among the mourners moved to cover the grave with the rusty-smelling soil, she asked them to wait a moment more.

THAT NIGHT, after Echo fell asleep finally, Fabrisse sat beside the window in the ungiving light of the moon, staring at the chest within which she had once hidden her red glass. She had not opened it since Pons's death, afraid of finding the glass missing, of knowing her full role in the story of Pons's parting. Her head throbbed, and in a moment of impatience she flung the chest open, snatched up the wedding dress inside, and shook it over the linens beneath.

The glass slipped as smoothly as water from the sleeve of the dress onto the linens. How innocent it appeared, how harmless—trustworthy, even. She picked it up and pressed it to her cheek, soaking up its coolness. For more than seven years she had carried the weight of culpability for Pons's death. She had tormented herself without reason, and it seemed to her now that her real torment was only just beginning.

At dawn, the house would burn. She had not even accepted the rector's gift of Esclarmonde's house, she realized, and yet she set about packing. She pressed the linens, the wedding dress, and the glass deep into the chest, then gathered belongings she could not bear to leave behind—the baptismal clothes she had worn as a child, the brush Pons had given her, the clippings of his hair and nails, the little shift Echo had worn and tripped over when she was first walking.

As she piled together what foodstuff and supplies remained in the house, her headache faded. The dim blue light that preceded dawn filtered through the windows, and with it, the pockmarked henchman came knocking on the door. She fretted, thinking the burning had nearly begun, but the boy explained that the rector had sent him to help her move to her new home. She thanked the boy and offered him a cup of water, which he gratefully accepted.

She woke Echo and the three of them carried the chest and the chicken coops down the road to the house of Esclarmonde. While the house was decrepit on the outside, the old woman had kept it well within. Indeed, there were little jars containing dried lavender and roses by each window. The hooks over the hearth were brimming with utensils, and not a scrap of food or waste or spittle could be found on the rushes over the ground. Fabrisse inspected the two bedrooms off the kitchen and saw that each was appointed with not only a pallet, but a chest and a stool and a shelf built into the wall. She and Echo would have their own beds now. On the shelf in one of the rooms, beside another jar of dried flowers, was a flagon. She withdrew its plug, sniffing inside. *Wine.* She had never sold a cup to the old woman—afraid of approaching the house—but she felt her heart move out to Esclarmonde.

BY THE TIME they had returned up the road, a small crowd of villagers was gathered in her yard. The other henchman had summoned everyone to watch the burning, and the village men were to torch the house themselves.

There was nothing Fabrisse wanted from the house, save her foodstuff, her wine-selling ware, and the animals in the pen and the stable. She entered the house one last time with Echo, and they gathered what they could before leaving quickly.

Still more of the village had appeared outside, sleepy children leaning against their mothers or curled up on the ground. How children were saved by this wondrous capacity for sleep, thought Fabrisse, as she herded the goats from the stable, the pigs from the pen.

She stood with Echo among the animals at the edge of the crowd, looking from the village men holding branches to be torched, to the rector with his eyes still yearning toward Echo, to the barren fields below them all. She was alone and unwanted, and what was there to do but remain living in spite of that?

Fire spread from branch to branch, and she endured, even as the roof was alight, even as the flames reached like angry tongues toward Heaven, an insult to God's eye.

TWELVE

THE HOUSE COLLAPSED in a heap of fire and smoke, and Pierre did not take his eyes away from the seven-year-old Echo. He watched her pressed against her mother's side, her two front teeth biting the plump, red flesh of her bottom lip, her grubby fingers pushing hair from her eyes, behind her ear—hair that fell in an unbraided tangle down her back. He saw her feet, pink and filthy, her plump toes peeking out from beneath her shift, stitched together from old scraps. . . . It was awful, mad, contemptible, this thing he felt for the child, this desire beating in his chest, burning through his loins. But for all the power of will he had come to know after confessing to the Good Men years before, he could not harness his drive to possess Echo with his eyes now. He gazed at her, this lovely live creature, and thought that despite all reason, his dead bride had come back to him in Echo's form; Marquise was incarnate once more.

He had seen Echo over the years, of course. Her mother rarely attended Mass, but when she did, Echo was always by her side—clinging to Fabrisse or gazing up at her rather than listening to the words of the sermon. He had heard gossip of late that the girl had gone mute, and when he had seen her about the village—wine-selling with her mother, or pulling up carrots in their yard—he had noticed the silence that seemed to surround her like a shroud, so different from the noise that burst from other village children. But he had never really *looked* at her. It had always been Fabrisse whom his eyes had lingered on—Fabrisse who had transformed from a tender-eyed maidservant to a weary widow, with tangled, uncovered hair and the look of drunkenness beneath her skin.

Long before he had come to know Fabrisse as his illegitimate niece, he had felt haunted by what she knew of him: not even the women he had made love to in his life had seen him from the vantage point she had by the dungeon door. She had watched as he undid his vows of celibacy—desperate, floundering, sometimes lost in ecstasy, all too often humiliated. And when she had led him back out to the stables each night, he had felt the weight of having stolen away yet another piece of her innocence. Still, he never saw judgment in her eyes. Perhaps because of this—because he had bared his wretched soul to her and yet remained somehow accepted—he felt at once ashamed in her presence and comforted. He carried the memory of her shy, mysterious eyes in the shadows of his mind long after he had stopped visiting the dungeon, and when she caught him watching her burying her husband on the hillside, he felt that his very soul had been recognized. Later—after he had learned that she was the Fabrisse he had baptized as his spiritual daughter—he sometimes yearned to embrace her in a gesture of both paternal consolation and boyish greediness for solace. Never had he felt lust for her, however. His feelings for her were too complicated by regret for that.

If he had been pressed to acknowledge why he was relieved each year when she did not appear at his confessional, he might have admitted to having sensed her growing desire for him, and his own fear of being confronted by as much. In truth, when he saw her gazing at him now and then, a sick feeling like guilt spread through his gut. Was it not his fault if she had come to desire him? He had been her first education in wantonness, and he had never gathered his courage to tell her that she was his brother's bastard child. What was he afraid of? Humiliating her, perhaps. Humiliating himself for what he had revealed to her. He kept his distance, helping her when he could, ignoring the small voice in his mind that warned him that her passion was mounting, mounting, and soon it would loose itself from her containment, parading naked before his eyes.

It was thus not without hesitation that he went to her house on the night after Pons's remains were exhumed and burned. After the henchmen had announced that the house was to be torched as well, he made haste for Prades d'Aillon and knocked upon the door of Esclarmonde's married daughter. He had been the one to accuse Esclarmonde of sorcery. The Inquisitor had threatened him again with arrest for collusion, and in a desperate effort to satisfy both the Inquisitor and the

Good Men, he had scrawled Esclarmonde's name across a slip of parchment and shoved it into a messenger's hand. He had suspected that the old woman was innocent of sorcery, and assuaged his guilt with the thought that her innocence would be evident. If nothing else, the fact that she had mistakenly murdered a Good Man would win her favor in the Inquisitorial Court. And indeed it had; she was imprisoned for less than a season. The Inquisitor sent Pierre a chastising letter, suggesting that Pierre had made a false accusation in order to protect the truly sinful, and stating that Esclarmonde had been advised to leave the corrupt parish of Montaillou at once.

Without much in the way of haggling, the old woman and her daughter accepted Pierre's money in exchange for the deed to the house in Montaillou. They fed him supper and he paid them more and then made his way slowly back toward the village. He returned to Montaillou by the midnight hour—the hour of his sin with the Châtelaine—and when he saw Fabrisse sitting in the moon glow on her roof, he felt suddenly ill. He wanted to flee, but she opened the door and he was obliged to enter.

He would have left immediately after consoling the dying Old Woman Rives had it not been for the sleeping figure of Echo he glimpsed on the floor—her pale legs jutting out from beneath her blanket, her hair a tumble of curls hiding all her face but the dimple on her chin. Her breathing was deep and regular, and he was reminded of Marquise listening to its rhythm—Marquise had breathed that way as they had stood together before the Virgin, little Fabrisse kicking in his arms. It was the sound of life itself, he thought, and he could not bring himself to leave the girl.

"You are not frightened to be alone?" he asked Fabrisse, knowing already what her response would be.

"No," she said, and in the darkness he saw her nod yes.

Later, when he returned with the candles and cross and vessels of holy oil and water, he saw the flash of Echo's body naked in the moonlight, and it seemed to him a miracle. Though he had never seen Marquise without clothes, he knew absolutely that *this* was his beloved's form—younger now than it would have been if he had known it, but still hers. This was her belly, tight as a drum. These were her knees, slightly turned in. These were legs, long and downy and milk-white. And her navel. And the crease of her sex. How furious he was when Fabrisse snatched up the blanket and hid away what was his.

He bit his tongue and watched as the girl wandered to her grandmother's bedside, the blanket falling from her naked shoulders. She stood across from him, her head drooping down. She brushed hair away from her cheek with a sleepy toss of a hand, and he saw her eyebrows lift in reluctant expectation of death's approach. She glanced at him, blinking through long lashes without a shadow of reserve or caution, and he saw that hers were Marquise's eyes—portentous, heavy, knowing. Gazing at them, his very soul was captivated. He had been dead, or as good as dead, and now he was suddenly alive—delivered from the void of his former lifeless life.

Fabrisse came round from behind the girl and drew her away from the bed. For a long moment, the girl stared at him, her unfathomable silence passing between them. Her lips parted, and he saw her two front teeth, splayed slightly. She reached up and tugged on her earlobe, and then glanced down, bumbled away from the bed, and dropped onto the floor in a sleeping heap.

If he had not wanted to face Fabrisse before, he simply could not now. He stood and went to the window and knelt down, looking through the darkness past the poplars breathing in the night, to the stars—as vibrant with excitement as he, it seemed, and as naked as Echo beneath the blanket, so close. His mind buzzed with the pulse of the stars and the leaping in his heart and the low burning at the base of his spine and the sound of the girl breathing steadily in sleep, dreaming into him as he ached his dreaming thoughts into her. It was mad! For the first time in his life, he felt the desire to become a father. . . .

Sitting by the old woman again, he closed his eyes and dreamed of slipping fingers beneath the blanket's edge, tasting the girl's bright red mouth, the lobes of her ears, plump and soft. He woke with a phrase on his lips—*forty years,* and he realized that he was at least that much older than she; but as he glanced over at her, lying on her belly, her blooming breath filling the air, he knew utterly and without much remorse that he would do anything to have her.

SEVEN YEARS BEFORE, he had confessed to the Good Men, and for six of those seven years, he had kept his promise to walk away from sin. He had remained celibate, finding ways to avoid Ax and the whores he had come to know there, and seeking counsel with the Good Men before every season of confession, when—in order to avoid suspicion among the faithful of his parish—he was obligated to listen to the hushed divulgences of women as well as men, and so to feel the warmth of feminine shame radiating from their skin.

It was not that celibacy came easily to him, but that after so much trepidation about living in a state of mortal sin, he felt sustained by the thought that he was gradually purging himself of wrongdoing; he had embraced a new faith—older in his heart than that he had preached by—and he clung to its abhorrence of the flesh and all things material as if it were a raft saving him from a raging river.

"Repulsive giver of spoiled rot," he told himself when confronted with the swelling breasts of confessing women. He tried to imagine yellow mire spilling from their nipples, but then the nipples were soft and dusky pink in his mind. Round. Beautiful. *Not beautiful,* he told himself: wicked, created by the Devil to lure him in. He gave the women heavy penance and told them to pray for forgiveness for their womanly sins.

AVA GUILHABERT was the first peasant woman with whom he trespassed.

When the newly appointed Inquisitor summoned him to the Sermo Generalis—demanding that he both present a list of wayfarers, and notify the brothers Authié of their own summons—he did not deliberate for long. He sent word to the brothers in Ax that they should stay clear of Montaillou for a time, and he crafted a "list" of the only wayfarer he felt justified implicating; of all the Believers and parishioners he knew in the village, Philippe Guilhabert was without question the most culpable as a man. Over the years prior, Philippe had confessed to him about the bastard family he had engendered in Catalonia, about the frequent lashings he had given Ava, and about the women he had seized on the road, raped and beaten—killing one in the end. Philippe had cried gently as he confessed, repenting truly and asking for forgiveness. Pierre had given penance to him, but he had found himself, at heart, unforgiving.

At the conclusion of the Sermo Generalis, the Inquisitor paused by Pierre before proceeding down the nave of the Cathedral. "Expect henchmen to come for your man in six days," he said. And then, "I shall expect a list from you in less." That afternoon, Pierre set off from

Toulouse, journeying down the Ariège toward Ax. He stayed at an inn in Saverdun, and then in Tarascon the night after. When he finally arrived in Ax, he found Jean Marty and Prades Tavernier in hiding with the brothers beneath the house of their mother's cousin. Rather than confess to having submitted Philippe's name, he told them that the Inquisitor was already conducting a trial against Philippe and that henchmen were coming for him within the week. The brothers helped him forge a plan of escape for Philippe, and it was of this plan that he meant to speak with Philippe when he returned to Montaillou the following day. But Philippe was absent, and Ava greeted him with a bruise on her cheek. . . .

Later, he would blame that bruise for his fall. Blue and broken by veins of red, it seemed to call to him. He felt bruised, too—caught between the Inquisitor's threats and his own promise of aid to the Good Men, between his desire to maintain his position of power in the village, however meager that power was becoming, and his urgency to live a life of faithfulness to his true beliefs. At one time he had been the lord of all things spiritual in the village; now both the Inquisitor and the Good Men were lording over him, and he hated how small it made him feel, how vulnerable.

When Ava said that Philippe was out, he walked to her bedroom without thinking. He told her of the henchmen's coming, and when she denied that Philippe had housed the Good Men from time to time, he said that all the village knew that Philippe was both a Believer and an adulterer. He studied the bruise, longing to kiss it.

"Who struck you, Ava?" he asked.

She touched the bruise but did not answer.

"Philippe," he said.

"No," she said.

"Yes," he said, and he put his fingers over hers on the bruise, thinking she, too, was caught between conflicting desires: to save her husband on the one hand, and to be saved from him on the other. He stroked the bruise and she allowed him.

"Stop," she murmured. "Stop, please."

It all happened as easily as a breath of air. She was sweet, relenting, and he was achingly grateful to her. She opened and he entered her, entered the peace of her peaceful center. In her, he relaxed, body and soul, and the question of his stature in the village was a question no longer. For a lingering moment, he was healed.

. . .

HE DESPAIRED for this crime of the flesh and longed to enact it again, wallowing in the miserable thought that he would never achieve salvation. Then the henchmen came and his torment turned to suspicion. They were looking not only for Philippe, but also for both the brothers Authié, Jean Marty, and Prades Tavernier. He had not submitted a list to the Inquisitor since the Sermo Generalis, and he had no idea how the Inquisitor had obtained the names of Jean Marty and Prades Tavernier unless a spy was lurking in the village. Was the Inquisitor trying to frighten him into surrendering the names of all the Believers by suggesting that he had a source other than him—a source who might reveal Pierre's own collaboration in the heresy? He was stricken with a sweat that would not leave him, and his bowels bubbled for days. He searched his mind for a way to dig himself out of culpability, and he feared that in the awful end he would have to betray the Good Men or be imprisoned himself, burned perhaps for heresy.

Ava was summoned to Toulouse and left without consulting him. He had wanted to convince her to flee from the Inquisition, so afraid was he that she would reveal not only their lovemaking, but also his part in her lie as to Philippe's whereabouts. For the six weeks that she was gone, fear devoured him, and a horrible darkness such as he had never known spread like a shadow over his soul. He dreamed that he found Ava alone in her house. There was a knife in his hand, and as she opened her mouth to speak, he grabbed hold of her tongue and sliced it out. When he woke, he could still feel the slippery warmth of blood on his fingertips, the strength of her tongue as it fought against him. He remembered how firmly he had had to cut against the muscle, and he wondered for an instant if it had not been a dream at all but a memory of an act he had actually performed. He could have performed it, he knew, and yet knew nothing of himself at all.

During Ava's absence, the Inquisitor sent him a second letter, demanding that he add to his "list of suspect brevity," and it was then that he submitted the name of Esclarmonde. He braced himself for the appearance of more henchmen, sent word to the brothers and their companions to remain far from the village, and warned the Believers whom he trusted that there was a spy in Montaillou.

Frightened by this possibility, Old Man Belot decided to flee with his family. Late one night, Pierre helped them sneak to the bushes at the southern edge of the village, over the Col du Pradel and through the Val d'Orlu, where they could run for a mountain pass and escape to Catalonia. He ran with them as far as the steep slope of the Col, wanting never to stop, the pain in his hip so severe he stumbled on a rock. Old Woman Belot reached down to help him stand. "Come with us," she said, gripping his arm. "We'll slow to a walk."

Old Man Belot stared into the darkness ahead and Pierre held his hand up to the old woman, gesturing that he would stay. "Careful of the bears," he said, and she frowned. He watched her turn and run, taking one of her grandsons by the hand. They were free, he thought, as they disappeared into the darkness.

HE KNEW he had to find a way to prevent further villagers from testifying; once in the Inquisitor's presence they would likely divulge all gossip, and he would be swept with a flood of Believers into prison. He told the family Benet that if the henchmen arrived with a surprise summons for any of them, they should strangle the dogs and cats and feign affliction with the plague. As for Na Roqua, he told her to moan in her bed, complaining of broken bones. "You were working on the roof," he told her. "And you fell from the ladder and broke all your bones. 'I cannot move,' you will say. And they will leave you. They must."

Several of the women among the Believers he counseled cried to him of their fears, and despite the feeling in his deepest soul that he must not take advantage of them in their weakness, he plotted to visit them again when their husbands were gone—out shepherding or plowing or carrying what little grain was left from the year before to the water mills along the Hers. It was not that he had noticed particularly the attributes of any of these women, but that he could not face the void of aloneness that seemed at every moment to be consuming him. In his heart, he knew that the occasions when he had felt truly filled by another had presented themselves to him; he had not searched for the Virgin, for Marquise, for the Châtelaine, each of whom had held him for a time from the agony of solitude. He knew he could not force his loneliness away, but he tried to force it nevertheless.

One day at noon, he walked into the kitchen of Alissende Roussel without knocking. She looked up from the bowl of eggs and salted carrots that she had set on the table before her boys, and wiped her hands on her dress. "Are they coming for us?" she said.

He told her that he had to speak to her alone, and she paused for a moment before leaving the boys. "Eat," she said to them. "No need to worry."

She led him down to the cellar. "Are they coming?" she said again.

He laid his hand on her shoulder, and her shoulder began to shudder. She covered her face with her hands. "I don't want to go to prison," she cried. "Even if I go to Hell, I don't care. Just not prison."

"I will take care of you," he whispered. He noticed the plumpness of her arms, the fabric of her rust-colored dress against her hips. He ached to lose himself in the peace of her soft, feminine center. Gently, gently, he let his fingers fall from her shoulder to the curve of her back, to the slope of her haunch. She pulled away, staring at him with frightened eyes. "I will take care of you," he said again.

She shook her head, silently telling him to stop, but still he stepped toward her and bent to kiss the silken hair behind her ear. He tasted the salt of her sweat. "Do you understand?" he said to her.

She breathed without moving. "You will take care of us?" she said at last.

"Yes," he said, his fingertips reaching for hers.

"Mama!" one of the boys called from above.

She gasped and stepped away from him, staring wildly into his eyes. Finally, she turned to look up the stairs. "I'll be up in a moment," she called. "Eat your eggs for now."

"I ate my eggs already, Mama!"

"Then your carrots!" she said. "Stay there."

Slowly, she turned back to him. "How shall it be then?" she whispered, a small sweat breaking across her brow.

When he did not answer, she said, "From the front or the back?"

He felt his cheeks burning with color. "The back," he said, too ashamed to face her.

She turned around and lifted her dress over her haunches, bare and pale and round as two moons. "You will take care of us," she whispered. "Tell me again."

"I will take care of you," he said, and for a fleeting moment, he actually believed he had such power.

· · ·

WHEN THE HENCHMEN came for not only Esclarmonde, but also Na Roqua and the family Belot, he was both relieved that he had prepared the Believers and further convinced a spy was near. The only person to have testified openly from the village was Ava, and if she had not disclosed the names of the healer and the family now in exile, someone had done so in guise.

Ava returned from her penitential pilgrimage three evenings before Easter and he did not allow her a moment of rest before pounding on her door. "I have never thought you guilty of heresy," he said once inside, "and I will not now if you tell me the names of those you accused to the Inquisitor." They were standing in her entry, and Ava kept looking from him to Béatrice, who peered at them from within the kitchen.

"Please," Ava whispered. "She is frightened enough that her father will be burned."

He grabbed her wrist and led her past Béatrice to the bedroom. "There," he said, shoving her inside.

"You are not like this," she said. "Please." She rubbed her wrist and sat down on the bed. "What is it that you want? I'll give it to you. Whatever it is."

"The names," he said. "Those you discussed with the Inquisitor."

She squeezed her wrist, then glared up at him. "He asked about Philippe for one," she said. "On and on about Philippe. Whom he met with, and what they spoke of and so on. You don't think that was easy for me to discuss?"

"And whom did you say he met with, Ava?"

Her lips pursed. "The brothers," she said. "And Prades Tavernier. And Jean Marty—but he knew about them all. You know he knew about them. The henchmen said they were hunting them when they came for Philippe. You heard."

"Yes," he said. "And who else?"

She shook her head. "I didn't want to," she whispered.

He waited. "Didn't want to what?"

"Tell them of Pons," she said.

"Pons Rives?"

She nodded. "But what was the harm in it, since he is dead?"

He did not answer.

"He asked if Pons had a wife, and I said yes, but that she was an honest Christian. No heretic. But still he wanted to know her name. . . . I had to tell the truth, Pierre. I could not lie if I wanted to be saved."

"And who else, Ava?"

Her eyebrows lifted as she thought. "The healer," she said. "She visited some nights for supper and talked with Philippe of the Good Men and how blessed they were. But she's such an old woman. What will the Inquisitor do to her? A man of compassion like him."

"And the family Belot? Did you tell him of them?"

She frowned. "Philippe never got on with Old Man Belot. . . . But he told me once that Old Man Belot and his kin were Believers." She paused. "And I told the Inquisitor that, yes. I wanted to be gone from there, Pierre. You understand."

He stared down at her, his teeth clenched. "And what of me, Ava?"

Her lips parted. Suddenly she smiled. "Nothing," she said. "Nothing. I promise." She held her hands out to him. "He asked if you were protecting the heretics. If I had ever seen you with the Good Men. But I said no. Because I had not. And you are not. Are you? You are not, no. And so I did not lie." She laughed. "He never asked me if I had made love with you, so it was not a lie to keep that quiet, was it? I told the truth, didn't I? And I paid penance for my crimes."

"And did he ask who warned Philippe that henchmen were coming?" he said.

She bit her lip. Slowly, she shook her head. "Strange," she said at last. "Strange, but he did not."

She lay back on the bed, staring up at the ceiling. He lay over her and took her then, took her badly, because he did not know whether to punish her for betrayal or thank her for sparing him.

ALTHOUGH AVA had been the one to accuse Na Roqua and the family Belot of heresy, there was still another who had betrayed Jean Marty and Prades Tavernier, and Pierre determined to root out who that other was. During the Easter season of confession, he held his own Inquisition in miniature—summoning villagers to the chapel one by one and questioning them as thoroughly as he could without revealing his own association with the Good Men. He hissed that lying in confession was an unpardonable crime, and even made teenage boys weep with fear. Thus it was that when the father of the late Bernadette Marty knelt before him and confessed at once to having divulged the names of Jean Marty and Prades Tavernier to the same friar who had become Inquisitor, Pierre almost did not believe him.

"What did you say?" he asked the old man.

"I told him," the old man said. "Jean Marty was no kind of husband at all to my Bernadette. Would she have died if he hadn't been a heretic? If there was no brother Authié? No Prades Tavernier? No heresy?" He gazed at Pierre, his blue eyes round and brilliant. "Tell me, Domine," he said. "Would she?"

He asked the old man to repeat every detail of his encounter with the friar, and with each retelling, he pictured the Inquisitor more clearly—his hungry, birdlike eyes, his sneering mouth, his large hands folding together in a sign of pity. He remembered the Inquisitor standing over him at the pulpit in the Cathedral Saint-Étienne and he knew that if he wanted to hold on to any sense of dignity as a man or as a rector, he could not smite Bernadette's father for walking in the way of Christian duty. The old man seemed neither to know of his involvement with the Good Men nor to have any desire to inform the friar of others in the heresy. He was simply at a loss in the wake of his daughter's death, and angry with the men he perceived to have taken her.

Pierre told the old man to say several Paters and advised him to try to forgive those who had led his daughter astray. "Remember Our Lord's compassion," he said. "Unclench yourself from what anger you can."

A MONTH PASSED and Pierre held the old man's secret in his throat like a taste no drink of water could cleanse him of. The Inquisitor sent him a letter, notifying him simply that Philippe Guilhabert had been apprehended—as if he were trying to suggest that, one by one, the beams of support holding Pierre from imprisonment were falling to the side.

Two months later, Bernadette's husband, Prades Tavernier, and the younger Authié were apprehended, and rumor spread in the village that Pierre himself may have been responsible for their arrest.

One evening, when he was lying on his pallet in the loft of the barn, looking out the high window at the roundness of the moon, the eldest son of Old Man Maurs—an immense, long-armed youth named Thomas—came knocking. He did not allow Pierre a moment to question him at the door, but barged in and stomped through the chickens, kicking up the straw, as if searching for evidence to prove Pierre's treachery.

"Stop," Pierre said to him feebly.

Thomas swung around to face him, his eyes torpid, his face red and perspiring. "What are you telling me?" he said.

"I am the rector of this parish," said Pierre. "You shall not question me. Or make a mess of my straw." He was trembling. "Get out if you are here to devastate my barn."

Thomas chortled. "Your barn?" he said. "The barn of your brothers, I think. While your brothers reap for their grain in the heat, you lie in the chapel and ask for tithes. Well, I won't give you tithes anymore." He stepped through the straw toward Pierre, his fingers gathering in a fist. "And if you have been a double-crossing liar, I will devastate something more than this barn." He bared his teeth like a dog.

Pierre felt his hip let go beneath him and he crouched down to the straw-covered floor. What point was there in even pretending to be this youth's superior when he was a weakling in the village. "I—" he said, and he meant to say, "I have gone to so much trouble to defend you. I have lied for you and risked my life and name. I have lost my power." But he knew such self-pitying would only further enfeeble him, and so he glared into the eyes of Thomas and spoke what little power he had left. "I have heard confession, as you know," he said. "And there is only one man in this village who has betrayed our trust. Our trust."

Thomas relaxed his fist.

"If you are a pleasant fellow," said Pierre, "I will tell you the name of this man."

Thomas kicked some of the straw that he had displaced into a pile.

"Father of the late Bernadette," said Pierre. "Our Bernadette."

Thomas nodded and retreated to the door. When he tripped over a pitchfork and nearly fell, Pierre shouted that he should be more careful.

ANY SATISFACTION Pierre reaped from humiliating the youth dissipated when the old man was discovered dismembered three days later. In one violent gesture, the power of the Maurses had been flung in his eyes, and the shame of having betrayed a confessor cut him so deeply to the quick he told himself any knife wound would be a source of relief to him. For more than a week, he performed Mass in a daze, and sat from sunset to sunrise with a knife on his lap, staring at his wrists, at his ankles, feeling the thumping of his heart. And then one day, news of Philippe's part in the apprehension of Bernadette's husband and the Good Men reached the village, and he charged up the road from the square to Ava's house. He did not know whether he wanted to wield his power by killing her before the Maurses had a chance or by warning her of the wrath coming her way. He knocked lightly on her door.

"You," she said, smiling, the tip of her long braid brushing against her hip.

He leaned toward her to kiss her mouth, but she stepped back from him. "Not now," she said. He followed her into the kitchen, and noticed that her cooking spoon and knife lay on a square of linen on the table, as if about to be wrapped away. Beside them, a bowl and a cup were stacked within her pot.

"Where are you going?" he asked her.

"Pierre," she said. "Please leave me to pack up my things."

"Without so much as a kiss?"

"A kiss, then," she said. "And then you must leave."

"Don't go, Ava."

Her lips parted. She did not speak, but gazed down at his hand, which was resting over the knife on her table. He had not realized he had moved his hand there, and he shuddered, remembering the feeling of her tongue straining against the knife in his dream.

"You have me scared, with all your seriousness," she said. "Give that to me." She held his forearm and carefully slid the knife out from under his hand. "You'll cut yourself if you don't watch out," she said. "Mind your own things. It's taken me time to put everything in order."

"Ava," he said. He had become so weak, so desperate, trying to keep himself alive in the peace of so many women, and drowning himself within them instead. It seemed to him that without Ava, he would die. "Don't go, Ava," he cried, dropping onto the bench by the table. "Don't go, please. Please."

She knelt before the bench, taking his face in her hands. She kissed his cheeks and wiped his eyes with her thumbs. "You've heard about Philippe I'm sure," she murmured. "You should be happy that he's on the side of the right."

He moaned.

"He came to me," she said. "Not exactly he, but a messenger in his place, with the news that Philippe wants me to come. Me and Béatrice. He wants us again. And it is to him that I am going."

"But, Ava," he said. He leaned his forehead into her neck and caressed her soft breasts. "I love you more than anyone in the world. Like no other, Ava. Please don't leave me."

She laughed and cooed at him as if he were a child. "Foolish man," she murmured. She kissed his eyes. "You're one to talk with all your women, you."

"No women," he said, "only you."

"Foolish, foolish," she said. "Foolish with your talk. Don't you think I know you, dear?"

She held him for a long time, and when he would not go, she made love to him sweetly. He sobbed with thanks, and allowed her afterward to sponge his limbs and his member as if he were no more than a baby.

IT WAS SOON after Ava left that the henchmen came with the news of Pons's sentencing. Pierre had been so mired within the misery of his ever-deepening ineffectualness and solitude, he had not even thought to warn Fabrisse of the possibility of her own summons. Though Ava had claimed to defend Fabrisse to the Inquisitor, she had revealed Fabrisse's name along with Pons's, and Pierre had known well enough that a summons would likely follow. What he had not anticipated was that Pons's body would be exhumed and burned, and that on that very night his life would begin again with the vision of Echo.

He passed the night by the bedside of the dying Old Woman Rives, the thrill of Echo glowing like a sensual flame in his spine. After the old woman died, he forced himself to leave, telling Fabrisse he would see to the coffin.

"I have no money for a coffin," he heard her say, his hand already on the latch of the door. He turned to her, tried to reassure her, but then the passion he had feared in her flared. She stared at him with untamed eyes, then fell on her knees, clutching at him in spasms. "I know," he heard her feral moaning, and he saw the top of her tangled hair. He struggled to break away from her grasp. "You love me," she said. She spoke with such blind certainty, he thought for an instant he had been mistaken—perhaps he loved her indeed.

As much in horror as in an effort to gather his thoughts, he looked up from her wretched figure. In a flash, by the door to the dead old woman's bedroom, he saw Echo standing naked, ever more lovely in her remoteness. She was tugging at her ear, as she had the night before, staring at him as if she understood him somehow. He felt her compassion drift like a vapor through the air, and all the self-doubt he had felt a moment before drained from him. The girl was his life. She was his life, entirely.

He glanced down at Fabrisse, and saw that she had become quite still, her eyes wide with surprise and shame. He could not bear to see her in such a state anymore. "Prepare yourself for the viewing," he said, leaving his life for the moment.

Nothing would be the same for him ever.

IN THE WAKE of the burial of Old Woman Rives, the Believers turned on Pierre, claiming that he had slighted not only the deceased with his words during her interment, but also God—who knew the words for lies. Thomas Maurs, who had been pleasant to him since their encounter in the barn, stopped Pierre in the road the day after the burial, scratching his groin as he spoke. "You don't imagine that holy water has any power?" he said.

Pierre could not bring himself to respond in the face of such insolence. He turned to proceed down the road.

"And the host!" shouted Thomas. "Do you really believe the host is anything but a slice of turnip?" He laughed, and Pierre turned around to face him. "And yet you consecrate it in the Mass as if it were God! Why do you perform what you do not believe?"

Pierre studied the youth's burning eyes—eyes that reminded him of his late brother Guillaume, seducer of Marquise. "You know very well," he said finally. Again, he turned down the road, and as he walked, he thought that—for Echo's sake—Thomas should be exiled from the village. Such rage, such virulent ill will, could only be harmful to an innocent girl.

ALTHOUGH THE FREQUENT PRESENCE of the henchmen and the burnings had augmented villagers' fear of being accused of heresy, the faith of the Good Christians itself appeared to be engulfing yet more of the village every day. When Pierre delivered Mass, he had the feeling increasingly that behind the watchful eyes of his parishioners was the spirit of mocking, and he could almost hear their silent jeers.

One evening after vespers, he was pausing to sit under the elm in the square as he sometimes did, when he heard a trickling, then felt something on his head—a wetness pouring down. He jerked away, and looked up into the tree. "Who's there?" he called, seeing the shadowy shape of a boy among the branches. The boy did not answer, and Pierre stood, wanting to shake the high limbs of the tree, but he could not reach them.

"Papa says you are nothing but a chamber pot!" the boy said finally.

"And you believe everything your father says?" Pierre demanded.

The boy did not answer, but jumped down the other side of the tree and scurried away. In the darkness, Pierre could not see him. A Maurs probably, he thought, wiping the urine from his cheek.

FALL ARRIVED, and for lack of water, the hemp did not sprout and grow for the women to crush and comb in the winter. The villagers were desperate, hungry, and Pierre wondered if perhaps it was because of this that the Church—through the mouth of the Bishop of Sabarthès—decided to levy a new tax on all within the region. The people were to pay tithes on products that came of their livestock and an additional tax of one-eighth on grains—the latter of which nearly equaled the yearly harvest tax. The Bishop wrote Pierre a letter stating that if he did not collect the tithes with strictness, he would have the Inquisitor to face. There was no money or surplus to be gathered, but Pierre went knocking from house to house all the same.

Not even the steadfast parishioners greeted him with kindness, and the Believers looked him in the eye and refused to pay. "If you are one of us," said Old Man Maurs, "you will find a way around your obligations." And his son Thomas went so far as to suggest that Pierre give what tithes he had gathered from the parishioners to the Good Christians rather than the Church. "We are hungry like the rest," he muttered, "and more worthy of living."

Though Pierre allowed the Maurses to go without paying this once, he was determined to exact what he could in order to avoid suspicion. He had to remain a free man, he told himself, a man free to love Echo.

·   ·   ·

IN THE SPRING the rain came, but happiness did not return to the village. Unrepentant, the younger Authié and Prades Tavernier were relaxed to the secular arm and burned in Toulouse. Pierre's presence at the burnings had been requested, and although he feigned illness so not to attend, rumors spread that he was on the side of the Inquisition.

One morning, he woke to a note slid under the door of his barn. *"You will be killed if you persist to walk the fence between us and them,"* it read. *"Assassins from Gerona have already been hired."* There were few in the village other than Pierre who could read or write, and he was nearly certain that none of the Maurses could have penned the threat alone. He wondered if it had been composed by the elder Authié, with whom he had lost contact after the younger had been apprehended.

Terrified, he decided to move his bed to the house of his brothers, who—he suspected—were at once sympathetic to the Believers and disappointed that he had failed as a priest to keep the village within the legitimate faith. He had never spoken to his brothers of his own disillusionment with the Church, but he had caught them occasionally eyeing him in Mass with an expression of distrust, or even disdain. When he arrived at the door to their house with his pallet and sheets, they scowled but did not question him, and he did not bother to explain.

Night after night he lay in their cellar, listening to every creak in the floorboards above, searching for a way to avoid imprisonment by the Inquisitor and yet to stay alive. During the light hours, when his mind was tricked into thinking he was safe, he mounted the bell tower of the chapel and watched Echo playing in the distance in Esclarmonde's yard. His fervor to survive intensified as he watched her, so much in the thick of life. How he wanted to live by that milk-white fawn with lazy limbs and dimpled chin.

THE INQUISITOR was quiet for a time, and Pierre was untested, and as such survived. But then, when he was at last tiring of passing nights beneath the rocking beds that his brothers shared with their wives, a messenger of the Inquisition arrived at the chapel after a vespers service. The letter he came bearing read:

May this be your warning, Pierre Clergue. I know that you are a false priest, of a parish teeming with heresy. Someday soon, your village will be surrounded, your people rounded up like sheep. We are coming, and you have a choice to make. Aid us in our attack, or be rounded up as a lowly beast. You know as well as I what your fate shall be in the latter case.

If the Châtelaine had been in Montaillou, he would have run to her now. What other woman had known him for who he truly was—a heretic in hiding—and cared for him nevertheless? Only Fabrisse, and the thought of her was no comfort to him. He sensed that there was yet another, and then he remembered the Virgin—she who had taken up so much of his heart at one time. Yes, though he had betrayed her as he had betrayed no other, he would pray to her for guidance now.

He asked the messenger to wait for him in the vestry, and then he knelt down before the altar, gazing up at the Virgin. *What power you gave me once,* he prayed. *I was small. I would not grow. And you smiled that I might follow your way.* She looked down at him with eyes at once sad and merciful, and it seemed to him that whether or not he believed in the goodness of the flesh and of the material world, he owed all the power he ever had to her. When the village had been bound to her, he had led the people in her name. To survive, to lead the people again, he must help the Inquisitor bind them to her.

He nearly wept, he was so thankful for the insight. He crossed himself and stood, making haste to the vestry, where—as the messenger looked on—he sat at the table, spread out a fresh sheet of parchment, and took up his quill to write:

On the Feast Day of the Virgin all the village will be gathered in the square at high noon. There is room enough in the dungeons of the fortress to house everyone for a time.

Before the heresy had come to Montaillou, the Feast Day had been celebrated in honor of Sancta Maria, but in the years since, it had become nearly a pagan holiday—when parishioners and Believers together feasted and danced until night fell, praising what God they would. In Pierre's mind, there was no day more fitting for the village to be reclaimed in the Virgin's name.

He gave the response to the messenger and watched from the bell tower as the man rode down the hill, past the wheat fields, and out under the fiery, setting sky. While he wanted to rejoice that at last he would be redeemed as priest, darkness stirred in his soul and he knew that he had fallen further still: he was using the Virgin to save his own life and, in the process, slaughtering the only faith he believed could save him spiritually.

NOT A FORTNIGHT LATER, in the golden warmth of a September morning, he stood in the churchyard, watching the villagers bustle in preparation for the midday feast—men carrying tables and benches on their backs, women bearing pots of fruited custards and stewed hare, adolescent girls prancing about in their finest dresses, poised to dance with the boys of their hearts until darkness fell. Now and then, he looked from the square down to the fields below the village, and the skin on the back of his neck prickled. He saw no henchmen, and prayed to God that the Inquisitor's letter had been nothing more than a test of his faithfulness. What miserable faithfulness he had demonstrated in the end. . . .

Noon approached and though there was a breeze in the air, he was damp with sweat, sure he would be sick on sacred ground if he remained in the churchyard. He limped closer to the square and saw Thomas Maurs standing under the elm with a pretty, stout girl whom he recognized as the grandniece of Na Roqua. Was the young Maurs courting her? Boys raced from table to table, playing some sort of game of chase. Pierre recognized Alissende's two among them, ruddy-faced and grinning from ear to ear. A flock of old women including the healer sat nearby, clucking with talk. As if Na Roqua sensed his eyes on her, she turned her old head his way and nodded.

He mopped his brow with his sleeve and glanced back to the fields—still as innocent and empty as before. When he looked to the square again, he saw Fabrisse descending the road, a jug of wine in her arms, and Echo trailing behind her, half-hidden in the wildness of her hair. He felt a rush of sympathy for the mother and child. What breach of faith had Fabrisse ever committed against him to deserve his betrayal of her now? And Echo . . . He could not bear the thought of the henchmen touching her, wounding her. In a moment of passion, he wanted to warn the mother and child to flee the village at once; just as quickly, however, he realized that if Fabrisse were caught on the run, her conviction in the Inquisitorial Court would be assured.

Glancing down to the square to be certain no one was watching, he walked to the bushes at the southern edge of the village, from where he had run for a time with the family Belot. Instead of following their path to the Col du Pradel—which he knew the henchmen would likely scout—he climbed up the rocky, forested side of a nearby hill. He had not planned to flee, but confronted with the languid ignorance of the villagers, he knew he could not face them as they came to recognize him for a traitor.

He walked and walked, until he was not far from the summit of the hill. Peering out from behind a boulder, he saw the village below. In the square, the villagers were already feasting at tables lined in rows. They bent their heads down to their bowls and leaned toward one another. He could almost hear their mouth-filled chatter, and thought he saw Echo's dark head at the end of a table.

Looking beneath the village, he saw nothing but fields extending to the base of the distant hills. His heart quickened with hope, but then he made out a soldier, galloping toward the village from the direction of Prades. Could it be that the Inquisitor had sent a single henchman? He searched the fields again, hoping to find nothing more. He spotted a soldier approaching from the west, and another from the east. And then the fields came alive with armor glinting in the sunlight, horses hurtling forward. Henchmen were coming from all directions across the Pays d'Aillon.

The villagers ate merrily, still unaware. He nearly shouted out a warning to them, although he knew any shouting would be ineffectual from such a distance. He saw one of the men in the square stand from his table and step in the direction of the lowlands. Suddenly, the man's hands gestured wildly above his head and the square was a jumble, villagers scattering like ants, tables toppling over, children screaming. *Run*, Pierre whispered. He saw several men racing past the houses on the north side of the hill.

At least fifty henchmen charged past the chapel and into the square, nearly stomping over those in their path as they sped to circle the colliding villagers. Pierre heard the din of distant uproar as women bent to pick up their young and men gestured over the heads of others. Beyond the raving crowd, two horsebacked henchmen forced the fugitives back to the square, crossbows pointed at their heads. A henchman kicked one of the men to the ground. As the man struggled to stand, Pierre thought he recognized him as Thomas Maurs. He felt his lungs sucking for air. *Dear God, what have I done?* he thought.

A henchman at the head of the square raised his fist, as if issuing a command, and the crowd—stiller now—parted slightly. Pierre saw the overseer in his dark, fur-lined cloak approach the henchman and pause by the foot of his horse. Pierre knew the overseer was being told of the inquisitorial order that he jail the villagers in the dungeons until they could be transported to the prisons of Toulouse. The overseer lowered his head, the henchman gestured to his fellows in arms, and then the crowd seemed to contract as villagers were corralled up the road—like beasts, as the Inquisitor had written.

The crowd neared the fortress, and Pierre thought he heard wailing on the wind, a moaning so pitiable his heart should have stopped beating from its sound. He wished it would stop. He remembered the villagers weeping on the first day he had preached as rector. It seemed to him now that they had already known he would break faith with them in the end. Agony replaced every last peace in his soul. There was no way out.

In part to torture himself further for his treachery, he watched as the villagers were shoved through a narrow door in the fortress that led directly to the underground. Those at the mouth of the door were flailing, as if someone at their feet had been crushed, and he feared for Echo in the mass of tightly packed bodies. If she was being crushed, how—in her silence—would she make herself known?

He let his head fall to the ground, and lay still for a time. When he finally had the courage to look up, he saw several henchmen stationed around the fortress and several others positioned at the edges of the village. A single unarmed man walked in the square among the overturned tables and benches, the spilled pots of feastly food. The man was wearing a habit, and even from the distance, Pierre could see that he was tonsured. The Inquisitor had come to Montaillou.

As if he sensed Pierre's eyes on the back of his head, the Inquisitor turned south, his face cocked up to the hills. *I know you are there,* he seemed to be saying with his steady gaze. *You have been beaten, Clergue. You have failed as a heretic, and failed as a man.*

PIERRE DID NOT WAIT to be found. In a daze, he tramped through the rough, untrodden terrain of the hills, knowing only that he could not face further humiliation. Vaguely, he pointed himself west, toward the grottoes near Tarascon, where, he had heard, heretics hid themselves from time to time. If not henchmen, then assassins from Gerona would surely be on the hunt for him. He climbed through the steep woods, slipping over moss and limping past leaves that shook as if with fright, past needly pines bristling when he brushed by. The very air around him seemed to weep for his crimes, and he wanted to join in, to beg for empathy. He realized that if he had been a young rector he would have been able to cry; but crying could be accomplished only with a measure of self-pity, and there was none of that left for him. He walked on, his body urging him to flee, his mind strangely unafraid of the wolves and the bears and the snakes that had always terrified him.

A taste like darkness gathered in his mouth as the forest became dim and his mind more frenzied. He sat and leaned his cheek against the scratching bark of a pine, the moisture of the earth spreading through his robe and along his thighs. He pictured the villagers heaped together in the underground, where he had first defiled his priestly vows. He saw their tearful faces, Echo clawing for space to breathe, Thomas Maurs, hurt and slumped over in a dark corner.

He slept briefly, and fragments of skin and bone inhabited his restless dreams. When he woke, he realized that if the village was devastated, he would have no parish for which to preach. He imagined himself, as if in memory, wandering alone among the gaunt remains of what was and never would be.

He did not seek shelter, though it rained softly through the night. When dawn finally licked its ashen light over the trees, he continued west on his journey, running among the dripping leaves, tripping over his vestments, wet and muddy. His hip throbbed, as did his ankle, which he had twisted so many times that his shoe had torn; and yet he was somehow distanced from the pain. He reached a bracken-covered crest and the angry northwest wind blew against his back as he ran to escape the Hell brewing in his mind. Until now, he had conceived of Hell as something removed from his life; stuffed with culpability, however, he understood Hell to be within him—caught within his very soul, and he could not imagine its black clutch ever leaving him.

Sometime after noon, he came upon a lake, shallow with still salt-water. Bathing his ankles in the reedy bank, he realized how thirsty he was, and knew he must find a stream if he was to survive. Mosquitoes bit at his feet, and he watched them have their drink before he carried on toward the caves of Tarascon.

Dusk had nearly arrived by the time he found a stream. He did not feel his thirst anymore, but his legs thrust him toward the muddy bank, and soon he was drinking from a pool of sunlight, taking sun into his mouth, it seemed. The stream was serene. He saw trout knifing through its clear water, and he thought how awful and yet wonderful it was that there were mercies in this world where there should not be. His hands reached into the cool water, groping for the fish, and then he was splash-ing after the trout as they slipped from his fingers, one after another.

When he was too chilled to move, he retreated to the bank, think-ing he would look for a branch to spear the fish, and warm himself in the dying light. As he walked to a patch of sun, he caught sight of a camp, or what seemed to be a camp, not far from the bank, before the mouth of a small cave. There was a pile of ash surrounded by a ring of stones. And a long spear, made from a knife tied to the end of a branch, rested against the trunk of a tree. No one was in sight, so he approached vigilantly, assuring himself with the thought that he would not steal the spear, merely borrow it to catch his dinner.

With the spear in hand, he limped upstream. He threw the knife down into the water, missing the trout as they flitted past him. Finally, he moved into the center of the stream, singled out a trout several spans upwater, and held the spear up in the air, poised to hurl it down. The trout neared, nearly passing him, before the knife nabbed its flapping tail. He shouted out with jubilation, and held the fish by the gills with his free hand, spinning around.

Someone was watching him from the bank. At first glance he thought it was a kind of beast, for all the pale hair that hung around its face and grew from its chin. But then he realized that it was a man, and a young man at that, with penetrating blue eyes and an unlined brow. The man was quite tall, or appeared to be, standing with one hand grip-ping the trunk of a beech tree, the other holding something slim and black—a book, Pierre realized. He wore the clothes of a townsman, though they were ragged and torn in places. If this man was not a her-mit, he was undoubtedly in hiding, and undoubtedly would be angry at having been discovered.

Pierre held the spear out in front of him, the fish flipping from the tip. "I saw your camp," he stuttered. "Please forgive me. I've been traveling for days now without food. I was so hungry." With the spear in front of him, he walked up the bank.

"You are not a Dominican," said the man, looking him over. "Not a friar."

"No," said Pierre.

"But you are a priest."

"No," said Pierre again. He glanced down at his soaked, priestly vestments. "I mean to say, yes." He held the trout farther out. It had grown quite still, and it hung from the tip of the spear pitifully. "Please, take the fish by way of apology," said Pierre. "I'll be on my way."

"Is there anyone with you?" said the man.

Pierre shook his head.

"Bring the fish, then," said the man. "We'll cook it over the fire."

AS PIERRE WARMED himself by the fire, the man speared several more trout. Under the fading sky, he cleaned the fish with a spare knife, then held them one at a time on a stick over the flames. Pierre watched as the man cooked the fish. He did not move as one accustomed to the rigors of the wild. The peasants of Montaillou were rough-mannered, their hands in the habit of breaking the necks of chickens, of skinning daily kill without pause. But this man turned the fish over the fire with precision, his fingers supporting and rotating the stick as if it were a sophisticated mechanism. No, he was not of peasant stock, thought Pierre; or if he was, he was of a family wealthy enough to hire others to do their labor. Wealth would explain his ability to read.

The man handed Pierre a bowl filled with roasted fish. "We will share the bowl if you don't mind," he said.

"Of course," said Pierre, taking a piece of the oily trout with his fingers.

"You are running from something," said the man, turning another fish over the fire. "Not the Inquisition, if you are a priest."

Pierre pulled a bone from between his teeth. "The Inquisition?" he said. "No. No." Was this man, too, running from the Inquisitor? Pierre held the bowl out to him, but the man would not take it, and so he ate again.

The man roasted the remaining fish, and finally accepted the bowl. They took turns eating in silence. After the meal, Pierre followed the man out to the stream, where they washed out their mouths and drank for a while. On the way back, the man spoke again. "I make my bed in the cave," he said. "Moss is a fair pillow if you want to make a bed for yourself." Near the fire, he stopped and looked down at Pierre. " I see that you are tired," he said. "There is no reason not to rest here."

The man sat again by the fire, taking up his book and beginning to read. Pierre wondered if it was a book of the Good Men. "It is not easy to be alone in the woods," he said to the man. "Are you not afraid?"

The man glanced from the book up at him. "When I first arrived," he said. "But not much anymore."

"And how long has it been that you have been living here?"

The man shrugged. "I followed time for a while, but then the following didn't seem to help me."

Pierre was nearly certain that this man was a heretic in hiding. He crouched by the fire, across from him. "I have heard your accent before," he said. "It is the accent of the people of Foix, is it not?"

The man raised his eyes from the book and squinted at Pierre. It was the first time that a shadow of fear had passed over his features. "I have not lived in Foix for a long time," he said.

Pierre held his hands up to the heat of the fire. He looked up at the starry sky. "Do you believe?" he said in a half-whisper.

There was a silence, and then Pierre heard the man shut his book. "I am not a heretic, if that is what you mean," said the man. Pierre lowered his eyes and saw that the man was studying him. "Though I don't suppose I would have anything against a heretic if I met one." He ran his fingers through his beard. "Did you steal the vestments you wear?"

"These?" said Pierre. "No . . . no. I am a veritable priest. . . . Though not much of one it seems." Away from the village and the Inquisitor and everything he had come to know as a man, he felt strangely freed, as if there were no price to be paid for absolute honesty. He nearly confessed everything there was to confess about himself, but he did not, and the man seemed to be grateful for his silence.

"You needn't tell me why you are hiding," the man said, gathering up his book. "I will sleep now. If you wouldn't mind covering the fire with ash yourself."

The man nodded to him as he turned to leave, and Pierre recognized something in his eyes—not fear, not restlessness, but a heaviness that came with being burdened deeply. "Is there something I can do for you, son?" Pierre said, without knowing he would speak.

The man seemed to be surprised. His mouth opened, as if he meant to respond, but then he shook his head, bidding Pierre good night.

THEY SPENT the following day in silence for the most part. The man gathered berries and nuts in the morning, killed a squirrel for their meal at midday, and read during all other times. Pierre knew better than to ask him what he was reading. He walked along the stream, telling himself he must leave and give the man his peace despite his own longing to remain. The thought of continuing on his solitary journey through the woods was terrifying to him; he knew that when he came to the Châtelaine seeking refuge, he would have to decide if and when he would return to Montaillou. With that decision, he would have to look his humiliation, his remorse, in the eye, and he would have to consider the grave threat of assassins' having been hired to murder him. But here in the woods, in the care of a man whose very name he had not been asked to shoulder, he was free from all that for a time.

They passed the evening meal as they had the night before, Pierre eating as the man roasted fish on the spear. Pierre expected that after the meal the man would again begin to read; instead, he folded his hands together and stared down at his lap, as if considering something weighty. "There is just one thing," he said at last, in a voice barely audible.

"One thing?" said Pierre. It had been so long since he and the man had conversed, he was not sure of what the man was speaking.

"Last night," said the man, "you asked if there was something you could do for me. And if it is not too much trouble, there is just one thing."

"Yes," said Pierre. "What is it, son?" He felt a surge of paternal feeling for the youth—not the feeling he felt for all parishioners, but something deeper, more personal, even physical. Yes, he felt it in his chest, like a root that reached into him, down to the quick.

"I have never been able to make a proper confession," said the man. "I left the home of my father when I was still young, and then there was never a priest to trust."

"And you want to make confession to me?"

The man nodded, his eyes wide.

"I have made mistakes as a priest," said Pierre. "I confess that to you. . . . But I pledge to keep your confidence."

"Do you pledge it really?"

"It is my obligation," said Pierre.

The man seemed to be reassured by this. "Well then," he said, sighing. Pierre saw that his eyes were moist.

Pierre took one of the sticks he had gathered during the day and prodded the fire to build up its flames. "I am an old man," he said as he prodded, "and I have heard much in the way of sin." He thrust the stick into the fire. "If you are carrying the burden of your sins, give the burden to me."

The man wiped his eyes. "My father sent me from Foix when I was a boy," he began, smiling vaguely at Pierre. "You were correct about my homeland. . . . He sent me to a school in Pamiers. 'For the purposes of learning grammar and so on,' he told me. But really, it was simply to send me away from him. . . . He was a doctor and wanted to train me, but I couldn't endure the sight of people in pain. Women bleeding." He squinted at Pierre. "Are you certain this isn't any trouble?"

"No trouble," said Pierre. "Keep talking."

Again, the youth wiped his eyes. "In Pamiers," he said, "I was made to share a bed with another boy." His face contorted, as if he were suddenly pained. He fell silent.

"And this boy," said Pierre at last, "did he do something to you, son?"

The youth shook his head, then nodded, then shook his head again. "He did," he said, "but, Father . . ."

"You needn't be afraid. Tell me."

"I didn't . . . resist him. I was lonely, you see, and . . ."

"You were a boy. That explains it well enough, I think. And you are remorseful."

"But I am not really, Father. That is just the thing." He looked up at Pierre with wild eyes, more piercing in the firelight. "I loved him," he whispered. "Not as a brother, you understand? As everything."

Pierre was quiet, waiting for the youth to continue. Long before, a confessing shepherd had told him of his love for another man. The shepherd had spoken of the vulgar acts they had performed, and Pierre had been so repelled by his descriptions, it had taken all his will not to scoff rather than administer the shepherd penance. In the forest now, however, by the mouth of the primeval cave, Pierre was filled with the knowledge of his own fallen nature—a nature he was not resistant to somehow. He felt opened up, and nothing the youth spoke of struck him as anything more than a consequence of humanity. He felt a compassion deeper than he had known possible, and he realized that he might have felt such compassion all along in his life, as a priest and as a man, breathing the air of many.

"It is not a crime to love another," said Pierre. "It is God who gives us such a capacity."

The man glanced up at him, surprised. "The master of the school was not as forgiving," he said. "He is a friar now, with the Inquisition of Toulouse, and he made it such that I had to flee."

"From the school?"

The youth nodded. "And it was then that I learned my trade. Shoemaking. I am a cobbler, not a doctor. And it was then, too, that I began to walk in the way of real darkness. Sinning, Father."

"What kind of sinning, son?"

"Of the flesh, Father."

"With prostitutes."

"Of a kind." Suddenly, he covered his face with his hands and stood from the fire. "I'm sorry," he muttered. "Thank you for your trouble, but I must carry this burden alone." He retreated to the cave, and Pierre did not try to stop him.

Later that night, as they lay across from each another in the darkness, Pierre spoke finally. "A whore is a whore," he said. "A sinner, like the rest of us."

He heard the youth begin to cry. "But there were so many of them," said the youth.

"Yes."

"So many. And I was only trying to find some comfort."

"Yes."

"But still I knew that it was evil."

"Was it evil, really?"

"Help me."

"I want to help you. Help me to help you."

The youth cried more fervently, and then his crying seemed to wear itself out, and then there was only the sound of their breathing and turning now and again over the moss, only the sound of the creatures of the forest outside, twittering and calling. After a time, the youth told him of how he had gone to Toulouse when the lepers were burning, of how he had sinned with men until one night by the river he had blistered like a leper and God had flashed His starry face his way and made a miracle on his skin—a miracle in exchange for a vow that he marry. But how was he ever to realize that pledge when he had no courage with women, when he was hiding from the Inquisition? And what woman with a gentle soul would want a sodomite for a husband?

THE NEXT MORNING, Pierre woke to find his shoes mended, resting by the mouth of the cave. The cobbler was nowhere, and Pierre took his absence as a cue to be on his way. He was putting on his shoes, when he noticed a sack hidden behind a stone near the cave. There was a wooden tablet lying on top of the sack, and a bone stylus peeking out from within it. Though Pierre knew it was not in the form of discretion to interfere with his host's things, he withdrew the stylus, took up the tablet, and etched a message into its green wax: "It is not safe in my parish now, but if there comes a day when the Inquisition dies down, you will find a home in Montaillou. Ask your way there from Ax-les-Thermes." He nearly added a request that the cobbler rub out the message after reading it, but then he reminded himself that the youth knew well enough that he was a man on the run. He set the tablet and stylus back on the sack, tempted only for an instant to look for the book the cobbler had been reading.

He followed the stream west until it met the Ariège, and then he walked north, curving to the east when he saw the mighty turrets of Foix due north, and then curving west again to the river and Varilhes. The first peasant he stopped in Varilhes told him where to find the Châtelaine, who was living now with a new husband. Rumor had it that she was dying of a faulty heart. "If you have any last words for her," the peasant said, "you'd best make haste."

Pierre did not pause to wash his face at an inn, but proceeded directly to the Châtelaine's house. He walked up the path through her garden, telling himself that if her husband was there and questioned him, he would say he was a priest to deliver last rites. An old servant woman came to the door, and when Pierre announced that he had come to see the Châtelaine, the servant eyed him with suspicion for only a moment before showing him inside. "She's resting, Domine," the servant said, as she pushed back the door to the Châtelaine's room and waved him within.

The Châtelaine lay sleeping in a bed in the corner, her face pale, as if all the color had been rinsed away. He approached her tentatively and knelt by her side. He saw tiny veins in her eyelids. Why had he never noticed those veins before?

He took her hand and she opened her eyes. "Pierre?" she said. "Have you come really?"

He sat on the bed beside her and stroked her arm. "You're unwell," he murmured.

"Dying," she said. Tears budded in her eyes.

"You must not be," he said, feeling something in his own chest let loose. There was a bowl of half-eaten broth on a table by the bed. He reached for the bowl and held a spoonful of broth up to her lips. "Take it," he said, and she opened her mouth for him.

He fed her in silence, and she cried gently, struggling to swallow. "All finished," he said, when the bowl was empty. He set it back on the table.

"All finished," she said, and closed her eyes, reaching for his hand. "Pierre," she said, after a moment. "I have heard about what you did to the village." She opened her eyes and gripped his hand firmly. "Why did you do that to those you defended before?"

He held her hand to his forehead, and then pressed it to his eyes. He could have said it was because of the tithes the Believers would not pay, or because of their threats against him, or because of his love for the Virgin or his unquenchable thirst for a power forever receding from him. But he knew the real reason lay elsewhere. He was painfully in love for the first time since Marquise had died, and if it had not been for that pain, he would have doggedly followed the Good Men's way, sacrificing his freedom in the end. How could he hope for a peaceful, fleshly future love with Echo without the promise of his freedom, of his life?

"I am sorry," he said, and he truly was.

1308 — 1322

Part III

THIRTEEN

THE VILLAGERS OF MONTAILLOU were separated by sex into cells of the fortress dungeon, and then all the children under fourteen years of age were released back onto the emptied slope of the knoll to fend for themselves. Of those villagers who remained imprisoned, some wept incessantly, some stormed with rage, some tried to flee, some shrank into themselves—stunned and pale. They were to be questioned individually by the Inquisitor, who had installed himself in the fortress banquet hall, and until a determination had been made about each of them, they would remain sequestered together, as if a plague were upon them all.

There was little talk among the women in the cell in which Fabrisse was kept. The air was too stifling, the flies too persistent, the putrid drinking water too scarce. What words passed between them were exchanged in the first few days, before hunger and exhaustion had firmly set in, and those words reflected the women's concern for their children, free now but undefended, and their nagging suspicion that the rector had turned on them, turned them in—innocent and guilty, no matter.

On the Feast Day of the Virgin, the day the village had been surrounded by henchmen, Fabrisse had seen the rector as she descended the road toward the square with Echo. He was standing at the edge of the churchyard, and even from a distance she could see that his face was pallid and glistening with perspiration. For a moment, their eyes met, and she thought she saw anguish in him, terror.

She and Echo entered the square, and she set the jug of wine she was carrying on the end of a table and told Echo to sit and be still. When she glanced back at the churchyard, the rector had disappeared. During what followed of the feast, she looked for him up and down the road. Then she caught sight of a flash of armor in a pale stubble field below the knoll. In an instant, she understood that a henchman was on the approach, and that the rector was somehow responsible. Had he denounced one of the Believers he had formerly defended? Dread gathered in her, and she imagined him hiding somewhere nearby, like a timid hunter who had laid a trap and feared the rage of his prey.

Only later, in the confines of the hot, stinking cell, did she allow herself to grasp that the rector had betrayed the village as a whole. Her feelings of protectiveness toward him turned to anger, and she recognized the tremendous pain he had caused so many people. As though she had woken from a long sleep, she saw with alert eyes that the same heretics whom she had come to resent for stealing away her husband were themselves victims now, that the man with whom she had yearned to share an all-absorbing love was the true enemy of them all. Whereas once the rector had protected the Believers, had protected and taken care of her, now he had led the wolves into his pasture. He had left his parishioners to testify against one another, to betray one another, to betray him, or to betray their own hope of salvation by telling lies to the Inquisitor, and she hated him as she never thought she could hate a man whom she also loved and desired.

FOR FIFTEEN DAYS, she endured with the others in the underground. In each cell was a meager bucket of warm water, a troughlike bowl from which they ate what was served out to them like dogs, and an excrement tub into which they relieved themselves when their urgency grew greater than their shame. The henchmen had rationed out one blanket to every five or six souls, and all communal kindness between the prisoners quickly vanished—the strongest or most demanding in each cell claiming the louse-infested blankets for themselves. Friendship, pity, and fellow interest faded. The ground crawled with vermin, sleep became impossible, tempers flared.

When at last Fabrisse was called to sit before the Inquisitor, she rejoiced weakly. She craved space and light and clean-smelling air, and had lived for days in the hope that if the Inquisitor saw her parched lips in the clarity of the hall, he would take pity on her and give her some cool water. She followed the henchman up the spiral steps of the tower, too fatigued to hold up her aching head. She did not need to look where the henchman was leading her; she had traveled the distance from the underground to the hall again and again as maidservant to the Châtelaine.

The Inquisitor was sitting at a large trestle table in the hall, whispering to a slightly younger friar by his side. Neither man greeted her when she entered the room, and so she stood at the door, silently watching them. The Inquisitor had aged significantly in the years since she had last seen him. He was something of an old man now, with straggly, graying hair and softly creased features, as if he had spent much time squinting and frowning and fretting. On the table between him and the younger friar, beside a candle flickering in a tarnished copper stand, she spotted a pitcher and a cup. She licked her lips and stepped forward into the room to make her presence further felt. The Inquisitor craned his head around to look at her, his black eyes darting birdlike over the length of her body. He scowled, as if repulsed by her, but she was too thirsty to be bothered.

"Fabrisse Rives?" the Inquisitor sputtered.

She nodded.

"Sit down," he said.

She sat on the bench facing him, and his eyes followed hers to the pitcher. He took it up, poured water from it into the cup, and drank deeply, wiping his lips when he was done. "Your husband," he said huskily. He coughed into his fist, and was momentarily overpowered by a violent fit of hacking. Then he cleared his throat, looked at her with listless, almost uninterested eyes, and spoke again. "Your husband was tried in my court. Convicted of heresy. He took his own life, did he not? Took his life according to a heretic rite?"

She licked her lips, and her tongue made a dry, sticky sound. "It is true, my Lord," she said. She did not know quite what appellation to call him by, but he did not correct her and so she continued to speak, the younger friar inscribing her words on a page of blank parchment. "If I had known what he was going to do," she said, "I would have done everything in my power to prevent it."

The Inquisitor's eyes narrowed. "But you must have known that your husband was engaged in heretical activity."

"Yes. But I did not approve of it, and I never took part in the activity I saw."

"And what activity did you see?" he asked.

She remembered the baptisms by the Good Men she had witnessed. How weary Bernadette had been from the bad birth of her baby boy. And Pons . . . He had reached to feel her pregnant womb before promising never again to touch a woman. She realized that the first baptism she had witnessed had occurred in this very hall, and that Prades Tavernier, too, was dead now—burned by the order of the Inquisitor himself. . . . How much had come to pass since the day she had stood in this room as a new bride, watching Prades Tavernier fervently commit himself to the Good Men's faith.

"I saw baptisms," she said, trying to conserve the moisture in her mouth. "Bernadette Marty's, my husband's, Prades Tavernier's. But they were sad occasions to me." She glanced at the pitcher, and the Inquisitor poured himself another cup.

"And who else was present at these rites?" he asked, raising the cup to his lips as if to taunt her.

She did not want to be part of another's conviction, but she knew silence would win her neither water nor freedom. "My mother-in-law," she said. "But she is dead now." She remembered that Jean Marty, Bernadette's husband, was as good as dead himself—imprisoned for life, it was said, in the Inquisitor's tower. "Bernadette's husband," she went on. "And the brothers Authié."

"Surely there were others," he said, and sipped from the cup.

She remembered that Na Roqua had been in the kitchen when the Good Men blessed Pons before he died, but she could not bring herself to speak against the healer. She tried to think of who had been at the baptism of Prades Tavernier, but the only presence that remained strong in her mind was that of the rector. She had sniffed out his scent and known he was hiding somewhere in the shadows by the entrance to the hall. "Perhaps Old Man Benet and his wife," she stammered. "But I cannot be certain. Old Man Benet is dead now, and his wife is old and certain soon to die."

The Inquisitor drank deeply again, and she regretted the words she had just spoken. "You wouldn't imprison an old woman, would you, Lord?" she said. "Old Woman Benet is frail, very frail, and surely innocent of heresy."

He set the cup down, regarding her with suspicion. He sighed, then, in a rushed manner, began to ask her a series of questions pertaining to the incarnation of Christ, His resurrection, and ascension. What did she believe a real Christian to be? Did she think the real Church was that over which the Pope presided? Did she trust that it was indeed the body of the Lord Jesus Christ on the altar? She tried to answer with care, but several times he cut her short, as if disinclined to listen; and she had the sense that the spirit of conviction was absent from his questions, that what he truly, passionately cared for lay somewhere beyond the bounds of the Roman Church.

He rubbed his face, as if to cleanse himself of the exchange that had just taken place between them, and then he refilled the cup and pushed it slightly toward her, his cheeks flushing with color. "Do you trust that your rector, Pierre Clergue, is innocent of all heresy?" he asked. Something about the tremor in his voice, about the way his eyes flashed with sudden vigor, told her that he was intensely concerned with the rector. He nudged the cup farther toward her, and she understood at once that the water would be hers if she confessed what she knew of the rector's heretical sympathies.

"The rector?" she said, unable to go on.

"It has come to my attention," the Inquisitor said, breathing rapidly, "that Pierre Clergue may have protected the very heretics who most threaten his Mother Church. That he may be guilty of lewd and unpriestly acts." He nodded to her, and she saw sweat glistening under the sockets of his eyes, on the skin of his upper lip.

Her devotion to the rector had only caused her pain in recent years. Still, she knew she could not forsake him, much as she was dying for drink, much as her fidelity to him infuriated her now. He was her love. Her fallen fool of a love. What choice did she have but to ardently defend him?

"Do you trust," the Inquisitor went on, his tone urgent, "that Pierre Clergue is innocent of such mortal sin?"

She felt her face become hot with emotion. "I trust," she said. "But of course, I trust!"

FOURTEEN

WHILE THEIR PARENTS were imprisoned, the children of the village sustained themselves together. Echo, however, remained alone. She had been ridiculed by fellow girls and boys since she first lost her capacity for speech; but she had never much wanted to join their fold in play and prattle. It had always been her mother who captured her attention, her mother whose attention she could never quite capture. And now that her mother was gone, she carried on with her chores as if a ghost of her mother were there— collecting eggs from the chicken coops, drawing water from the spring, and gathering kindling, nuts, and snails from the edge of the forest beyond the wheat fields. Every evening, she covered the fire with cinders and crawled onto the roof in imitation of her mother, gazing up the slope of the knoll, past the house in which she had been born—a rubbish heap now—toward the fortress in which her mother was imprisoned. Was her mother, somewhere in the dark, yearning toward her?

Before her mother had begun to drink, Echo had not recognized her face and form and words as distinctly separate from her own; but with wine, her mother started to speak about her own body's unmet needs, complaining that widows didn't have the chance to sin, as no one in the village wanted to couple with a dead man's wife. Sometimes when her mother undressed for bed, she would parade around the room naked. "And what am I supposed to do with all this?" she said, throwing her arms into the air and showing off her breasts. Echo knew it was a man her mother wanted. She wished her mother wouldn't speak about such things—things that meant her mother needed something other than her, that meant her mother was a kind of animal who could nudge her away and wander off free.

With the recent drought, her mother had sworn off wine for a time, but even then it seemed to hold power over her. Rather than regarding Echo over supper, her mother would gaze up from the table at the flagon on the shelf, licking her lips as if in hunger. And when their old house had burned and they had moved down the road, her mother had taken to sleeping with the flagon cradled in her arms, insisting that Echo sleep by herself. Sometimes late at night, Echo crawled into her mother's bed, the flagon between them. She listened to her mother's dreamy, drunken murmurs. "Pierre, Pierre," her mother said, and Echo understood that her mother was speaking of Pierre Clergue, the rector. She had seen the way her mother cried to him on her knees the morning Grandmother Rives had died, the way her mother turned her eyes in his direction whenever they passed him in the square. She knew her mother was breaking apart for lack of love from him, just as she herself was breaking apart for lack of love from her mother. Already, Echo's own voice had broken. What piece of her would break next? All she wanted was to be whole again—whole and within the comfort of her mother's all-encompassing comfort with her.

ONE AFTERNOON, when she thought she could not stand her mother's absence any longer, she went out to gather kindling, tramping through the tussocks of broom beyond the fields. Instead of stopping at the edge of the forest, she wandered into a shady stand of pines, her hands searching like eyes for a path through the trees, her heart beating wildly. She had never ventured so far away from the house alone.

Soon, she came upon a clearing, lush with fiddlehead ferns and a narrow, winding stream. She set down her basket and drank of the cool water. As she drank, she had the sense that someone was watching her, and she looked up from the water at the old, moss-covered pines all around. How silent they were, and yet alive. Their silence was a comfort to her, and without understanding why, she found herself acknowledging them with a nod, as if they were great beings she was passing on a journey.

She tramped on, not knowing quite what she was looking for—

not kindling anymore, and not her mother, but some relief from the misery of missing her. She heard a bough break in the distance, and she was suddenly afraid that a bear might be near. Though she knew it was said bears could climb, she dropped her basket and jumped up onto the low branch of a stunted pine. From there, she climbed to a higher branch, and its needles scratched between her thighs as she squatted down.

She listened, allowing only her eyes to move as she searched the forest for signs of wildlife. She saw a chough peering down at her from between the leaves of a nearby beech tree. Something rustled in the brush below her feet, and a rabbit bounded out, disappearing into a thicket of holm oak a moment later. She leaned against the sappy trunk of the tree, bracing herself. She waited.

Noon came and went, darkening the forest. Though her heart continued to beat firmly in her chest, she began to be aware of a feeling like peacefulness blooming in her, spreading through her thighs and down into her toes. Her breathing slowed, and she felt as if she were disappearing into the tree, or becoming part of the branch and the trunk, the smoothness of the bark. She heard the calling of crows nearby, and their sounds, too, seemed to move through her, to be an echo of her own silenced voice. The more she listened, the more she heard—insects buzzing, rabbits and squirrels rustling in the brush, the bells of the sheep in the faraway meadows, and the ringing of the high wind through the trees. It was thrilling, the sounds of the hills heaping on top of one another, breathing in and out. All this life seemed to her now to be one and the same as her own small life, and she did not want this endless, floating sensation of disappearing to end.

For a long, long pause, her fear that her mother might not return left her. Then, a chill prickled the skin of her forearm and the fear returned. She leaped from the branch into the thistly brush below, picked up her basket, and ran through the forest toward the twilight of the open fields and the solitude of home.

SOME DAYS LATER, she returned from the forest to find her mother sitting on the floor in front of the hearth, sipping from the flagon. How pale she looked, and thin, and strangely older. Her eyes, though sad, were focused, present. She had not been drinking for long. When she saw Echo in the doorway, she pulled the flagon from between her lips and stretched her hand out. "Come and embrace me, then," she said, smiling quietly.

Echo eyed the flagon, resting against her mother's breasts.

"Oh, Echo," her mother said. "Now is not the time to be hard on me." Her brow pinched into a frown, and she set the flagon away from her on the floor. "Come," she said, stretching her hand back out. "I am tired. Too tired to stand." She sighed. "Don't you know that you are my very own?"

Without a moment's pause, Echo ran to her and pressed her face to her breasts, crying against her strange new smell.

That night in bed, by the light of a candle, her mother told her that two days after she had been questioned by the Inquisitor, henchmen had descended into the cells of the underground and read out the names of those villagers to be liberated. Nearly half the villagers' names were called, and Fabrisse's was among them. The remainder were to be led on foot to Toulouse, where they would meet their fate by trial.

In the dark, Echo saw her mother blinking up at the ceiling. She wished she had words to comfort her. *I will take care of you*, she said with her hands, stroking her mother's patchy, matted hair.

"You know now that people can be broken, Echo," her mother whispered. "More often than not, they are broken by life somehow."

IN MANY WAYS, the village returned to its patterns of old. More than half the children were no longer without parents, and those still alone were taken in by others. The winter wheat was planted in the fields, and one Sunday in late autumn when the winds were so fierce a stand of poplars collapsed to the ground, the rector returned without apology or explanation, and Mass was held in the chapel once more.

Still, there was a heaviness, a sadness that hung over the valley; there was exhaustion in the air. For as much as everyone feared being summoned to appear again before the Inquisitor, as much as they feared for those now on trial in Toulouse, the vital fighting spirit that had animated their fear and suspicion before had been sucked out of them in the dungeons of the fortress. Even those who had been enemies found themselves glancing at one another on the road, as if to say,

"Ah, we have both escaped this once," or "Yes, I am also afraid for my future."

The one person who still seemed to kindle the flame of fury in the villagers was the rector, who came to be called the Little Bishop, for he had wielded his power indiscriminately—not as a simple shepherd priest who loves his flock much as they stray from him now and then. The rector had strayed from *them*, and they had not the stamina, not the heart, to begin to trust him again.

WINTER SPREAD its snow like an endless sheath across the fields and up, over the rising slope of the hills, as far as the jagged peaks of the Pyrenees. Villagers retreated into the den of their homes, warmed by the hearth, by the scent of oak logs burning. They were shielded from the news of inquisition for a while.

When the snow began to thaw and the first leaves of green budded out from the trees, a group of villagers returned from Toulouse. Echo was with her mother, sitting at the hearth and stuffing pillows with fresh goose feathers, when she heard a crowd of footsteps crunching on the snow. She rushed to the window and cracked open the shutters, afraid henchmen had come for her mother once more.

Outside, a huddle of sullen-faced men and women were walking up the road; she recognized them as some of the villagers who had been missing. What caught her breath was not the sight of how gaunt their faces had become, but the enormous yellow crosses stitched to the front of their cloaks. They were a small sea of yellow rising up the road, and whereas so much warm color would have ordinarily delighted her, she felt chilled now. The crosses reminded her of bells roped around the necks of cows: she knew they meant these villagers were somehow owned.

THAT AFTERNOON, her mother bundled her in a wool blanket. With the flagon, they walked to the house of Old Woman Benet's son, who had been among those to return cloaked in a yellow cross. "I have come to apologize," her mother said to him at the door. The man squinted, then gestured them inside. He watched as they sat on a bench by the hearth.

"I told the Inquisitor," her mother said, "that I had seen your mother in the presence of the Good Men."

The man kicked a log in the hearth so that the fire sparked. "You should not have done that, Fabrisse Rives," he said.

"I— " her mother said, but he held his hand up in the air, cutting her short. He sat on a bench by the trestle table.

"Not only you, Fabrisse," he muttered, hiding his face in his hands.

For a long while, no one spoke, and Echo thought she had never heard a fire crackle with such force.

"I, too, told the Inquisitor of my mother," the man said finally. " 'My mother believes anything,' I told him. 'You cannot blame her. She saw the holy way the Good Men dressed and she believed. But as for me . . . I should have known better.' " His hands fell from his face, and Echo saw that his eyes were wet. "She is in prison now, my mother," he said. "Sentenced to life in a communal cell because she would not show remorse." A strange grin came over his face, even as his eyes gleamed with tears.

"And you?" said her mother.

"Me?" He chuckled softly. "You can trust that each of us who returned today showed much in the way of remorse. And for our remorse, we have been allowed to go, on the condition that we wear these crosses for the remainder of our lives." He pointed to the center of the cross stitched in yellow felt on his shirt. "Both indoors and out, in private and in public. For the rest of our lives, a humiliation. But nothing compared to what the imprisoned are suffering now."

Suddenly, his mouth opened and he breathed deeply, then looked at the fire in the hearth. "My wife," he went on. "She is with child and awaiting trial now. Being held in a squalid house outside the gates of the city."

Echo felt her mother stiffen. "She has not yet been tried?" her mother said.

"No," said the man, his eyes still on the fire. "She and many others from the village wait and wait to speak a word on their own behalf. And as they wait, they live in Hell." He closed his eyes for a long moment. "I am not sorry to have spoken against the Good Men," he whispered.

"They told us the *world* was Hell. . . . But even the ice, the snow is lovely. Even hunger is lovely when you are free to dig the soil yourself."

SLOWLY, MORE VILLAGERS crept back from Toulouse. Some had passed all their days away from Montaillou detained in a house outside the gates of the inquisitorial city, awaiting trial; others—after long periods in prison, either in communal cells or in fettered, solitary confinement—had been persuaded to convert back to the true faith and were shown mercy by the Inquisitor, who exchanged their sentences of life imprisonment for the vow that they remain faithful to the Church, forever to shoulder the burden of the penitential yellow cross.

However briefly or interminably villagers were imprisoned, once they had been found guilty, their property reverted to the Church, and increasingly henchmen arrived to seize land and livestock, to be managed by the overseer and those in his employ. Many houses were burned during this time, and for the children growing in the wake of inquisition, these burnings became something of a tragedy of nature: like a flood or a drought, they were observed as a source of great suffering, but accepted as part of the general difficulty of life.

In the year following the siege of the village, the elder of the Authié brothers was captured on the road from Beaupuy to Ax. Word traveled to the village that the Inquisitor—in the course of a single Sermo Generalis—had sentenced the Good Man to be relaxed to the secular arm along with seventeen other men and women. The only villager of Montaillou among them was Philippe Guilhabert, Ava's husband, who after spying on the Inquisitor's behalf, had relapsed into heresy and been caught attempting to flee to Catalonia.

Philippe and the Authié elder were burned in the square of the Cathedral Saint-Étienne, and it was said that in the moments preceding the Good Man's death, he proclaimed that if only he had been allowed to preach freely, the entire region might have been saved. Soon after the burnings, Ava wandered back to the village with her daughter to witness her house's being torched. It was to be the last time in a great while that the henchmen presided over the destruction of a home in Montaillou. After the Inquisitor's simultaneous sentencing to death of so many men, the Pope had become disapproving of his zeal and limited his power such that he could not pass severe sentence without the approval of someone in the ecclesiastic branch of the Church, such as a bishop of a diocese. With the news of this shift, the villagers of Montaillou breathed a sigh of relief. The Inquisitor had been dominated by another more merciful, and if an end to inquisition was not visible on the horizon, a paler version of it was near.

THROUGH ECHO'S ADOLESCENT YEARS, signs of the Inquisition left the village; henchmen ceased to arrive with summonses, and even the yellow crosses floating like ghosts up and down the hillside faded in their power to surprise and scare. What continued to haunt Echo was the loneliness her mother's wine-drinking inspired in her, a loneliness she fled from by escaping to the forest and the realm of comfort she had discovered as a girl.

Lying in the clearing on the moss-covered ground, she stared up at the silent, mighty pines and listened to the sounds of the stream, loosing itself quietly over stones. She relaxed into the pleasure of seeing—the silvery remains of spiderwebs, the dark green of vines melting up the trunks of trees. When it rained, she watched the trickle of water on the waxy green of the leaves, the little purple blooms among moss twittering under the falling water's weight. And when a flash of sunlight broke through the tops of the trees, she peered through sun-blotted eyes at the stream, stippled with so many points of light. She breathed, aware of the scent of sap filling her chest, her belly, of a feeling of expanding, dissipating. Here, she was free from the frustration of never being able to express herself in words, free from the hunger for a mother who never searched her eyes for a glimpse of the words she might have spoken. Occasionally, she felt the pang of loneliness in her breast, but then the sound of wind whispering through the trees carried her up, up, and she was tingling, warm, sun-filled, laughing. She was without herself, and yet strangely complete.

Deeper in the forest, and over a steep slope, she discovered a hole where water pooled before plunging down in a cascade. In the summers, she soaked her toes there, sometimes undressing completely to feel the sun on her back, the air under her arms, the wet bank beneath her thighs, beneath her buttocks. Once, quite by hazard, she caught a glimpse of her face reflected in the pool, and she was mesmerized by the reality of her own physical presence: she squinted into the water and bunched up her features, watching as her reflection instantly did the same. Over time, she continued to study her reflection, and noticed her nose becoming more prominent, her cheeks going slack. And when she examined her nude body—her swelling thighs and breasts and belly—she saw her mother's body emerging in her own. Dimly, she was aware that her body was growing toward fertility, toward coupling, toward what her mother had yearned for all these years, and a part of her was terrified that when she finally did become a woman, her mother would want nothing more to do with her. Still another part of her exalted in the changes overcoming her body. Like a fruit, her body was ripening, and she had the sense that when it finally, fully burst forth, the silence gathering in her would somehow be released. Yes, her body was preparing for something enormous to take place.

IT WAS NOT until the summer before she turned fifteen that she first began to suspect that her body was preparing for the rector. One hot evening at dusk, when she was tending to the cabbages in her mother's garden and could not seem to cool herself down, she noticed a figure standing on the bell tower of the chapel below. The figure was obscured in the dying light, but quickly she made out the smallness of its stature and the shape of priestly robes. The rector was facing her, as if staring at her, and for a long moment she stared back. Then the skin between her shoulder blades prickled and she was suddenly shy. She glanced down at the cabbages. A moment later she glanced back, but the bell tower was empty.

That autumn, she worked for wage in the fields of a wealthy peasant farmer, digging small holes in the soil into which the seeds of winter wheat would be planted. In the middle of a field, she heard the voice of the rector. She peered up from the soil and saw him not far off, speaking with the farmer about tithes owed to the Church. As if he sensed her eyes on him, he turned his head slightly, gazing past the farmer at her. Their eyes caught, and she thought she saw something of pain in his features before he turned back to the farmer.

Not long after, she was entering the forest, finding her way through a thicket of branches, when she sensed someone behind her. She saw nothing and continued on to the clearing, where she kneeled by the stream for a drink. Still, she had the sense that someone was near, and she looked up from her cupped hands, past the trees from where she had come. A marmot scuttled over a pile of fallen leaves, startling her, and she braced herself against a large rock. Her heart thumped madly in her chest and she was sure the rector was watching. She was breathless, yet unafraid somehow. She knew the rector would not hurt her, and a part of her thrilled at having been found.

IN LATE AUTUMN, the rector disappeared for the fourth time since the village had been seized, leaving the chapel bells silent and the Mass unheard. With each disappearance, the villagers grew more divided in their sympathies for him—those who persisted in calling him the Little Bishop claimed he was in league with the Inquisitor, spying on parishioners and hatching a new plan to root out what remained of heresy; others rumored that assassins were after him, and argued that he should be shown compassion, for he was a lowly man of the Church and could have done nothing to defend them from the fury of the Inquisitor.

With the rector's disappearance now, Echo noticed her mother's drinking deepening. It was as if, by steeping herself in wine, her mother were trying to drown out the terrifying thought that the rector might never return. Echo, too, felt the pinch of fear. Staring from the road up at the newly fallen snow on the peaks of the mountains in the distance, she wondered how he would survive through the winter if he stayed away for long. She prayed that he return, with his predatory, mournful, embracing stare.

One evening during his absence, when snow had begun to fall lightly in the village, her mother spoke of her own fear of dying. She was spinning by the fire, her eyes glazed over from wine. "When it comes to dying," she said, "never count on a man, Echo. . . . My mother died without a man by her side. Not even the priest who gave her rites remained. . . . No, a man won't be there when you are dying. Or he will be there, and he won't give you what you need."

She pulled fibers of flax toward the spindle. "What you need is someone large," she said. "Not a small man, no. They cause too much pain. Someone large, with a large ear to listen, and a large mouth to kiss. A large hand to stroke your hair. Someone strong. But a man is never strong like a woman. It isn't in him not to think of himself." She touched her head, found a hair near her temple, and plucked it. "As much as I tell you, you'll expect something more."

She squinted at Echo, as if in an effort to detect desire for the rector in her. Echo's cheeks became hot and her eyes fell to the floor. She had done nothing but exchange glances with the rector, nothing but sense his furtive presence in the wood, but she felt as though she had betrayed her mother—stolen away her only love.

WHEN AT LAST the chapel bell sounded with the rector's return, Echo waited for him to seek her out. Through the days, she peered from the kitchen window to the bell tower, forever desolate, and when she ventured through the drifts of snow into the forest, the lack of human tracks other than her own confirmed her sense that the rector had not come. Several times, she passed the chapel during vespers and felt the urge to enter, to force her presence upon the rector, but as strong as her temptation was, she walked on. She told herself that if the rector had felt any kind of passion for her once, it was passion no longer.

Winter passed, and then spring slipped away. When summer arrived, with its long, sunny days of reaping, she put her mind on the color of the wheat that she gathered, on the sound of sickles slicing through the stalks all around. Then one day, around the time of her sixteenth birthday, she bent down to pick up a bundle of wheat and noticed a smudge of blood on the instep of her heel. Squatting in the privacy of uncut stalks, she traced a line of red that ran to the opening between her legs, and she knew at once that her first blood had come, her first change in life. She rubbed the line of blood away, dread gathering in her. Was she a woman now? Would her mother soon try to be rid of her? She crept through the fields toward home, hoping the farmer to whom she had hired herself out would not catch her.

That afternoon, her mother returned from wine-selling as she was soaking her stained linens in a bowl of water, trying to scrub the blood away. "So it has happened to you," her mother said, staring at the stains.

After supper, her mother was kinder. She boiled a cup of wine mixed with water, saying the warmth would soothe Echo's womb, and she demonstrated how a woman might fold a square of cloth into her linens to catch her monthly blood as it fell. "Many things to look after," she said. "Someday, you will teach this to your own daughter."

Echo felt her throat tighten. It was the first time her mother had acknowledged the possibility that one day she, too, might give life.

That night her mother's kindness turned sour. After drinking through a flagon of wine, she began to speak words Echo had never heard her utter before. "If a fuck is what he wants, he'll get a fuck," she said, staring into the hearth. She glared at Echo. "And don't think I don't know that you want one!"

Echo shook her head and covered her ears.

"I've seen the way you look at him!" her mother snapped. "Stare at him. And he—no, he can't stop himself from staring in return. . . . Nice, fine body like yours. What would he want with old meat? He'll get a fuck if he wants one. I'm no miser."

Suddenly she flung the flagon to the ground and stood, grabbing Echo by the wrist and dragging her out the door. Echo fought against her, but her mother dug her nails into her skin and yanked her down the road.

"Domine!" she shouted at the chapel, beating against the latched door. "Come out and see what I have brought for you! Fresh meat that is ready to be taken!" Echo broke away from her, cowering among the graves in the churchyard. "Domine!" her mother shouted again.

Slowly, the door opened. The rector stood within, his face ashen. When he saw Echo hiding among the crosses in the yard, he frowned. "Take your mother home," he said.

"Home!" her mother cried. "Do you think home is any comfort to me? Nothing but alone for all these years and the thought in my mind—" She beat her forehead with her palm. "That you stared at her and not me!" She pointed at Echo, and her mouth curled. "So take her! You've ruined my life! Go ahead and ruin hers! I give her to you! And don't think she's as innocent as she seems! Always overheated, with that look of hunger in her eyes."

"Fabrisse," he said.

"Don't!" her mother cried. She stormed past Echo toward the square.

Before following her mother, Echo nodded quickly to the rector. How else, in a moment, could she have indicated that she was at once sorry to have troubled him, ashamed of her mother's words, and aware of the bond that had been forming between them—a bond that even on this miserable night, the first of her womanhood, had been strengthened.

HER MOTHER did not speak a word to her about that night, but Echo saw by the quivering, unsettled look in her eyes that she had not forgotten what had happened, and that what had happened had been a grave humiliation to her. When Echo had been a child, her mother had told her of how she had battled to preserve her own vergonha—a woman's honor, a woman's pride. Now Echo saw only sadness, only defeat in her eyes, and she feared her mother's vergonha had been lost entirely.

She passed the days of her first blood tucked away in the house, and her mother brought her bowls of broth and bits of bread, never pausing to smile at her. *Mama,* Echo said with her hands, catching her mother by the sleeve, but her mother would not look at her.

At last, the blood came to its conclusion, and Echo flew from the house to the forest. Was she not expecting to find *him* there, waiting for her in the clearing? When she saw him, sitting on a rock by the stream, then standing up to face her, his arms held out from his sides and the same look of deep concern in his eyes, she smiled and covered her face with her hands. She felt as though—for the first time in her life—she were being seen, fully recognized. In his look was boundless understanding, and all the frustration she had felt of late, all the pain, poured up from her soul and out her eyes. She began to weep.

"Yes," she heard him say. "I am sorry for what your mother said in the chapel."

How much her mother's words had wounded her, she realized. It struck her suddenly that she would never have the closeness with her mother that she craved, and she cried with further abandon.

"Yes," he said again.

Through her tears, she saw him walking tentatively toward her. He came within an arm's reach, and for a moment they stood facing each other—she sobbing fitfully, and he shifting his weight from one foot to another.

"Would you mind—" he muttered, and without thinking, she fell against his chest. She smelled the musky scent of his robe, heard his heart beating quickly. *His heart*—how fragile and human he seemed.

His fingertips touched the back of her head. She felt them begin to pet her hair, and she relaxed into his embrace. It was strange, so strange touching him, this man she had only seen.

Soon, he was leading her to the bank of the stream, drawing her down, and then she was lying on her side, he sitting over her, stroking the tears from her cheek. She turned blindly toward him and glimpsed his eyes, green and alive.

"What do you need from me?" he said. The thoughtfulness behind his question made her tears come more quickly.

His cheeks were chapped from the sun, his hair more gray than black. There was sweat on the bridge of his nose and stubble that she had never noticed over his lip and along the ridge of his jaw. She searched his eyes, calm and unabashed in their gaze, and she had the sense that his life had been much wider than hers, deeper with complication and loss. What frustration and pain she felt was diminished in the face of his greater life, and she yearned to bridge the gap between them, to leap all at once over the precipice of their awkwardness, their strangeness, to find the relief of knowing each other fully.

As if he felt her urgency, he pulled her head to his chest and kissed her hair. "You are a mystery, such a mystery," he murmured. "And you will have to tell me if I am ever mistaken about what you need from me, Grazida."

The sound of her name startled her—it had been so long since anyone had referred to her as anything but Echo. She remembered that her mother had told her it was he who had baptized her as a baby, spoken her name as he welcomed her into the family of the Church, and it occurred to her that he had likely touched her body then, when she had been defenseless, a new creature in the world. She would not yet have known to be ashamed; she would not yet have learned to be silent. Perhaps she had cried aloud with the touch of his hands on her naked body.

"Grazida," he said. His eyes implored her for permission. Permission to be near her, she thought. Permission to look upon her, to speak her name. She felt his trepidation, his yearning for her, and she wanted to ease him as she longed to be eased. She felt for his arm and gently drew him down.

"I don't want to hurt you," he said, his eyes full of anguish. "I am an old man and no good for you."

Yes, you are good for me, she wanted to say. She watched as his eyes widened, traveling down the length of her body.

"You are beautiful . . . beautiful," he said. "A woman now."

She drew his face to hers and tasted the warmth of his mouth.

He kissed her, then suddenly sat upright, lifting her skirt and pulling his own robe over his hips. For a fleeting moment, she saw his nakedness, then he leaned over her, crushing her down.

Though she was surprised by what he did, never for a moment did she think she might not want just this from him. She closed her eyes, giving in to his weight, to the pain of him striving to be within her. This pain, this breaking through of her body was her opening to him, becoming him, yes. She allowed him to spread up through her belly and down to her toes, and she became the air he exhaled, the dampness of his sweat, his moaning pleasure. She saw the face of his soul, trembling and eager, wounded.

"Forgive me," she heard him murmur. But what was there to forgive? For he had come to her, endeavored to know her in her silence, exposed his own silence to her, and in all her life, she had never felt so *with* another.

FIFTEEN

N EARLY EIGHT YEARS BEFORE, when Pierre had fled from Montaillou for the first time, he remained with the Châtelaine in Varilhes until she died, and then—when he heard rumors that not a henchman remained in Montaillou—he wandered home through a violent windstorm, half-hoping the trees collapsing in the forest would knock him down. He returned to the cold silence of the villagers, and their blinking, distrustful eyes. Weary of his own cowardice, of his unpriestly urges and weakness of spiritual ardor, he did not attempt to rekindle their devotion to him. He was a traitor, a filthy old man, unworthy of respect or pleasure. He tried to smother the flame of desire burning in him for Echo, and without ever pausing to defend his honor, he relaxed into his tarnished reputation, performing his priestly obligations without passion—as might one far from the benevolence of God.

Two years later, the healer Na Roqua—who had recently been released from prison in Toulouse—stole into the chapel while he was biding time in the vestry, her cloak of yellow crosses wrapped around her middle. With an expression of exhaustion on her lined features, she warned him that assassins would be coming for him by daybreak, hired by those members of the family Maurs not rotting in prison with the others. "You know I am not proud of you anymore," she said, her eyes moist. "But I have loved your mother. And I suppose I have cared for you in some way. I don't want to see you dead, God knows."

He was neither stunned nor self-pitying, but grateful for her honesty. When she fled from the chapel, he did not stop her with the question of how he was to know when it would be safe to return to the village. Such a question would have suggested that he thought himself worthy of saving, and of the risk he knew she was taking by betraying the Maurses now. He watched her disappear, unable to speak his thanks, and when the night was black he slipped into its deadening embrace, frightened of the wilderness, and yet unafraid of death somehow.

Then, and once thereafter, when the healer again came to him with caution, he fled to an inn in Tarascon. Dressed in the clothes of a layman, he drank in a tavern and hid from the memory of the whores he had once taken, the little Mondinette he had abused. What eased his mind were thoughts of the cobbler he had met while escaping the village for the first time. How kind, how honest the cobbler had been, and where was he now, with his bright, troubled eyes, and his noble hands? In many ways, their discussions seemed to him to have been the most uncloaked exchanges of his life. He had not been trying to gain anything through them. He had heard the cobbler, and without a thought he had offered him a piece of his heart.

EACH TIME he returned to the village, unsure if it would be only to meet his killers, he was weaker of body and spirit, less able to stifle his longing for Echo. Despite the countless times he reminded himself that he was the uncle of her mother and a decrepit old man, undeserving of her bright newness, he spied on her more and more—from the bell tower of the chapel, from the edges of the wheat fields, through the parted shutters of the window in the room where she slumbered. Occasionally, when he lost all temperance, he followed her from the fields to the forest, where he hid behind a boulder and watched as she silently slipped into a kind of waking sleep. She lay with open eyes by the bank of the stream, and her presence, her stillness, seemed to silence the very forest: the great trees, the birds mating, the leaves falling to the ground. Now and then, he could imagine himself lying beside her, but it was a shadowy self—a self that might have come into the light if only he had been younger, better.

Then, during the autumn of what would have been her fifteenth year, when he was nearly fifty-eight, he began to notice her staring in return, and his mind was cast into an oblivion of uncertainty—was she silently inviting him to approach, or suggesting that his staring was a burden to her? In a fever, he followed her to the forest again, trailing too closely behind. She seemed to sense him near, and sat with wide eyes rather than reclining along the bank of the stream. Though he desperately wanted to break through the tangle of trees and confess himself to her as he could confess to no one now, he retreated, hating himself for stealing away her only solitude.

THAT SAME AUTUMN, Na Roqua gave him the signal that assassins were again on the approach, this time hired from Ussat rather than Gerona. Instead of fleeing west toward Tarascon as he had before, he headed east, inspired to save himself only by the thought of Echo. Without a destination in mind, he walked and walked, down among the lizards and wet rocks of the steep Gorges du Rébenty, along the broom-banked River Boulzane, and out into a hazel copse, where he found a spring for drinking and an abandoned grange for a night of shelter. The next day, he ventured farther east, through forest and vineyard, to the sacked fortress of Quéribus, carved above the sheer face of the highest crag in view. When he had been in favor with the Good Men, they had told him about this fortress—"the last citadel of the Good Christians," they called it. Most of a century before, the fortress and those within it had been defeated by battalions crusading against heresy, now the hollow immensity of the fortress was a dizzying reminder that he was powerless not only in the face of his own Believing parishioners, but also in that of the larger Inquisition—capable of crushing who and what it would at will. He watched the sky setting violet over the ravaged ramparts and felt very, very small.

That night, he came upon a hamlet and paid to board with an old woman who told him the sea was not far off. He had never seen the sea before, but he had heard of its great, blue swells, like ripples in a lake, only larger. The sea was said to be loud, roaring in places, and quiet as a reedy, shallow pool in others. Vaguely, he had the sense that this was what he had traveled so far east for. In the morning, he thanked the old woman and carried on, through fields of green grasses and past a large saltwater lake that, at first, he mistook disappointedly for the sea.

When at last he mounted the crest of a rocky hill, he was struck by a vision that squeezed all breath from his body: blue, gilt with shimmering light, crashing in waves on the rocks below, and extending to the end of the world. It was the most unencumbered sight he had beheld in all his life. He felt as if he were witnessing the unfathomable vastness of God.

Carefully, he made his way along a precipitous path down to a narrow cove of sand, where he stood terrified. When he had the courage, he kicked off his shoes, approached the water's edge, and touched his toes to the foamy, white surf. The sun glinting off the waves beckoned him to enter further, and he did, stunned by the forceful tug of the sea pulling him in and down. He was knocked over, and as he struggled to stand, gasping for air, the thunderous sound of the waves crashed in his ears and the troubled waters of his own soul broke open. He had been living a kind of death, he realized, slowly killing himself in all his shame and remorse. But he did not want to be dead. No, he wanted to live!

He clawed his way to the shore, fighting to breathe, and when he stood again on the sand, he laughed loudly, his belly heaving. Wet and shivering, he rested on a sun-warmed shelf of rock and fell asleep. He dreamed of drinking water from a trough, of Marquise sleeping beside him on a bed of waving sea. He was alive, still alive, with the chance to live more. When he opened his eyes in the early light of dawn, he told himself that life was not to be squandered.

HE FORBADE HIMSELF to spy on Echo, allowing her life to thrive in private and his own regretful soul to heal. So it was that one hot night the following summer, as he was sitting in the vestry, preparing the first sermon in years he felt to be divinely inspired, he was truly aghast when Fabrisse pounced upon the chapel door with the news that Echo was ready to be taken. And when the girl looked at him with her dark, anguished eyes, acknowledging a secret bond between them, he was frightened of the torment such an acknowledgment would bring to both of their lives.

The torment set in without delay, and the following day, and for five days after, he waited for her in the forest between the midday Mass and vespers. Then, on the seventh day, she appeared, pale, her hair still uncovered and wild. What was there to be done but comfort her? When she cried, her tears were as understandable to him as any words of grief—she was pained by the embarrassment her mother had caused her, pained by the awkwardness of this very moment, and pained perhaps, too, by the knowledge that he had spied on her in this secret place. Though he knew there was an element of fear in her tears—fear of what was to happen between them imminently—he sensed that there was also an element of relief: the pretense that they were not already intimately yoked together was over at last, and now she could let all the strain of pretending fall from her.

He was careful at first not to be more than fatherly in his affection, but each touch of her hair, of her cheek, seemed to burn with the fire darting up from his loins. He led her to the bank of the stream, and when she looked up into his face with half-open, teary eyes, she seemed at once a child and a woman.

"What do you need from me?" he asked her, and then asked again, and then regretted asking when he saw a flash of distress pass over her features at not being able to respond in words. As much as he had been inhabited by thoughts of her for years, he had never truly considered the difficulty voicelessness presented for her. He had never considered that she might be frustrated within silence rather than sheltered by it.

Without warning, she drew him down to her, and he moaned without meaning to, told her he couldn't bear to hurt her. "I am an old man, and no good for you," he muttered. She kissed him, and despite all reason, he gave way to recklessness, uncloaking her, himself, without seeking permission. He lay against her, trembling, terrified of breaking her open. For a moment, he felt the beat of her life in him. Then the moment was over.

"Forgive me," he murmured, and he thought of how he had watched her in the clearing from behind the boulder, how he had imagined a better version of himself lying at her side.

Afterward, she drew her shift up and off, as if she wanted to reveal still more of herself to him. Her body was milk-white as it had been when she was a child, but gleaming now with fertility—her breasts budding up small and rosy, her hips slipping out from the curve of her waist like hills. She took his hand and pressed it to the places that pulsed with her secret, warm life, and he rubbed his cheek against the tender skin of her belly, kissed her until he was moved to move within her once more.

In silence, they huddled together until the hour of the vespers service had come and gone and the moon came up over the pines. "May I see you tomorrow?" he whispered, and she looked up into his eyes with a wistful expression, nodding.

Do you like me? she seemed to ask. He drew her closer, kissed her hair.

"I will walk with you as far as the forest's edge," he told her. "And then you run along, and I will watch to be sure you are safe."

When she left his side, he stood in the shadow of the trees, watching her lope through the moonlit fields. She turned back to look at him once—perhaps to be sure that what had happened between them was more than a dream—and he stepped out from the shadows into the moonlight, waving to her with abandon.

SHE WAS WAITING for him in the wood the next day, smiling, jubilant. Before he approached, she pulled off her shift and stood, naked and shivering. He undressed without a word, shy even in the presence of her unabashedness. She took his hand, examined it for a moment, then pressed it to her cheek, to her lips, to her cheek again. Her lips opened and her eyes squeezed shut, as if in silent laughter. Then her eyes darted open to meet his.

Through the weeks that followed, they met again and again to make love, and she thrust him closer, thrust their bodies together, as if to make up for the words she could not speak. Within her, he basked in a kindness, a warmth that seemed to him at once carnal and spiritual. She was far sweeter than he had imagined. She wanted to be happy. She wanted to give to him. She watched him like an animal aching to please, to put a smile upon his face. And in her utter openness to him, to the love that passed between them, she was defenseless, tender as a growing shoot.

Always when he withdrew from her body, she studied his eyes, as if for a sign of his satisfaction, and sometimes, holding onto his hand, she fell into a deep sleep. He watched her breathing steadily, and it seemed to him that her body—her wheat-worked hands, her hair like black water, her glowing eyes and fertile mouth, the swelling slope of her haunch—reflected not only the unguarded goodness of her soul, but the goodness of the world.

He had spent most of a lifetime believing that his imperfect body was a prison to his soul. Even when he had turned against the Good Men in the name of inquisition, he had remained faithful to their belief that the world was corrupt, all matter the work of Darkness rather than Light. But now, he could not distinguish the end of flesh from the beginning of Spirit, the end of Echo from the beginning of God. One balmy Sunday after Mass, when Echo led him naked up to a shallow pool, he caught the reflection of trees in her face, and in an instant the distance between soul and matter disappeared for him. Later, lying with his ear to her belly, he heard the distant echo of God's pulse, and increasingly he saw God in everything living and thriving—in the roots of the trees and the nests of the choughs. His entire sense of truth dissipated: if God shone in the world, then the world must be good, flesh must be good. And what sense was there in shunning the body if the body shimmered with the beauty of the soul, if the soul shimmered through the senses of the body?

The days grew colder, and soon even the heat he made with Echo was insufficient to keep them warm out of doors. They began to meet in the house of her mother while Fabrisse was out selling wine. In the evenings, when he passed Fabrisse on the road, he saw by the heaviness of her stare that she knew he was taking her daughter as she herself had drunkenly enjoined him to. She was suffering, but he did not allow himself to suffer for her. He lived in ardent carelessness and in joy, his thoughts far from inquisition and assassins and remorse.

Now and then he wondered if he should not extract the amulet from behind the statue of the Virgin, where he had hidden it through the years; then the thought of his life moving into Echo's, the thought of their child beating within her center, was too thrilling. He chose not to think about how he would be able to remain in the village as a father. He chose not to think at all. Unlike so many of the women he had known, she touched him and gazed at the shapes of his body as greedily as he touched and gazed at her. His kisses seemed to nourish her more than fruit, and very often when he moved within her, he had the sense that she was on the verge of calling out in pleasure. He called out for her, and she was soft and strong and endless as the sea, her liquid warmth swelling in waves through him, through her, until he was lost and gasping, cleansed of himself like a newborn. He saw her open face smiling beneath him and knew that she had been born, too—she, a child once, now a woman.

THE FIRST BLOOMS of spring appeared, echoing Echo's own blooming. Then the Easter season of confession began, and he listened unrepentant and overflowing with compassion, unafraid of touching, of
taking the hands of those who were sorrowful and in need of touch.
Oddly, he felt himself a truer priest than he had been since he was a
young man.

On the last day of confession, after he had extinguished the candles on the altar and was cloaking himself in preparation to meet Echo
in the wood, the youngest of the brothers Maurs appeared in the chapel
door. The youth was no more than nineteen or twenty, and had been
too young at the time the village had been seized to have been arrested.
After the inquisitorial raid on his family's land and possessions, he had
hired himself out as a shepherd to wealthy noblemen in Aragon, and
was thus absent from the village most of the year.

"Have I come too late to confess?" he said, and Pierre wondered if
the members of the family Maurs had abandoned the idea of assassins in
order to kill him with their own hands. The youth did not appear to be
armed, but Pierre readied himself for attack nevertheless, reaching for
the brass snuffer on the altar.

"I will only be a moment, Domine," the youth said. His gaze
moved to the snuffer. "Please, Domine. I need to be heard."

Slowly, Pierre set the snuffer down. The youth wiped the rain
from his face and approached, crossing himself and glancing up at the
statue of the Virgin with a frown. He knelt, and when Pierre sat across
from him, he folded his hands together.

"It was I," the youth said, in a voice more of a boy than a man.

"You?" said Pierre.

"I . . . You were sitting under the elm in the square," he said. "And
I . . . I used your head as a chamber pot."

Pierre remembered now. Years before, he had been sitting under
the elm when a boy urinated on his head, then raced away before he
could be caught.

"I am sorry, Domine," said the youth.

Pierre cleared his throat and coughed into his hand. Was this part
of the Maurses' plan—to soften him to them, to make him unsuspecting?

"Last night," said the youth, "the old woman Na Roqua died."

"Died!" said Pierre. He had been so taken up with Echo, he had forgotten the healer, forgotten her allegiance to him. And now she had slipped away, or even worse, been killed on his behalf. He had not had a moment to thank her, or to seek her advice on how he might survive without her cautionary kindness.

"You know there are few of my family now free," said the youth. "And those of us on the outside of prison, those of us in Montaillou still, blame you." He paused. "For a long time, we have wanted you dead, Domine. But throughout, the healer never ceased speaking of your good side. . . . Last night, when she was in a fever, she called us all around. She said an angel of the Lord was at her ear, whispering that none of us would have peace if you were killed. . . ."

The youth fell silent, and Pierre heard his own heart thudding in anticipation.

"I would not have believed her, were it not for a man I met in the winter pastures of Peniscola," the youth continued. His eyes fell to his hands. "A shepherd called Michel. I told him of the assassins my brothers and I had hired to kill you. That we would not be at peace until our family was avenged. . . . But he . . . he said that if we succeeded in killing you, we would kill all hope of our own peace. 'Sorrow, hate, that is within you, not without,' he said. 'It is not possible to kill your anger by killing another.'"

Again he fell silent, as if deep in thought. "I told my free brothers that the time had come for peace with you." He squinted up at Pierre. "Perhaps if you trust us, Domine, you will help our father, still in prison. You will help our brothers."

Pierre reached forward and squeezed the youth's shoulder. "You have my trust," he said, and even as he spoke, he wondered whether, if he did not succeed in helping the Maurses, they would turn on him again.

BY THE TIME the youth left, the day had turned stormy, and Pierre made haste to meet Echo, his mind a blur as he limped through the wet wheat fields. He was humbled by the knowledge that the healer, even in the throes of death, had battled to preserve his life.

When he arrived in the wood, he spotted Echo crouching under a tree that wept with rain. She, too, was weeping, soaked through and gripping her skirt in her fists, her teeth chattering together. Without words, he went and kissed her wet, miserable face, her eyes—wild and afraid—that latched onto his.

Do you like me still? she seemed to ask him.

"You should not have waited for me in the rain," he told her. He stood and tried to pull her up, but she resisted, shook her head violently. "You should be home in front of the fire, Echo."

She inhaled sharply, then broke into a fit of tears.

"What is it?" he asked. "Echo, please." Again, he tried to pull her up, but she fought against him. In exasperation, he stepped away from her, and she clutched the edge of his cloak, clinging to his leg.

The rain beat down, cold as winter, and though he knew they both would likely suffer the consequences of remaining in the wet outside, he sat down in the mud and held her. She shivered and cried and made short, breathy coughing sounds, and for the first time, he hated her silence. How could he hope to comfort her if she could not give him the words he needed to understand her grief?

She nestled against him and fell into a strange sleep, mouthing words he could not read. He kissed her forehead, burning to the touch. Why had he not noticed before that she was in fever?

"Echo!" he said, shaking her awake. She opened her eyes, startled, and when he dragged her up from the ground, she did not resist him.

HER MOTHER was spinning by the kitchen fire when they entered. She watched with bland eyes as he led Echo to the hearth, removed her dripping shoes, and stripped off her shift.

"Something to dry her with," he said.

Fabrisse rose from her spindle, left the kitchen, and returned with a fleece and a bundle of coarse cloth.

Together, they spread the fleece on the floor and began to dry Echo, who stood in a kind of waking sleep, eyes closed, teeth chattering.

"She is with child, you know," said Fabrisse.

Echo opened her eyes and gazed at him, a queer, hopeful look on her face.

"No," he stuttered. "She is in fever. She is ill."

"She is with child," said Fabrisse. "Vomiting for days now."

He stood speechless. As much as he had known that pregnancy

was possible, inevitable even with all the lovemaking they had done, he found himself stunned to the core. He blinked dumbly at Fabrisse, waiting to be chastised for Echo's fall. But Fabrisse was as silent as her daughter.

"I will fetch the healer," he said, and then corrected himself. "A doctor. Someone."

HE WASTED NO TIME, but journeyed to Prades d'Aillon, hoping to find a healer there. As he walked, his hip aching intolerably, he wondered how he ever could have delighted in the thought of a child beating incarnate within Echo when he was a priest with priestly obligations— obligations not only to the Church but to the Inquisitor, to the Believers, to the Maurses.

For an awful moment, he wished the young Maurs had indeed taken his life. It had been so many months since he had considered the villagers imprisoned due to his betrayal, so many years since he had received word from the Inquisitorial Office, and he did not know if the Inquisitor had forgotten him since his powers had been curtailed by the Pope, or if the Inquisitor was observing him still from afar, waiting for the right circumstances before pouncing.

He remembered the old rector, who had lived openly with his lover and their daughter in the village. Nothing was the same now. The only hope of fathering as a priest without attracting scrutiny was to run to Palhars, a diocese between Aragon and Comminges-Couserans and out of reach of the Inquisitor, where it was said priests still kept mistresses publicly. But fleeing could be a grave risk: if he and Echo were caught by anyone motivated to feed the Inquisitor with information, their lives would be made intolerable. And she was the daughter of his niece. Even in Palhars, they could be condemned harshly.

He found the house of the priest of Prades and knocked on his door. Without much in the way of regret, the priest told him that the only woman known to heal maladies in the village had been living with her sister in Baga since winter. "As for a doctor, I have heard there is one who attends to peasants in Ax," he said, frowning at the puddle of rain Pierre left on his kitchen floor.

Pierre knew it would be impossible to make his way down the steep path to Ax in the dark and the rain, and he limped back to Montaillou, punishing himself all the while with thoughts of Echo dying like Marquise. He must pray to the Virgin, he told himself. He must pray fervently for the life of Echo and their child.

Approaching the village, he saw lights flickering through the apertures of the chapel walls, and he mumbled self-reproof, thinking he had forgotten to extinguish the candles on the altar in his haste.

He found the door to the chapel partly open. Within, a man lay at the foot of the Virgin. He sat up with a start as Pierre stepped onto the chapel floor.

"The door was unlatched," the man said, his voice tired.

For a moment, Pierre could not speak for emotion. "My friend," he managed to stutter. "Cobbler."

SIXTEEN

THREE DAYS AFTER the cobbler Arnaud had last seen the rector in the wilderness, the odor of solitude had become too much for him to bear, and he packed up his few belongings and left the cave and the woods that surrounded it. He walked south, toward the mountains and the pastures of tall grasses, where shepherds and those fleeing Inquisition were said to roam. He intended to find a village out of the domain of the Inquisitor, where he might work as a cobbler and by some miracle of fate or will attract the attention of a gentle-hearted would-be wife.

He left the Ariège for a time and followed a web of streams flooded with rainbow trout and char. When he descended a mountain pass, entering into a lush valley, he met the Ariège once more, and then the river lost itself in the Segre and he came across the summer dwelling place of a group of shepherds preparing their herds to go south for winter. Sitting with the shepherds around a fire crackling with pine branches, the smell of sheep dung sharp in the air, he ate enormous slices of garlic pie, drank cupfuls of wine. Curiosity gleamed in the shepherds' eyes, and he knew they suspected him of heresy. *Better heresy than sodomy*, he thought. Though he had ached for human contact for what seemed like years, he kept his distance, careful not to touch the hands of one of the men filling his plate, not to brush the knees of another sitting beside him before the fire—as if through contact with him they would be able to surmise his tainted history.

As it happened, the eldest of the shepherds, a man named Baudoin, was soon to be married and was now on his way to Baga to return sixty-three sheep to the noblewoman of whom he was in the employ. "She will need another to lead the sheep south," he said to Arnaud. "You could shepherd them. And these old rascals could teach you how."

Too intoxicated by the company of others to refuse, Arnaud followed Baudoin the next day to the home of the noblewoman, who struck the shepherd's name from her book and frowned in surprise when Arnaud bent down to write in his own. "You can write, Arnaud Lizier," she said, turning her dark eyes to meet his, searching—he thought—for traces of heresy or lost privilege in him. "You will find that the life of a shepherd is one of liberty." She smiled. "When it comes to sheep, you are answerable to me now. But as for the rest, you are free."

SO IT WAS that as quickly as he had sworn on bone to apprentice to Jean the Cobbler, Arnaud came to be a shepherd. With the sixty-three sheep in tow, he followed the others and their flocks over rangetops and through valleys, the bells of the sheep clanging, wind whipping the tall grasses and his beard and his hair. In the evenings, they erected fences to contain the sheep, and slept under the trees or in hastily constructed dwellings of branch and stone. Arnaud listened to the men snoring in sleep beside him and tried to hide from the memory of Master de Massabuçu snoring across from him and The Small. He knew he must never allow himself to feel as much as a flicker of desire for one of the shepherds. He had made a promise to God, a promise that—he knew in the depth of his heart—he was in part neglecting by choosing to reside with only men in the wild now.

Along the journey south, he came to enjoy the company of a shepherd called Michel, a man of forty-odd years, with rugged hands, silver black hair, and a mouth that ceaselessly filled the air with words. Often, the two of them would watch their sheep browsing the bracken of the plateaus together, Michel talking as Arnaud listened.

"If you ask me," Michel said one afternoon, after bemoaning Baudoin's decision to marry, "even if Baudoin returns to shepherding, he will be a shepherd no more."

They were sitting on a wide stone, and the breeze was so soft and dry, Arnaud thought if he closed his eyes and lay back, he would fall into a languorous slumber. "No?" he murmured.

"By God, no!" said Michel. "For what do you think a shepherd is?"

Arnaud turned to him, remembering the noblewoman's words. "A free man?"

"By God, yes!" said Michel. "You've learned quickly! A free man!" He paused for only a moment, and Arnaud noticed his cheeks flushing pink—with the wind or exhilaration. "The men who are most free are men burdened by sheep!" he went on. "With sheep, a man must move constantly. What can he own that he cannot carry on his back?"

Arnaud did not answer, and Michel stood on the stone and howled. "Nothing! Nothing!" Not a sheep paused to look up at him, accustomed to such outbursts of jubilation, perhaps. "Some clothes, an axe, a pot to cook with, a sack of grain if a man is strong! And for the rest of it—fine house, fine land, fine wife—" His face contorted in an expression of revulsion. "He cares not a stitch for it!"

He sat with a huff and leaned toward Arnaud. "I will tell you a secret," he said, lowering his tone. "More than one man has offered me his daughter for a wife. But I am a shepherd. What would I do with a wife but die unto myself?"

For a brief time, Arnaud wondered if Michel was the same sort of man as he. Then they passed San Mateo, and Michel left camp to find a woman of the night, returning at dawn, bleary-eyed and mumbling about the pleasures of women with hips fleshy enough to grab hold of.

IN THE VAL D'ARQUES, they settled into the winter cabane, a single room with a meager chimney and a floor of trodden dung. Though Michel was in name the chef de cabane and so in charge of cooking, Arnaud quickly came to assume responsibility for the evening meal each night. He enjoyed watching the men eat the mutton and eggs, the liver and fish he had prepared. And busying himself with the cleaning after the meal, he listened to their conversations without having to speak a word himself.

It was in the evenings after supper that he learned of the Good Men, and in doing so, of the shepherds' own beliefs. Four of the six of them were sympathetic to the Good Men's ways and thought that at all cost they should be given charity. "Why give your fleeces to Saint Anthony and the Virgin," said one, "when the Good Men are in need? Give the Good Men a fleece, and you will benefit far more greatly. For they pray for those who give them charity. And pray with unsurpassed effect!"

"It is true," said another, "that their bodies are like those of any other men alive. They have flesh, yes. And bones, yes. And noses just like the lot of us. But they alone live as the apostles did. They never lie. Never take what is not given them. Even if they found a gold coin on the road, they would not take it unless someone offered it to them first. Surely peace is better reached through their faith."

Michel was not one of those to speak ardently on the Good Men's behalf, but neither did he argue against their supporters. Because he was so rarely silent otherwise, Arnaud found himself wondering if Michel had something to hide with respect to the heresy, or if he considered the matter of faith too grave to debate aloud. Only once did Michel address the subject of the Good Men, and his words were measured. "It is true," he said, "that the Good Men practice the ideal of poverty. It is an ideal once preached by the Dominican friars. An ideal the friars no longer seem to live by."

ONE NIGHT in late autumn, a boy on muleback came laden with supplies and gossip. Over supper, he told the shepherds that the rector of Montaillou had returned to his parish after a long absence, and that he had been tight-lipped and lofty when questioned as to his previous whereabouts.

"The rector of Montaillou?" said Arnaud, turning from the rabbit stew he had been stirring over the fire.

"You know him?" said one of the shepherds.

"Know him?" said Arnaud. "No—I . . . Very distantly."

Another shepherd who often spoke in defense of the Good Men eyed Arnaud as if he were a stranger. "He locked all his parish up and gave the Inquisitor the key," he said. "They call him the Little Bishop of Sabarthès, because he is destroying the country with his little power, conspiring with the Inquisition so."

There was a long period of silence, and then Michel clapped his hands together, as he often did to raise spirits at the break of day. "More stew, I think!" he exclaimed.

"Yes," said Arnaud, his voice shaking. He turned back to the fire, wondering if it was possible that the same gentle priest who had welcomed his confession with comfort could indeed be in league with the Inquisitor. He remembered the wheezing sound of the rector's breath in the cave at night, the quiet way he had watched their supper fish being skewered over the fire. No, he would not blindly believe what these men had to say of the rector. Even in this place of liberty, he knew, men could be slandered unfairly.

THE DAYS GREW SHORTER, the nights of men snoring in sleep stretched on, and the ewes grew fat with unborn lambs. Then, during the season of Christmas, the ewes fell into labor, and Arnaud watched in agony as Michel reached into their bodies, easing out one slick, bloody lamb after another.

When all the babes were delivered safely, Arnaud experienced an elation such as he had never known. He felt that in some way he was part of the great spirit beating in the babes, in their tired mothers, in Michel and the others who had boldly pushed their hands into the mothers' centers. How alive they all were, and dependent on the earth for continuance! The lambs were nourished by the milk of their mothers, who grazed the earth for food just as farmers sowed the earth to cultivate wheat. The lambs, their mothers, the farmers, the shepherds— all would return to the earth, and how would they be any different from one another then? Together, they would provide sustenance for new life.

Soon after the lambs were born, Arnaud dreamed of being born himself. He had the sense of being suspended, enveloped in a kind of viscous warmth, and then he felt violent pressure, yearning. He woke in a state of rapture, and knew with absolute certainty that he had remembered his mother. He had been within her womb, had wanted to leave her, but she had not wanted to let him go.

FOR THE NEXT EIGHT YEARS, he remained in the employment of the noblewoman of Baga, straying from the trampled path between the summer cabane in the Pal Pass and the winter cabane in the Val d'Arques only when wars between neighboring lords forced him and the others to move their flocks to a new camp for a season.

With time, he learned to birth lambs himself, to make cheese as pungent as it was soft, and to detect the presence of wolves before as much as a distant howl. He felt ever more a sense of belonging, not only with the shepherds—whom he came to regard as brothers, not only with the sheep, but also with the flowering meadows and the biting winds and the thistly bracken always prickling at his toes. Though he understood more and more about the heresy and agreed with its premise that the realm of the senses was forever one of change, and thus of loss and desire and grief, increasingly he could not deny the invigoration such loss and desire and grief inspired in him. In truth, his awareness of his own life was heightened when he suffered sadness at the loss of a shepherd to marriage, or when a sheep he cared for died. There was something tragic and yet beautiful about the moaning of the ewes as they labored, about the sounds of a faraway shepherd grunting as he freed himself of his seed. Even the desire for Michel he sometimes could not smother struck him as being as lovely as it was dangerous. And he did not want to leave the wildness of the wild, much as he sensed God's eye upon him, much as he knew he must attend to his promise to marry and reproduce.

Often, he and Michel were the last to remain awake at night, and they would sit before the fire, warming the bottoms of their feet, thinking. The Inquisition had been quiet for many years, and he knew there was no longer reason for him to remain in hiding in Catalonia. He remembered the invitation the rector of Montaillou had inscribed on his tablet long before: *If there comes a day when the Inquisition dies down, you will find a home in Montaillou.* Perhaps the rector would know of a young woman suited to be his wife. . . .

One night, Michel interrupted his thoughts with a question. "What is burdening you, Arnaud?" He continued without waiting for a response. "In all these years, I have never seen you lose your temper. You've never taken a whore, and you don't laugh when we tell lurid jokes. . . . There is sadness in your eyes. Are you trying to be a saint?" He raised his hand. "No," he said. "No. Don't answer."

They were quiet, listening to the fire sputter, and Arnaud felt his heart quickening. He wanted to excuse himself to sleep, but Michel spoke again.

"My grandfather told me something that I suppose someone told him," he said. "I think I will tell it to you now. . . . If you are searching for God up there"—he pointed to the ceiling—"forget it. You will never know when this world was created. You will never know the face of God by looking away from yourself." He gestured to Arnaud. "Look within. Learn about who is in there, what you truly love and hate. And fear. Learn what gives your eyes their strange stare."

Arnaud felt heat rising to his cheeks. He wanted to tell Michel that he knew himself well enough, and that part of what he was could not be in the world.

"If you look, really look," continued Michel, "you will find God in yourself, Arnaud. Or that is what my grandfather told me. That the distance between Him and you and me is an illusion. 'The kingdom of the Father is spread out upon the earth, and men do not see it,' he said. . . . 'I am thou, and thou art God. . . . We are brothers, nature our Godly blood.'"

Arnaud could restrain himself no longer. "I do feel that we are brothers, Michel," he said. "But I cannot believe that I will find God by examining myself. . . . God wants me to be other than I am."

"Impossible," said Michel.

"It is true," said Arnaud.

"I don't believe it," said Michel. "No. What would He want you to be that's so different?"

"I cannot tell you."

"Perhaps I already know."

Michel studied him with soft, almost longing eyes, as if he did know Arnaud's secret and shared it. Arnaud was suddenly ashamed and he looked down, covering his groin with his fist. He sensed Michel moving toward him, felt fingertips brushing against his cheek and gently taking hold of his chin, as if to draw him forward in a kiss. How easy it would be to give in. . . .

"No!" Arnaud shouted, standing suddenly.

Michel gazed up at him, bewilderment in his eyes.

"God wants me to marry!" Arnaud said. "To marry a woman!"

Michel's face fell flat. "You know nothing about freedom, Arnaud," he said. "It is you who believes you should marry. . . . So marry. You are not much of a shepherd anyhow."

HE DID NOT WAIT for the lambs that had been born that year during Christmas to be weaned, but packed up his old shoe-making supplies and the earnings he had saved, and convinced one of the shepherds whose flock had dwindled to accompany him quickly to Baga. There, he struck his name from the book of the noblewoman, who shook her head as she pressed a small purse of change into his fist. "I thought freedom suited you, Arnaud Lizier," she said.

From Baga, he traveled through the moist meadows of the Llobregat River valley, crossed a mountain pass still wet from winter, and walked until he found the Sègre and then the Ariège. At night, he slept under the fierce spring stars and tried not to think of Michel—of the easy, untroubled manner in which he had opened himself to tenderness and touch with another man.

When at last he arrived in Ax-les-Thermes, he followed the advice the rector had written in his tablet, and asked his way to Montaillou from there. The day turned stormy, and the climb up the mountainside to the village was almost impossibly steep. By nightfall the village was in sight, perched in the moonlight on top of a hill surrounded by newly cultivated fields. Even in the dim light, he saw that the fortress was not insignificant in size. Below it, among the houses holding fast to the hillside and twinkling with firelight, he saw large black piles, too angular to be dung heaps. For a moment, he was overcome by a feeling of dread and wanted to flee. Then he saw a little chapel at the base of the village, and he pressed himself to continue.

Not a soul was to be seen on the road or in the square by the graveyard. He decided to crouch down beside the door to the chapel to shelter himself somewhat from the rain. As soon as he leaned his weight against the door, it opened, and he entered the chapel, stepping over points of moonlight falling from the apertures of a wall. He made his way to the altar, lit three candles, and gazed up at the flickering features of the Virgin's face, crossing himself as he had when he was a boy.

He removed his wet cloak and shoes, and lay on the floor by the Virgin's feet. "Good Mother," he whispered, and though he felt vaguely frightened and displaced, a heavy peace crept over his eyes, and he could do nothing but close them.

HE WAS AWAKENED by a creaking sound, and he sat blinking at the shrunken shape in the doorway before recognizing the rector. "The door was unlatched," he stuttered, and it occurred to him that the rector might not remember him.

"My friend," the rector said after a moment's pause. "Cobbler."

Arnaud sat in silence, stunned, as the rector rushed toward him, kneeled down, took his hand, and clutched it in both of his own. He was soaking wet from the rain, his cheeks flushed from the cold, his eyes gleaming softly in the candlelight. "How good it is to see you," the rector said. He smiled and stroked Arnaud's hand. "And how changed you are. A man now."

The rector, too, was changed—grayer, with an older, more wearied face. "I cannot tell you how often I have thought of you," he continued. "But I don't even know your name."

"Arnaud . . . Arnaud Lizier."

"Pierre Clergue," said the rector. "Call me Pierre and I shall be pleased."

"I will try."

"Arnaud," said the rector. "The sight of you now is a tremendous comfort to me." His eyes darkened, and Arnaud wondered if he was ill, or suffering in some way.

"Father," he said. "Is something troubling you?"

The rector turned to the Virgin. "A girl in the village," he said. "A dear young woman. She has fallen ill with fever, and I have been to Prades in search of a healer, but there is none." He gestured gloomily toward the door behind him. "Tomorrow I will go to Ax at the break of day to search for a doctor. . . . It is for the girl that I came to pray."

"I should leave you," said Arnaud, moving from his place before the Virgin.

"No," said the rector, reaching for his hand again and grasping it firmly. "Stay."

Arnaud watched as the rector crossed himself and folded his hands together. He had never observed a priest moved to tears over the illness of a parishioner, and he wanted to help the girl as he might. It had been years and years since he had accompanied his father to the bedsides of ailing patients, but he remembered well enough what he had learned of fever and disease then.

He waited until the rector crossed himself, signaling the conclusion of his prayer. "Father," he said. "I may not have mentioned to you before that my father was a doctor. Is a doctor still, perhaps. In Foix."

"A doctor?" said the rector. "Yes. I believe you did tell me."

"And I learned much from him before we parted ways. . . . I know something of fever. I could do my best to help the girl."

The rector's eyes brightened. "My friend," he said, "again you save me."

THEY RUSHED from the chapel through the muddy graveyard, the smell of rain saturating the air. Arnaud stopped at the roadside to pick some wild lavender. "For the fever," he explained, but the rector did not seem to hear.

The girl's house was at the very edge of the village. She lay on a fleece before the hearth in the kitchen, blankets piled over her. Her teeth chattered together, but her open eyes were placid, moving to the rector as he and Arnaud came near.

"Echo," the rector said to her, and she smiled distantly—as if, in some way, she were gazing upon him from afar.

On a bench by the hearth sat a woman whom Arnaud took to be the girl's mother. Her face was bloated, pink, as if she had been crying for weeks, and her unconcealed hair was thin, almost balding. She wrung her hands together, standing from the bench. "I have covered her and covered her!" she said. "But still she shivers!"

"Fabrisse," said the rector to her. "I have brought a man who knows something of fever. Arnaud Lizier. He is an old friend."

The woman nodded to Arnaud, and he nodded in return. "May I go to your daughter, Madame?"

"Do as you must," said the rector before the woman could answer.

Arnaud bent down over the girl. She smelled of grass and soil and sweat. For an instant, he was reminded of the ewes and the smell of their fleeces after a shower. He pushed away the hair stuck in curls to her flushed face, and she gazed back at him without a shadow of shyness, as if she did not recognize him as someone she had never known. He felt her forehead, her cheeks, far hotter than he had anticipated.

"Your fever is quite high," he said to her. "Do you hear me? Do you hear?"

The girl nodded dimly, shifting her gaze again to the rector.

"She does not speak," her mother said. "Has not since she was a child."

Arnaud studied the girl's eyes, still mysteriously placid. Her pupils were contracted, her eyelids a bruised purple, and the veins at her temples engorged. His father had told him once that a woman's eyes were the mirrors of her health. But what did these signs mean?

"We must uncover you," he said to the girl. "These blankets are only raising your fever." He turned to the rector, meaning to ask him to leave so that the girl's privacy might be guarded, but the rector stooped down and threw the blankets off himself. Neither the girl nor her mother seemed in any way surprised by this action, or troubled by the rector's continued presence in the room.

Naked, the girl shivered more violently. Arnaud glimpsed her pubic hair, her breasts, the dark recess of her navel. He had not seen a naked woman other than the woman his father had cut open to extract the nonborn, and fear threatened to overtake him as it had when he was a child. The girl curled onto her side, knees against her chest, as if to protect him from her nakedness somehow.

"How long has she been hot?" he asked her mother.

"Since this afternoon," the rector answered. "Or at least since then. She was sitting in the wood in the rain when I found her."

"And has her fever broken?"

"No," the woman said. "It seems only to have risen."

Arnaud took the girl's wrist in hand, counting steadily to himself as he listened to her pulse—shallow and concentrated, and a bit fast. He remembered that his father had once diagnosed a man who had a shallow, fast pulse with incurable infection. That man's tongue had been coated with a thick, white substance.

"May I look into your mouth?" he asked the girl. She turned her face toward him, opening her lips and exposing her wet, red tongue. "Normal enough," he said to her, and she smiled at him slightly. Something about the manner in which her eyes watched his made him feel as though she understood his fear of her body. He smiled at her in return.

He touched her abdomen, probing her appendix as his father had taught him. He asked if she felt any tenderness, and she shook her head no. He felt for swollen glands under her arms and over her chest—a practice he had watched his father perform when plague was in question. He felt no lumps, but noticed that her breasts were firmer than they appeared. He asked if she had urinated in recent hours, and then asked to see the chamber pot in which her urine was contained. As he had almost suspected, the urine was cloudy, so brown it seemed burnt. His father had always said that a man or woman with cloudy, burnt urine was a man or woman no longer pure, and as such at risk of infection. He knew he ought to examine her genital region for signs of redness or inflammation, but he could not bring himself to do so yet. First, he would try to lower her fever.

"I'll need a bucket and some cloth," he said to her mother. "And a cup, and the coolest water to be found."

When the supplies were brought, he filled the cup with water and held it to the girl's lips, raising her damp head from the fleece. She drank a few sips, then closed her eyes, laying her head back down. In the bucket, he soaked the lavender, plunged the cloth into the mixture, and sponged her forehead, her shoulders, the back of her neck, her arms and fingers. He moved to the bottom of the fleece and sponged the base of her feet, her ankles, the gaps between her toes.

Cloth in hand, he stood and went bashfully to her mother. "Her back and chest and womb should be cooled with the lavender water," he said. "And the skin under her arms. And much heat accumulates between the thighs. It would be best if you treated her there." He paused. "And you would help me much if you searched her genitals for redness and irritation. I fear infection."

The woman stared at him for a moment before speaking. "She is with child," she said, her teeth clenched.

"Fabrisse!" cried the rector.

The woman glared at him. "You'll have me be quiet about your sin now?" she said. "Now, when my daughter is ill? Dying from infection? It is you who infected her!"

For an awkward moment, the three of them stared at one another, the rector shamefaced, the woman flaring with anger, Arnaud comprehending the words she had just spoken.

"She is not dying as yet," Arnaud said finally. "And in any case, we should not speak that word in her presence. . . . In all likelihood, she is not infected. I simply want to be sure." He faced the woman. "The rector and I will leave the room, and in the meantime, you will examine her and cool her down further. . . . Fevers do not like the light. If she is better by morning, we won't need to go to Ax for a doctor. . . ."

"And the child within her?" said the rector, his features knotted together.

Through the window by the hearth, Arnaud saw that the rain had stopped. "Let us go to the garden," he said. "Soon we will know more."

Outside, the air was soft and cool, and they stood for a time in silence.

Arnaud gazed into the distance at a stand of poplars bathed in the blue light of the moon. "I have been meaning to thank you," he said to the rector, hoping to ease the awkwardness between them, "for the kind note you left me in the wood. . . . I have been shepherding since, and without a home in a manner. . . . Not that it was a hardship for me. I adored the freedom shepherding allowed me. But I wasn't attending to the promise I made. . . . You remember . . . Do you? . . . The promise I made to God to marry."

But the rector was not listening. He was gazing up at the moon with pleading eyes. "She must not die," he murmured. "She is a dear girl. Dear to me."

FABRISSE FOUND no visible sign of infection upon examining her daughter, and by morning the fever seemed to have left Echo's body entirely. She was able to walk to her room, where she sat propped up by pillows, covered with a sheet and eating salt-pork broth with such vigor Arnaud had to caution her to slow down.

Relieved and thankful, the rector invited Arnaud to the house of his brothers for a morning meal. As they walked up the road, they passed the charred remains of what appeared to have been houses—the same black heaps, Arnaud realized, that he had seen the previous night from afar. Littered with dung and waste, the ruins were as ghastly to smell as to behold. "Inquisition," the rector said without further explanation.

The wife of one of the rector's brothers cooked them a breakfast of eggs and fatty pork, and they sopped up the runny yolks and grease with bread still hot to the touch. "Now you must sleep," the rector instructed him, showing him to the barn behind the house. When Arnaud refused to take the rector's bed as his own, they pitched together a pallet of straw beneath the loft, and Arnaud spread out upon it without pausing to remove his clothes.

It was dark when he awoke to find the rector standing over the pallet, a lantern in hand. "Has the fever returned?" Arnaud stuttered.

"No," the rector said, but there was sadness in his eyes even so. "She is up and about already. Wanting to return to the wood, I suppose."

"She must rest," said Arnaud. "Three days of rest after high fever. It may still return. And with the child inside her . . ."

The rector paced to the other end of the barn, his lantern casting light from side to side. "Arnaud," he said. "I have been considering what you said last night."

Arnaud did not remember what he could have said worth consideration.

The rector turned to face him. "As a priest," he said, "I made a vow to be celibate, never to marry. . . . I was a young man then . . . even younger than you, I suppose. How old are you now?"

Arnaud shrugged. "Thirty. Thirty-two."

"Yes, I was younger," the rector said. "I was twenty-three, and didn't know what I was promising. . . . Isn't it odd that God wants his priests not to take a beloved other than Himself, other than His Church, and yet wants the rest of men to fill the earth through reproduction? You made a promise to marry, to reproduce. I've never forgotten the miracle He gave you for that."

He knelt beside Arnaud, set the lantern at the edge of the pallet. "If I knew of a woman who would be your wife," he said, looking Arnaud in the eye, "would you have her? Do you truly want to marry?"

Arnaud was so taken aback, a moment passed before he could answer. "I made a promise," he said. "Of course."

"You made a promise, I know," said the rector. "But do you *want* to marry? Could you spend the rest of your days as a loyal husband?" He sighed. "I wish I were a better priest, Arnaud. I wish I did not have to disappoint you and others with my weakness. . . . But I have never wanted to be celibate. And I ask you to ask yourself what the point of a promise is if one cannot keep it. If one does not want it from the bottom of one's heart."

Arnaud studied the rector and recognized him for the first time as a kindred spirit, a man similarly torn between two loves: love of God and righteousness on the one hand, and love of the things of the earth on the other. Did Arnaud himself want to marry? He wanted to be at peace with God, at peace with himself. And could he be a loyal husband? He knew well enough that if he willed himself to be loyal in deed, he would; but to be loyal in heart . . . that depended on the woman he shared vows with.

"Who?" he asked, and even as he spoke, he knew the answer.

"Echo," the rector said. "She is a good girl. And she would do you well as a wife."

Arnaud gazed up into the shadowy eyes of the rector, and saw what Michel must have seen in him: the weariness of a man unable to live his life fully. The rector loved Echo; she was the wife he could not marry, carrying the child he could not father in the light, and he needed a man to provide his child with a name.

"But will she have me really?" Arnaud whispered. "Will she want me? Have you asked her?"

"She will have you," the rector said. "She must."

WHEN ARNAUD was a child, he had been witness to the betrothals of two female cousins, and in each case, the groom-to-be had presented his intended with a kiss and a ring and a promise that he would indeed take her as his own. Arnaud wanted to see Echo before the wedding, to present her with a ring, if not a kiss, and to assure her mother that he was a master of his trade, fully capable of earning an honest living. But the rector would not allow him to pay the girl a visit. "She is in no state to be seen, Arnaud," he said, as if he had forgotten Arnaud's capacity for healing, and the state the girl had been in when Arnaud had seen her before. "She is still weak from fever. . . . And as for a ring, you need not spend what money you have saved. My mother's ring will do. Echo is not a girl for finery."

So it was that Arnaud did not see Echo again for the remainder of the week. Then, on Sunday, in the calm light of late morning, he stood beside her at the door to the chapel, a crowd of gossiping villagers gathering behind them as they waited for the rector to emerge. Arnaud could not help but steal glances at Echo, at her eyes, dark with illness or remorse, at her hair, uncovered but crowned by a coronet of dusky pink flowers. She wore a threadbare, dingy blue tunic, trimmed with fur falling off at the collar. The dress gave Arnaud the impression of fallen, ancient splendor; Echo, whom he remembered as a woman not slight of shape, seemed shrunken within it, withered. She hung her head, would not return his smile with the same kindness she had given him when she was truly bare, and he understood why the rector had not allowed him to see her. He never would have agreed to the wedding had he known it would grieve her so.

The rector appeared in the chapel door, an open book in one hand and a vessel of holy water in the other. He stared at Echo as if at an apparition, and she glanced up at him, fingering her tear-stained cheeks as if to give him testimony of her sadness. The rector's eyes fell to his book. "Does anyone present know of an impediment why this man and this woman should not be joined together in matrimony?" he asked. A rumble of whispers passed through the crowd. Echo lifted her chin as if to speak, and Arnaud nearly spoke for her, but the rector continued with a brief prayer.

When Arnaud was told to repeat the vow the rector uttered, he was obedient. "I, Arnaud," he said, "give my body to thee, Grazida, in loyal matrimony."

"And she receives it," the rector responded. "And as she cannot speak the vow herself, I bless you now in matrimony, in the name of the Father, and of the Son, and of the Holy Ghost." He sprinkled them with holy water, blessed the ring that he took from his pocket, and gave it to Arnaud, telling him to slip it over Echo's thumb, index, and middle fingers with the words, "In the name of the Father, and of the Son, and of the Holy Ghost."

The girl spread her fingers out, and Arnaud pushed the little ring over her knuckles. "In the name of the Father, and of the Son, and of the Holy Ghost," he said.

"Now place the ring on her fourth finger," said the rector.

Arnaud did so.

"With this ring, I thee wed," said the rector, gazing at Echo. "This gold and silver I thee give."

"With this ring, I thee wed," repeated Arnaud. "This gold and silver I thee give."

"With my body, I thee worship," said the rector. "And with this dowry, I thee endow."

Echo peered down at the ring on her finger and Arnaud repeated the verse, wishing to God the ring had truly been his to give.

THE CEREMONY was followed by a nuptial Mass inside the chapel, during which Arnaud and Echo were made to join hands before the altar as the villagers untied her hair, veiled them both with a pall, and

bound them together with a cord of white and purple. After the benediction, the rector lifted the pall and gave Arnaud the Kiss of Peace,
telling him to convey it to his new bride. Shyly, Arnaud turned to Echo.
He kissed her quickly on the cheek. When still she would not look at
him, he feared his lips had repulsed her.

There was a grand feast after the Mass. As Arnaud learned, the
rector had taken it upon himself to purchase goods and hire servants
for the affair, and Fabrisse's house was strewn with garlands of white
blooms and rosemary. In the garden, tables were assembled and covered
with legs of mutton and oranges and apples, jugs of spiced wine, roasted
ducklings, and a swan still in plume. A jester entertained the feasting
villagers with mock birdcalls and tricks of acrobatics, and a jongleur accompanied by the thin, sharp sounds of a viol sang of noble ladies and
their suffering, knightly suitors. It was the most splendid banquet ever
held in the village, Fabrisse told Arnaud, her cheeks ruddy with excitement, as if she had forgotten that her daughter was carrying the child of
another. Arnaud could not take joy in the day's splendor: he knew the
rector had prevented him from joining in the preparations because he
wanted to give Echo Paradise by himself. And he saw that Echo did not
take joy in the festivities either, but sat at the end of a long table, staring out at the fields and the woods beyond, as if to lose herself in their
distance somehow.

That night, villagers threw wheat upon Echo's head as she proceeded into the house to her chamber, led by her mother. When Arnaud entered her dimly lit room with the rector, he found her already
tucked in bed, only the collar of her linen nightdress showing over the
covers. Fabrisse stood by the door, her expression somber. "For you,"
she said to Arnaud, pointing to a pile of nightclothes folded on the pillow by Echo. Had the rector employed a tailor to make these, too?

Arnaud searched the room for a dark corner in which to undress
privately, but the rector stopped him. "Not yet, not yet," he said, and
then murmured a prayer, blessing the nuptial bed and sprinkling holy
water up and down. He leaned over Echo to sprinkle her, and she
latched onto his arm, refusing to let him go. Her mouth spread open as
if at any moment she would cry out.

"Echo," Fabrisse said. "No. No."

Abruptly, the rector pulled away from her and left the room. Fabrisse gazed at him through the open door, and then turned back to

Echo. "You have the chance for something real, now," she said. "Something lovely." She looked to Arnaud. "Bless you," she whispered, and stepped from the room. She shut the door behind her.

Alone, Arnaud and Echo stared at each other, the flickering light of the bedside candle the only movement between them.

All at once, the door burst open and the rector entered, panting as if he had run from far off. "A marriage need not be consummated immediately for it to be genuine in the eyes of God!" he stammered. His mouth moved as if he meant to say more, but then he shook his head and retreated. The door slammed.

Again, they were alone.

Arnaud nodded at Echo, and she turned away from him, curling into herself. Was she weeping silently? He chastised himself for having scared her with his nod. He wanted to comfort her. To comfort her, that was all. "Echo," he said. "I understand what you are feeling."

She did not move, and he lost his courage to go on. He was angry, he realized. Not at her, but at the rector. *You love him,* he wanted to say to her. *But you must forget him now. He is an old man, and not your husband. Listen to your mother. You—we have the chance to right our wrongs together.*

He saw a pitcher of water on a small table at her side. Softly, he walked around the bed to pour her a cup. He held the water out to her, and she wiped her eyes and propped herself up. She took the cup, watched him as she drank.

"I will try to be a good husband to you," he said, smiling at her hesitantly.

Her eyes remained fixed on him, but she did not return his smile. He walked around the bed and sat on the edge across from her. For a time, he remained with his back toward her, feeling the weight of her stare. Then, he glanced over his shoulder and their eyes met. In the darkness, he thought he saw in her gaze a glimmer of surprise that he had not tried to make love to her, a glimmer of confusion and something akin to disappointment. Could it be? He turned his back to her again, kicked off his shoes, and lay back on the pillow, aware of her nearness, of her eyes on him still.

Little by little, he heard her breath become regular. He blew out the candle at his bedside. "Good night," he whispered. She could not have known that the idea of them making love was more wrought with fear for him than for her.

He found them lying together beside a stream, under the shade of a moss-covered tree. Peering out from behind a boulder, he forced himself to watch, as if to punish himself for not being the one to please her. And how pleased she was. Arnaud had never seen her in such a state of abandon—stark naked under the rector, and yet all around him, embracing him with her legs, with her arms, with her hands in his hair. She alternately smiled, became serious, and opened her lips as if to cry out, her movements melting into his, her body containing and being contained. Arnaud had to hold himself from barging into the clearing to stop her. This woman, whom he had not even wanted, had given herself over entirely to another, and he could not help yearning for a piece of her affection, could not help but feel hatred for the rector.

HE DID NOT WAIT for Echo to undress privately before he entered their room that night. He found her standing beside the bed, half-naked. She stared at him, her mouth agape as he surveyed her body. Her belly was still slight, but her breasts were fuller and darker of color than they had been when she was ill. He realized that he had been so caught up with the idea of marrying her since then, he had nearly forgotten she was carrying a child. . . . A child was growing within her now. What hostility he had felt upon entering the room faded, and he sat on the bed, facing away from her, allowing her to finish undressing.

When she was under the covers, he lay down, keeping his distance from her. He looked at the back of her head, dark with curls. "Echo," he said. "I want to read to you, if you will allow me. . . . I know you have been interested in the book that I have been reading at night."

She scowled over her shoulder at him, as if in disagreement.

"Perhaps you haven't been interested then," he said. "But I would like to read to you nevertheless." He took the book out from under his pillow. "There is a story in here," he said, "of a girl with your name. A girl called Echo . . . I first read the story before I knew you. . . . Would you like to hear it?"

She squinted, hesitating, and it seemed to him that she wanted both to hear the story and to demonstrate her lack of interest in any-

*W*ITH HIS SAVINGS and the purse of change the noblewoman of Baga had given him, Arnaud was able to purchase a good amount of leather from a tanner in Ax, and he set about making replicas of the master shoes he had constructed as an apprentice long before. The shoes in hand, he followed Fabrisse door to door as she sold wine, offering his services, and soon enough villagers were coming not only from Montaillou, but from Prades and Camurac and as far as Ascou, proposing trades. A few chickens here, a fleece there, a sack of millet and rye— payment for the shoes was far less in value than what he had received in Toulouse; but it was far more than what Fabrisse was bringing in for wine, and he was happy to contribute as he could to the household.

At night, he waited to enter the bedroom until Echo had changed into her nightclothes and slipped into bed. Then, fully clothed, he lay across from her and read. Over the years he had spent shepherding, he had abandoned reading for the life of the immediate, of the senses, of the open air, and his slim volume of Ovid, his tablet and bone stylus— once so beloved to him—had become empty of significance. As a husband, however, with a wife who could not speak to him and whom he dared not touch, reading became a solace again, and he took to studying passages until the light of day broke through the leaves of the shutter. Sometimes it seemed to him that Echo was feigning sleep, peering out from half-shut lids at the book in his hands, at the side of his face. He wanted to read to her, to talk to her if only through the words of another. But the moment never seemed appropriate, and he remained in silence, Ovid's words mounting in his soul like too much unspent love.

*F*OR OVER A MONTH, the rector kept his distance from them, or so Arnaud thought. Then, one afternoon in the heat of summer, Arnaud was returning from a trip to the tanner in Ax, laden with leather, when he spotted Echo crossing a fallow field below the village. There was something of determination in her gait—as if she were trying to *get* somewhere, rather than simply wandering for pleasure. She disappeared into the dark mouth of the wood beyond the field, and he followed, knowing well enough that she would likely lead him to misery.

Echo. "You have the chance for something real, now," she said. "Something lovely." She looked to Arnaud. "Bless you," she whispered, and stepped from the room. She shut the door behind her.

Alone, Arnaud and Echo stared at each other, the flickering light of the bedside candle the only movement between them.

All at once, the door burst open and the rector entered, panting as if he had run from far off. "A marriage need not be consummated immediately for it to be genuine in the eyes of God!" he stammered. His mouth moved as if he meant to say more, but then he shook his head and retreated. The door slammed.

Again, they were alone.

Arnaud nodded at Echo, and she turned away from him, curling into herself. Was she weeping silently? He chastised himself for having scared her with his nod. He wanted to comfort her. To comfort her, that was all. "Echo," he said. "I understand what you are feeling."

She did not move, and he lost his courage to go on. He was angry, he realized. Not at her, but at the rector. *You love him,* he wanted to say to her. *But you must forget him now. He is an old man, and not your husband. Listen to your mother. You—we have the chance to right our wrongs together.*

He saw a pitcher of water on a small table at her side. Softly, he walked around the bed to pour her a cup. He held the water out to her, and she wiped her eyes and propped herself up. She took the cup, watched him as she drank.

"I will try to be a good husband to you," he said, smiling at her hesitantly.

Her eyes remained fixed on him, but she did not return his smile. He walked around the bed and sat on the edge across from her. For a time, he remained with his back toward her, feeling the weight of her stare. Then, he glanced over his shoulder and their eyes met. In the darkness, he thought he saw in her gaze a glimmer of surprise that he had not tried to make love to her, a glimmer of confusion and something akin to disappointment. Could it be? He turned his back to her again, kicked off his shoes, and lay back on the pillow, aware of her nearness, of her eyes on him still.

Little by little, he heard her breath become regular. He blew out the candle at his bedside. "Good night," he whispered. She could not have known that the idea of them making love was more wrought with fear for him than for her.

bound them together with a cord of white and purple. After the benediction, the rector lifted the pall and gave Arnaud the Kiss of Peace, telling him to convey it to his new bride. Shyly, Arnaud turned to Echo. He kissed her quickly on the cheek. When still she would not look at him, he feared his lips had repulsed her.

There was a grand feast after the Mass. As Arnaud learned, the rector had taken it upon himself to purchase goods and hire servants for the affair, and Fabrisse's house was strewn with garlands of white blooms and rosemary. In the garden, tables were assembled and covered with legs of mutton and oranges and apples, jugs of spiced wine, roasted ducklings, and a swan still in plume. A jester entertained the feasting villagers with mock birdcalls and tricks of acrobatics, and a jongleur accompanied by the thin, sharp sounds of a viol sang of noble ladies and their suffering, knightly suitors. It was the most splendid banquet ever held in the village, Fabrisse told Arnaud, her cheeks ruddy with excitement, as if she had forgotten that her daughter was carrying the child of another. Arnaud could not take joy in the day's splendor: he knew the rector had prevented him from joining in the preparations because he wanted to give Echo Paradise by himself. And he saw that Echo did not take joy in the festivities either, but sat at the end of a long table, staring out at the fields and the woods beyond, as if to lose herself in their distance somehow.

That night, villagers threw wheat upon Echo's head as she proceeded into the house to her chamber, led by her mother. When Arnaud entered her dimly lit room with the rector, he found her already tucked in bed, only the collar of her linen nightdress showing over the covers. Fabrisse stood by the door, her expression somber. "For you," she said to Arnaud, pointing to a pile of nightclothes folded on the pillow by Echo. Had the rector employed a tailor to make these, too?

Arnaud searched the room for a dark corner in which to undress privately, but the rector stopped him. "Not yet, not yet," he said, and then murmured a prayer, blessing the nuptial bed and sprinkling holy water up and down. He leaned over Echo to sprinkle her, and she latched onto his arm, refusing to let him go. Her mouth spread open as if at any moment she would cry out.

"Echo," Fabrisse said. "No. No."

Abruptly, the rector pulled away from her and left the room. Fabrisse gazed at him through the open door, and then turned back to thing he had to offer. Gradually, she turned toward him, and rested her cheek against her hands.

Though he did not have her affection, he had her interest; he had her attention. He opened the book, skipped over the introduction of Narcissus, and silently read through the Latin in preparation. He would have to insert words here and there in the translation to make the story of Echo seamless. He cleared his throat, glancing up at her eyes, set on his.

"Once," he began, "there was a certain nymph of strange speech, resounding Echo, who could neither hold her peace when others spoke, nor yet begin to speak until others had addressed her. . . ." He smiled as he read, echoing the delight creeping over her lips.

THERE WAS NOT a night afterward when he did not read to her, and he found he loved watching the play of expression on her face as she absorbed Ovid's tales. Now and then, he pointed out patterns of story or fatal flaws of character, and she listened intently, as if memorizing his words in order to consider them at greater length later. He was glad for what he had of her, glad to give her something she had not had before.

Still, he could not be content knowing her days were free for the rector's taking. He proposed that she give up working for the farmer in the fields. "With the goods and money I am earning," he told her, "you need not hire yourself out, Echo. Stay home and guard your health." Happily, she abandoned the fields, but after three days under his watchful eye, she set about wine-selling with her mother. As he worked on his bench in front of the house, he caught glimpses of them passing up and down the road, like shadows of each other—silent, dark, unassuming of manner. He felt like a predator, incapable of letting his prey go.

There were days—almost more than he could bear—when he was forced to leave the village for the tanner in Ax. Despite his own moral sense, he lied to Echo once, told her he would be gone the following day. Instead, he hid out below the village, testing her fidelity. Faithfully, she descended the road and crossed the fields to the mouth of the wood. He followed, and watched in agony as she and the rector fell into each other. How could he deprive her of such bliss, such comfort? How could he allow her to go on torturing him so?

ONE EVENING in June, during a rare, hot shower, he walked the steep incline from Ax, pain shooting like lightning down his limbs. He told himself the pain was merely from the climb, but deep inside he feared he was falling ill. The pain seemed to issue from within his spine.

Fabrisse was weaving a basket at the table before the hearth. When she saw him, she scowled and shook her head, then gestured toward the fire. "Put another log on for me," she muttered. "Your soup is in the kettle."

He set down his pack, removed his wet cloak, and did as he was told, raking the fire a bit, breaking in kindling, and adding a few slender logs. The scent of the wood burning was a comfort to him, sweet and warm. He rubbed his aching hands over the flames before stirring the bubbling cabbage soup in the pot.

"Your wife is not home," he heard Fabrisse say, and he braced himself for the word that Echo was with the rector. He served himself a bowl, then sat at the table across from Fabrisse, blowing into the bowl to cool the soup and calm his nerves.

"This afternoon," she said, squinting as if straining to see him, "I found a book on your bed." She paused. "I threw it into the dung heap. . . . I can't have a book in my house. A book killed my husband. . . . I can't have heresy." She waved her hand in front of her face, as if to cast Arnaud away.

"I am not a heretic, Fabrisse," he said. "There are only tales in my book. Nothing of Scripture or faith. Nothing of heresy. You must believe me."

The old woman squinted at him again. "What do you take me for, a fool?" she said. By the manner in which she sniffled and shook her head, he knew she believed him and was sorry for having thrown the book out. "Echo is angry with me," she murmured. "She left in a rage when she found the book missing."

Her eyes became moist, and he reached across the table to take her hand. "I can get another book," he said. He studied her worn features, and saw something of her daughter's beauty in her face.

"There was a time when my daughter used to echo me," she said. "She was clever. . . . I used to wonder how she could make so much meaning just by repeating after me."

He had wondered why Echo, a mute, should be named for a tendency of voice. "And why did she stop speaking?" he asked.

Fabrisse sighed. In the glow of the hearth, he saw that thinking of such things pained her. "She was six," she said. "Seven, maybe . . . She just stopped. Never uttered a word again. . . . Sometimes I think she took a vow to punish me. Her silence is more like a fast than a disease."

ECHO RETURNED LATER that night, while he was stretched out on their bed, rubbing leather for a pair of shoes he meant to make. She held the wet, soiled book out to him, an expression of self-reproach on her face.

"Your mother told me she found it," he said.

She grimaced and sat across from him on the bed, and he handed her the cloth he had been using. Slowly, she began to wipe the dung away from the cover. Then she opened the book and turned from page to page. Some of the lettering had run together, but the tales largely remained intact.

"I can teach you to read, Echo," he said. It was an offer he would one day regret.

SEVENTEEN

ECHO COULD NOT DENY that from the moment Arnaud had entered her world, she had felt calmed by his presence, reassured. The evening before he had tended to her fever, she had been retching over the chamber pot in her room when her mother burst through the door. "You're pregnant," she said. "Don't expect the rector to want you now."

Though Echo did not believe that anything would cause the rector to reject her, she knew a child could be nothing but a humiliation to a man of God. Several years earlier, she had heard that a village girl singed an unborn child from her womb by sitting over a tall jar of smoke. The rector need not know she was pregnant, she told herself.

The next morning at dusk, she rolled the jar in which she and her mother made butter out among the bushes behind the house, filled the bottom with sticks, and set the sticks ablaze with a thin log from the hearth. She sat over the jar and imagined smoke cradling the baby inside her in pretty swirls. *Take the baby away,* she thought, and then it seemed as if her loins caught fire and she jumped, surrounded by smoke and coughing so violently she was ill.

Her mother found her cleaning up the mess. She eyed the smoldering sticks next to the mouth of the tipped-over jar. "That is not the way to do it," she said, then paused. "I wanted you, Echo. Don't you want your child?"

· · ·

ECHO NEVER KNEW whether it was the smoke or the rain that sent her
into fever, or the words her mother had spoken the night before. When
the rector brought Arnaud to see her, she feared only that the strange
young man would uncover the blistering burns between her thighs. If
the rector did not resent her for carrying his child, surely he would for
trying to rid it from her body.

Arnaud was gentle. He had gentle, pale-blue eyes, rimmed with
long, pale lashes. He looked squarely at her, but never in a forceful manner, and his hands passed over her belly and breasts firmly, but without
desire. Though he did not appear to be more than ten years her senior,
she felt like a child to him, her body sexless and familiar. When he
asked her mother to inspect her genitals rather than demanding to do
so himself, she was endlessly grateful. She knew well enough that although her mother could be cruel, she would never betray her by men-
tioning the burns—they were self-inflicted; her pregnancy involved the
shame of another.

AS SHE SOON LEARNED, her mother's warning that the rector might
no longer want her was as true as it was false. In wanting her so much,
he explained, he had to give her to another. To Arnaud. "But you will be
his only in name," he told her. "And our child is ours. Ours."

She cried, thinking she would rather be his unwed mistress than
his wedded whore. He had become her body, she his. What would become of her, them, if her body was split open by another?

At the wedding, she was cruel to both the rector and Arnaud,
and also to her mother, who, thrilled by the pomp and plenty of
the day, wanted her to take joy in her good fortune. "What other
bride of Montaillou has been greeted by a swan in plume on her
wedding table?" her mother said. "Clap, dance, be merry, Echo." It
was the first time in what seemed like forever that her mother glowed
with happiness instead of wine, but Echo could not oblige her.
She sat at the end of a table and sulked, wishing she could escape
to the forest, to her other self—the self away from this pregnant
self-wife.

SHE WONDERED what kind of man would marry a woman he knew to be pregnant with the child of another. On the wedding night, her respect for Arnaud dwindled further when he did not try to claim her as his own. She had expected to have to put up a fight, fending off his desire; she had expected to lose. But he did not assert his masculinity in the slightest. He fed her water like a good father might, then sat facing away from her.

Sometime in the middle of the night, she woke to find his arms around her, his body—still clothed—pressed up against her side. He was sleeping, snoring softly, and she lay in silence, listening. Though his arm was heavy over her hip, she did not move it, did not want to wake him, to break the mysterious comfort she drew from the thought that some deep part of him had hungered to touch her, and moved through dreams to do so.

When, the following evening, he lay over the covers, opened a slim, black book and began to read, she was as irritated at him for feigning disinterest in her as she was terrified. The only books she had seen were those in the hands of the rector, although she had heard of heretic books and had been warned by her mother to avoid them at all cost. "The one thing more dangerous than laying eyes on a heretic book is laying eyes on a Good Man reading," her mother had told her when she was a child. "If a Good Man catches you spying on him, he will spin you into his web and pour words down your throat and flood your heart with heresy. And then there is no escaping. You are his supper fly."

Echo knew her mother's greatest grief had sprung from her father's reading, from his heresy, but she could not bring herself to snatch the book from between Arnaud's hands and cast it away. Night after night, she spied on his pale, placid eyes moving over the shapes on the pages with ease, and during the day, when she entered the room alone, she gazed at the pillow beneath which she knew the book was hidden, yearning to approach.

PERHAPS IT WAS the presence of the book in her life, or the healing gentleness of Arnaud by her side, but the sickness in her stomach faded, and her joy in the child growing within her increased like the roses coming into flower and the summer vines creeping over the twined branches on the hillside. Another self was inside her, more tender than she but equally alive—a little bud, blooming. She felt proud to be containing a part of the rector, and ever more hungry for his affection.

When her burns healed, she sought him out in the chapel, and he greeted her with restrained delight, telling her to be gone to the wood, where he would join her after a time. Waiting for him to arrive, she wandered up to the pool above the cascade and gazed at the reflection of her nude body, as ripe as a blushing pear. The rector met her below by the stream, and she drew his attention to her swelling belly, to the tips of her breasts, turning color. His eyes were bland, his words unfeeling. "I see," he said. "I see."

They made love awkwardly, and she feared that the togetherness they had once shared was slipping away. Though he kissed her, stroked her, his touch was rough, his movements measured, and she did not sense his soul nearby. She heard the crickets humming, woodpeckers knocking on their evening trees, and her spirit reached for the spirit of the forest so not to remain solitary.

ONE NIGHT, soon after she had returned from the rector feeling as lonely as she was aware of the life becoming in her body, Arnaud tramped into their room without warning. Partly undressed, she was aghast, ashamed, and also, oddly, relieved. Perhaps he would prove to be nothing of a Good Man; perhaps she would come to enjoy the man he showed her he could be.

Instead, he told her he wanted to read to her, and she feared he was about to spin a web of heresy. "There is a story in here," he said, drawing the book from beneath his pillow, "of a girl with your name. A girl called Echo."

Something about the evenness of his tone convinced her that he was not speaking lies. She lay on her pillow, her heart thumping madly. She had always supposed that because books reflected truth, they had been written by God. Could it be that God had penned a story of her life?

"Once," he read slowly, "there was a certain nymph of strange speech, resounding Echo, who could neither hold her peace when others spoke, nor yet begin to speak until others had addressed her." He paused, as if gathering words in his mind.

"Up to this time," he read on, "Echo had form and was not a voice alone; and yet, though talkative, she had no other use of speech than now—only the power out of many words to repeat the last she heard. . . . Juno had made her thus; for often when she might have surprised the nymphs in the company with her lord upon the mountainsides, Echo would cunningly hold the goddess in long talk until the nymphs were fled. . . . When Juno realized this, she said to her: 'That tongue of thine, by which I have been tricked, shall have its power curtailed and enjoy only the briefest use of speech.' . . . The event confirmed her threat. She merely repeats the concluding phrases of a speech and returns the words she hears. . . .'"

Echo only partly conceived of what she was hearing—a nymph with her name, a goddess called Juno, a spell that restricted a tongue's speech forevermore—but she could hardly contain her ecstasy. She moved to Arnaud and leaned against his shoulder in order to study the shapes on the pages—shapes that seemed suddenly to breathe.

THAT NIGHT, she learned the tale had been written by a man called Ovid. Though she knew it was said that a great divide separated God from His creatures, she could not help regarding the book as something almost Godly, a powerful keeper of truth and lives.

Arnaud suggested that she abandon her work in the fields, and she spent three full days hidden in their room, the book open on her thighs. She loved the dark smell of its leather cover, the clarity of its first page, open like the face of an egg. She ran her finger against its rough edges and examined the little brown marks strewn across each page—like so many broken twigs, with red spots like bugs squatting here and there, and lines spinning out in leaves. Despite her reason, she wondered if the marks might not burn to the touch, and she felt them quickly, first the black—which she found cool, and then the red—which she found vaguely warmer. Then, on the evening of the third day, she dreamed the book came alive. Little brown bugs crawled across twigs and she squashed them with her fist, making bloody stains. The next morning, she joined her mother selling wine, afraid the dream had been a warning that she ought to leave the book in peace.

. . .

FOR A TIME, she stayed away from the breathing shapes, merely listening when Arnaud read to her at night. When she closed her eyes or
ventured through the fields or into the woods during the day, however,
the shapes appeared to her like apparitions—lovely as they were dangerous. She saw them in the grain of the wheat, in the bark of the trees,
among the yellow spots behind her eyes.

Then, one day when Arnaud was in Ax, she returned from the rector feeling despondent and heard Narcissus and Echo, Jove and Juno
calling. She drew the book out from beneath the pillow and flipped
through the pages, feasting on the shapes until her stomach growled
and she left the book on the bed to find something to eat. Her mother
found the book and flew into a fury. "So I have a heretic for a daughter
now, do I?" her mother cried.

Echo thought the lives she had only just discovered in the pages
would die with the night, but her mother confessed to having hidden
the book in the dung heap, and after a gruesome search, she came upon
it, sodden and stinking.

Arnaud was working at his shoemaking when she entered their
room that night. His eyes gleamed with a heat she had not seen in them
before. "I can teach you to read, Echo," he said, and just as suddenly
blurted out, "But you cannot tell a soul. Not a soul. Not even the rector."

She found herself smiling. *Not even the rector,* she echoed in her mind.

THE FOLLOWING AFTERNOON, she and Arnaud wandered down the
hillside, past tufts of pink primrose and through a part of the wood she
did not know, arriving finally in an exposed, light-filled meadow. Here,
too, primrose ran wild, and geranium also, and they sat among the pink
and the purple, the green-brown of brawny bracken that waved its curly
tops as if to whisper secrets to the wind.

Arnaud opened the sack he had brought, and withdrew a flat piece
of wood, covered with what looked to her like green wax. He set the
wood in his lap and smoothed the wax with his thumb. Then he
reached into his sack and withdrew a bonelike stick. "A stylus," he
told her.

She wondered why he had not withdrawn the book, and he explained himself as if he had heard her thoughts. "Before teaching you to read Latin," he told her, "I will teach you letters. How to write words in our own language."

She wanted to read, to read the book, but she nodded in assent to be polite, watching as he held the wood against his lap and took the stylus between his fingers. He pushed the pointed tip into the wax, dragged it down, lifted it, and dragged it around. "Do you recognize this?" he asked her.

She stared at the white scratches in the wax. It seemed to her they were like many of the twiglike marks she had seen in the book, all of them perhaps.

"This," he said, holding the wood up to her, "is the first letter of the alphabet." He said "alphabet" as though she ought to have understood the word, and she nodded, pretending she had.

"The letter *a*," he said, pointing to the scratches with the stylus. "It stands for the sound 'aaa.'" He opened his mouth, and she saw his tongue, raised slightly at the back of his throat. "Aaa," he said. "Say it with your lips. Aaa."

She moved her lips to mirror his. *Aaa,* she thought.

"Yes," he said. "Aaa. Like 'animal.' Aaanimal."

Aaanimal, she thought, marveling at how the sound could look like the scratches.

"And what else?" he said. "What else begins with the sound 'aaa'?" He paused, observing her as she thought. "Ass," he said. "Aaass."

She imagined an ass's rump. "Aaass," she mouthed.

He smiled at her. "Now you try to make the shape on the tablet." He set the tablet on her lap, held the stylus out, and pushed it into her palm. It was warm in places from the pressure of his skin; she put her fingertips on the warm parts, but the stylus dropped into her lap. "Pick it up," he said, "and I will show you how to hold it."

She held the stylus by the end and he slid her fingers toward the tip. He moved her thumb to the underside and pressed her forefinger above. "The other fingers support it as you write," he told her, then drew his hands away from hers. "Go on," he said. "Try to make the letter."

She lowered the stylus toward the wax, but became timid when the tip stuck. "Here," he said, moving behind her and kneeling down. He put his fingers around hers, and she looked at the top of his hand— large and sunburnt. It was the hand that had touched her when she was in fever. She felt shy suddenly, aware of the wind of his breath on her neck. His fingers pushed against hers, dragging the tip down, lifting it out of the wax, then dragging it around. "There," she heard him whisper. "You have made a letter."

His hand released hers and the stylus sprang back. She steadied it between her fingers. "There are many more letters," he said. "But you must master *a* first. Go ahead. Try on your own." He watched from behind as she pressed the tip into the wax, drew a line, and then a curve attached to it. The curve was pointed—nothing like the one they had made together.

"Start again," he said, and she drew yet another *a*—still too short and fat, but better. "Again, again," he told her.

She breathed in the sweetness of the wax, and made another letter, and another. With every *a*, she thought of the words animal and ass, and smelled the stench of her mule's rump. By the time the tablet was filled, the letter *a* was brown like fur in her mind.

THE NEXT DAY, Arnaud taught her five new letters, then five the day after, and ten the day after that. Her fingers grew sure over the stylus as she practiced into the evenings, until the light of early autumn drained from the sky. At night, she etched letters into the pallet with her fingertip, and onto her pillow when the candle was out. And during the day, when she was out walking or alone for a time, she etched letters into the earth—*a, b, c* . . . The earth itself no longer seemed as simple.

The more letters she learned, the more vividly she sensed them, and they began to cluster in different parts of her body. The letter *a* was under her arms—furry and musty like an animal in the wild. The letter *b* curled between her legs, rough and earthen like the bark of a branch, *branca*, or the itchy feel of a man's beard, *barba*.

There were green, verdant letters that ran up through her nose and under her eyebrows—the *v* of valley, *valada*, and the *p* of plant, *planta*, or paradise, *paradis*. The *l* of lake, *lac*, was liquid cool and beaded across her back and shoulders like rain. The *m* of memory, *memoria*, burned in her chest—the distance of a mountain, *montanha*, of a morrow, *matin*, of a mirror, *miralh*, never as clear as a face.

Certain letters signaled warning and she felt them in the sockets of her eyes—the *d* of distress, *destreisa*, and deception, *decepcion*, and the *n* of night, *noch*, and "No!"—a frightened cry. The letter *r* floated in the back of her mind—the most solemn letter, she thought, the letter of ritual, obliging her to recite and repeat, *recitar* and *repetir.*

Her favorite letters were *f* and *c,* warm and glowing orange down her insides. *F* was for flour, *farina,* to make a cake, and for fruit, *frucha,* the sweetness her tongue craved. *C* spread like a candle, *candela,* through her thighs, *coisas,* through her opening like a cave, *caverna,* her *con.*

Of all the letters, *s* slipped around her body most, never sure of its place. Sometimes it slithered like a snake, *serpen,* sliding around her rib cage and squeezing the breath from her. Sometimes it sucked softly at her breast, *sen,* making her nipples hard. *S* was regular as the seasons, *sazons,* and new as a shoemaker, *sabatier,* who had come to Montaillou swearing to give her his body, and suffering in solitude at her bedside.

ONE NIGHT in late summer, she could not sleep for all the letters in her mind and the thought of Arnaud beside her. He still slept fully dressed and found his way through dreams to her night-clothed body. And she had begun to hold him in return, feeling shame for taking what he gave unknowingly, and for breaking her fidelity to the rector.

On this night, he had not yet moved to her when she heard him moan, as if in pain. A moment later, he sat, hunching over the side of the bed before rising. He took the candle from the bedside and left the room. She heard him fumbling with the pot in the kitchen, then the sound of water pouring. The pot clanked onto the trivet. Was he preparing a broth? She wanted to prepare it for him, but the thought of standing with him alone before the fire filled her with unease.

After a while, the front door creaked open, and she went to the window and parted the shutters slightly. She saw him in the moonlight by the bushes out back, limping against the weight of the water-filled pot. He was going to take a bath, she realized. He walked to one of the empty barrels kept for grain, then poured the water from the pot into the barrel. Steam rose into the night. He removed his shirt, and she saw his broad, white back. He bent down and kicked off his trousers, exposing his buttocks, his long legs. He hunched over, massaging his shins and calves and thighs, then he sat on the lip of the barrel and swung himself inside.

The water must have been near boiling, for his mouth opened in the expression of a silent scream. She watched his slender arms grip the sides of the barrel, then reach down into the water as he lowered himself to splash his face. It seemed to her for the first time that he was her equal in silence, in seclusion. He had spoken of himself and his wants and needs no more than she had been able to. All she knew of him was that he was kind, that he could make shoes and read—but where he had learned such things, why he would have wanted to tie his life to hers, she still did not know.

She felt something move in her womb, a fluttering sensation. The baby. In a curious way, it seemed as though Arnaud had tickled her inside. The bones of his arms and shoulders, the splashing movements he made, his human frailty had touched her. Yes, he was as alone as she— as alone, it seemed to her suddenly, as every creature alive. Since she had lost her speech and the gap between her thoughts and her words had widened immeasurably, she had come to assume that no such gap existed for others. But now, seeing Arnaud in pain, in the midst of a suffering of which he did not speak, she heard his silence, and longed to give him comfort.

Again, she felt a flutter and she left the window and crawled under the covers. She slept for a time, until she heard him enter the room, a lighted candle casting an orange glow on his face. He stood at the foot of the bed, fully dressed, looking down at her with his wide, blue eyes, warmed by the light. She had never noticed how lovely he was of face, how sympathetically he gazed upon her, and she was suddenly stricken with the pain of never having had him as her own. *What are you thinking?* she wanted to ask him. *Tell me. And I will tell you. We will spend the whole night telling. Holding.* But she could only return his look, his small, sweet smile. He lay beside her over the covers, and when he jerked asleep, she felt for his hand in the darkness and tucked her fingers inside its embrace.

The next day, she crept down the hillside. She found the rector in the chapel vestry and implored him with her eyes to steal away with her for a time. Once in the wood, she pulled him down over her, within her, never minding the haggard expression on his face. For a moment, she thought she felt the presence of another nearby, and allowed herself to imagine it was Arnaud—he who, though her husband, she felt she should not want, but wanted anyway. Arnaud . . . She pretended to be comforting him, taking comfort. She pretended to want the rector in all sincerity.

Such pretense was new to her life.

．　．　．

AUTUMN ARRIVED with its unrelenting wet and mud, and she noticed Arnaud's face taking on a strange, greenish pallor. Despite the cold, he rose from bed to bathe himself almost nightly, and often, as he worked at his bench during the day, she saw him gripping his limbs as if to soothe a pain spreading through his body.

When he was giving her lessons, his pain seemed to fade. Together, they had found a grange in half-ruin beyond the road to Camurac where they could continue in private and in shelter, and there he taught her to write whole words—first in their own language, and then in Latin. Water—*aiga, aqua.* Tree—*arbre, arbor.* Child—*enfan, infans.* Bread—*pan, panis.* Rain—*ploia, pluvia.* Mother—*maire, mater.* Priest—*capelan, capellanus.* Voice—*votz, vox.*

Her experience of life was no less sweet for learning the spelling of words, but it was changed. For the longest time, she had not sifted her feelings through the filter of language, as she had no need to communicate them precisely, and now, she was taken aback by the limiting quality of words. How, she wondered, could the yearning she felt for the rector, for Arnaud, for her mother's love, for knowledge, be expressed in eight letters—*volontat,* yearning. How could the suffering she recognized not only in herself but also in Arnaud, and the rector, and her mother, be contained by the word *pena*—pain, suffering; *poena* in Latin, Arnaud told her. And life! That force of inhalation, exhalation, the blooming she sensed in every bud on the tree! How inadequate the word *vida* seemed to be in relation to the vastness of the condition of being alive. *Vida, vita*—life was a word, the word a concept, different from the sense of life and the love for life she experienced in her body, different from the feeling of life growing in her womb.

One afternoon, Arnaud taught her to write the word for love— *amor*—and he became so still and quiet, she felt as though she could hear his heart beating. She rubbed the words from the wax, wanting to leave this one thing unbounded by letters in her mind.

The baby kicked within her, and she took his hand and pressed it against her belly, as she had often done with the rector. *Feel,* she told him with her eyes. *Feel with me.*

An enormous grin spread over his face. He blushed to the tips of his ears, but did not take his hand away.

. . .

AUTUMN TURNED into winter and her belly became heavy as a sack of grain. Still sometimes she met the rector—in the house when her mother and Arnaud were away, or in the chapel after vespers. She did not suspect that the rector sensed her growing coldness toward him; he was growing so cold himself, he could not have sensed much, she thought.

Then one night, in the dead of winter, when they were lying under a blanket before the altar, snow falling in swirls through the sky outside, he surprised her. "You have fallen in love with him then," he said, and she stared at him blankly, unable to deny his words. *Amor.* Love.

"And I suppose you have—" He paused. "Shared yourself with him on many nights." She shook her head violently, and he laughed, so sharply she thought at any moment he would sob, or shout at her. "I know he prefers men, Echo," he said. "But he is a man. And men take what they can get."

She was so stunned by the harshness of his words, so confused by their meaning, she could do nothing but sit. He stared up at her with a cruel, trembling smirk. "It is against the rules to reveal another's confession," he said. "But who will you tell?" Again, he laughed, falsely, terribly. "I have taken my share of women, Echo," he said. "And your husband has taken his share of men."

She shook her head. She did not believe him. It was mad, what he was saying. She had never heard of such a thing. It made her want to laugh. And she did, silently, even in her anger. *I love him,* she thought. *And I don't care. I don't care what you say.*

He rolled away from her, covering part of his cheek with the blanket. "I received a letter today," he said, his tone quiet, even. "From the Inquisitor . . . Do you know what that means?" He looked back at her, and he seemed suddenly to have shrunken to the shape of a boy. "It is all beginning again. A new bishop of Pamiers was appointed. And he is eager to crush the heresy in our diocese. . . . They have their eyes on us. Their eyes on me."

Again, his lips trembled. "I am not strong enough to go through it without you," he cried. "Don't leave me, Echo. Don't love him instead of me."

She could not help feeling pity as she watched him weep, and she lay by his side again, and took him in her arms. She soothed him with kisses, petted his hair as he had often petted hers. Still, she was aware of a feeling of disgust for him rising in her. He was cruel, crueler than she had known he could be, and quick to put his own need for solace before hers, before Arnaud's. Solace, *conort. C-o-n-o-r-t.*

He clung to her like a baby, and she held him until he became very still in sleep. Gently, she untangled her limbs from his and stood, wrapping her cloak around her middle. She paused a moment before leaving his side, noticing a book sitting by the chalice on the dimly lit altar. She had never thought to look through his books, but in the wake of his spitefulness toward Arnaud, she felt a sudden and sharp urgency to take something of his for herself. She would look at the book. Merely look. She glanced back to be sure he was asleep, then stepped softly to the altar.

The cover of the book was cracked and brown with age, and she fingered it for a moment before turning it back. The first pages were filled with rows and rows of perfectly inscribed words, gilded in places and decorated by tiny representations of the Christ story. Following was a section of pages written in a hand far less precise. Was it the rector's script? she wondered. Near the top of one of these pages, she saw a word she recognized—*Fabrisse.* Arnaud had taught her to write her mother's married name, but *Fabrisse* in the rector's book was not followed by *Rives.* She struggled to sound out what followed instead, and a chill moved up her spine. She had never heard of another Fabrisse in the region. . . . *Cl-er-gue. Clergue.* She was nearly sure she had come upon the rector's surname.

For a moment, she was reassured—she found it almost amusing that the rector had a relative who shared her mother's name. But then a terrible thought occurred to her. Among the words written after *Fabrisse Clergue,* she recognized a form of the verb *baptize,* and the nouns *year, Lord,* and *December.* Her mother had been baptized, she knew—but by what name? She had been without a surname before marrying.

Echo tried to concentrate, to etch the words she read into her memory. Then, breathless, she shut the book and fled, pretending not to hear when the rector woke and called after her. Outside, the snow had turned wild. The wind blew fiercely, and she ran up the road, clutching her belly, trying to catch enough air in her mouth.

When she arrived home and stumbled into the kitchen, her mother was drinking by the fire. "You are killing your poor husband," her mother said, waving her away, as if she couldn't bear the sight of her. "Belly past your nose and you can't stand to be without what your husband, too, has to offer."

She left her mother in the kitchen and made her way to the bedroom in the back, shivering. Arnaud lay in bed, pale and bleary-eyed. "Echo," he said to her, a look of concern crossing his face.

She went to the corner of the bed beneath which the pallet and stylus were hidden. Taking the stylus between her numb fingers, she inscribed the words she had memorized into the wax. She thrust the pallet before Arnaud's eyes, and he squinted down at her imperfect letters.

"Where have you seen this, Echo?" he said.

She pointed to the tablet. *Read it. Read it. Tell me*, she demanded with her eyes.

Again he studied her letters. "Fabrisse Clergue," he read slowly. "Baptized in the year of Our Lord twelve hundred and eighty-two, the twenty-ninth of December." He paused, and then frowned, as if the same awful thought that had occurred to her had flared in his mind. "Is Clergue your mother's family name?" he said, a pained look in his eyes. "Is your mother related to the rector? Are you—"

But she could not listen anymore. She stared at the wall in front of her, feeling the baby in her shift as if suddenly it hated her body. She hated her body, knew nothing, nothing, but that the rector could be her blood and knew as much and had kept it from her, wanted to keep her as his own anyway. He had married her to a lover of men to keep her from another's embrace, and she was angry, hated them all, hated her body, the baby inside.

She could not remain—in the room, in the house. She was suffocating, in a mad daze. She stood and walked from the room, past the kitchen. "You'll catch your death in the cold," she heard her mother say.

The wind froze her face, and little flying pieces of ice stabbed her eyes as if to blind her. In the snow, the world was mute—covering over the sound of her footsteps crunching on the ground below. Moonlight illuminated the snow, enveloping the hillside in a misty evening whiteness, and she wanted to enter the white, to disappear within it somehow. . . . Where was she walking? To the wood, perhaps. Yes, to the only place of comfort to her that remained.

Suddenly she was seized with pain so violent she doubled over, gripping her belly. She tried to stand, told herself she must walk. Walk to the wood. Find a place to breathe. But again pain seized her, and she fell to her knees, snow on her cheek and wrists and ankles. She closed her eyes, bracing herself against the pain. A sound broke the night's silence. An awful sound, piercing, but also as full of hope as a sound could be. It was the sound of her screaming, and then screaming in astonishment and agony.

Something pushed against her legs and neck. She opened her eyes and saw Arnaud bending over her, and, behind his face, the brightness of the moon and the stars, with all their little points of light. She screamed more loudly, as if to say, *Do you hear? It hurts. Hurts! Listen! Hear me!* And he cradled her in his arms, standing, grinning and grimacing with the sounds that she made.

He walked with her to the house and she fought against him, against the surging pain. He held her more firmly against his body. "Be still, Echo," he said to her. "You are going to give birth soon, and I am going to help you."

EIGHTEEN

A DECADE BEFORE, Bernard had begun his inquisitorial campaign with a fervent eye on Pierre Clergue, prepared to destroy him and all his vulgar wantonness little by little. How he had wanted that false leader of piety to suffer for neglecting to contain his lusts, to contain his flock within the true faith. Six days after he first mounted the pulpit of the Cathedral Saint-Étienne, claiming his power to convict and forgive, six days after Clergue presented him with a meager "list" of wayward parishioners consisting of the single name Philippe Guilhabert, Bernard sent henchmen to Montaillou in search of Guilhabert, hoping not only to impress Clergue with the swiftness of his action, but also to subdue him into submission. The henchmen returned to Toulouse, however, with the paltry tale that Guilhabert had died somewhere on a mountain pass, and Bernard silently cursed Clergue. He sent the henchmen back to the village, commanding them to summon the "widow" Guilhabert to Toulouse, where she would be made to testify under oath as to her husband's whereabouts.

Bernard's headquarters in Toulouse were in an unadorned brick house that had been given long before to Saint Dominic. When Grégoire had served as Inquisitor, he had lived and worked in the house, which was adjacent to the grand Château Narbonnais, home of the Count of Toulouse and of the notorious mur—the prison in which felons of both the Church and the county were held. It was between the musty walls of this house that Bernard questioned Ava Guilhabert, who confessed almost immediately that Clergue had warned her of the henchmen's coming and told her of the particular mountain pass her husband should travel along to escape arrest. Though Bernard was pleased to have an official accusation against the rector recorded in his register, he knew well enough that a single piece of incriminating evidence was not sufficient to summon the rector to stand trial. As with the inquisitorial process Moses had put forth, two or more lay denunciations were necessary for any action to be taken against a man.

By the grace of God, Philippe Guilhabert was apprehended in the region of Lordat soon after, and for three days Bernard interrogated him mercilessly, aiming to pressure the heretic into exposing Clergue's involvement in his attempted escape from arrest. By law, Bernard could not reveal to Philippe the names of the witnesses who had spoken, or written, against him—in this case, that of his wife and his rector—but he attempted to inflict the sting of betrayal on Philippe in order to prompt him to betray Clergue. "You must know that you have been accused by others," he said. "Others who have suggested that the rector warned you of the henchmen's coming."

As willing as Philippe was to point fingers at his fellow parishioners and to admit that he had indeed been seduced by the words of the Good Men—words, he claimed, he now recognized as blasphemy—he would not utter a word of reproach against the rector, refusing to acknowledge that his own flight to Catalonia had been anything other than a routine journey to visit the second wife and family he had there. "I am not proud of my infidelity to my first wife," he muttered flatly, "but I have done my best to serve both of my families. I cannot tell you how often I have walked the mountain passes just to bring a bit of wool and some needles and some coins to the mother of the children I did not father legitimately."

Exasperated, Bernard determined to use Philippe to his own ends rather than submit the trifling evidence against him to the inquisitorial jury—a group of thirty upstanding and learned Toulousan men who studied the evidence presented to them without knowing the name of the accused, and then recommended an appropriate sentence to Bernard. Because Philippe had confessed to having once been a Believer, abjured his faith in all heresy, and expressed remorse and sought forgiveness for his infidelity to his wife, the jury, at best, might sentence him to a term of imprisonment for having fled arrest. Instead, Bernard released Philippe on the condition that he pledge forever true to the true faith and aid the Inquisition in its quest to find the brothers Authié, Prades Tavernier, and

Jean Marty. In capturing these men, Bernard hoped, he would not only make great strides in stamping out heresy in the land, but also secure the evidence against Clergue necessary to send him to the stake.

Philippe's release proved fruitful. One of the brothers Authié, Prades Tavernier, and Jean Marty were apprehended on a mountain pass in Aragon, Philippe by their side. Try as Bernard might to convert them back to the true faith, however, try as he might to convince them to confess their wrongdoing, they were as mute as if their tongues had been cut out. And when Bernard's questions turned to the subject of Clergue, the men said nothing but that he was an honorable Christian indeed, a response Bernard interpreted to be a frustratingly snide affirmation that the rector was a heretic in guise—"an honorable Christian" in their view was surely a Good Christian or a Believer in the Good Christian's faith.

Infuriated that the men would not denounce Clergue plainly, Bernard locked them into the *murus strictus*—the narrowest of the prison cells, meant for solitary confinement, where they were shackled to a wall, kept in darkness, and fed only the scantest quantity of bread and water. From time to time, Bernard descended into the pit of the mur to threaten them with burning and test their faith with a scrap of freshly roasted meat, but his efforts proved futile. Even worse, he was left with the awful sensation that it was *he* who had somehow abandoned the teachings of Christ, *he* who was merciless. Was he not laboring to spare these souls from the fire of eternal damnation? He tried to shake off the image of Clergue shackled to a wall—an image that surged in his mind whenever he laid eyes on the men rotting slowly under his command. Pausing in the confines of the straight corridors between the cells, he breathed in the moldy air and could almost smell Clergue nearby, his body shackled and vulnerable, compensating for the indulgences it had once feasted upon. In his deepest heart, he could not deny that part of the passion that fired his efforts to force the Good Men into confession was not Christ-like at all.

EVEN AS HE CONTINUED to interrogate and sentence suspects throughout the province, he exerted ever more pressure on the tiny parish of Montaillou—sentencing those proven to have died in a state of heretical sin to be exhumed and burned, and urging the Bishop of

Sabarthès to levy a new tax on livestock and grains. With the surplus from the tithes, he was able to send still more henchmen throughout the province, and to erect elaborate scaffolds in the Cathedral square in Toulouse for the purpose of a public burning of the Good Men Authié and Tavernier, whom the jury had determined to be incontrovertibly and obdurately guilty of heresy.

On the day of the burnings, Bernard watched as the Count urged the men, tied to stakes, to confess their sins or face final judicial penalty. Just as they had in the mur, they kept their silence, and the execution- ers lit the fagots and straw piled around them to the chin. Soon smoke heaved into the air, and it seemed to Bernard to be strangling him, singeing his lungs so he could not breathe. He remembered the first burning he had brought about long before, the burning of Jean Maulen in Carcassonne. He could not feel more certain now that such coming apart of life in smoldering ash and scarlet half-burned limbs was not a grave misstep. Moses had saved his people from blasphemy by killing off those guilty of idolatry, and God had allowed for the bloodshed; but could such severity be justified after the compassion of Christ? Christ had lost blood for the forgiveness of the sins of others. How could God thence look upon the killing of His creatures as anything but a tragedy of those he had trusted with life?

Before the fires burned themselves out, Bernard retreated to his brick-lined bedroom. He was uncomfortably hot, and his limbs and back were racked with pain. He threw the blankets off his pallet, lay down on the warm sheets, and curled onto his side, coughing uncon- trollably, as if to purge his body of the filthy smoke he had inhaled. He waited for the oblivion of sleep to save him. If it had been Clergue on the stake, would he have felt so defeated?

THAT NIGHT, the scent of the burning bodies still sharp in his mind, agony crept like a shadow across the clarity of his soul, and he was pol- luted by dreams as he had been in Albi—dreams of a young woman's body containing him, his flesh foaming with an abandon so profound he was dizzy upon waking.

Through the weeks that followed, the dreams persisted in all their virulence, and he began to resist sleeping at all—sitting up in bed rather than reclining or pacing the floor until his feet were aching. He grew thin and irritable, and in the light hours, thoughts of Clergue grew tree-like in his mind. Now and then, he found himself venturing down into the pit of the mur, wandering through the moldy maze of walls worn smooth by heretic hands of old. How he longed to face Clergue, to excise the impurity swelling in his own body and soul by beating Clergue into priestly submission. Clergue must be made to desire God to the exclusion of others! He must be chastened!

One day, he lost all temperance, and hastily wrote a letter to Clergue:

> *May this be your warning, Pierre Clergue. I know that you are a false priest, of a parish teeming with heresy. Someday soon, your village will be surrounded, your people rounded up like sheep. We are coming, and you have a choice to make. Aid us in our attack, or be rounded up as a lowly beast. You know as well as I what your fate shall be in the latter case.*

He regretted the letter as soon as the messenger drew it from between his fingertips. If Clergue was frightened into fleeing by the letter's ruthlessness, he might escape the clutches of the Inquisition forever. Four days later, however, the messenger brought him a response from the rector:

> *On the Feast Day of the Virgin all the village will be gathered in the square at high noon. There is room enough in the dungeons of the fortress to house everyone for a time.*

Bernard was alternately elated, thrown into a cold sweat, and consumed by dread. The confrontation he had been awaiting was finally to come, and so soon. . . . For all the time he had spent pondering Clergue's motivations, his cunning, he had never expected him to turn over his parish with such little resistance. A strange haze of disappointment spread through him, and rather than immediately draft a plan to take the village, he crawled onto his pallet and slept.

WITHIN A FORTNIGHT, he had spent the remaining money from the tithes to hire more henchmen, and on a particularly sun-drenched day in September, they took Montaillou by force. Was it any surprise that Clergue was nowhere to be found among the celebrating crowd? After the henchmen corralled all the peasants into the dungeons, Bernard walked among the disarray in the square—the overturned tables and plates of stinking stew. He gazed toward the hills, knowing he should be satisfied with the parish Clergue had lost to him, but feeling restless nevertheless, oddly distanced from himself—as if his soul had shriveled and he could not locate it, however much he tried. Was it fear that he felt? Fear that he had lost Clergue forever?

For three weeks he interrogated the villagers, while his favored scriptor—a friar by the name of de Massabuçu—took notes. For the most part, what he discovered lurking among the villagers was supreme ignorance—not heresy, precisely, but confusion, misinformation, a stupidity for which he blamed Clergue singularly. Seven villagers claimed not even to believe in the reality of the soul as they had seen nothing but air come from the mouths of those who had expired. One said she had come to the conclusion that nothing existed but the present world—neither Heaven nor Hell—and when Bernard asked if she did not then believe men would be resurrected after death, she answered that she had seen the way bodies putrefied in the ground. "What is there to be resurrected?" she asked. "Rot and bones?"

Bernard did not take the time to undo the damage Clergue's excesses had allowed, but pressed the villagers to articulate the rector's relationship to heresy, to the Good Men who propagated it, and to the Believers who had come under scrutiny. More than a few men and women acknowledged that they had heard that the rector had defended the Good Christians from arrest and used the Inquisition to his own ends, convincing village women to be known by him carnally if they wanted protection; but none would name names, and none would confess to having been personally shielded from the Inquisition by him, or to having been one of his reluctant lovers. Bernard was left to craft a list of those villagers denounced by a minimum of two others—a list that comprised nearly half of the village adults. Those not immediately arrested, but in whose eyes Bernard had recognized a flicker of untruth as to the question of the rector's guilt, would be summoned to testify against him later—when Clergue himself was shackled and suffering underground.

. . .

IN ORDER TO SAFEGUARD the reputations of the accused until proven guilty, the trials were furtive affairs, conducted in the brick house in Toulouse, with only Bernard and de Massabuçu in attendance. At the onset of each trial, the accused was invited to list his enemies; if the name of someone who had denounced him appeared on the list, the evidence that witness had provided was struck from the record. In turn, the evidence the accused provided against the enemies on his list was considered invalid. As ill luck, or fate, or God—Bernard sometimes feared—would have it, the only men and women of Montaillou who ultimately denounced Clergue, claiming to have witnessed him in an act of heresy or defiance against the Church, also listed him as one of their primary enemies. Their denunciations were thus worthless, like so many precious coins of gold suddenly rendered rubbish. Could it be that somehow the rector—despite his fall away from the Church and the tenets of the priesthood—was touched by the favor of God Himself? It seemed preposterous, and yet Clergue had escaped Bernard's grasp at every turn.

Increasingly, it became clear to Bernard that if he was going to pin down Clergue with a legitimate denunciation, he was going to have to obtain that denunciation from someone outside of his parish—someone Clergue had not recently betrayed in allowing the village to be overtaken. He set about writing a letter to the present Inquisitor of Carcassonne, Geoffroy d'Ablis, asking for his aid in the quest to locate the still unbound and unburned elder brother Authié. The Good Man, Bernard argued, was disseminating lies throughout the region with every free breath of his body, and he needed to be stopped as swiftly as possible.

Geoffroy d'Ablis obliged Bernard, and after a costly search the Good Man was captured. Unlike his younger brother and Prades Tavernier, he spoke at a quick clip, only too happy to converse on the subject of his faith, and to challenge Bernard's own interpretation of Scripture. It was as though he were inquisiting Bernard instead of the other way around.

"And how do you interpret the first verses of John?" he asked Bernard across the inquisitorial chamber. "'In the beginning was the Word,'" he continued, "'and the Word was with God . . . All things were made by Him, and without Him . . . *Factum est nihil quod factum est.*'" He smiled coyly. "How do you interpret '*Factum est nihil*'?"

"I should ask what you make of the phrase," Bernard retorted.

The Good Man waited for him to answer.

"Only because I want to convince you of the true path," Bernard conceded, "will I tell you my interpretation, the interpretation of the Church, I might remind you." He paused. "I take the phrase to mean that nothing was created without Him."

An expression of pity creased the Good Man's brow. "My brother," he said, more slowly. "You are gravely mistaken. . . . What the verse means to say is that without Him the vastness of Nothing was created. *The* Nothing. The domain of all evil—matter, flesh, all that is corruptible . . . the domain of the absence of everything good and light and pure."

"Tell me about Pierre Clergue," Bernard said, knowing he should engage the heretic in debate and reason him out of his error, but unable to concentrate on the words of John for now.

Suddenly, the Good Man became tight-lipped. He would not denounce the rector, or any other man or woman for that matter. "I will not have the blood of another on my hands," he said. "Not blood drawn from your Church."

After five days of interrogation, the Good Man would not budge and Bernard threw him into the *murus strictus,* instructing the prison marshal to bring to his cell a seldom-used instrument of torture. Bernard would see to it that the Good Man had blood on his hands if he did not confess what he knew of the rector.

When the ground of the tiny cell was wet with blood, the dark walls streaked with the prints of bloody hands, Bernard left the Good Man to consider his impending doom. He did not want to submit the evidence he had amassed against him to the men of the jury yet, as he knew they would rapidly conclude Authié must be relaxed to the secular arm to be burned—and burned, the Good Man was of no use to him at all.

For several months, he continued to interrogate the villagers of Montaillou on trial, but he was distracted, heavy of mood, and uneasy, vaguely aware that something horrendous lay in wait for him. During the season of Lent, he embarked on another round of torturing Authié in his cell, and the Good Man retaliated with equal fervor. "You are no less evil than the Romans who tried to slaughter Our Lord!" he hissed, and then spat blood into Bernard's eye such that he was temporarily blinded.

The next morning, Bernard relinquished to the jury selections of what he had recorded against everyone on trial. On the fifth of

April, the Sunday of the Passion, he stood at the pulpit of the Cathedral Saint-Étienne—before Geoffroy d'Ablis, nine consuls, ten archdeacons, officials of the Count and the crown, their deputies, local lords and knights, specialists of law and judges who had served on the jury, and the body of those on trial surrounded by guards—and sentenced seventeen heretics to be relaxed and burned. Among them were the Good Man Authié and Philippe Guilhabert, who, found to have relapsed into heresy, were apprehended by henchmen near Junac.

The following Sunday ashes fell like snowflakes through the bright spring sky, and Bernard tried to comfort himself with the thought that Satan had slithered into the blood of those burning—men no longer, but souls who had once threatened to undermine the Good News of Christ. . . . How grievously Bernard himself had failed God.

UNTIL THIS TIME, Pope Clément V had not interfered with Bernard's inquisitorial processes—though he had, several years earlier, allowed himself to be persuaded by the people of Albi and Carcassonne to send two cardinals to investigate the prisons there. The report from the cardinals had been dismal. They had described the prisons as "Hell," the prisoners as "incapacitated" and subjected to the worst of tortures, some enduring misery for more than five years without yet being convicted. Clément V thus had ordered all but the principal jailers of each prison to be removed from responsibility, and second principal jailers to be added. Neither jailer was to converse with prisoners without the other present, and the prisoners themselves were—without fail—to receive from the jailers all food and supplies provided by the king and their personal friends and relations. Aged and sickly prisoners were to be moved to the upper levels of the prison tower, those fettered were to be unbound, and all were to be released from the confines of the cells daily, such that they might walk about in the corridors. Finally, Clément V ordered that all existing cells be made brighter, and he mandated the building of new, wider, and more light-filled chambers.

In April of the year 1312, Bernard held a Sermo Generalis on the Sunday of Saint-Georges, pronouncing a total of two hundred twenty-five sentences against those on trial: Fifty were to wear yellow crosses, eighty-eight to be immured, ten to be held in solitary confinement, thirty-six to be exhumed from the grave and burned, five to be relaxed to the secular arm. . . . Bernard had thought he was serving the Church, and thus God, as well as he could, but Clément V viewed his sentences as excessively harsh. Too often the guilty had not been given the chance to show contrition or be pardoned, he said.

Less than a week later, at the Council of Vienne, the Pope passed the bull *Multorum querela*, attempting to curb the fervor of the Inquisitorial Office as a whole by reducing the power of inquisitors to initiate trial, to submit a man to severe circumstances of confinement or torture, or to pass definitive sentence. In each of those cases, the *Multorum querela* decreed, the Inquisitor must have the accord of the bishop of the diocese of the accused, and under no circumstances was a prisoner to be tortured on more than one occasion. Each prison in which the indicted and convicted were held was to have two chief custodians—one assigned by the Inquisitor, the other by the local bishop—and these wardens were to abide by the same conditions of behavior already enjoined on the jailers of the prisons of Albi and Carcassonne.

Needless to say, Bernard was astonished and he objected vigorously, immediately addressing a letter to the Pope in which he argued that the only result of the *Multorum* would be to impede their efforts against heresy. The province of Toulouse, he maintained, included several dioceses, and to obtain the consent of a said bishop every time he wanted to put a man on trial or torture him into confession would only bring about inopportune delays. For example, occasionally one of his henchmen managed to apprehend an envoy of the Good Men. If such messengers were not swiftly made to disclose what they knew of the Good Christians' whereabouts, their usefulness to the Inquisition would be lost. Moreover, he reasoned, the Pope's bull was in breach of Pope Innocent IV's bull *Ad extirpanda* of 1252—a bull that established the practice of torture as admissible in the inquisitorial courts by stipulating that heretics be dealt with as secular criminals, "as they are truly robbers, and murderers of souls, and thieves of the Sacraments of God," Pope Innocent had written. And in 1262, Pope Urbain IV had supplemented Innocent's bull with the *Ut negotium*, in which he sanctioned the practice of torture by inquisitors themselves. In closing, Bernard reminded the Pope of Christ's words in Matthew: *"Do not think that I have come to bring peace on earth; I have not come to bring peace, but a sword."* The Inquisitor's power to slay the subverters of Christ's Word, wrote Bernard, ought to be buttressed, not limited.

Pope Clément indicated his disaccord by failing to respond.

. . .

AS IT HAPPENED, a new Bishop of the diocese of Pamiers—comprising the parish of Montaillou—was appointed the same year. Bishop Pelfort de Rabastens was his name, and rather than embrace the new inquisitorial power the bull *Multorum* gave him, he occupied himself with his dissenting canons and denied Bernard's accounts that the diocese was in a state of spiritual crisis. Bernard's inquisition against Montaillou and its surrounding parishes thus came to an abrupt halt, and the zeal that had fed his fight against heresy in the province faded. How astonished Grégoire would have been, thought Bernard, to learn that it was the Pope who was challenging inquisitorial authority now.

The summer was hot and humid, and Bernard was forever soaked with perspiration, his sheets sour, the pages of his register damp and moldy. A persistent, wet cough plagued him, and he feared he was drowning in impotence, too tired to seek out episcopal approval either to initiate new trials or to pass new sentences, and haunted by dreams inhabited by Clergue and the forms of women who might have been his lovers.

Then, in early fall, determined to rise up against sloth and temptation, he turned his gaze upon a group of subverters he felt he could legally and presently conquer. It was not that he hated the Jews or thought them essentially corrupt or unworthy. Indeed, the great Saint Paul had been of the seed of Abraham, and had called the Jews the natural branches of God's tree, broken off because of unbelief. The Gentiles, Paul said, were wild olive shoots grafted onto the tree in place of its natural branches. It was good and right and expected then that the Jews should be converted and grafted onto the tree once more. *"The Lord your God will raise up for you a prophet like me from among you, from your brethren—him you shall heed,"* Moses had foretold. How blinded the Chosen People of Moses had been, thought Bernard, when they rejected Jesus as the true Messiah.

Legally, Bernard had no authority over Jews who kept to the concerns of their synagogues and the Law of Moses; but if a Jew converted to Christianity only to give up the Faith, or disparaged Christianity or swayed another to deny his baptism, he could be denounced for heresy. The Bishop of Toulouse, unconcerned with the Jews of his diocese, allowed Bernard to initiate trial against all twice-denounced Jews, and Bernard went about attempting to convert lapsed Christians and convict their corrupters, who followed a specific path to "rejudaize" the baptized Jew, asking him if he would not like to wash in running water in order to cleanse himself of the blemish of baptism. Such corrupters were guilty of the greatest affront to God, and Bernard often quoted Paul during their interrogations: "*A man who has violated the law of Moses dies without mercy at the testimony of two or three witnesses. How much worse punishment do you think will be deserved by the man who has spurned the Son of God, and profaned the blood of the covenant by which he was sanctified, and outraged the Spirit of grace?*"

During this time, Bernard came across a book that included statements from the Jewish Talmudic writings, among them one asserting that Christ was neither God nor Messiah, but slayer of the law God had laid down, His followers no more than infidels. Bernard had found the book on a Jew who claimed that he and his brethren, at their September feast of conciliation, uttered a curse by which they insinuated that Christ was the bastard son of a whore, and by which they damned both Mother and Son, the Catholic Faith, and all its supporters. Disgusted as much by the writing as by the Jew's words, Bernard ordered that all the Talmudic texts in the domain of the city be seized. When two cartloads of books had been amassed, he publicly cast them into a raging fire in the Cathedral square. Rather than being spurred on to greater inquisitorial action by the burning, however, he took to bed, incapacitated for more than a month by a sweating illness that not even the Court doctor could diagnose.

IN APRIL of the year 1314, the Pope died suddenly, prompting a crisis of papal succession that was to last two years. On more than a few occasions, Bernard imagined himself stepping into the center of the Papal Court, and his very skin thrilled. To possess such power during a time of trial for the Church! To subvert the subverters of God's revealed Word by all means *he* deemed necessary! He had never served in an episcopal capacity, though, and he knew such imaginings were simply vanity.

On the seventh of August, 1316, an assembly of cardinals met in Lyons and elected the cardinal-bishop of Porto to serve as the next Pope. An esteemed administrator and doctor of civil and canon law, Jean XXII was a skeletal old man of seventy-two when he took the papal oath, and Bernard had the highest hopes that he would bend to his plaint that the bull *Multorum* be revoked. Despite the Pope's agedness, however, he proved hearty of will and repeatedly refused to overturn or amend the decree that Clément V had crafted. Instead, he delegated to Bernard and another, by the name of Bertrand de la Tour, the serious mission of establishing harmony in northern Italy and Tuscany. How could Bernard do other than his chief commanded, much as he knew that his heart would not be in the diplomacy?

He and de la Tour traversed the Alps, then journeyed from town to town for a year. Through it all, he missed the region that was his home, with its limpid air and quivering poplars, and clouds so fat and low, its sky so hovering, he felt sheltered at all times, blissfully protected from the scrutiny of . . . what? Here, light was wounding, the sky an abyss, wind forever at his back, and he sought out shadows within which to hide himself. When it rained, he did not feel refreshed, and when de la Tour commented on the beauty of the land and its colors, Bernard saw only white and black: white mountaintop, black firs; white boulder, black cloud; black road, black donkey hoof. Grass that had been burned.

At night, he could not sleep for the rounded sounds of the foreign tongues shouting on the streets—he wanted to bellow out for them to stop. In half-dreams, the voices echoed his daytime footsteps, leading him to the center he could hide from no longer, that deep cleft of desire, that blackness pawing at his flesh. "My God, why hast Thou forsaken me?" he asked each day as he walked, his joints aching. He looked right and left of the roads he walked, as if the face of Clergue would somehow appear. Oh, to be caught within the Paradise of a cell with the shackled rector . . . to be protected from the Hell of life uncloistered . . .

Wherever he and de la Tour appeared, they declared peace in the name of the Pope, but violence forever followed in their wake, and when they returned to Avignon the following winter, their mission was acknowledged to have been a failure.

WHILE BERNARD had been in Italy, another Bishop of Pamiers was appointed—one Jacques Fournier, twenty years Bernard's junior and a product of the diocese. Born in Saverdun, Fournier had studied theology in Paris and then succeeded his uncle as abbot of the Cistercian monastery of Fontfroide. Already, his precision and severity had gained notice; he was only too eager to embrace the inquisitorial power his successor in Pamiers had shunned, and had determined from the outset of his bishopric tenure to establish his own inquisitorial office for the purposes of detecting all deviance in the diocese—not only deviance of faith, but also sorcery, sodomy, and the propensity to drunkenness. In Bernard's absence, the Inquisitor of Carcassonne had assigned a Dominican friar of Pamiers to serve as an inquisitorial substitute in Fournier's office. The Bishop and the substitute could call a man to trial, interrogate him, and sentence him to wear a cross without consulting anyone. If they wanted to condemn a man to the mur or to relaxation, however, they were to call upon a Dominican inquisitor.

What a dark day it was when Bernard returned to Toulouse to find that he had lost his hold on the people of Clergue's parish, on Clergue himself. Now there was Fournier, young Fournier, who was said to be able to recognize a heretic from a true Christian with the glance of an eye, and to have already successfully tried and converted several from the parish of Pamiers. Fournier's patience, it was said, his earnest desire to communicate, allowed him to win souls back to the Faith so readily. He was known to have passed weeks with an indicted Jew of the diocese, explaining to him the mystery of the Trinity and persuading him to believe in the possibility of God incarnated.

Sixteen years later, this Fournier would become Pope under the name of Benoît XII. Had Bernard known as much, he might have shrunk away from inquisition promptly. He did not want to be second to an inquisitorial other. Already, the glorious dream that had been born in him with Grégoire's letter was dimming. He had tried to be unflinching, had sentenced hundreds upon hundreds who threatened the spiritual wellness of the Church. But a sense of accomplishment eluded him. . . . He could not allow this meager bishop to displace him yet.

Still wearied from his travels, he laid a fresh sheet of parchment across his desk and took a quill between his shivering fingers, preparing to write Clergue. . . . *You have not been forgotten,* he wrote finally. *Bishop Fournier and I will call upon you soon.*

He glanced up from the page and noticed a tiny mirror shining on the wall above his desk. The face of the man looking back at him was so ravaged, so thin, his hair so tangled and white, he could not bring himself to look away. At fifty-five, he had become an old man. He realized, startlingly, that death would be upon him soon, yet he was as far from the peace of Paradise as he had ever been.

NINETEEN

ECHO LABORED on a blanket before the hearth, her back against the end of a bench, her legs spread wide apart. She screamed and screamed, her mother gazed on in astonishment, and Arnaud cooed to her gently—as though her sudden vocalisms had not been unforeseen, as though her agony were a small, sweet thing needing only a bit of soothing. Arnaud lined a basket with straw for the coming child and then lubricated his hands with olive oil, explaining that he had delivered many a lamb in his life; now that Echo's fruit was ready to drop away, he would ease its passage from her body. He massaged her opening, patting and pulling her skin this way and that, softening and stretching her folds as she pushed and breathed.

Convinced suddenly that she needed to go to stool, Echo raised herself up onto her knees and Arnaud held his hands out to catch what fell from her. Moments later, his hands were drenched with her waters, then filled with her child—a girl, who slipped out easily, warm and wet and strangely at peace. In order not to tear the cord away from her, Arnaud asked Echo to lie back on the blanket, and he set the little girl between her thighs—her backside to Echo's opening and the cord over her tiny body. He soaked a square of linen in water and wine and sponged the baby.

When at last the little girl was clean, she wailed loudly, and Echo wailed with relief. What mercy, what mercy there was in the world, she thought, peering through tears at her daughter—*her* daughter, a small sweet thing, a new life asking only to bloom, to be, to flourish with her nurturing. Arnaud cut the cord and tied it tightly, then held the baby up for Echo to embrace. Echo kissed her daughter's pink, moist face. *"Merce" will be your name,* she told her silently. *M-e-r-c-e:* mercy, kindness, thanks, the power to forgive or to be kind. Already the little girl had given Echo back her voice, and with the wonder Echo felt in her breast, she could not be hopeless, could not harbor anger—not even toward the rector.

"We should keep her warm," Arnaud said of the child, and Echo passed Merce to him. He cradled the girl in his arms, then stood with her close to the hearth, holding his hand over her open, curious eyes so that the brightness of the flames would not wound her sight. At long last, Echo and Arnaud had become family.

ECHO SLOWLY BEGAN to speak—at first tentatively, and then with more assurance. Her writing had prepared her to express herself orally. It was only with Merce, however, that her words were copious. "I nearly took a vow of silence, little one," she whispered to the baby. "But your sweetness is so heavenly, how can I not tell you as much?"

Echo had heard many new mothers complain of how often their babies needed to eat, but she eagerly awaited Merce's feedings. She loved holding the girl in the crook of her arm, stroking the thin black fur of her hair, watching her lips purse and suck, her nose twitch, her large, dark eyes become heavy. Echo thought her heart would burst, she was so happy. *Dear God,* she prayed, watching the girl sleep. *Never take my girl away from me. Let my untroubled, heavenly, hopeful Merce stay.*

Though she knew the baby must be baptized, she avoided the rector, and the ever-falling snow of winter shut her and the child in the house for a time. As much in spirit and practice as in name, Merce became Arnaud's daughter. How he loved fussing over her, bringing a smile to her lips, watching her feed and yawn and sleep. Sometimes, as Echo watched him watching the child, she remembered what the rector had told her—that Arnaud had taken his share of men before. She told herself it did not matter whom he had been a lover of, why he had never taken her; with Merce between them, their flesh labored for the same purpose now—to keep the baby alive and contented. What greater togetherness could they forge?

Arnaud was still silent about himself. He never spoke of his needs or history or sadnesses, and because silence with him had also been her habit, she did not begin to question him now. She did not need to question him to know he was in increasing pain. Little soft tumors had begun to reveal themselves in the joints between his fingers, and his walk had become a shuffle. He squinted at the shoes he was making, as if his vision were slipping away, and at night, he moaned, throbbing in his dreams. She watched him as he slept, the light of the moon falling in streaks across their bed, across his face, across his arm tossed around Merce, between them. Echo was aware of his skin, of everything that lay outside of his skin and up against his skin, of the dark sickness that lay beneath. Would he soon be dying?

As much for his sake as for hers, she pressed him to continue their writing lessons. When spring came, they ventured with Merce into the nearly flowering meadows that had earlier served as their schoolroom. Arnaud lay back among the reedy grasses, sucking on the ends of sweet weeds and calling out sentences to her, and she inscribed their syllables into the tablet with greater and greater fluency, uttering the words aloud to give him pleasure.

Sometimes a phrase of song or thankfulness would come to her, and she would breathe its life onto the tablet or into the earth with the tip of her shoe or into Merce's ear: *"Ab l'alen tir vas me l'aire,"* With my breath I draw toward myself the breeze. *"Lanquan li jorn son lonc en mai m'es bels doutz chans d'auzels de loing,"* When the days are long in May I like a sweet song of birds from afar. *"N deman per un mot cen,"* In exchange for one word I ask for a hundred. *"En liey nays joys e comensa,"* In her, joy is born and begins. She did not pause to wonder why the verses were shaping themselves in her mind, but she was grateful for them. With their words beating in her body, the world appeared brighter, more worthy of song and prayer and praise.

AS THE WEATHER grew warm, the rector began to hound her. Sometimes in the morning, before Arnaud had awakened, she would find the rector sniffing at their bedroom window, and later in the day, as she tended to the garden or plucked chickens in the yard, she would catch him staring at her from the bell tower of the chapel. For as long as she stared back at him, he did not lower his gaze.

One afternoon, when Arnaud was looking particularly ashen,

Echo wrapped him in a woolen blanket, gave him a cup of hot honeyed milk, and left Merce napping with him. She ventured down the hill, through the fields and the grove, to the clearing that had once been the home of her love with the rector. There, in the midst of so much green and the arching old trees, the grandfathers of her desire, her heart warmed and she knew she cared for the rector despite the fact that they were no longer together. *"La nostr'amor va enaissi com la branca de l'albespi, qu'esta sobre l'arbr'entrenan la nuoit ab la ploi'ez al gel,"* she thought. Our love goes just like the branch of the hawthorn bush, that remains on the tree at night, in the rain and the frost.

A fierce wind kicked up and the branches of the trees began to sway together. The world was howling and she wanted to howl with it, but she turned and saw the rector not ten paces from her, standing beside the trunk of a birch, his arms crossed over his chest, his eyes wild, as if the wind had swept away his remaining sense.

I didn't see you, she said silently, afraid of sullying her voice by sharing it with him.

"Am I such a stranger to you, Echo?" he said. "All the village is talking about your regained speech. They say it is your husband, your child, the pleasure they have brought you. . . . Don't you remember I gave them to you, Echo? Gave your mother the house that shelters you?"

She looked down at the ground and lifted the hem of her skirt so not to trip over fallen branches. She wanted to leave.

"Why do you not speak for me?" he said, blocking her path. He held her shoulder with one hand and stroked her hair with the other. "You are still my girl, tell me."

She stared into his wild green eyes, unable to speak.

A cruel, animal sneer came over his mouth and he squeezed her shoulder. "So you *are* his lover now," he said.

She shook her head, no.

"I won't let you go back to him without having some of you," he said. He thrust his weight against her and shoved her to the ground. She cried out, and he smiled viciously, pinning her hands over her head and pushing her skirt up, her linens down.

"Putana," he muttered. *Whore.* "Putrid with the rot of so much putrid milk."

She fought against him for a time, but fighting only made his deed more painful. She tried to shut her body down—to numb it into nonfeeling. *It will soon be over, soon be over,* she told herself, containing the pain in silence, waiting. She smelled his rotten breath, heard his grunts distantly, as if she were somewhere else.

When he was through, she did not look at his face, but curled onto her side and stared at the tips of her fingers. How deadened they seemed to be, merely appendages of her deadened body.

"You can tell the Inquisitor what I did to you," she heard him say. "You won't be safe from inquisition now that you can speak. Now that you can stand trial." She listened to him step from her, breaking branches underfoot.

When she looked up at him, she saw that he was standing several paces away, a dark expression of horror on his features. It was as if, in violating her, he had murdered what lightness remained in his life, and now he was wondering how he might most quickly die.

"Did you baptize my mother?" she said, sitting and gripping the aching place between her thighs.

His eyes lifted to meet hers.

"Did you baptize my mother?" she said again.

"I never told anyone that," he whispered. "Who told you that?"

"I read it in your book," she said coldly. "Fabrisse Clergue, baptized in the year of Our Lord twelve hundred and eighty-two, the twenty-ninth of December." She paused. "Is my mother your daughter?"

"No," he said quickly. "Dear God, no . . . My niece . . . I had a brother who died long ago. Guillaume. But he never knew Fabrisse, and cared nothing for her mother." A small smile of defeat crept over his lips. "I suppose your husband taught you to read," he murmured. "I should have kept you from his heresy."

She was so surprised to hear the word "heresy" coupled with "husband," a moment passed before she thought to defend Arnaud, before she realized that the rector's assumption about him could lead to trouble with the Inquisition.

"He is no heretic," she said, but the rector had already turned to go, leaving her in the windy wood alone.

FOR DAYS, Echo kept quiet about the encounter, trying to purge herself of the festering hatred for the rector that had found its way into her breast. Even as she listened to the babbling Merce, however, her ears were hot with the memory of the rector's cruel words, and when she glimpsed her mother, glazed over from drink, she felt guilty—as though, in keeping quiet about the rector's blood relation to them, she were corroborating his crime of secrecy. For as long as she could remember, her mother had been suffering for lack of the rector's love; perhaps if her mother knew of her relation to him, the heartache that drew her to drink would subside.

It was still difficult for Echo to find voice in the presence of her mother, as she often felt her mother eyeing her with blame. Only two days after the birth of Merce—when Echo had first begun to form words aloud—her mother had accused her of never having tried hard enough to speak. "So you went on punishing me and punishing me when you could have tried harder," her mother had said, and Echo had been left with the shadowy thought that perhaps her previous silence had been as much a convenience as a curse. Perhaps she had shielded herself from her mother's disinterest by shutting up the words her mother might ignore.

In truth, her silence had been a blessing when she had taken the rector as a lover, for she had never had to explain her whereabouts to her mother, never had to justify her sin, to acknowledge her betrayal, to bear the burden of defending herself in the face of her mother's anger. Since then, the rector had cleaved them one from the other, and they existed within the cold, unspoken knowledge that he stood between them—one of them chosen, the other spurned.

No, Echo did not want to give him such power over them anymore. She would speak to her mother. She would risk reproach, rejection. She wanted her mother to know who they were.

One evening, while Arnaud was resting with Merce in the bedroom, her mother returned from wine-selling, complaining of all the tongues that had held her in talk through the day. Echo watched her sit at the table and pour herself an evening cup.

"Am I that hideous to you?" her mother said.

Echo realized she had been staring. "No, Mama," she said.

"Am I nothing more than a foul old woman now?"

Echo sat across from her. "No."

"Stop staring then."

Echo nodded, paused. "I want to talk to you, Mama."

Her mother sighed, poured another cup. "Have I not told you I've been held in talk all day?"

"I saw him," said Echo.

Her mother frowned over the rim of her cup.

"A few days back," said Echo. "In the wood. We—"

"I thought you had stopped all that," said her mother. "All that fucking behind your husband's back."

"Please."

"You're no kind of mother. Leaving your child with your husband all day."

"Listen to me, Mama."

"If I were your husband, I would take a mistress. Even my wife's mother. A woman is a woman, no? What with his sadness over you being gone all the time, he'll soon be dead. I should save him from his misery."

Echo felt her heart pounding. "The rector is your uncle, Mama."

Her mother peered at her, the corners of her mouth glistening with wine.

"His brother," said Echo, "a dead brother named Guillaume, is your father. And the rector baptized you himself. Your name is written in his book. Fabrisse Clergue. That is your name, Mama."

Her mother's mouth moved slightly, but her gaze was still frozen.

"We must put him out of our heads," said Echo. "He is a blood relation and no good for either of us. No good for Merce." Echo could not remember the last time her mother had listened silently to her, and the silence, the listening was such a comfort now, her throat hurt with coming tears. "He is a cruel man, Mama," she said, "and unworthy of our devotion." She reached out and took her mother's hand, but her mother snatched it away.

"I have no name," her mother said, standing from the table, a blank expression on her face. She grabbed the flask and cup, and left the kitchen.

That night, Echo was awakened by a loud noise coming from above. It was not the familiar creaking of her mother walking to the roof's center, but a heavy, blunt thudding, as if someone were trying to break through the roof with a plank of wood. Together with Arnaud, she ventured outside, Merce tucked into a blanket in her arms.

The moon was full, the sky more blue than black, the clouds illuminated and haunting. In the glow of the night, Echo saw her mother, stark naked on the rooftop, pacing back and forth, gesturing madly toward the fortress, muttering something about the Châtelaine, about how the Châtelaine needed her to prepare. How pitiful her mother's body looked, ravaged by age, her breasts and belly and buttocks hanging like withered fruit clinging too long to the tree. Echo wanted to hide her away from peering eyes.

"Mama!" she called, quietly as she could.

Her mother cowered down, covering her head, as if someone were about to strike her. "Please!" her mother cried, with such anguish Echo felt her own heart break.

BY THE TIME Echo was able to coax her mother down, dawn had almost broken, and—though a crowd had not gathered to watch the spectacle of her mother's losing her mind—Echo knew that by midday all the village would be clucking with feigned pity. Her mother had never quite kept to the fold, and the fold would be all too happy to cast her aside.

In a sense, the peace of mind Echo had hoped her mother would come to know with the knowledge of her name did descend upon her. She cared not a stitch about the villagers' newly unconcealed scorn for her; indeed she cared not a stitch for the daily affairs of life. She ceased to drink or sell wine, to cook, to speak audibly or sensibly, to sleep in her bed, to move about in the village. Instead, she sat through the days in a chair lined with pillows at the kitchen window, gazing up toward the fortress, the same blank expression on her face. And Echo knew she had failed her—rather than shielding her from pain, she had perverted her mother's prevailing dream. The peace her mother had come to know was a peace of having been not emancipated from illusion, but conquered.

BECAUSE HER MOTHER could no longer work, and because Arnaud no longer made shoes with much speed, Echo took up her mother's wine-selling trade, journeying to Camurac and Prades d'Aillon to increase business. Each morning, she set out with Merce slung across her hip, and weekly she paid a village boy to fetch wine on muleback. Without her mother draining supplies, the trade was more profitable than Echo had expected, and one day—when she noticed a lump forming on the side of Arnaud's nose—she told him to stop working. He refused her. "I won't be useless, Echo," he said. She saw his hands shaking and apologized.

The following winter, when Merce was a year of age, Arnaud woke up one morning with five new lumps around the bridge of his nose; by dawn he had fallen into seizure three times. From that day forth, he was almost continuously in fever, and he begged Echo to keep Merce away. "I may infect her," he said. "Or hurt her in seizure."

"You have been ill for a long time, Arnaud," she said. "The girl is fine. She wants to be with her father."

The three of them still slept together because Echo insisted upon it, and because Merce loved nestling between them. One night, when Arnaud was in a terrible sweat, Echo asked if he might not allow her to change his shirt, but he refused her, shy. Before blowing out the candle at his side, he grimaced and turned to her.

"I want to apologize to you, Echo," he said. "For being such a false husband . . . I never consummated my love for you." His pale eyes studied her without timidity, and she, too, became shy. She looked down and took his knotted hand from where it was clasping the sheet. "It wasn't that I didn't want to," he continued. "Only—"

"You needn't explain," she said. "Rest. Please."

His trembling thumb stroked her hand. "All my life," he said, "it has seemed I have been holding a secret inside." His hand moved from hers to the damp fabric over his chest. "The secret that I was not supposed to be. That I was contrary to nature. And it has made me terribly hesitant in life."

She looked up at him, returning his gaze.

"Did I tell you my father was a doctor to the Count in Foix?" he said, an uncertain, wavering smile playing at the corners of his mouth. "I don't even know if he is still alive. But he saved a good many people from death. And he taught me how to recognize when a life was beyond saving. . . . This life, my life, has come to the end of its time, Echo."

Though she had known, in her deepest heart, that his death was drawing near, his acknowledgment of it overwhelmed her. He was giving in to death, allowing himself to be overtaken, and it was not just. She needed him. "You are the father of my girl," she burst out. "You cannot die!"

Tears began to streak down his sweaty face. "I am sorry," he said, and then he said it again, and again, as if he were apologizing not only to her, not only to Merce, but also to all the loved ones of his life.

BY SPRING, Arnaud had exiled himself to the bed, banning Echo and the baby from his side. "Stay away! Away!" he called to Merce when she wandered into the room, craving his company.

The lumps that had appeared on his face softened further and began to eat away at his body—at his nose and then at the skin around the open wound where his nose had been, at his lips, at the skin over his forehead, inside his throat. He became so hoarse, he could barely speak, and what skin remained on his face turned a dark, crimson color. The room itself took on the sour stench of death, and though neither Arnaud nor Echo confessed as much, they both feared leprosy had taken hold of him. As the new Bishop of Pamiers was said to be scouring the diocese for lepers, they kept the shutters shut and the stench sealed in, afraid the illness would be discovered by ill-wishing others.

Late one night, when Merce was deep in sleep, Echo rose from the pallet in her mother's abandoned room and wrapped herself in her cloak. She lit an oil lamp and stole hastily down the road to the chapel. Long before, the rector had told her where to find the key to the chapel on the occasion that she came to meet him and found him nowhere. Just as he had promised, the key was pressed into the earth beneath a flat stone two paces to the right of the steps to the portal. As quickly as she could, she unlatched the door, slipped inside, and made for the vestry.

In the orange glow of the lamplight, she saw the rector's little desk, and, upon it, a jar of ink, several quills, a blotter, and a modest stack of paper. She pulled the stool out from under the desk, set the lamp on the table, and sat. The quill was similar to the stylus she had used with Arnaud, but she had never written with ink before, and she made several attempts at dipping the tip of the quill into the ink, blotting it, and setting it down onto the paper before producing a legible letter.

She knew none of the conventions of correspondence—neither how to address an intended reader, nor how to indicate her identity as author—but she scripted the content of what she had come to convey with rapid assurance:

You do not know me. I am the wife of your son, Arnaud. We live in a vil-
lage not more than a half-day journey from Ax-les-Thermes. Montail-
lou is the name. Your son is ill. Please come before he dies.

The next morning, before dawn, she knocked at the window of
the boy she often hired out to buy wine supplies. When he appeared at
the window, pink-cheeked and dreamy-eyed, she gave him the letter,
instructing him to deliver it to the court doctor of Foix. "A doctor by
the name of Lizier," she said, placing several sous on the frame of the
window. He smiled down at the money. "There will be more if you find
the man," she told him. He took the money and scampered away.

Soon after, she stood in her garden and looked out over the fields
and pastures gaining golden color as the early-morning fog faded. The
boy dashed by on his way down the road, his dark, fleecy hair bouncing with each leap he made. *Lizier!* she wanted to call after him, but restrained herself.

BEFORE THE BOY returned to the village, inquisition did, and this time
it was the rector who delivered summonses. First to be called to Pamiers
was the remainder of the family Maurs, then the entirety of the family
Belot—whose members had previously escaped to Catalonia only to return in recent years.

Occasionally, Echo caught sight of the rector on the road, moving
with the lethargy of a corpse, his eyes fixed indifferently in front of him.
It was commonly said that when a man plainly and passionlessly turned
against his brethren, death was at his door—he was generating the enemies who would soon slay him.

One morning the chapel bells did not ring at dawn, and Echo
knew the rector had fled for his life. She could not imagine him surviving away from the village for long. What was he but the priest of this
little parish, the lover of its women? How could he continue to breathe
apart from what he was?

She told Arnaud that the rector had fled, suspecting the news would
relieve him. Instead, he became grave, and cautioned her at once to flee
with Merce from the diocese. "He will be found, Echo," he told her. "The
Inquisition will find him. And he will spare no one. Especially not you."

"Why not me?"

"He lost you, Echo."

"And who will care for you?" she cried. "Who will care for Mama? And for Merce and me when we are alone? No, we will not leave you."

"Please," he implored her. "Go. And when I am healed, I will find you."

"You won't be healed, Arnaud," she said, not intending to be unkind.

THE BOY she had paid to deliver the letter returned with far less fervor than that with which he had departed. Having heard of Pamiers's new inquisitorial offensive against all heretics in the diocese, he had taken his time in Foix. "There weren't many who would talk to me there," he whispered to Echo in her kitchen on the evening of his homecoming. "And no one knew of a court doctor by the name of Lizier. I might not have found him if an old woman hadn't taken kindly to me. Took me in and let me stay in the servants' quarters of her grand old house. Said that Lizier was a fine doctor in his time, but had become sick with sadness worse than plague."

"And did you find him?" whispered Echo.

"Yes, yes," said the boy, his gray-green eyes flashing with irritation. "The old woman herself led me by the hand to his house—an enormous, dark thing. Half the size of our fortress. And so sooty, with all the windows closed. An old man came to the door—more phantom than man, I tell you. 'I have a letter for the Doctor Lizier,' I said, and he said, 'I am the Doctor Lizier.' And then I held the letter out, and he took it and shut the door." The corners of his lips lifted in a strained grin. "You told me there would be more money if I found the man himself. And I did. I did. And I'd like my money, please."

Echo paid the boy his sous and silently urged herself not to wait for the doctor's coming.

EVERY MORNING, before she set off wine-selling, she made a bread soup, fed her mother and Arnaud each a bowl, ate what she herself could stomach, and sat out in the garden with Merce at her breast, watching the day come to light. It seemed to her that despite the misery those she cherished were suffering, there was gladness to be found all around. Each piece of nature her eyes rested upon seemed to be a little offering, a little affirmation of beauty and life, beckoning her to leave her worries, to leave the solitude of her own mind. *Look to the things before you,* they seemed to say—*the wet, wheaten valley, the water trickling from the tree, the clouds so soft and bright, the breast swelling with cream. Look to what you can see, and you will find peace.*

And then, one morning, her eyes took delight in the shape of a man approaching along a footpath at the edge of the fields. He was neither woodcutter nor farmer, for he walked with an upright gait—as one unaccustomed to the burdens of carrying a heavy pack or bending over the plow. Repeatedly, he turned his gaze from the footpath up to the village, as a stranger to Montaillou might. He disappeared from view, and Echo pulled Merce from her breast and covered herself. She walked with the drowsy child down to the elm in the square.

The man emerged from the bend in the road by the chapel. He was carrying a small sack in hand, his gaze downcast as he trod wearily up the steep incline. Now and again, he paused to catch his breath. When he was close to the square, she stepped out from the shelter of the elm, and his eyes lifted to meet hers. From the distance, they surveyed each other. Then he bowed his head and continued up the road, and she ventured toward him.

They stopped an arm's distance from each other. His pale eyes studied her, and she noticed his white, unkempt hair, his haggard features. Something about the dullness of his stare gave her the impression that he had left the ardor of his life long before.

"Doctor?" she whispered.

His eyes fell to the sleeping child in her arms. He covered his mouth with his fist and nodded.

IN SILENCE, she led him to the house. As they passed through the kitchen, she noticed him staring at the hearth, at the half-eaten ham hanging from the rafters, at the straw-covered floor. Never had her abode seemed humble to her before. His eyes paused on the face of her mother, sleeping in a childish pose in the chair.

"I will show you to Arnaud," she whispered, at once ashamed of her mother and wanting to protect her.

She lay Merce on her mother's pallet and led the doctor to the bedroom where Arnaud slept, stretched out on the bed, his decaying mouth wide open and searching for air, the wounds around the hole of his nose oozing yellow water. When the doctor saw him, he burst into tears.

Without a word, he made his way to the window and angrily thrust the shutters open. "At least my son can have some air!" he cried out.

Echo dared not dispute him.

Arnaud's eyes batted open and he squinted at the man at the window. He pushed himself up in the bed and glanced at Echo, who was standing in the doorway.

"I wrote him a letter, Arnaud," she said softly. "I told him of your illness. I asked him to come."

Bewildered, Arnaud looked back at his father.

"My boy," the old man said. He walked around the bed and sat at Arnaud's side, looking down at his knotted, wounded hands that clutched at the covers.

Arnaud appeared at once tentative, terrified, and euphoric: he stared at the man, his mouth quivering. Echo feared he would die from shock.

"Arnaud," she said. "He needn't stay. If it is too much for you."

"Father," Arnaud murmured, and the man shuddered in another fit of tears.

For a time, they sat like that, the man crying into his hands, Arnaud staring tensely at him. Then the man wiped his face.

"When I learned that you had fled from the school," he said, his voice unsteady, "when I learned that you had run away in the night, I went to the Count, asked if he wouldn't give me some of his men, and he did. . . ."

"You looked for me?" said Arnaud.

"We searched for you everywhere," his father said. "In the most wretched places . . . But you were nowhere to be found. They said you must be dead." He shook his head. "I couldn't rest. Couldn't keep going on with patients and their illnesses wondering if you were in greater pain somewhere. Wondering if, by some miracle, you were waiting for me at home." His eyes searched Arnaud's. "Why did you never come home?"

Arnaud frowned. It seemed to Echo that his answer was too large for words.

"All these years," his father said, "the thing I have most wanted to tell you is that I was wrong to send you away, Arnaud. To send you to a place among strangers." He nodded through his tears. "You were my stroke of luck, my brightest star. . . . When you were small, I thought myself too lucky. How unjust it seemed that I had you—spent every day with your sweet smile, your sweet nature—when your poor mother, who had wanted you so much, was all alone. . . . And then I sent you away to be alone, too." He struck his thigh with his fist. "I knew from the start that sending you away was wrong, a mistake. I wanted to fetch you. But I was afraid you would think me a coward. That I couldn't survive without you. How cowardly I was."

"I didn't know. I didn't know," Arnaud murmured.

The man closed his eyes for a moment, as if reseeing the events of the past. "The boys at the school told me what the master had done to you," he said. "I should have killed that man then and there."

"But weren't you angry with me, Father?"

The man appeared confused.

"Didn't the boys, the master, tell you what I had done?"

His father's expression softened. "Oh, Arnaud," he said, "I was never for a moment angry with you."

They cried together then, embracing awkwardly, Arnaud turning his face so that his wounds would not touch his father's skin. "I thought," Arnaud said, "if I went home to you, I wouldn't be able to bear your scorn. If you hadn't wanted me—"

"Hadn't wanted you?"

"I preferred to be alone than risk being spurned."

"But I would never, never—" his father sputtered. "Can you forgive me? Can you forgive me for abandoning you?"

"I abandoned you," said Arnaud. "I need your forgiveness." Suddenly, he pushed away from his father's clasp and looked him solemnly in the eye. "I brought this, this horrible disease, this leprosy upon myself, Father. God is punishing me for wrongdoing."

"No!" his father cried out. He caressed the back of Arnaud's head, stroking his matted hair. "You have been struck down by an appalling, pitiless contagion. It is against the nature of God to be so merciless."

THAT EVENING, after the doctor had examined Arnaud, he came to the kitchen and Echo fed him a small feast of fig-stuffed chicken, garlic soup, and fried ham. He drank at least half a flagon of wine, regarded her staring mother with an equally blank expression, and asked Echo to sit so that they might speak together. Merce was busy trying to climb up onto the bench across from him, and Echo scooped her up onto her lap as she sat. Merce tapped her plump fingers against the table's edge.

"I do not believe he is ill with leprosy," the doctor said. He sniffed, and his red-rimmed eyes studied the baby's tapping fingers. "There is another contagion. Far rarer, and as yet unrecognized. I have seen two cases, a man and his wife, both decried lepers by other doctors and confined to a colony beyond the city wall. But they were not lepers, no."

Echo held Merce more tightly against herself, and the girl squealed, batting her arms to be free. "How do you know they were not?" Echo said.

The doctor's eyes met hers. "Every disease has its course," he said. "And in both of these cases, the man's and his wife's, the disease began with a single wound on the genitals." He paused, studying Echo as if to determine whether or not his words were too crude. "Later," he continued, "a rash appeared, an eruption of yellow pustules. In his case, over the entire body, and in hers, over the face and thighs . . . It was then that they were outcast, sent to the colony, but the pustules went away. The man and his wife were released, esteemed saints. . . . In three years, however, the contagion flared in a tertiary phase. Nodules began to form under the skin of his face, ulcerating his palate and larynx. His genitals, too, were eaten away. And she—" He stopped himself short, shook his head as if to tell himself to be silent.

"She?" said Echo, bouncing Merce up and down.

"She was seized with pain so terrible, so excruciating, her screams could be heard all around. She went quite mad. Became half-paralyzed. And then one night, her heart stopped entirely." His features squeezed together, as if suddenly he were enduring the woman's pain. "It would be quite normal, Madame," he said quietly, "if pustules had manifested on your body. On your vulva or thighs . . . Have you noticed anything?"

Echo shook her head. She had not. No.

"Forgive my indiscretion," he said. "But I must advise you then not to lie with my son as a wife might with her husband." He sighed, glancing again at her mother, who nodded to him as though, somehow, she were aware and appreciative of his advice.

"Let us pray that it is not too late for you, Madame," he said to Echo. "May you be spared."

OVER THE FOLLOWING DAYS, the doctor burned juniper berries throughout the house to purify the air he feared corrupted, gave Arnaud several courses of clysters to cleanse his bowels, and rubbed a cloth coated with an ointment of mercury over Arnaud's limbs and face. Against all hope and reason, he was doing what he could to cure his son.

During this time, Echo continued to sell wine, and on a journey to Camurac, she learned that massacres had occurred in the province of Toulouse and the dioceses of Albi and Cahors. Bands of peasants who called themselves pastoureaux had convened throughout the country with the purpose of claiming the Holy Land and ridding France of Jews. Without discretion or mercy, they had gone about slaughtering Jewish families and seizing their property, much to the horror of the authorities of the Church and the Comté. It was said that the pastoureaux were headed for Avignon to capture and disburse the wealth of the papacy. Already, several had been caught in Carcassonne. When Echo told Arnaud and his father the news, the old man hid his face in his hands. "Who do they believe themselves to be," he murmured, "killing God's creatures in His name?"

On the morning of the doctor's seventh day in the village, they were awakened by a heavy thrashing at the door. The last time Echo had heard such an avid, angry knocking, she had been a girl. That day, her father's body had been exhumed and burned. That night, her grandmother had stopped breathing. Vaguely, she remembered the rector murmuring prayers over her grandmother's half-dead body.

She covered herself with a blanket and went to the door. A single henchman stood beyond the threshold. He was stoutly built, and carried both a crossbow and a sword. Behind him, she saw several village men gathered in her garden.

"Grazida Lizier?" the henchman said.

She nodded.

"You have been called to Pamiers. You are to leave immediately. The Bishop will expect you to appear at the gate of the episcopal palace two days from now at noon. If you do not present yourself at that time, you will be arrested and imprisoned. And if you attempt to flee, you will be excommunicated and hunted down, and the property of your family will be confiscated to the Church." Without so much as a nod, he left, and she shut the door quickly, afraid he would return to summon Arnaud or her mother.

She found Arnaud sitting up in his bed, bracing the arm of his father, who was crouching beside him. "You are safe," she said, and tears sprang to her eyes—tears of relief and gratitude, she realized. Yes, she was the strongest of the family, and thus the one who ought to defend them now.

"And you?" Arnaud said quietly.

She knew his dread was for her, and she wished there were a way to protect him from the truth. "Me?" she said, unable to answer.

SHE HAD WANTED to take Merce with her, as the girl was not weaned and neither Arnaud nor her mother could tend to her, but the doctor assured her that the girl would be far safer left at his side. "The journey will be difficult on both of you if she goes," he said. "And if, God forbid, you are imprisoned, there is little chance the girl would live—what with the unclean water and the dysentery that almost always accompanies imprisonment with others. . . . You are strong enough to resist disease, but not the girl."

"She needs my milk," Echo argued.

"Not anymore," the doctor said.

She put together a bag of bread and cheese and fruit, and the doctor pressed a pouch heavy with coins into her palm. "That boy you sent with your letter," he said. "He seemed a good boy to me. Give him some money to accompany you on the journey. And be sure to stay at an inn that is clean—there are so many where undesirables hang about."

She thanked him for the money, and he told her not to worry about her mother. "I will watch over her myself," he said. "And I will hire a servant or two to tend to the house and the cooking and the girl. . . . We shall be well. We shall be well."

Later, the boy sat out in the garden with her sack while she bid the family farewell. She held Arnaud's unwounded fingers to her lips, to her cheeks. "Thank you," she told him, and could not say more. Arnaud nodded to her, equally mute.

The doctor followed her to the kitchen, Merce in his arms. She kissed her mother on one cheek and then the other, and then fell against her breast. *I am afraid,* she thought. *Mama, I am afraid.* She felt her mother stroke her back. "Can't you stay?" her mother whispered.

"I am sorry, Mama," she said.

She nodded to the doctor, then took Merce in her arms, kissing her fat cheeks. The little girl squealed with laughter and Echo broke into tears. She gave the girl back to the doctor and turned to go.

At the door, she looked over her shoulder and Merce giggled at her. Echo laughed through her tears. "Be a good girl now," she said. She forced herself to open the door. One last time, she looked at the girl, who squealed again with pleasure.

"Take her away, please," Echo said.

"We shall be well!" the doctor said, then disappeared with the girl into the bedroom where Arnaud lay.

SHE AND THE BOY ventured through the heat of the day past Camurac and Comus, and down along the River Hers, through the narrow, relentless Gorges of Fear. She tried to describe to herself the world they passed, to lose herself in the rhythms of words, to rest in the merciful sight of sky and crag and river. . . . But ridge after ridge blurred like shadow in her mind, the light looked dead, the trees dry, conveying nothing of fertile pleasure. She was left with fear, with heat, with the cloudless sky that offered no shelter. She tasted red dust in her mouth, smelled her own souring, spilled milk. She would have cried were it not for the boy walking before her, and the cheerful manner in which he glanced back at her. "Should we stop and rest?" he asked, concerned, and she told him no, told him they must push on.

They arrived in Lavelanet late that evening, and then, before sundown the following day, in Pamiers. As the boy scurried through the suffocating streets in search of an inn with a vacancy, she took shelter behind an abandoned cart and stared up at the great, crenellated walls of the fortress that dominated the city. Just below stood a smaller fortification, dark of color, and austere with its many windowless towers.

"I found a room!" the boy sang, bounding back toward her. It was as if, for his youth, he could not conceive of the gravity of her plight, did not understand that her life and liberty were in question, that this ashen view could be her last unencumbered experience of sight.

AS THE BOY SLEPT on a bed beside her that night, she realized suddenly that the rector might be in Pamiers. Perhaps, as Arnaud had feared, he had been caught and tried. Perhaps he had been the one to speak against her.

The next morning, the boy walked with her through the stuffy streets toward the palace of the Bishop, the same dark, windowless fortification she had seen the day before. She stepped along the dry stitches in the road, imagining the fertile plain and the freely flowing Ariège beyond the city walls. She had not known until now how fresh the mountain air of Montaillou was.

She was made to wait at the palace gate. The boy waited with her, kicking rocks to pass time. When at last a guard came to lead her within, she was seized with panic and stooped to embrace the boy, who stood passively, allowing her to take of him what she needed.

"Shall I wait for you here?" he asked.

"No," she said. And then, "Would that be too difficult?"

"I'll wait," he said, and stiffened while she embraced him again.

The galleries of the palace were narrow and dark and unadorned, and when the guard stopped at a small door, she prepared herself to enter a cavity as cramped as a cell. Instead, when the door was opened by a man within, she was ushered into a large, light-filled hall, with a wooden-planked floor covered with rugs, tapestries hanging about the walls, and a table long as a tree, behind which four men sat.

At the center was a man in elaborate, priestly garb—the Bishop, she supposed. He was younger than she had anticipated, and dark-featured, with a curious smile playing upon his lips and a gentleness in his eyes that almost embarrassed her. He stood, nodded, and gestured to the chair in the center of the chamber.

"Rest your legs, Madame," he said, his voice as placid as his regard. "You must be tired from the journey. I hear you were made to travel in haste."

She approached the chair, glancing at the others at the table. The eldest of the four was a gaunt, ill-looking white-haired friar. On the other side of the Bishop were two men with quills in hand. Before each were large sheets of paper, jars of ink, and blotters.

The Bishop sat as she did. "It is I," he said, "who will question you today, Madame. The man to my right is the very significant Inquisitor

Bernard of Toulouse. It is a rare occasion that he replaces the Dominican who usually assists me." He glanced at the Inquisitor, whose black, unblinking eyes did not stray from her. "The Inquisitor wanted very much to be here today for you. And I have invited him to be present on the condition that he allow me to conduct the interrogation."

There was a moment of silence, and then the scratching sounds of the scribes writing filled the room. She doubted their marks, feared the scribes were already condemning her with every mortal, imprecise stroke.

"To begin," said the Bishop, glancing down at a page of a thick book open before him. "I must tell you of what you are accused. In doing so I will ask you to swear to tell the truth." He smiled again at her, the corners of his eyes creasing together. "Do you, Grazida, wife of Arnaud Lizier, swear by the sacred Gospels of God to tell the truth, as much about yourself as a defendant as about others as a witness?" He paused. "You may answer."

"Yes," she said.

"And do you swear by these same gospels to tell the truth about the heresy of which you are strongly suspected, and about the incest and debauchery which you are accused of committing through the agency of Pierre Clergue, rector of the Church of Montaillou?"

She was so stunned by his words, by their coldness, she could not speak for a moment. *Incest. Debauchery.* No, those words did not reflect her experience of the rector, of what they had shared. She realized suddenly, and with the full force of certainty, that the rector had indeed spoken against her. Who else knew of their blood relation?

"Madame?" the Bishop prompted, and the Inquisitor coughed into his fist, frowning at her. The scratching sounds of the scribes continued.

"Yes," she said. "I swear to tell the truth."

"Finally," the Bishop said. "Is there any man or woman whom you consider to be your enemy?"

"Enemy?" she said. "No!" Certainly, there were villagers who had gossiped about her sudden ability to speak, or about her pregnancy—so soon in showing itself after her marriage—or about her mother's drunkenness, or madness. Certainly, since Merce had been born, she had shied away from the rector, resented his spying, hated him even—especially after he had forced himself on her. But she had never considered him—or anyone else—to be an enemy.

"Then," the Bishop said, "I will ask you to give us an account of how your carnal relationship with the rector began."

She paused, thinking. Though she had never felt shame with the rector, she was humiliated now, aware that these men considered their lovemaking to be a humiliation. Still, it did not occur to her to lie about what had happened. She had sworn by the sacred Gospels to tell the truth. "Four years ago," she said, "or five, I am not sure, I walked to the wood, to the clearing, as I had often since I was a girl. . . . The rector was there."

She listened to her voice as if it were not hers, as if the life of which it spoke were something other than that which she had felt, sensed, lived. When she and the rector had begun it had been spring, and he had looked at her as if not knowing how to comfort her, how to touch her, and there had been trees all around. He had smelled strange, like myrrh and cedar, was it? And she had cried, yes, because her mother had hurt her so. He had held her as no one in her life had held her, and they had lain together, in the clearing, by the stream, a stream whose water trickled down to the Ariège. And he had touched her, and she had been frightened and had wanted more. And there had been the sounds of the forest, the sounds of his breath, the pain in her center—how good it felt not to be alone anymore.

"He comforted me," she said, "as I was sad at the time. He embraced me, and I kissed him. I couldn't speak, you see. Since I had been a girl, words had failed me." Now, too, words were failing her. As much as she tried to be truthful, every utterance was an approximation, and thus a lie of sorts, a small murder of what had been. And the simple, plodding story of how she and the rector had begun sounded empty and awful to her ears. "It was then that he lay upon me. Not violently. Gently. With much kindness. He asked me to forgive him, but there was nothing to forgive."

The Inquisitor stood suddenly from his chair, an angry expression in his eyes. "Are you suggesting that Clergue told you it was not a sin for a priest to know a virgin carnally?" he asked.

The Bishop glared at him. "I implore you," he said, "to allow me to conduct the interrogation. If you have questions when I am through, you may ask them then."

The Inquisitor sat, plainly displeased, and the Bishop turned his gaze back to her. "Madame," he said, "when you knew this rector carnally, did you believe yourself to be sinning with him?"

"Sinning?" she said. "No, I did not think I was sinning. It gave us both great joy when we made love. Our joy was shared then."

"And did you not know," the Bishop said, "that this rector was a kinsman of your mother, although an illegitimate one?"

"I did not know until recently," she said. "My mother knew nothing of it herself. She had never known the name of her father."

"But if you had known that your mother was a niece of his," the Bishop said, "would you have so willingly been known by him?"

But that is not the way it was, she thought. "I do not believe so," she said, realizing that, after the birth of Merce, she had withdrawn from the rector not simply because they were related by blood, but because he had kept their relation a secret from her, because he had never told her mother, of all people, who her own father had been.

The Bishop turned a page in his book. "How long did you continue to know the rector?" he said to her.

She considered the question. "From one spring to another," she said. "We made love from one spring to another, and then—" Then Merce sprang to life inside me, she thought.

"Then?" the Bishop said.

"Then the rector gave me in marriage to my husband. . . ."

"And did your fleshly sinning with the rector continue?"

She felt her face become hot with shame and anger. Why should she have to reveal the intimacies of her life and love to these men? "Still sometimes we met in the wood," she said. "But less and less. Less and less."

"You hid it from your husband?" the Bishop said, scowling at her.

"I went to the wood when he was away," she said, "or occupied with his shoe-making." She remembered the conquered look in Arnaud's eyes when she returned from the wood some evenings. "I think," she said, "it is possible my husband knew about it. But he never chastised me, or asked me to confess as much."

The Bishop glanced at the Inquisitor, who regarded him with an expression of disgust. "You have conducted yourself badly with this priest," the Bishop said to her. "In particular, because you have a husband. Did you not think it a sin to know a man other than your husband? Did you not think such carnal deeds might displease God?"

She tried to remember if there had been a moment—a fleeting moment—during which she had felt a shadow of Godly judgment descend upon her and the rector. She had felt the presence of the trees, of the wind, of the leaves, of the moss making her back damp. She had felt the rector's trepidation. But never for a moment had she thought that their mingling was an affront to God.

"No," she said. "I did not think our lying together should displease any living being."

The Bishop pushed his book away from him, toward the center of the table. "Suppose your husband had told you it displeased him," he said. "Would you have believed it to be a sin then?"

"He did not tell me it displeased him."

"Suppose he had," he said more firmly.

"I still would not have thought it a sin," she said. Surely, she would have felt more sorry, sorry to hurt Arnaud. But sin was bad, evil. Her lovemaking with the rector had been bliss. "If any man lies with any woman," she said, "whether he is a priest or a cobbler, whether she is a virgin or a widow, whether in marriage or outside it, if their joy is shared, I do not think they sin. I do not think I sinned with the rector."

"And who taught you this great error, woman?" the Inquisitor broke in. His face had become red and wrathful.

"You will answer the question," the Bishop said softly, studying his hands, clasped over his book.

"No one but myself," she responded.

The Inquisitor groaned, pushed his chair back noisily, and began to pace behind the others. One of the scribes stopped writing, but the Bishop pressed on, smiling at her in a strained, unhappy manner. "And have you spoken of your ideas about carnal union to anyone else?" he said.

"No," she said. "No one has ever asked me about them." She glanced up at the Inquisitor, who was mumbling quietly to himself as he paced.

"Do you believe that those people who live a good and saintly life will go to Paradise after death and that sinners will go to Hell?" the Bishop said. "More shortly, do you believe there is a Hell, a Paradise?"

She hesitated, trying to concentrate on the question rather than on the indecipherable mumblings of the Inquisitor. "I have heard it said there is a Paradise," she said. She could imagine Paradise—something like the wood, but wider, with bending trees and streams with glistening trout to eat and the sounds of leaves and wind and water dripping, running. Yes, she could imagine it. Paradise would be as good as love with the rector had been. "I believe it," she said. "I have also heard there is a Hell. Although I cannot imagine it." She had never seen a place where no brightness entered in, where nothing but nothing of goodness could be found.

"Do you believe that people shall be resurrected?" the Bishop asked.

"I've heard that we shall rise again after death," she said. "I see no reason to question the idea. . . . But I have not seen as much, and so I cannot believe in it with certainty."

The Bishop slid his book toward himself and considered the open page. "Do you believe that God made all the things of this world?" he said, his eyes lifting to meet hers.

The things of this world . . . She thought of the valley below Montaillou, the pastures and fields she looked upon while nursing Merce each morning as the day came to light, drenching the world in ever deeper color. "I believe God made those things that are good to the eye and ear and mouth," she said, "those things that are useful and bring us pleasure, peace of mind. Flowers and fruits and oxen. Goats and mules. Men and women and children, of course. And the trees and wind and water." She thought. "But I do not believe God made those things that hurt us— drought and madness and sickness."

"And who do you believe made those things?" the Bishop demanded. He was staring intently at her, the Inquisitor poised behind him, listening.

"No one," she whispered. "They happen. Pain happens, in spite of God."

SHE WAS MADE to wait with a guard outside the hall, in the bleak, confining corridor. As she leaned against the stone wall, staring down at her feet, she realized that neither the Bishop nor the Inquisitor had asked her about Arnaud. Because the rector had accused Arnaud of heresy upon learning she could read, she had thought he would accuse him to the Bishop, accuse her of having been caught in the web of his ways. She had expected to have to defend Arnaud and to demonstrate that the gods and goddesses of his book were not of the Good Christians, but of fancy.

There was a sound at the door to the hall, and then the Inquisitor appeared—looking more ancient in the corridor's shadows, more weary, his thin face covered with wrinkles. His eyes flicked over her body, and then he turned and walked away from her down the corridor.

The same man who had ushered her into the hall came to the door and beckoned to her. This time when she entered, the Bishop did not stand to greet her, did not gesture her toward the chair. The scribes peered up at her.

"Grazida Lizier," the Bishop said, "you have chosen to speak sparingly, and it is the opinion of this Office that you have not confessed in full. You will be held in the Tour des Allemans until the time you see fit to speak openly."

"I will speak openly now," she said, her voice rising to a shrill pitch. "I will tell you anything, anything you want to know. My husband taught me to read, but his was a book of Ovid, not heresy."

The Bishop's eyes narrowed. "Your husband taught you to read?" He stared at her in bewilderment, as if he did not know how to proceed. "And how," he stammered, "did your husband learn to read? Did a Good Man teach him?"

She hesitated, stunned by her own ignorance of Arnaud's history. She had never thought to ask him where he had learned to read. "We know nothing of heresy," she said meekly.

The Bishop shook his head, his lips pinched together in an expression of disbelief. She realized that in confessing to have been taught to read, she had all but admitted to being seduced by heresy. And she had endangered Arnaud, innocent Arnaud.

"You will be held in the Tour for a minimum of six weeks," the Bishop said. "The guard will take you at this time—"

"But my baby," she said. "My husband. He is very sick and cannot care for her. And my mother—"

"You have brought this upon yourself, Madame," the Bishop said, his gaze unyielding. "In six weeks, you will have another opportunity to speak." He gestured for the guard.

"Do not resist me, Madame," the guard murmured. He took her roughly by the arm and pulled her toward the door.

She craned her head around to look at the Bishop, who was whispering to his scribes. "Is the rector being held in the Tour?" she called to him. She needed to know if the man who had stolen her from her daughter, from her ailing husband, was suffering, too, for having failed the Church.

The Bishop looked up at her, a crease of exhaustion on his brow. "In the worst kind of cell," he said. "Yes. He is there."

THE TOUR DES ALLEMANS was outside the gates of the city, and as the guard led her there, his demeanor softened. She told him about the boy waiting for her by the palace gate, and he took pity on her and promised to find him.

"Tell the boy to go home," she said, trying to swallow down her terror and grief. "Tell him to tell my husband that I confessed he taught me to read. And I am sorry, and worried for his safety, worried they will come for him now. Tell him I will be imprisoned for six weeks."

The prison warden was a large, gentle-eyed man, whose wife, Honors, led her to the room where she would be lodged with twenty-three other women, some still standing trial, most already sentenced. "The Bishop is not all bad," Honors whispered to her as they mounted the stairs. "He had the Tour built himself, and to the requirements of the Pope. There are ample beds, and a high window here and there, and as much air as can be found in the best prisons anywhere."

From the moment Echo stepped into the cell and saw the filthy, faded faces of the women, she felt suffocated, overpowered by the stale stench that permeated the room—the stench of spilled blood and urine, of dysentery and despair. She sat on a dingy pallet in a corner, hiding from the women's gazes, from the sight of their threadbare dresses. She knew her own dress was as worn and miserable, her own aspect as muted of cheer, but she did not want to see the reflection of her image, did not want to be reminded that she was poor and powerless, revoltingly frail, revoltingly human.

As a child of Montaillou, she had been nurtured on the golden-green colors of fields and meadows and groves, on the intense blue of the endless sky. Her eyes had thrived with the view of mountain vastness nearby, and her body was accustomed to the pleasures of roaming unencumbered up and down the hillside. In the confines of the cell, she plunged into a melancholy such as she had never experienced in life. The air was hot and close, offering no breath of wind to cleanse her of mourning. The only two windows were narrow and high, and mounted each by a ledge jutting out from the prison's exterior, such that not even a slice of sky could be viewed, bringing no relief of color or distance to her newly deprived eyes.

As her spirit faded, so did her body, which through the weeks upon weeks that followed was slowly eaten away by hunger and dysentery and fatigue. There was not enough bedding, and she slept restlessly. Sometimes at night, she would unexpectedly burst into a bout of uncontrollable sobbing, or her heart would begin to beat so quickly she thought she would surely die. She ached for the comfort of Arnaud by her side, for the sweet mercy of Merce feeding of her body. Never again would she feed her precious little girl; her breasts had become small and dry.

With every passing week, she spoke less, until finally she chose muteness, as muteness once had seemed to choose her. She listened to the women sharing stories of their children, of their husbands, of their sisters, of their ailments. If she had not thought that the women wanted most to be heard, she would have felt ungenerous meeting their words with silence. She felt dead inside, as if she were already in the grave. She had doubted the notion of Hell before, but she began to believe in it now. Perhaps Hell was when one could no longer recognize the goodness of the world, when one's despair was so black and absorbing that the very dream of future light was blotted out.

Occasionally, as she lay on her pallet during the day, watching the women think and breathe and softly commiserate, a feeling akin to hope would wash through her. Then the misty dream of freedom would take shape in her mind—Arnaud would be healed, her mother joyful, Merce strong and healthy; together they would find a grange in Aragon, with a flock of fluffy sheep and a house to call their own. She and her mother would cultivate grapes as Arnaud cobbled, as Merce grew into a girl, learning the tongue of Aragon. And during the summers they would reap golden fields in the sunshine. . . . The dream dissipated as quickly as it arrived, however, and she was left with the gnawing fear that she might never escape the Hell that was consuming her.

ONE MORNING, an autumn leaf blew in through one of the windows. For a time, she and the other women simply gazed at it—a brilliant eruption of orange and red on the dusty planks of the prison floor. A woman picked up the leaf, then passed it around. When at last Echo had the chance to hold it, she touched its crumpled smoothness to her cheek, to her mouth, breathing in its sharp autumnal smell. A small miracle had occurred, and she did not want it to go unheeded.

That afternoon, the warden's wife, Honors, came to the cell with a small, thin package for her. She took it and sat on her pallet, facing the wall to hide from the prying eyes of others. She unwrapped the package and found several sheets of paper folded within—two letters, she realized, one from Arnaud, the other from his father. She read:

To my dear wife, your husband.

I have asked my father to write this, as my hands cannot seem to keep steady.

Several weeks ago, the boy came to us with word of your imprisonment. I hope you will not be upset that I immediately drafted a letter to the Bishop, testifying as to your innocence. If I did not fear my condition would aggravate his case against you, I would go to see him at once.

Often, my father and I pray for your safety, but I have been unable to find the words to write you.

Merce has spoken her first sentence. Where Mama go? She asks the question and her hands lift up to her ears and her shoulders shrug as she looks about the room. She misses you so, but she is well, very well. She is drinking goat milk and eating much in the way of cooked grains and fruits.

My father is taking good care of us all, attempting to treat your mother for what he calls an ailment of mood. Perhaps she will improve.

When you left, I did not know what to tell you. In truth, I still do not. Only that I wish I could take your place, that I would give anything to protect you, and that I am sorry, deeply sorry, if by teaching you to read, I further endangered you. If I had not been ill, we could have fled together. You could have been free now and Merce could have her mother.

When you left, you thanked me, but it is I who have the right to be most grateful. I was selfish in marrying you. Any man would stand by you as a husband. Thank you for the many days you stood by me as a wife.

I will write again soon.

I love you. I love you. I love you.

To my daughter, beloved wife of my son, your Father.

I penned the previous letter to you several days ago. I meant to send it along, but Arnaud became so ill, I could not leave his side. He ceased to speak, and retreated into the depths of his soul, moaning out, his breathing labored and slow. Then, last night, he became calm. His breathing was shallow, spare, his hands and feet growing ever more cold. I thought he would go during the night, and I sat by him, Merce in my arms. She was a great comfort to him, you know.

Just as dawn was coming, a gentle wind picked up outside. I looked through the window and it was as if the poplars in the distance were breathing in the light of the breaking day. What a glorious morning it was. More beautiful than any I have seen in my life. Merce woke. She knows me as Grandfather now. Where Papa go? she said, and I looked down and saw that indeed he had left us. He has left us, Echo. Thanks be to God he is out of his suffering now. He shall rest in hallowed ground, here in Montaillou if I am able to arrange it. It was Montaillou that was his home.

As I told you before, you must not worry for a moment about Merce and your mother. Both are progressing steadily, and I shall never abandon them, even when the Bishop realizes he has wronged you, as he must if he is truly a man of God and humility.

The Lord be with you, child. I am sorry for the heartache I know you must be enduring now. Ever yours, farewell.

She could not hide her grief from the women who shared her cell. . . . Arnaud, her sweet Arnaud, had passed into the arms of death, had lost everything known to him, and lost it all at once, and lost it all alone. Where was his voice, his wisdom, his soul? Had he realized, upon drawing his last breath, that he was a moment away from dying? Would he know a paradise other than that of this world, with its pain and pleasure and promise of death? How he had suffered unfairly . . . Arnaud . . . Even in the face of death he had been gentle, concerned for her and her mother and their child. . . .

Forgive me, husband, she prayed. *I have been caught in this hell, this hell of despair, and I did not remember the life I have still. I did not sense that you had died while I lived.*

For days she wept, and the women were good to her, comforting her with tender looks and kind words, and she found the voice to thank them.

NOT A FORTNIGHT LATER, the same guard who had escorted her to the Tour came to the cell. She was to be interrogated again, he announced. He led her outside into the light of day, and she gulped in the clean, brisk air, stretching her lungs and legs and eyes as they walked the distance from the Tour to Pamiers. How high the poplars reached from the banks of the shimmering, deeply green river! How vast the clouds were, and shot through with golden color! The fields and meadows to her side reached immeasurably to the distant, yellowing foothills. She looked back over her shoulder and vaguely made out the far-off, white-capped peaks of the Pyrenees against the sky, immoderately blue, it seemed to her now. She felt as if her senses would break with the sheer size and brilliance of the world, and she burst into tears—overwhelmed at once with delight and sorrow and fear.

In the Bishop's palace, the guard led her down the shadowy corridors to the chamber in which she had been tried before. The first thing she noticed when she entered the chamber was the window along the wall—wider than she had remembered. Through it, she saw the busy, darkened streets of Pamiers, and the yellow-green pastures beyond the city walls. Life! Life was thriving everywhere.

"Grazida Lizier," the Bishop said to her. He was sitting, as before, at the center of the table, the scribes to his left, and a young friar she had not seen before to his right. All of the men were staring at her, and in their eyes she recognized an absence of the begging hunger, the hopelessness she had come to know so well in prison. How clean these men were, well groomed and well appointed. Even the friar, though humbly robed and gentle-eyed, had the aspect of privilege and comfort and assurance about him.

The Bishop pointed her to the chair, and his expression soured as he looked her over. "I have asked the Inquisitor Bernard of Toulouse," he said, "to allow me to conduct this interrogation without him. I fear his outbursts may have intimidated you before." He cocked his head toward the friar to his right. "The Dominican who usually assists me, Brother Gaillard de Pomiès, will attend in the Inquisitor's place. I assure you that you will hear no outbursts from him."

The young friar nodded, as if in assent, and the Bishop cleared his throat, touching the open book before him. "Since you last appeared," he began, "I have received a letter from your husband. He has written in your defense. Along with the letter, he sent a book that he claimed to be the only text from which you read. A filthy book. Filled with deviant behavior . . . I saw it fit to send a copy of the letter to the Inquisitor Bernard, who was in Toulouse at the time. His scribe received the letter and recognized your husband's name. Arnaud Lizier."

"He is dead now," she interrupted him.

The Bishop appeared to be surprised that she knew as much, and he squinted at her for a moment. "The Inquisitor's scribe was a master of a school before," he went on at last. "And your husband, your Arnaud, was his pupil. . . . Did your husband tell you about the school he attended as a boy in Pamiers?"

"No," she said.

"He was punished for deviant behavior there," the Bishop said. "Sodomy. Do you know what that is?"

"I do not," she said.

The Bishop's features stiffened. "Something unspeakable," he said. "An unnatural offense. When a man unites himself carnally to another in the foulest place the body knows. . . . Did your husband commit this sin with you?"

She tried to make sense of his words. "No," she said. How could she explain that Arnaud had never united himself carnally to her?

"As you must understand," the Bishop said, with an expression of severity in his eyes, "I cannot trust the testimony of a man capable of such mortal wrongdoing. I sent my men to have him arrested, and they found him as you have mentioned. Dead. Dead of leprosy."

"Not leprosy," she said. "Another contagion. His father is a doctor and knows about such things."

"He died only the day before my men arrived," the Bishop retorted. "And my men saw his body. Rotted away. God Himself deemed him spiritual rot."

She wanted to cry out, *If God could be so cruel, I hate him!* But she knew that if she wanted to see Merce, she must be silent, accept the judgment these men passed on Arnaud, on her. She studied the dirty grooves in the planked floor, thinking the chamber was not as pure as it had first appeared, thinking Arnaud was safe from these men and their words now.

"When you were last here," she heard the Bishop say, "you confessed that your husband had taught you to read. . . . Do you swear now by the sacred gospels that he never read or spoke of heresy to you? That you never laid eyes on a word of heresy with him?"

She looked at him fixedly, wanting him to see her sincerity in her gaze. "I swear with all my heart," she said. "I never laid eyes on a word of heresy with him or without, and he never read or spoke to me of anything of the sort."

The Bishop nodded to himself, and his eyes became soft. He seemed to believe her. "I have never known a laywoman to read," he said quietly. He studied her for a long moment, as though she were a mystery and he were searching for a way to comprehend her.

"Even so," he said, "you have sinned gravely. Not only have you committed adultery, you have believed, in error, that your deeds were not sinful. You have doubted, heretically, that Hell exists and that God rules all the world. And you have demonstrated lack of faith in the teaching of the Church that men shall be resurrected. You must embrace the truth the Church teaches, Grazida, for it is nothing but heresy to think otherwise."

What did it matter anymore, talk of sin, talk of truth, what once she had felt in her heart. There had been bliss, bliss with the rector, but it would never be again. There had been freedom, freedom in the wood, freedom in her body from thoughts of sin, but now, after inquisition, after so much talk, the notion of sin would always be present for her. Arnaud had died, and these men of God had sullied him with their words, and she would never again trust they knew all. She would pretend to believe what she was told to believe: it was a small price to pay for the freedom to nurture her child.

"I will embrace it all," she said, "and confess my error."

"Do you promise to believe now and into the future that any carnal union of man and woman outside of marriage is a mortal sin?" the Bishop said.

"I promise," she said. "I believe it now and evermore."

"And do you promise to believe that there is a Hell, in which bad men and bad demons are perpetually punished?"

"Yes, I do," she said. "I believe there is a Hell, and I pray to God that he might spare me from it."

"And do you believe that men shall be judged according to their acts, and resurrected in the same flesh as they have now?"

"Yes," she said. "I was not certain of it before. But I am now. I believe it fully, and always shall. And I will teach my daughter as much. Please release me to her so I might mother her well, Monseigneur."

The Bishop gazed into her eyes as if sincerely considering her plea. Then his expression darkened, and he glanced at the young friar at his side. "Brother Pomiès," he said, "please have the prisoner repeat Formula A."

The friar straightened in his chair and opened a thin text on the table before him. He smoothed down the first page in the book and, with an even, almost soothing voice, proceeded to speak the formula, pausing at every phrase so that she might echo it back. According to the formula, she promised to abjure all heresy, to pursue heretics to the best of her power, to aid the Bishop and all inquisitors in their endeavors, to keep, guard, and protect the Catholic faith, to obey and defer to the orders of the Holy Roman Church, the Bishop, and all inquisitors, and to accept what penance was imposed upon her.

The Bishop sighed with the conclusion of the formula, and told her that her case would be presented to a jury, who would advise him on how she should be sentenced. "The Inquisitor Bernard will have something to say in your sentencing, of course," he said before ordering the guard to take her away.

SHE RETURNED to the Tour and the despairing, hungry eyes of the women in the cell. Then, several weeks later, she and a mass of others from the prison were ushered by men of arms toward the Cemetery Saint-Jean, where the Bishop was to pronounce sentences. The day was cold and gray and foggy, and she had to strain to see through the gloom. As she walked, she looked for the rector among those bound hand and foot, their chains clanking and chilling her to the bone. She made out faces dark with fatigue and fear, but none was familiar to her, none was the face she needed, the face of someone beloved, if only beloved before.

Many men and women were already standing among the cold crosses in the cemetery, before a platform that had been erected, and she realized that not all those awaiting sentence had been imprisoned as she had, not all had been deemed guilty of crimes as grievous. The Bishop emerged from the mist with his flock of officials and the Inquisitor of Toulouse, who stood at the foot of the platform, glancing furtively this way and that, as if he were awaiting judgment.

Though she knew her fate was about to be decided, she felt

strangely distanced from the proceedings. Through the gray air, she saw a crop of poplars bordering the cemetery, and in the distance she made out the frozen gray spires of the Cathedral, rising up above the walls of Pamiers.

The Bishop began to receive oaths from the officials, and she considered the corpses beneath their feet, the bones, the bodies no longer vital, the blood frozen underground. Death was near, as was the possibility of freedom. She strained to see the Bishop, his men, puffing out cold air—the same air she and the others inhaled, exhaled. They were breathing in and out together, living at once, but death was near. In the Tour, blood had been spilled; in the Tour, bodies were being made to suffer, to flounder so that souls could be liberated. Who among them would be freed to go?

The Bishop spoke in a sedately decorous voice as he read the names of men and women allowed to lay aside the crosses they were previously condemned to wear, as he commuted sentences of life imprisonment in exchange for lighter penances. His tone became sharper, the rhythm of his speech more frenzied as he called out the names and crimes of those to be signed with the cross on their clothes. "Isabeau de Burlatz, guilty of receiving heretics in her home on one occasion, and of eating bread blessed by heretics twice." . . . "Adélaide Peyrat, guilty of listening to heretics preaching on two occasions." . . . "Napoléon de Bavière, guilty of attending a heretical baptism." . . . The Bishop's voice spread like a wintry draft through her soul as she waited, understanding awfully that her penance would be greater than that of those whose names had already been called out.

The Bishop proceeded to review the confessions of those to be sentenced to the Tour—those whose property would thus be confiscated—and she turned her gaze to the Inquisitor, whose thin, pale face drifted toward her. "Grazida Lizier," she heard and looked back to the Bishop. "Guilty of adultery, incest, deviance of thought, heresy, withholding information from the Court . . ."

If there was more, she did not hear; she had become a ghost, a ghost unto herself, a ghost as she had been when violated by the rector. She could not feel the cold, clean air her body inhaled, exhaled. There was the whiteness of the sky, and the gray of the ground, and the shapes of the crosses among the shapes of men and women before her. There was a numbness in her heart.

"Grazida Lizier," the Bishop uttered, "sentenced to life imprisonment in the Tour."

THAT NIGHT, the Inquisitor paid her a visit in the Tour. As the warden
held up an oil lamp to light the corridor in which they stood, the Inquisitor thrust a heavy, coarse sack between her hands. "I have the
power to lighten your sentence," he told her. "But you must provide me
with more information than you have thus far."

In the glow of the lamp, his skin appeared almost transparent. His
eyes were clouded with age, and his cheeks and chin were whiskery. He
seemed mad, as hungry and doomed as anyone in the Tour.

"You can read," he said, glancing from her breasts to her mouth to
her eyes. "But can you write?"

She nodded, too fatigued to lie.

"Then write," he said heatedly. "Write of the rector, of how he seduced you, of everything he spoke to you. Write of why he married you
to your husband, of his relation to your mother. Tell the story he cannot deny."

He coughed into his fist. His lungs seemed to be filled with thick,
wet fluid. "I will send someone for your testimony," he choked, and
then, abruptly, he turned away from her, telling the warden to lock her
again in the cell.

THROUGH THE FOLLOWING WEEKS, she stared at the contents of
the sack—a mound of scrolled paper, a quill, and a jar of ink—unable
to find the life inside her necessary to save herself from dying to the
world. Here, in the midst of so many living things going to waste,
kept apart from the wind and the wood and the fresh water of rivers, kept
apart from the rest of life, she could not hope to invoke the optimism of
respiring letters, the pleasure of their colors, sprouting like shoots in her
once pleasure-loving body—under her arms, between her thighs, in the
sockets of her eyes. No, she had nothing to say. Nothing except stains
of ink, stains of blood. Somewhere in the Tour, the rector was bloody,
dying, and who could save him? Not she. Not if she proved him guilty.
Words broke apart in her mind, their syllables shadowy. And there was

nothing to defend her against the night—no Merce, no phrase, no lightness.

Then, nearly a month after she had been sentenced, a letter arrived:

My daughter, your forever Father.

We were devastated by the word that you have been sentenced to the Tour. Henchmen came to seize the house, and we fled to Foix, where we are living now. I have written an appeal to the Comte. Surely, he has sway over the consuls of Pamiers. Surely, he has sway over the Bishop himself.

Merce is a beautiful girl, and talking quite fluently. She tries to engage your mother, who seems to be progressing. Sometimes, I catch her smiling at the little girl, but I know she aches for you, Echo.

Do not lose faith. Please, my child, hold onto hope for your daughter's sake.

She read the letter through several times, then read it aloud for all the women to hear. There *was* still hope; they were still residents of this world.

The following morning, by the soft light threading through the window, she held the quill in hand, all the women watching as she dipped its tip tentatively into the jar. She knew there was not enough ink to tell the story of the rector and her mother and Arnaud. She knew there were not enough words to tell the history she carried in her body, a history that with her death would and must fade away. But she could gesture toward what had been. She could try to be as truthful as ink and words would allow. . . .

TWENTY

IERRE CANNOT SEE in the darkness of his cell. He is shackled to a wall, his hands over his ears. He is aware of pain cutting through his back and shoulders and legs, through his head. His skin is hot, his breath parched, coming sharply, quickly. But in his memory, he is free, being carried under the twilight sky against the softness of his mother's body. She takes him to the chapel, nudges him forward to stand beside the priest, and he smells the scent of holiness in the air, grows dizzy with the mist of incense and the flickering light of candles and the chanted words *"Lord, let this boy grow."* His mother carries him home. He notices a little moon shining over the chapel. Its mysteriousness fills his heart, mingles with the sound of his mother's breathing, sharply, quickly. He knows there is a chance he may sleep and wake to find himself grown. His life is still limitless, reaching to the dark edges of the moonlit horizon. He believes everything will be good in time.

He tries to adjust his shoulders against the wall and the irons cut deeper into his wrists. When henchmen captured him on a mountain pass, they taunted him with a sword, cut his forehead, his cheek, the underside of his jaw. Though he was frightened, unprepared for the death he knew would follow, he was strangely relieved to be captured, strangely relieved to see the Inquisitor sitting next to the Bishop at his trial. He had come to the end of his horizon; he had lost the woman of his life, and he gazed into the depths of the Inquisitor's eyes and wept bitterly, confessing the sin he had committed in taking her, the daughter of his illegitimate niece. Unmoved, the Inquisitor blinked and coughed and demanded to know more. What other women had he crossed carnally? What heretics had he defended? What heresy had he committed? Was the Inquisitor blind? Pierre wondered. Did the Inquisitor not see that he had laid bare the heart of his wretched heart?

He refused to say more and was thrown into a cell, stripped naked, and shackled to the wall. Deprived of more than the scantest amount of bread and water, deprived of the freedom to move his limbs as he would, he grew monstrously gaunt, crusted in his own excrement, and infested by maggots. He tried not to blame God for his suffering, tried to accept the mortification of his flesh as penance for his sins. Had he not sinned terribly? He had broken every promise of faithfulness he had made to the Virgin, to the Church, to the Good Men, to the Maurses, to the Believing women he had taken. And he had violated the woman whom he loved beyond all others. . . . Echo . . . Her sweetness lay like a shadow over his heart, caressing and wounding him further. He remembered her small, sweet smile, speaking more than words, her teeth smooth as stones in the river, her hair black and radiant as dark water. He tried to be as silent and blameless as she was, blameless as the bud that opens and flowers.

Then one day the Inquisitor appeared in the cell with word that Echo had been sentenced to a life term in the Tour. "I can shorten her term, have her released," the Inquisitor muttered. "I *will* have her released if you confess the full extent of your crimes, confess what you know of others." In an instant, Pierre understood that he would betray all those whom he had sinned against for the sake of his love for her.

He was carried back to the hall of interrogation, where he confessed every detail of his life against the Church. How long ago his sinning had begun . . . He remembered the Châtelaine, how she had moved her mouth to his, breathing into him the essence of being human, of being fallen, of being one who gives way to the passions of the heart and the flesh, even at the cost of being good.

Since confessing all, he has been sentenced to relaxation to the secular arm. He is afraid, and not afraid. He longs for life, and awaits the release of death. He finds enduring comfort in the knowledge that Echo will be spared. He licks his dry, bloody mouth. He hears the door to the cell creak open, and then the voices of several guards. They tell him he is to be taken to the square, and he is too weak to groan in fear or assent. He is unshackled, shrouded in a thick, coarse blanket. He cannot move his legs and arms, and they hang from the trunk of his torso like dead animals. The throbbing in his body dims, and he hears the heavy breathing of the men who carry him. His own breathing becomes more labored. He tries to calm himself by pretending he is in his mother's arms.

He hears the humming of many voices, like the faraway bleating of sheep in the fields. When he was a boy, he wanted to be a great shepherd, a great leader of a flock, but he lost his body to one woman after another, lost his heart and staff along the way. His sheep spread out over the slanting mountainside, and he did not try to save them. They were shepherded by others, others who blamed him. Who among them had really loved him at all?

He is pushed up against something hard and rounded, a stake, he realizes. He nearly collapses before he is pushed up again. He feels tightness around his ankles, is aware of his arms being pulled behind him, his wrists being bound together. Suddenly, the blanket is torn away from him and he is blinded by the glaring light of day. He blinks, makes out the impression of a crowd. There are men piling fagots around him. He closes his eyes and feels the pressure of fagots being piled up to his chest. His breathing becomes more labored still. He hears a noise like moaning in his mouth. He is frightened. Frightened of more pain searing through his body. Soon he will be dead.

Behind the darkness of his closed lids, colors begin to form. Is he dreaming? He seems to be standing in a pasture, high in the mountains somewhere. There is green and gold, and clouds, white and luminous. There is the tickle of breeze in his hair, and a pain flooding over his skin, as agonizing as it is exquisite, a pain such as he has never known, a peace, a freedom.

BERNARD IS IN TOULOUSE, resting in bed between the sour sheets, flies biting at his cheek. The scriptor de Massabuçu has given him the testimony of Grazida Lizier, brought by messenger from Pamiers. He holds the single page before his eyes, straining to read the woman's letters in the dim light. A month ago, he might have interpreted her terseness as disrespect, an outright act of insubordination against him. Now her words strike him as guileless, and he accepts them as he would a drink of warm water—with neither enthusiasm nor distaste. Again, he reads:

> *There was a priest, and a woman who was a bastard, and a mute, and a cobbler who died, and they loved one another greatly, about which much could be written.*

A month ago, he went to the Tour in Pamiers to see Clergue. He took the warden's lamp and keys and ventured down into the furtive curves of the underground, frenzy spreading through his limbs. In the previous two years, he had held six Sermones Generales, pronouncing more than two hundred judgments. The battle against heresy had, for all purposes, been won; his beloved Mother Church had been defended. Yet there was no peace in him. It seemed that if he could not crack Clergue's silence soon, he would lose the most important battle of all, sink into the hellish sweat of his lurid self—the self he knew in dreams.

The cell in the underground reeked, and Clergue hung perfectly still. He felt a surge of pity for the man, his body still warm, but fading quickly. "Your whore Grazida Lizier has been sentenced to life in the Tour!" Bernard shouted, more violently than he had intended to. He held the lamp up and saw Clergue open his eyes with an expression of dismay. His lips began to tremble, and then his head drooped down, hanging from his neck. The manacles binding his hands to the wall creaked. "I can shorten her term, have her released," Bernard blurted out, more in pity than in conniving. "I *will* have her released if you confess the full extent of your crimes. . . ." Even as he spoke, he knew he was lying.

Later, in the palace of the Bishop, Clergue confessed without asking for mercy, merely frowning when the Bishop urged him to seek forgiveness from the Church. And Bernard felt strangely defeated by Clergue's unwavering admissions of fault. Clergue seemed suddenly to be a man strong enough to bear the burden of his own wrongdoing, whereas Bernard was nothing more than a coward, hiding from his imperfections, from his human failings. Was he not guilty of committing acts of equal lechery, if only in the darkness of his dreams? Had he not abandoned his passion for God in cultivating such a heated antagonism for Clergue?

He was the first to arrive in the cathedral square of Pamiers on the day Clergue was to be burned, and as a crowd slowly gathered before the scaffold, he found himself gasping to breathe. Clergue was bound to the stake, fagots piled up the length of his body. *Repent!* Bernard nearly shouted. He realized he did not want Clergue to die just yet. The henchmen lit the fagots, and a curious whimpering smile came over Clergue's lips, as though—with much agony—he were witnessing his own salvation. How alone Bernard felt, alone as a baby abandoned on the bank of a reedy river.

He lays the testimony of Grazida Lizier beside him in the bed, curling around it. Somehow, the ink on paper is a comfort to him, a clear though fragile link to Clergue, to the time in his life when he felt mighty. In two days, he will leave his station as Inquisitor. He has written the Pope, reminding him of the many years he has served in Toulouse, and the Pope has responded by naming him Bishop of Tuy, in Galicia, south of the Pyrenees, and far from Avignon—an appointment, Bernard knows, to be neither proud nor ashamed of.

He fingers the smooth letters on the paper. There is no longer a reason to keep Clergue's lover from the world. He will write the Bishop that he was mistaken in urging that she be sentenced so harshly. *Go and sin no more,* he will write her. *Sin no more,* he tells himself, pushing her paper away from his mouth.

He remembers the vow he spoke as a young novitiate. *I, Bernard, make profession and promise obedience to God, and to the blessed Maria, and to the blessed Dominic. And I pledge to be obedient to you, Brother, master of the Order of the Preaching Brothers, and to your successors until death.* How it seemed then that he was entering the ecstasy of oneness with God Himself. How it seemed that he would never, never again know loneliness. . . .

Perhaps he would have found contentedness if he had been less dutiful. Perhaps he would have been happier if, like Clergue, he had more to repent.

ECHO HAS BEEN RELEASED. She has stood over the yellowy grass in the Cemetery Saint-Jean and been told by the Bishop that she is free. She must wear crosses—two of them on her front, and two of them on her back. She must make pilgrimages and appear at her parish church on feast days to receive lashings from the priest. But she is free, walking in the wide world, in the shade, along the woody bank of the Ariège, headed for Foix. By sundown, she will reach her daughter. And what will she say?

She has left the quill and ink and paper in the cell. She does not want to write for a time. She wants to think with her feet on the soil, and her fingers on the breeze, and her nose in the hair of her daughter.

The sun peeps through the leaves of the tall trees and she pauses for a moment, lifting her wet eyes to the light. She is alone. She knows it and accepts it as she never did before. But she feels a beating liveliness all around. She hears the whispering breath of wind in the trees, the clean rush of river water by her feet, two birds calling, calling. . . . They do not know her, but they are of the earth just as she is. Inhaling, exhaling, hungry, yearning, they are of life, and so, she senses, everlasting.

THE TREES ARE unaware of her below, unaware of the city she has come from, of the Inquisition she has endured, of the joy burgeoning in her breast. They have never spoken of love, do not know why they are living, do not wonder why they should be. They ask only to feel the sun when the sun touches their leaves, to drink the rain their roots are drinking. They trust languidly.

Live, live, bloom, be . . .

AFTERWORD

FOR AS LONG AS I can remember, I have been fascinated by the split in Western culture between the spirit and the flesh—a split that echoes the deeper chasm between heaven and earth, and God and man. I have been troubled and intrigued by these dualisms because they do not exist as such in one culture I was brought up in, that of my mother's people, the Karen. The largest ethnic minority group in Burma, the Karen are primarily animist. They are at once profoundly spiritual and in touch with the earth, and view these tendencies as indistinguishable.

When I began my undergraduate studies, I knew I wanted to probe questions of God and faith and the possibility of transcendence, yet I had no idea that these questions would resonate most richly for me in the literature of medieval France. During a year abroad in Paris, I was introduced to two medieval courtly novels in which quests for honor and spiritual salvation were thwarted by earthly passions. I soon discovered that in many narratives of the period, themes of righteousness and duty intersected with themes of sensuality and illicit desire.

I began to read medieval mystical texts and was drawn particularly to the writings of a group of women who described the flesh not in opposition to the spirit, but as an instrument through which the spirit could flourish, and merge ecstatically with the Divine. In Peter Dronke's *Women Writers of the Middle Ages*, I read Grazida Lizier's deposition, and was struck by her ardently nondualistic, almost mystical worldview. Her moral and spiritual sensibilities were shaped by her physical experience of the world. She seemed an Edenic figure, free from shame even in her metaphorical nakedness before the men who deposed her.

In the fall of 1996, I entered the MFA program at the University of California at Irvine. Grazida's voice continued to haunt me, and I started to write a book that I imagined would be a slim, lyrical volume of ecstasies, a highly fictionalized account of her life. The more I tried to summon the past, however, the more duty-bound I felt to do so authentically; and the more I delved into research, the farther from me the past appeared.

I received a research grant from the School of Humanities and the Department of English at Irvine in June 1997, and set off on the first of two trips I would take to Montaillou. From Paris, I drove south to Toulouse, and then to Pamiers and Foix, dramatically situated at the foothills of the Pyrenees. I walked through the fertile, wooded Arget valley and along the tributaries of the Arize. Then one day I drove from Ax-les-Thermes up a steep pass to the pastures of the Pays d'Aillon, where Montaillou lies. Climbing the narrow road to the remains of the medieval fortress was an emotional experience: for years, the village had existed for me merely in the space of my imagination, and suddenly it came alive. The mayor of Montaillou, Alain Fayet, spent a good deal of time with me that day. He spoke passionately about the history of the village and the spirit of heresy, and advised me to visit the Archives Départementales de l'Ariège in Foix, where I eventually did essential research.

Another year passed before I began to conceive of the novel in its present form, as a narrative spanning three generations, not just the life of Grazida. I have based many of the characters on real people from medieval Montaillou, but their stories differ, in varying degrees, from those I have portrayed. The authentic Grazida Lizier was likely neither literate nor mute. Her mother, Fabrisse, was Pierre Clergue's illegitimate cousin, not his niece. Pierre Clergue was a lover of women, a heretic at heart, and a traitor to his parishioners. His life ended as a result of the Inquisition, although he died in prison and was burned posthumously. Two brothers by the name of Authié did in fact introduce heresy to the village; the circumstances of the introduction, though, were different from those I describe, as were the particulars of their arrests and burnings. The character of Bernard is a compilation of several inquisitors, especially Bernard Gui, who was not abandoned as a baby and who was not the first but the second Inquisitor of Heretical Depravity for the

Province of Toulouse. While the character Arnaud is primarily imagined, his experiences as a student in Pamiers have been drawn from those of a real Arnaud, who similarly feared himself diseased by leprosy.

Until recently, it was assumed that syphilis did not appear in Europe until the end of the fifteenth century, after the discovery of the New World. Evidence has come to light, however, suggesting that the disease was present in England in the 1340s, and may well have been mistaken for leprosy even before then. In rendering the character Arnaud's illness, I was helped tremendously by descriptions in Claude Quétel's *The History of Syphilis*, and inspired by Quétel's approach to syphilis as a social disease, as charged with meaning as AIDS is today.

Throughout *The Good Men*, minor characters bear the names of veritable medieval villagers, but any similarities between them beyond that of faith are, generally, unintended. Here and there, I have changed dates or shifted the order of events, and I ask scholars of the period for their tolerance. To those readers who would like to learn the stories of the real people of medieval Montaillou, I recommend two works that have been invaluable to me: Jean Duvernoy's *Le Registre d'Inquisition de Jacques Fournier*—a translation into modern French of the depositions taken by Fournier between 1318 and 1325—and Emmanuel Le Roy Ladurie's *Montaillou: The Promised Land of Error*—a brilliant study of life in and around Montaillou at that time.

CHRONOLOGY

1206	Saint Dominic determines to wean the people of Languedoc[1] away from the Cathar[2] heresy by preaching the gospel to them in the humble manner of the Good Men and the apostles.
1208	The papal legate Pierre de Castelnau, having excommunicated the Count of Toulouse for refusing to oust heretics from his domain, is murdered; Pope Innocent III consequently calls for the Albigensian[3] crusade against the Cathar heretics of Languedoc.
1209	A crusading army of nobles and their supporters from the Kingdom of France marches south and besieges Béziers; a bloody massacre ensues. Carcassonne surrenders to the crusaders soon after.
1210	Under the shrewd leadership of Simon de Montfort, the crusaders capture Minerve. In the first of many mass executions to take place during the crusade, 140 Good Christians are burned.
1211	Lavaur is captured by the crusaders; 300 to 400 heretics are burned. Attacks on the region of Toulouse begin.

1. Domain in which the language now called Occitan was spoken, part of what is today the Languedoc-Roussillon region of southern France.
2. The Cathars, dualists who conceived of the material world as evil, proliferated primarily in Languedoc and Lombardy from the twelfth to the early fourteenth centuries.
3. Term for Cathars in Languedoc, initially denoting the Good Christians and their supporters in the region of Albi.

1215	At the Fourth Lateran Council, the Count of Toulouse is dispossessed of his lands by Pope Innocent III. The Order of Saint Dominic is sanctioned.
1218	Simon de Montfort is killed during the siege of Toulouse.
1226	Louis VIII of France, eager to expand his kingdom, leads a siege of Avignon and takes most of the Rhone valley. He dies in November, and is succeeded by Louis IX (Saint Louis).
1228	Systematic destruction of the Toulouse countryside by royal troops.
1229	The Treaty of Meaux signals the end of the Albigensian crusade; the Count of Toulouse is reconciled with the Church in return for agreeing to terms that will eventually make the King of France heir to his county. Toulouse University is founded, and entrusted to the care of the Dominicans.
1233	The era of inquisition begins, when Pope Grégoire (Gregory) IX calls on the Dominicans to seek out and prosecute heretics.
1234	Riot by citizens of Albi against the Inquisitor.
1235	The Inquisitor of Toulouse is ejected from the city by the consuls.
1244	The Cathar castle of Montségur is surrendered to an army of bishops and royal soldiers; 220 Cathars are burned.
1252	Pope Innocent IV approves moderate torture in the inquisition of heretics.
1256	Surrender of Quéribus, the last vital Cathar fortress.
1262	Pope Urbain (Urban) IV allows inquisitors themselves to practice torture.
1271	The county of Toulouse reverts to the French crown.
1284	The consuls of Carcassonne scheme to steal inquisitorial records.
1294	Accession of Pope Boniface VIII and beginning of his power struggles with the French king, Philip IV (the Fair).
1296	Pierre Authié travels to Lombardy, where he will become a Cathar Good Man.
1302	Riots by citizens of Albi against Bishop Castanet and the Dominicans.
1306	King Philip IV expels Jews from France.
1307	Bernard Gui becomes Inquisitor of Toulouse.
1308	The population of Montaillou is arrested, on September 8.

1309	Pope Clément V moves the papacy to Avignon.
1310	Bernard Gui sentences seventeen heretics to be relaxed to the secular arm. Pierre Authié is sentenced and burned at the stake soon after.
1312	Pope Clément V issues the bull *Multorum querela*, limiting the power of inquisitors.
1317	Jacques Fournier becomes bishop of Pamiers, and establishes an inquisitorial office.
1320	Bands of peasants known as *pastoureaux* rise against Jews in France.
1321	The last known Good Man is burned.
1329	Last burning of Believers in Carcassonne.
1334	Jacques Fournier becomes pope, as Benoît (Benedict) XII.
1337	King Edward III of England claims the French crown; the Hundred Years' War commences.
1347	The Black Death arrives in Languedoc.
1377	The papacy returns to Rome under Grégoire (Gregory) XI.
1478	Establishment of the Spanish Inquisition.

AN EXPLICATION
OF THE CATHAR HERESY

THE GOOD MEN have been known since the Middle Ages as Cathars, a designation likely derived from *katharos*, the Greek for "pure." Many scholars have convincingly argued that Catharism originated in part from the dualistic heresy of the tenth-century Bogomils of Bulgaria, who conceived of the material world as the creation of Satan and thus inherently evil. The faith of the Bogomils could well have spread to western Europe in the twelfth century, as trade between East and West was increasing. By 1143, an organized sect of Cathars had established itself in Cologne; by the late twelfth century, Catharism was a serious threat to the Church and flourishing predominantly in the regions of Toulouse, Albi, and Gascony.

The Cathars were cosmic dualists. They believed in two co-eternal principles: God, creator of light and spirit, and Satan, creator of darkness and matter. According to their cosmology, Satan had lured many souls away from God's heavenly realm and imprisoned them in corruptible, decaying human bodies into which they were to be eternally re-incarnated. When God mercifully sent Christ to earth, the dominion of Satan over these souls was threatened. Christ—whom the Cathars believed to be a pure spirit and merely the illusion of a man—had delivered a message of salvation, which the Cathars alone had preserved in its pristine form. By the Cathar rite of baptism, prisoners of the flesh were cleansed of sin and promised resurrection of the soul. If baptized during the course of their lives rather than at the moment of death, they became Good Men or Good Women—preachers of the faith who lived in extreme asceticism, not eating meat, or holding property, or engaging in that most devilish of sins, sexual regeneration.

So rampant was Catharism in Languedoc by the dawning of the thirteenth century that in 1208, Pope Innocent III called for a crusade against it. Armies of French nobles marched south and launched the holy war with a bloody massacre at Béziers. By the spring of 1229, the war was over; soon thereafter, Pope Gregory IX established the Inquisition that would exterminate any remaining heresy. What flickers of Catharism arose after 1325 would be apparitions, remembrances, evocations of an earlier age.

ACKNOWLEDGMENTS

THIS BOOK HAS benefited from the work of many scholars. I am grateful to the following for their research on aspects of medieval and peasant life: Philippe Ariès and Georges Duby, general editors of *A History of Private Life II: Revelations of the Medieval World*; Jacques Gélis, author of *History of Childbirth: Fertility, Pregnancy and Birth in Early Modern Europe*; Geneviève d'Haucourt, author of *Life in the Middle Ages*; Ralph B. Pugh, author of *Imprisonment in Medieval England*; and Frances and Joseph Gies, authors of *Life in a Medieval City* and *Life in a Medieval Village*, which introduced me to such far-ranging subjects as the education of boys, the wiles of urban doctors, the treatment of lepers, and the tools of a tanner's trade. I am, of course, also indebted to Jean Duvernoy, whose edition and translation of Jacques Fournier's inquisitorial register I consulted frequently, and Emmanuel Le Roy Ladurie (and his translator Barbara Bray), whose seminal work on Montaillou and shepherd life was a source of much clarity for me.

The following served as my education in Catharism, the Albigensian crusade, and the medieval Inquisition: *Le Vrai Visage du Catharisme* by Anne Brenon; *The Cathars and the Albigensian Crusade* by Michael Costen; *Cathares, Vaudois et Béguins: Dissidents du Pays d'Oc* and *La Religion des Cathares* by Jean Duvernoy; *Inquisition and Medieval Society: Power, Discipline, and Resistance in Languedoc* by James B. Given; *The Mediæval Inquisition* by Jean Guiraud, translated by E. C. Messenger; *The Medieval Inquisition* by Bernard Hamilton; *Medieval Heresy: Popular Movements from Bogomil to Hus* by M. D. Lambert; *The Albigensian Crusade: An Historical Essay* by Jacques

Madaule, translated by Barbara Wall; *Écritures Cathares* and *La Vie Quotidienne des Cathares du Languedoc au XIIIᵉ Siècle* by René Nelli; *L'Inquisiteur Geoffroy d'Ablis et les Cathares du Comté de Foix* by Annette Pales-Gobilliard; *Heresy* and *Authority in Medieval Europe: Documents in Translation* and *Inquisition* by Edward Peters; *Histoire des Cathares: Hérésie, Croisade, Inquisition du XIᵉ au XIVᵉ Siècle, Les Cathares: De la Chute de Montségur aux Derniers Bûchers, 1244–1329,* and *Mourir à Montségur,* all three by Michel Roquebert; *The Albigensian Crusades* by Joseph R. Strayer; *Heresies of the High Middle Ages: Selected Sources,* translated and annotated by Walter L. Wakefield and Austin P. Evans; *Heresy, Crusade and Inquisition in Southern France: 1100–1250* by Walter L. Wakefield; and *The Albigensian Heresy* by the Reverend H. J. Warner. In particular, I am beholden to Jacques Madaule (and his English translator Barbara Wall), Joseph Strayer, and the Reverend Warner for their translations of Cathar liturgy.

Three books introduced me to the world of Bernard Gui, and I owe a great deal to each: *Between Church and State: The Lives of Four French Prelates in the Late Middle Ages* by Bernard Guenée, translated by Arthur Goldhammer; *Bernard Gui et Son Monde,* edited by Édouard Privat and the Centre d'Études Historiques de Fanjeaux; and *Characters of the Inquisition* by William Thomas Walsh. Much of the writing of the character Bernard is based on that of the real Bernard Gui, whose *Practica Inquisitionis Heretice Pravitatis* was edited in the nineteenth century by Célestin Dovais. I am also grateful to G. Mollat for his translation of Bernard Gui's edited manuals, *Manuel de l'Inquisiteur.*

Without William D. Paden's *An Introduction to Old Occitan* and Emil Levy's *Petit Dictionnaire Provençal-Français,* I would have been unable to find the Old Occitan for many words. I am especially grateful to Professor Paden, who generously verified the Occitan in the book, and whose translations of troubadour poetry were so lovely I felt compelled to quote several lines.

The majority of the Catholic creeds in the book are from *The Catholic Encyclopedia.* Biblical lines are from the Authorized King James Version and the Revised Standard Version. I have also drawn from *Instructions for Parish Priests* by John Myrc; *Preaching in Medieval England: An Introduction to Sermon Manuscripts of the Period, c. 1350–1450* by G. R. Owst; *The Gnostic Gospels* by Elaine Pagels; and the baptismal liturgy of the Book of Common Prayer, which I have used in the scene of Fabrisse's baptism, willfully ignoring the fact that it would have been more appropriately included in a narrative set in sixteenth-century England.

All quotations of Ovid's *Metamorphoses* are from Frank Justus Miller's translation, revised by G. P. Goold.

THROUGHOUT THE WRITING of this novel, I was assisted by various institutions and people. I am grateful to the staff of the Archives Départementales de l'Ariège in Foix, the Bibliothèque Municipale in Pamiers, and the library of the Centre d'Études Cathares in Carcassonne; and to the people in France who patiently answered my questions, among them Alain Fayet, mayor of Montaillou; Frère Elie Pascal of the Dominican convent in Toulouse; and Michel Roquebert, historian of the Cathar heresy.

The Donald and Dorothy Strauss Endowed Thesis Fellowship provided me with much-appreciated financial aid. Thank you to Duncan and Colleen Strauss, Nancy Strauss Tietge, the School of the Humanities and Department of English at the University of California at Irvine, and Arielle Read for her continual support. Thank you also to Gail Davis, who guided me through many a Latin line and the original text of Grazida's deposition, and Willis Barnstone, who never tired of discussing the Cathars with me.

I am indebted to the teachers at Harvard who introduced me to the medieval period and directed my studies, in particular Nancy Jones, Deborah Jenson, and Sandra Nadaff. My mentors in the graduate fiction-writing program at Irvine nurtured this book in its early life. I thank Margot Livesey, James McMichael, and Michael Ryan for their guidance; Melanie Thernstrom for her encouragement and professional advice; Michelle Latiolais for her faith in this story and her suggestion that I tell it chronologically; and Geoffrey Wolff for urging me to write a book ruled not by history, but by the imagination. My peers in the fiction workshop helped me find the voice and scope of the story; my thanks to them for their friendship and close reading.

I am grateful beyond measure to my agent, Eric Simonoff, for his enthusiasm, wisdom, and kindness; to my editor, Cindy Spiegel, for believing in the book and ushering it into the world with such intelligence and sensitivity; and to the publisher of Riverhead, Susan Petersen Kennedy, for giving generously of her insight and support. I am also tremendously thankful to Erin Bush for her helpfulness and good cheer, to Dorothy Vincent, and to Mih-Ho Cha, Paul Crichton, Marilyn

Acknowledgments

Ducksworth, Anna Jardine, and everyone else at Penguin Putnam who helped the novel and its author throughout the publication process.

For their warmth and understanding, I thank Tony Barnstone, Janet Cortellessa, Ayame Fukuda, Peter Hedges, Emily Tucker, Matthew Shaw, Jennifer Wang, Arthur and Judy Winer, the Benson clan, and my brother and sister, Bradford and Colleen.

To Andrew Winer, who contributed so much to this book, thank you for your humor, steadfastness, clarity of mind, and caring. And to my parents, Glenn and Louisa Craig, your loving support has been my greatest source of creative vitality. Thank you.